The Splendour

It was then that she saw her father. His face was smoke-blackened and so was his clothing, but she recognised him as soon as he stepped into the street lights. She was almost sure he had the money; there was a swiftness in his walk, which spoke, to his daughter at any rate, of success.

It did not last long. A couple of storm troopers detached themselves from the group and walked purposefully towards him. She saw him hesitate, then turn and grasp the blackened edge of the window as if for support. Then he drew himself up once more and walked, steadily, towards the men in brown.

Judith Saxton is a well-loved novelist who has had almost fifty books published in the last twenty years. She was born and brought up in Norfolk and now lives with her husband and family in North Wales. She has always been keenly interested in country pursuits – the family own several dogs, cats and horses – and enjoys cooking, despite having to cater for a large family.

D0860704

Also by Judith Saxton
*available in Mandarin

The Pride
The Glory
Full Circle
Sophie
Jenny Alone
Chasing Rainbows
Family Feeling
All My Fortunes
A Family Affair
Nobody's Children
This Royal Breed
First Love, Last Love
*The Blue and Distant Hills
Someone Special

JUDITH SAXTON
The Splendour

Mandarin

A Mandarin Paperback
THE SPLENDOUR

First published in Great Britain 1983
by Hamlyn Paperbacks
This edition published 1994
by Mandarin Paperbacks
an imprint of Reed Consumer Books Ltd
Michelin House, 81 Fulham Road, London SW3 6RB
and Auckland, Melbourne, Singapore and Toronto

Copyright © Judith Saxton 1983
The author has asserted her moral rights

A CIP catalogue record for this title
is available from the British Library
ISBN 0 7493 1792 2

Typeset by Deltatype Ltd, Ellesmere Port, Wirral
Printed and bound in Great Britain by BPC Paperbacks Ltd
Member of BPC Ltd

DEDICATION
In memory of Pat Woolstone, whose looks and charisma I shamelessly borrowed to enhance my heroine, Val Neyler.

Author's Acknowledgements

As this Saga progresses through the years, so does
my indebtedness to the people who have helped me
with advice and reminiscences, and I would like to
thank in particular the staff of the International
Library, Liverpool, for their help in discovering books
and maps which dealt with Germany in the thirties
and the staff of the Wrexham Branch library,
particularly Lynne Butler, Marina Thomas and
Margaret Bird, who worked very hard on my behalf.
In Norfolk, Captain Meyer of Dereham answered
my appeal on Radio Norfolk for anyone who knew
anything about the 1936 Olympics. His detailed
memories of that event and the colourful way in
which he described them helped me enormously to
get the background and, I hope, the 'feel' of the
stadium at that time.
Adelaide and Alan Hunter lent me books and
newspaper articles on the thirties in the run-up to the
war and last but not least my mother, Dorothy
Saxton, guided my footsteps along the paths which
she had trodden herself in 1939, when she helped to
get Jewish refugees out of Nazi Germany.

THE NEYLER AND ROSE FAMILIES

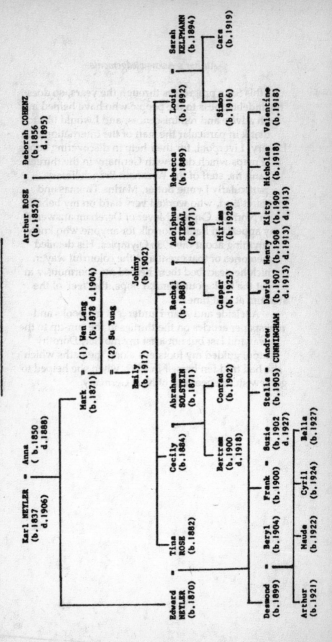

PART 1: 1931

Chapter One

April in Paris. A clear day with a fresh breeze and sunshine spilling down through the branches of the trees which line the left bank of the Seine and turning the river into a thousand winking, shifting points of light.

Somewhere, there was a bird market. Tina Neyler cocked her head, listening, and heard the liquid notes of cage birds mingling with the soft murmurs and cheeps of the sparrows and the burblings of the pigeons which swooped and hawked above the paving stones. She stood still for a moment, drinking in the atmosphere, revelling in the foreignness of it all, but then the breeze caught her little hat with its big cluster of artificial violets, and she began to walk once more. Her cream-coloured coat with the dark fur collar and big, turned-back fur sleeves was warm, but it was still very early in the morning and she had no desire to get chill, not on the very first day of their longed-for continental holiday!

Tina had left the hotel early, leaving Ted to have his lie-in and his breakfast in bed; for at forty-nine, she supposed, one was less anxious to lie in bed than at sixty-one. She had told him that she was going to buy presents for the family, and that had brightened his sleepy eye because he thought it would mean he would not be trailed around the shops in search of trifles. He *would* be trailed round the shops, of course; Tina had no intention of letting her husband escape from a tour of

3

the big stores, but at least he would not have to burden himself with most of the presents. He should help her choose Poppa's, but she had already made up her mind that grandchildren, great-nephews and nieces and those servants who merited it would get boxes of nougat, and that her sisters and sister-in-law would receive scarves, costume jewellery and other knick-knacks. She would reserve her more imaginative presents for her own children.

Though not for Stella. Stella, her eldest daughter, had gone to Australia two years earlier after a colossal family row, and Tina did not even know her address. She still agonised over Stella, but what could she have done? Andrew Cunningham, Stella's totally unsatisfactory husband, had actually been wanted by the police for fraud – in connection with fraud, perhaps she should say – and it had seemed only sensible to buy him a one-way ticket for Australia before he brought black disgrace on them all.

They had not realised that Stella would go too, that she would rage and storm at them, blame them for everything, even Andrew's behaviour, and then simply disappear. It was loyalty, of course, but mistaken loyalty, surely? Andrew, to Tina's personal knowledge, was a thief and a blackmailer. How could Stella continue to love such a man?

However, it was no good letting thoughts of Stella darken this bright day. She cast one more affectionate glance towards the river bank, where the artists were already setting up their easels beneath the trees, and then plunged across the road and into the maze of small streets which made up Montmartre. She would indulge herself with a good look at all the fascinating little shops and stalls and then head for the Galeries Lafayette, where she would be able to get most of her shopping done under one roof. She knew they sold magnificent boxes of nougat – she blessed the young for having the good sense to enjoy sweets – and very good costume jewellery, gloves and stockings. She would find something for everyone there.

Halfway down one particularly fascinating street, she remembered the twins. Val and Nicky were twelve and neither would thank her for clothes, and one did not give nougat to one's favourite children. For them, it must be something more personal. She slowed before a window displaying a wide variety of hunting, shooting and fishing equipment and almost at once saw the penknives. They were the very thing. A big one for Nick, as full of gadgets as an egg is of meat, whilst Val would be enchanted by one of the smaller ones with a mother-of-pearl handle and not only all the usual appendages of a first-rate penknife but also a teeny pair of scissors slotted into one side.

She went into the shop, reflecting smugly that it was not every Englishwoman who could have anticipated buying the penknives without a qualm. She was fond of telling her children that languages were important – though teachers these days did not seem to place the same emphasis on French and German as they had when she had been at school – and now she went quickly and confidently over to the counter, secure in the knowledge of first-rate French.

She had no difficulty and in fact made a friend of the shopkeeper, who cast admiring eyes over her small, trim figure and slender legs and actually went out with her into the street which ran along one end of the Place du Tetre and hailed a cab for her. The driver, too, was happy to oblige her when she told him she wanted to go to the Galeries Lafayette to do some shopping, and asked him to wait for her before taking her back to her hotel. Expense did not bother Tina, for Ted, most generous of men, was even more so on holiday and her grey suede handbag was heavy with francs. She climbed into the elderly cab, therefore, and leaned back against the cracked leather of the seat. Not being a driver herself, and having been used for more than thirty years to sitting in the front seat of various motor vehicles whilst Ted narrowly missed lampposts, grazed other vehicles and murdered foolish chickens, the driving of an elderly man in an elderly cab who had illusions of winning Le Mans did not worry her. She climbed out when they reached the store as calm and collected as she had climbed in, never having noticed the seven close shaves they had had as they tore through the city.

'You will wait, won't you?' she said as she left the cab. 'I shan't be very long.'

She was, of course. The brilliant lighting, the little booths set around the circular foyer with the galleries rising, tier on tier, above her, wooed her into spending both time and money. But even so, she chose with care and with pleasure the gifts that each recipient would enjoy.

Sarah, the divorced wife of her only brother, Louis, was to have a pair of earrings shaped like tiny black velvet gloves, and a large bottle of exquisite French perfume. Sarah was rich and beautiful and wore Paris clothes anyway as of right – or perhaps on her elegant figure all clothes looked like Paris models – but Tina loved Sarah, and felt guilty that Louis had treated her so badly, hence the bottle of perfume as well as the earrings.

She chose a soft evening wrap for Cecy, pale blue with silver stars embroidered on it. It was soft and cuddly, like Cecy herself, for even at forty-seven Cecy was given to dewy eyes and romantic novels and large boxes of turkish delight. Tina had no doubt that the stole would fit perfectly into Cecy's picture of herself as a delicate, pastel creature.

Rachel, on the other hand, was a gay and much more definite person, lacking Cecy's delicate colours perhaps, but with a verve and strength of character which she shared with Tina. Tina bought her a scarlet umbrella with an ivory handle because she could see how Ray's vivid face would glow beneath its shelter, warming and brightening the dullest of rainy days.

Becky, the only unmarried sister, was a hospital matron. She had very little time for her sisters, nor they for her, but Tina bought her a handsome silver brooch made in the shape of the Sacré Coeur, because it would look nice on the dark clothing that Becky favoured.

Grown-up sons were always difficult, so she brought them both large boxes of cigars. Desmond, the eldest, did smoke sometimes though Frank never did, but both were in business for themselves and both would offer the cigars to good customers. Des's wife, Beryl, was nothing like Sarah, but she also merited two presents. A rose-pink silk blouse because she was so colourless and defeated, and a flask of perfume because Des was a bad husband. Odd, Tina thought, as her purchases were wrapped, that the two men she loved most after Ted were both womanisers, yet Ted himself was such a wonderful person.

After dealing with Des, Beryl and Frank it was natural to turn to Josette. A Belgian refugee during the war, Josette had been rescued by Louis, and then adopted and brought up with their own children by Tina and Ted. She was a nurse, just as Becky was, but how different! Josette was small and brown and friendly, Tina thought now, an ideal nurse with her quick and ready sympathy. She merited two gifts, one because she was Josette and did not have many pretty things and one because she had never, in any way, imposed on her adopted parents. A silk dress in her size was expensive, but Tina did not grudge the money, knowing what pleasure it would bring, and a bottle of that same perfume which she intended to bestow on Sarah would give Josette not only pleasure but a considerable morale-boost, after days spent nursing in the atmosphere of carbolic and sickness. Conscience-perfume, Tina thought, and dismissed the thought quickly.

The nougat nearly defeated her. Boxes and boxes of the stuff had to be purchased, individually wrapped by the neat little assistants, and then carried out to her waiting taxi. A small pageboy, staggering beneath the weight of her parcels, had accompanied her from booth to booth and from tier to tier, but a second one had to be enlisted to cope with the nougat. Tina, with a mixture of pride and embarrassment, told the assistant on the sweet counter that the nougat was for her many grandchildren and then led the pageboys out to the pavement where her taxi waited. With mutual compliments and a large tip she and the boys parted company, and she climbed into the taxi beside her shopping. She told the driver, rather grandly, to take her to the Grand Hôtel, in the Place de l'Opéra, where Ted had insisted that they stay. They intended to lunch today at the Café de la Paix, if the terrace restaurant was sufficiently sheltered to make such a meal enjoyable.

Glancing through the window as Paris whisked past, Tina felt all the weariness and complacency of one who has had a successful morning's shopping. Ted would be pleased with her; almost as pleased as she was with herself!

'Madame, monsieur awaits you in the office.'

Tina, hurrying across the foyer, a retinue of staff following with their arms full of her parcels, paused, her eyebrows rising. What on earth could the young man behind the desk mean – Ted would be in their room still! Probably the young man's English was at fault. She spoke to him, therefore, in her best French.

'My husband is in our room, monsieur. I'm just going to join him.'

'No, madame; he awaits you in the off –' The young man stopped as Tina's hand flew to her heart. 'It is all right, madame, but a telegram came . . .' He deserted his desk and came over, taking her elbow. 'This way, madame.'

Tina accompanied him, dumb with imagined horror. Who was ill, dying, dead? Telegrams had terrified her ever since the war and even now, a dozen years later, she could not view one with equanimity. Des drove fast cars, Frank messed about in boats, the twins were always up to some devilry. Her heart began to bump unevenly. Who could it be? Poppa was eighty-one, it was a good age . . .

The office was large, imposing and over-furnished. There were three telephones on the desk and Ted was sitting with the receiver of one of them to his ear. He said, *'Oui, oui. Merci, monsieur, nous arriverons à deux heures,'* and then he replaced the receiver and turned to his wife.

'The children and grandchildren are fine.' He stood up and came round the desk, a fine figure of a man still, and put an arm round Tina's shoulders. 'Sit down. It's your father, love. Arthur's had a stroke.'

'Poppa! Oh, Ted, is he . . . ?'

'No. But the doctor doesn't hold out much hope. Still,

9

we'll see. I've got two berths on the boat train leaving the Gare du Nord at two today. We'll be back in Norwich in time for breakfast tomorrow.'

'Good. Is he in hospital?'

'I rang Cecy, but all the Solsteins were out, at the Bishopsgate house, so Arthur's not in hospital. Then I rang The Pride and Des was there as . . . as luck would have it. He told me Poppa was alive and Cecy and Alice were coping.'

'Alice would. She's been Poppa's housekeeper now for a lifetime. What else should we do?'

Tina knew, without asking, that Ted would not have asked Des to involve himself too much, even though Des was at home. Ted did not trust him as he trusted Frank. Frank ran a boatyard thirty miles from Norwich, where his grandfather lay dying, but it would be to Frank that Ted would turn for help.

'It's all in hand, love. I rang Frank and he's ringing Con and between them they'll do everything that needs to be done.'

Tina nodded. She was glad that Con was helping. Her nephew was a barrister as well as being Frank's closest friend, and they both loved Poppa.

'That's good. Frank and Con are so practical.'

'True.' Ted nodded and linked her arm with his. 'They'll get a professional nurse in and ask the Rabbi to come and see Arthur. Mr Crewe can manage everything at the factory, though later he may need a power of attorney. And now, my love, we're going to have a glance at the shops and a bite to eat before we leave.' He kissed the top of her brow, knocking her smart hat back a bit and then straightening it remorsefully. 'Poor darling, our one-day continental holiday, eh? Never mind, I'll make it up to you.'

*

Arthur lay in his big bed, the bed he had lain in every night, or damn' nearly every night, for the past forty-five years. He was propped up with pillows and could see, through his good eye, the window. Outside, there was a laburnum tree which would presently delight him with its showers of golden rain, and beside it an apple tree which, in a few weeks, would be crowded with pink and white blossom. But now everything was still, the branches bare, and his one good eye unbalanced without the other, inexplicably sightless. Someone or something had attached weights to the right side of his face, the corner of his mouth, eye and nostril, so that he could neither blink nor twitch the flesh on that side.

He turned his attention from the winter view to himself. Yesterday was a muddled nightmare, but now he knew who he was and where he lay. If it had been yesterday. Days seemed endless, nights longer. Earlier, he had searched every face that came to his bed for Deborah, his dear wife, but now he remembered that she had been dead for . . . could it really be thirty years? A tear filled his good eye and rolled down his cheek, into the thickness of his beard. A woman leaned forward and wiped the tear away, a handsome, white-haired woman whose hair, he knew, had once been corn-coloured. Who was she? No child of his. Cecy was his child. She kept coming across his line of vision, red-eyed and weeping. Little ninny! He would have snorted if he could, but such a sound was beyond him.

There were several woman in the room, but where were his other children? Where, above all, was Tina? When he needed her most, where was she? Gone, run away with that young *schlemiel* from New Zealand, who had stolen his eldest, best loved daughter from him. The boy was not even a Jew but a *goy*, so now his grandchildren were *goyim* and he should have cast them out, trampled them underfoot. Another tear formed. He wanted his Tina, Jew or Gentile, and he wanted her now! Tina would know what he most wanted, even if no one else could understand him.

He tried to shout at the foolish women, to move, gesture, but the lead weights were not only on his face but all down his right side, and his left side was lethargic, unwilling to move more than a fraction. The women, grouped by the window, were talking amongst themselves, damn their impudence. Taking no notice of him. He shouted, and a tiny, mewing sound emerged. Faces turned towards the bed. Little fat Cecy moved forward, bent over him, spoke. But her words made no sense and whilst he was still trying to speak again she turned away, shaking her head as if he were already dead, of no account.

Dead? Was his right side dead, then? He made his noise again, but they had gone from his vision. Panic seized him. Suppose they thought him dead already, did not realise that Arthur was very much alive inside this stupid shell which lay in bed and cried tears out of one eye and made sounds which he could hear even if they could not? He struggled to call out, to move, and imagined he did both; at any rate, a face swam into his line of vision again. It was the woman whose hair had once been corn-coloured – it was Alice! How could he have forgotten her, even for a moment! Now that he knew her he found immense reassurance in her presence. She looked into his eyes, and then, as if she could read the thoughts there and see the rawness of panic which threatened to overwhelm him, she took his left hand in her own warm clasp and spoke.

'Tina's coming, Mr Rose. She'll be here soon, you see.'

His relief was so great that he let his eyelid droop over his one active eye. Someone understood, someone knew that he was alive and that he desperately wanted Tina. Favourite daughter. Beloved child. Wicked, wilful, pain-giving, when she had run away from him all those years ago. But always there when needed, understanding his greatest desire, always dependable.

He began to doze, but his thoughts continued. True as steel, Tina was. She had married out and broken his heart but . . . favourite child. Beloved daughter. Coming. Coming.

Arthur slept.

'He's in there. Oh, Miss Tina, I think he's very ill!'

Tina was in her coat still, and a small velvet hat with a short veil. She shrugged out of her coat, then pulled the hat off, running a hand across her hair which, after the long journey, was wildly untidy despite the hat.

'I know, Alice. But he's still alive?'

'Maybe. Better go in, Miss Tina. He wants you.'

Tina entered the bedroom. A room of childhood memories still, not all of them happy, for her mother had died in this room. But then it had had linoleum covering the floor and cheap, dark curtaining at the windows, the paper on the walls dark and sombre, and a marble-topped washstand. Now it was carpeted, light and bright, the furniture chintz-covered, the fire crackling on the hearth, a brass and copper coal hod standing near.

'Poppa? It's me, Tina.'

He was propped up with plenty of pillows and the first thing she noticed was the drag on the right side of his face, the sightless eye. She might have wept, as Alice told her the other girls had, but she knew Poppa too well. Weeping women he abhorred!

'Is there anything you want, Poppa?'

He could neither nod nor shake his head, they had told her, but his good eye quivered slightly and she sat on the bed, facing him, and took his big, cold hand between her small warm ones. Then she released his hand to caress his cheek.

'Dear Poppa, get well for your Tina!'

He made his sound again, which Alice and Cecy, Rachel and Sarah, had assured her was meaningless. To Tina, it was not meaningless at all.

'Louis? You want us to fetch Louis, all the way from Australia?'

He sighed, a deep gusty sigh which stirred his beard. It gave Tina an idea. She leaned forward and spoke, looking deep into his eyes.

'That meant "yes", didn't it, Poppa? But should we say one sigh for no, and two sighs for yes? Now, you want Louis to be brought home, is that right?'

The pause seemed unbearable before he breathed heavily twice. Tina beamed at him, then released his hand and stood up. Her heart lifted. He was not quite lost to them whilst they could communicate!

'That's marvellous, Poppa! I'll go and send a cablegram to Louis right away. Becky, too, is coming to see you, and Josette – do you remember Josette, the refugee we adopted during the war? Only Stella cannot come, and she will send her love, I know that. Now you must wait for a little while, and then your family will be round you once more!'

Leaving the room, Tina distributed autocratic messages that the others must hurry, hurry, hurry; though she knew, as she had always known, that it was Louis Arthur most longed for. He had so many daughters! Four girls had been born to poor Deb before the long-awaited son, and then Louis was the sort of son a man could not but be proud of. His war record, his marriage, his beauty, charm, athletic prowess! One simply had to forget his womanising, his leaving of Sarah and the children, Simon and Cara, his abandoning of his elderly father and the shoe factory eleven years before. And remember his lovingness, his generosity (even, occasionally, with other people's money), and his genuine kindness. Louis would put himself out for anyone, do anything in his power to make things easier for others.

Tina, who knew Louis well, though not as well as she thought she did, was sure he would come back. He had, it is true, done little enough since his flight to earn Poppa's devotion. His letters had been brief and few, and though he had sent a few smudged snapshots of his flat, his house, his hospital and colleagues, he had never let anyone feel, for a single moment, that he regretted leaving.

Tina believed that Australia and his life there had been the making of him, but she also believed that Louis had loved Poppa as they all loved him. Whatever the difficulties, he would surmount them, and come back to see Poppa now, before it was too late to see him ever again.

His attitude to Sarah was, of course, an enigma. Sarah was beautiful, highly intelligent, and faithful. A better wife one could never hope to find. But he had never suggested that she might join him in Sydney now that he was established as a surgeon there; never, apparently, longed to have his wife and children under his roof. The fact that leaving now would be very difficult for Simon and Cara, to say nothing of Sarah, running her father's business and coping with her aged mother, was beside the point. When Louis had first gone Simon had been four, Cara a babe in arms. Their

15

minds had been sufficiently elastic, then, to have taken the change in their stride. But he had not wanted them. Or Sarah. And if he had asked them to go to Sydney now, Tina was sure it would be too late. Simon was very happy at Pursell's school, Cara adored the High School, both had myriads of friends and ploys. Besides, two years ago, Sarah had divorced Louis for desertion. Not to remarry but, as she said, to 'regularise the situation'.

With a sigh, Tina swept into Poppa's study to write out her telegram. It would not take much composing, for her belief in Louis's innate goodness was too deep to let her waste time, or words.

Poppa dying stop Come home Tina.

'Simon, would you please be nicer to your sister? Now that you're away at boarding school you only have to put up with her during vacations, which shouldn't tax you *too* much!' Sarah, seated in front of her dressing-table getting ready for an evening out, glared crossly at her son through the glass. Bicker, bicker, bicker, that was all Simon and Cara seemed to do these days. Over the most childish things, like who was to have the first bath, who should sit beside Dickson, the chauffeur, when they went for a ride in the car, who had the last remaining cream cake at tea.

Cara, leaning on her mother's shoulder, gave her a sweet, woman-to-woman smile through the mirror. Men, it seemed to imply, were only children at heart after all!

'He can't help it, Mother. He's naturally bossy and swollen headed, and as Gran says . . .'

'Cara, just stop making trouble!' Sarah's voice was crisp and edged with annoyance. Despite Cara's pretty looks and charm, she did not fool her mother for one moment. 'You deliberately aggravate Simon and I know it. It's just that he's fifteen and you're only twelve, so I thought I'd ask him to behave first.'

'Oh, Mother, I do-o-on't!' The whine in her voice was enough to set Sarah's teeth on edge. 'You ask Gran if . . .'

'Out! You're annoying Mother, you spoilt little brat!' Simon caught a handful of his sister's abundant black curls, pulled them up until she was on tiptoe, then ran her out of the room, slamming the door behind her and leaning against it. Through the mirror, he grinned half apologetically at his mother. 'Sorry, Mum, but you did say you wanted to talk, and you know how impossible it is to say anything in front of Cara these days without having it repeated in all quarters.'

'Yes, but that was a bit high-handed.' Sarah was wearing a charcoal grey dress with pearls in the low neck, and a pink chiffon scarf tucked into the waist-band. She picked up her powder puff and lightly touched her nose with it, to hide the seven pale gold freckles which warmed into fourteen at the first sight of the sun. 'Still, Simon, the fact remains that you're almost grown up and Cara's still very much a child, and you shouldn't plague her and quarrel with her the way you do. Especially now.'

She meant especially now, with your grandmother living here. Last year her father had died. Killed by his wife's nagging, Simon said when he thought his mother was not listening. In any event, after a mere four months of widowhood, Mrs Kelpmann had sold her mansion, dismissed her servants, and informed Sarah that she intended to move into the house on Ipswich Road.

'Your father would have wished it,' she told Sarah impressively. 'So fond of us both he was, my Ernest, he wanted you to come to us when that wicked Louis first

17

left you; only your obstinacy stopped us living together then. I'll move into your little guest suite and share expenses and be no trouble. No interference you should suffer – I know better than to interfere with the young!'

She did interfere, of course. She idolised Cara and disliked Simon, and she moved, not into the guest suite but into the old nursery suite at the top of the house. She came down to breakfast each morning and never went up again until last thing at night. The stairs, she complained in her most senile tones, were too much.

Because of her mother's presence Sarah's life had changed completely, and for the worse. Whilst never missing an opportunity to tell her daughter that she was far too young and beautiful to waste her life alone, she was rude to any man who came to the house to take Sarah out and had no qualms about inventing ailments, engagements or prejudices which meant that Sarah should, in fact, remain at home with her.

'If you mean Grandma, it isn't my fault that she lives with us,' Simon said reasonably, now. 'You should have put your foot down at once, Mother, when you saw that she was going to move in. You know you can't let her stay or she'll ruin our lives. She hates me and she spoils Cara to death, and there are times, honestly, when I don't believe she loves you anywhere near as much as she pretends. She's always picking and finding fault with you and then pretending she does it for your good. What's more, the cousins won't come visiting any more because she told Val she was a heathen, just because she isn't Jewish. She's been ever so rude to Auntie Tina and all the Neylers because they aren't Jewish, and you know you said you wouldn't stand for it. She's bigoted, narrow-minded, and really rather nasty. You should find her a little flat, close if you must, and make her move into it. You know I'm right!'

'Yes, I do know. But she's my mother, and I don't want to seem an unnatural daughter,' Sarah said, applying glycerine to her eyelashes with a tiny brush. 'Anyway, Simon, I asked you up here to tell you something rather special. It concerns Grandpa.'

'He's dying. I do know, Mother,' Simon said gently. 'He's a grand old boy and I'll be sorry to see him go, but he *is* eighty-one.'

'It's because of Grandpa, but it isn't . . . .' Sarah put down her make-up and turned to face her son squarely. 'Darling, Grandpa's asked your father to come back.'

There was the sort of silence that speaks. Sarah knew that the small Simon had idolised his father, but she had no way of knowing how he would take the news. Simon's face, she could see, did not know whether to smile or frown. It made up its mind and frowned.

'Well, he won't come, will he? I mean he wouldn't come for you! Or for me and Cara.'

'This is different, though, Simon. Grandpa is unlikely to live long, and Louis adored his father. I think he'll come back.'

'Yes, but suppose Grandpa had been killed crossing the road, then Daddy couldn't have been here in time,' Simon protested with unanswerable logic. 'I don't see why he should come now, hoping to be in time.'

'I know Louis a bit better than you do, darling, and I think he'll come. He'll want to see us, of course, particularly you and Cara. I want him to see how well you've been brought up, so be nice to him, welcome him. I've divorced him, so it's pointless bearing a grudge.'

'Yes, but that could be set aside, couldn't it?' Simon said with youthful optimism. 'You still like Daddy, don't you?'

'Indeed I don't. He behaved very badly towards me –

towards us all. Well, I suppose I like him, but I couldn't bear to get involved with him again. I'd never trust him, you see. Remember, he never told me he was leaving me and going to Australia. He told me he was going to London on business!'

'All right. What's this got to do with Grandma living here, anyway?'

'Well, Louis is bound to come here, and I thought I might ask him to speak to Grandma, make her see that she must move out.' A faint, reminiscent smile curved Sarah's lips. 'Louis was always a charmer, even to cross old ladies; I don't suppose he's changed in that respect.'

'Grandma doesn't like charmers,' Simon remarked. 'Look how she hates me! Are you going out tonight, Mother? Is that the reason for all this dressing up and jollity? And why Grandma muttered something rude to me as I came past the drawing-room?'

'I'm dining with Con. It seems rather awful to go when your grandfather's so ill, but I've done my share for today and so has Con, and I did hope Con might tell me how to treat your father. So, he's running us down to the coast, Great Yarmouth actually, where there's a new little restaurant which specialises in seafood. It will be good for us both to get away.'

Simon laughed and lounged towards the door. He had always called Con Solstein Uncle Con, but he was strictly speaking a first cousin, and his friendship with Sarah amused Simon rather more than his mother thought was warranted.

'You're cradle snatching. Uncle Con can't be more than thirty! You've gone out with him several times since he came back from London, haven't you?'

'He's twenty-nine,' Sarah said acidly. 'Why don't you point out that he's also a good two inches shorter than me and make my evening perfect?'

Simon, for all his faults, was a percipient youngster. He turned and came back to his mother, giving her shoulders a comforting squeeze.

'You don't look thirty-seven, you know you don't, and what do a couple of inches matter when you're as brainy as Uncle Con? Tell you what, ask Uncle Con about Gran. If anyone can tell you how to get rid of her without causing any fuss it's him. Give him my love when he calls for you.'

He left the room so quickly that, by the time Sarah reached her bedroom door, he was halfway down the stairs. She leaned over the banister and called down to him.

'What do you mean? You've not asked me if you can go out!'

'No, I don't believe I did! I'll be home before you, I daresay, and tucked up in bed by the time you're seeing Uncle Con off, so be good!'

He turned to grin up at her with that glint in his eyes and mischievous curl to his lips that wrenched her heart with memories of Louis.

'Simon, come back at once! You aren't . . .'

But he was across the hall and through the front door before she had finished the sentence. Sarah, with a defeated sigh, turned back to her room. Much good it did her to order him about! Grandma Kelpmann's constant presence had meant that the relationship between Sarah and her children had steadily deteriorated. Seeing her powerless to make Grandma behave herself, Simon took it for granted that she could not make him do as she wished either. And what was more, though in the old days he would have obeyed her from affection if nothing else, he seemed to think that, because she had allowed her mother to enter their lives, she had forfeited her right to such filial obedience.

21

He needs a father's hand, Sarah thought, sitting down in front of her dressing-table again. Being so rude about Grandma, then insinuating that she was chasing Con, then just walking out like that! Louis would never have allowed such behaviour – but then Louis had never had to deal with a young man, and the child had not been beyond Sarah's own capabilities to control. The very fact that Simon and Louis were so alike might make it easier for his father to control him or more difficult: she was in no position to say.

She outlined her mouth carefully with dark lipstick. Some people might think it her duty to marry again, not because she wanted to do so – one dose of the pains of marriage had so outweighed the pleasures that it had put her off wanting to catch the disease a second time, she told herself – but so that her children would have a more normal home life. And it was certainly true that no father would allow Simon to speak to her as he had just done.

However, there was more to marriage than providing a father for her offspring, she reminded herself, and since she had no one in mind and since wild horses wouldn't persuade her to take Louis back, the question was an academic one. She got up, checked her stocking seams, and made for the stairs. But at the very back of her mind she knew that, for the first time in many years, she was considering the possibility of marrying again.

Con, sitting opposite Sarah in the small restaurant, her beauty mellowed and enhanced by the rose-shaded lamps which lit their small alcove, leaned across the table and took her hand. She had beautiful hands, the filbert nails polished to perfection. Looking at them, it was impossible to guess that she had driven ambulances, nursed the sick and scrubbed floors during the war. She had reverted to being a lady of leisure in one sense, though she had taken an active interest in her father's business ever since Louis had left, and more particularly over the past five years. Not that you would think, to look at her, that she was anything but a beautiful, idle woman with a great deal of money.

Con knew that Sarah was worried at the thought of Louis's return, and wondered how best to comfort and advise her. For twelve months he had most urgently wanted her for himself and had only been held back from asking her to marry him by the certainty that she would turn him down. He could remember her wedding day, when she had graciously and charmingly kissed the eleven-year-old Con, who had scrubbed the kiss vigorously off his cheek with his handkerchief and blushed red as a tomato. It had not, he thought ruefully, been a propitious beginning for the sort of relationship he now had in mind. Indeed, he had actually called her 'Auntie' until five years since – he blushed all over again at the thought. Auntie, and a mere eight years older than he!

Now, the unbridgeable gap had diminished with the years, and had ceased to matter, probably, to everyone but him and Sarah. When he had been offered a place in chambers near the Inns of Court by a Solstein uncle whose own son had, disappointingly, not taken silk, he had jumped at the chance and certainly never thought about Sarah. She had been no more than his Uncle Louis's wife, five years ago.

But four years in London had been enough and back to Norwich he had come, to find on his very first night at home that things had changed more than he had ever dreamed. Sarah had come round to discuss a household problem with Cecy, Con's mother, and he had stood up, taken Sarah's hand, and then, with a laugh, claimed

23

a right to kiss her. She offered a cheek, smooth, faintly perfumed, and as his lips touched it he had known such a surge of desire that he had been quite shocked. She's Uncle Louis's wife, he had thought, she's eight years older than me, unattainable.

He had stepped back from her and known that he was fooling himself. She was no longer either Uncle Louis's wife or unattainable. Once, before he went to London, there had been something about Sarah which forbade closeness. He could not have said of what it consisted, or why it had been strong enough to make him consider her completely out of the running, but that had been how he had thought of her. Now he could sense that the constraint had gone. She was . . . waiting. Perhaps not for him, but for someone.

He had made sure, after that, that she never thought of him as her little nephew again. He took her out, listened to her problems, bided his time. Louis's return might be unwelcome to Sarah, but it was doubly so to Con. That wedding in the Shul, with himself, his brother Bertie and the Neyler cousins all watching Louis, the wonderful Uncle, and the woman who was fortunate enough to be his wife, came before his eyes every time he looked at Sarah. He remembered the furtive jokes which he had not fully understood and the stories of Louis's sexual prowess. He had gazed at Uncle Louis with wonder and awe, scarcely noticing Sarah save for the awful embarrassment of that kiss. Was it all going to happen again? Would Sarah be swept off her feet for a second time by the thoughtless, selfish Louis? Con's sympathies for his uncle had thinned with the years. It was all very well being a rake and a devil for the women, but to abandon your wife and children, to refuse tacitly to return to the country to see them, and then to come running because your father lay dying –

well, some would say that Louis was offering Sarah a subtle insult by such behaviour.

Con had been held back from asking Sarah to marry him by the fear that she would refuse and also, a little, by the roar of disapproval which he knew would deafen them both if she did accept him. The congregation of the Shul would be outraged and disapproving. Her nephew by marriage, they would say, eyes glittering. It shouldn't be allowed. She's leading that nice young Solstein boy astray with her experienced ways! That he was neither nice nor young Con would have been the first to assure them, but to a Jewish mother any young Jewish man must be both. There were never enough Jewish youths to supply all the available daughters with husbands at a given time and always, lurking at the back of every matriarchal mind, was the fear that a girl would 'marry out'. It was bad enough when a boy did so, but boys usually brought their brides to the Shul after a time, converts either before or soon after the marriage. Girls were different. It was the defection of girls which hurt.

So a marriage between Con and Sarah would not give rise to one bright matriarchal smile. Old Mrs Kelpmann did not want to see her daughter married to anyone, whatever she might pretend, and the rest of the congregation, with their unmarried daughters heavy on their hands, would think it a waste. He could almost hear the murmurs: a married woman she is, with children of her own already, no need of a husband she had, not like my Rhoda. Or Jessica. Or Deborah.

'Well, Con? You take my hand, turn it over, gaze into my palm like a fortune teller, and say nothing! What are you thinking about?'

'I'm thinking about you, of course. How could I think about anything else when you're with me?' Con had a singularly sweet and understanding smile and he bestowed it on Sarah now. 'Your problems take some solving, my dear!'

'If only you could think of a way to get Mama into a little flat without sorely offending her! And tell me how to behave with Louis, too. I know him so well: he's going to come home and expect everything to be as before, with me wanting him, loving him. I won't have him to stay at my house, but that won't stop him . . . Oh, Con! Do you know I can't sleep at night for worrying?'

'We can't talk here.' Con indicated the other alcove tables nearby, though he was very sure that no one could overhear their quiet conversation. 'We'll drive down to the front and go for a walk when we've finished eating, and we can talk then.'

The meal over, Con was as good as his word. He drove down to a point where he could park the car within a foot or so of the dark beach and he and Sarah got out. It was windy and brisk, if not actually cold, but Sarah said that after the sybaritic atmosphere of the restaurant and the bottle of wine they had shared, a bit of air and exercise would do them good, so she clung on to Con's arm and they battled their way against the wind for the length of three breakwaters before turning tail and letting it blow them back to the car again.

Flushed and invigorated, Con bundled Sarah back into his Rover 10, grateful for once that he was driving the saloon since his sports model had a tendency to let a gale like this in with you, which did not encourage intimate conversation. But in the snugness of the car, with the wind howling and the sea crashing outside, one could relax. He unwound the scarf in which he had muffled himself and tossed it on the back seat. Sarah decorously unfastened the top button of her heavy coat, then turned hopefully towards him.

'Well, Con? Have you found a solution to my problems?'

Con nodded, then leaned forward and unbuttoned the rest of her coat. She looked a little surprised, but allowed him to ease it off her shoulders without protest. When he slung it in the back seat on top of his scarf she looked at him again, her eyes wide with enquiry, her mouth a little open to repeat her question. Con pulled her roughly into his arms and kissed her. She sensed the difference in this kiss at once, used to the merest brushing of the lips from Con, and pulled back against his encircling arms, suddenly tense.

'No, Con! We're friends. Let's keep it that way.'

Con might be shorter than Sarah, but he was broad-shouldered and strong, and her struggles got her precisely nowhere. He had never cared enough about a woman before to try to overpower resistance, but he cared now, and was pleasantly surprised to find how easy it was to hold Sarah against her will. Or was she, perhaps, not putting her heart into her opposition? He kissed her mouth again, whilst it was still trying to complain, then crushed her in his arms, wriggling and ill-at-ease, and kissed her until he had the felicity of feeling her relax against him, of her mouth gradually softening beneath his, gently opening.

They were both breathless when he broke the kiss. He found her breast with one hand and felt her heartbeat increase as he fondled her. She sighed and caught at his hand but it was a token objection only, and they both knew it. He moved her so that she lay comfortably in the crook of his arm and then he kissed the softness where neck and shoulder joined, murmuring against her flesh: 'If you married again your mother would have to move into a flat. He would insist on it, I can promise you that. And if you married again,

27

Louis would scarcely try to . . . ingratiate himself with you.'

She said nothing, but gave a little sigh of pleasure as his mouth moved on her and he knew she wanted his lovemaking to go on, though how fast or how far he was as yet in no position to say. He realised that, though Uncle Louis's affairs had been a talking point for years, though there had been salacious whisperings of his fantastic abilities in that field, there had been no whisper about Sarah. Now, holding her, he knew that she was a passionate woman whose passions had been neither cooled nor extinguished by Louis's desertion. Quite the opposite, in fact. Self-control had been asserted against all her natural inclinations and now that it was lifted she wanted lovemaking as a right, a pleasure denied for too long.

When he moved back from her she made no attempt to follow him, though. She patted her dishevelled hair, and then, for the first time, appeared to consider his remark.

'If I married? But I'm not going to marry. Once bitten, twice shy, that's my motto!'

'Oh? I think you're going to marry me.'

'Con, how could I? I'm eight years older than you.'

He put out a hand and caught her neck, turning her so that she faced him. He rubbed his fingers up into her hair, then sat back again, and sensed a disappointment emanating from her. Not that she moved or spoke or allowed her face to fall, but he saw her eyes darken, knew how she felt.

'That's a bloody silly thing to say, sweetheart. Next you'll say you can't possibly marry me because you're an inch or so taller than I am, and really lacerate my feelings!'

'Well, I am taller than you.' She sighed and leaned

towards him, taking his hand. 'Don't be cross or hurt or anything. You know we couldn't get married. It just wouldn't work. There would be screams of outrage from your parents, for a start. Cecy and Abe would be horrified. You're their only son and they want grandchildren from a nice little daughter-in-law who'll cherish and obey you. Not a woman with a son of fifteen and a daughter of twelve, and, worse, a mind of her own!'

Con was not a barrister for nothing. He recognised the desire in Sarah's voice to be argued out of her resolution, and knew already that she wanted his lovemaking. He had lit a small flame; now he must feed it until it became a raging inferno, and then she would not care that he was Con who had been a little boy at her first wedding, Con who had been a good friend but was unthinkable as a lover.

He took her in his arms again, kissing her far more passionately and comprehensively than he had done before, and her quick response was both a delight and a confirmation of his suspicions. When at last he put her tenderly back into her own seat, draped her coat round her shoulders and started the car, it was because he knew the battle was as good as won. But he was far too wary to continue now. No matter how much she might want him to carry his lovemaking to its natural conclusion, she would not expect him to do so. Con, with a knowledge of human nature culled from years of working in court, knew that he could go ahead and possess Sarah here and now but knew also that it might do more harm than good to his cause. If she believed herself to be morally lax, eager only for physical satisfaction, then God knew if he would ever persuade her to marry him, and it was marriage he wanted, not a casual affair. However, if he could make her see it was

29

only through marriage that she would win the loving relationship she craved, ah, then . . .

'Con, what *am* I to do?'

'Give me the right not only to advise you but to interfere on your behalf, protect you, fight your battles, and you won't have to do anything, because I'll do it all for you.'

There was a long silence. The car's engine was sweetly tuned, the night breeze hummed with their speed as they drove along the main Acle road. Con, with his hands on the wheel, where they belonged, resisted a fearful temptation to pull Sarah close. He waited.

'Is that . . . Con, are you asking me to marry you?'

'Naturally. I love you, dammit, what else should I ask you?'

'Oh, Con, I wish . . . but you *know* it isn't possible!'

'And you know you're talking rubbish. I've loved you for a year, ever since I got back from London, but I've waited, letting you get to know me as a person and not just as a relative by marriage. I knew you couldn't and shouldn't be rushed. I believe you love me, I know, sweetheart, that you need me, so why not make it legal?'

Out of the corner of his eye he saw a shiver pass over her and knew that she wanted him, perhaps more desperately even than he wanted her. Eleven years of abstinence, after Louis's constant, hungry attentions for the previous half-dozen years! She had courage, and more self-control than most, his Sarah! For she would be his, he was sure of it at this moment, driving along in the windy darkness with her sitting beside him.

'I can't make up my mind just like that. I've got to have time to think. Just remember, Conrad Solstein, that when we first met you were ten and I was eighteen

30

and engaged to . . . oh, there's so much to think about!'

He said nothing and they drove home without mentioning the subject again though they talked on other, lighter matters. He drew up in front of her house and kissed her all over her face, down across her throat, to the tops of her breasts. She responded with ardour, and when he held her back from him, flushed and lovely, her mouth bee-stung from his kisses, he knew he had won.

'Well, darling Sarah?'

'All right, Con. Come round tomorrow morning, at about ten. We'll talk about it.' She put her hand on his cheek. 'I don't know about love any more, not after . . . but I like you better than any other man I've known.'

He grinned at her, understanding her compulsive honesty. So much easier to use the conventional words of love, but that wasn't Sarah. She couldn't say something she was not sure she meant. Getting out of the car, he helped her out of her seat and accompanied her into the hall, though he refused her offer of a cup of coffee. He was going to play the game to win this time, now that he was sure of the line to take.

'No thanks. Goodnight, my love.' He kissed her so casually that her eyes shot open, disappointed, he could swear, by the lightness of the caress, and then he drove away, leaving her standing silhouetted in the doorway, waving a little desolately.

It would not be simple or straightforward to win and wed his love, he knew that. She had been far more bitterly hurt and wounded by Louis than he had ever dreamed. It would take time, and love, to give her back that ebullient self-confidence that she had once possessed in such measure. There would be parental objections too, as she had forecast, both from his parents and from her crossgrained old mother. The children, Simon and Cara, would scarcely react complaisantly to the news that their mother was going to marry their Uncle Con! What would the cousins think? Stella would not know until it was an accomplished fact, of course, but Frank and Des, who had also attended the wedding, would probably kid him a bit. His Neyler cousins, those tall, yellow-haired, handsome relatives, *goyim* though they might be, mattered to him more than most, but even they would be pushed aside if they tried to stop him marrying Sarah. She was a woman to worship and to enjoy, to share with, to rejoice in. Whatever the losses in friendship, to possess Sarah would be worth it.

The family came. Becky, who had been away from Norwich for more than a dozen years, arrived and cast a critical eye over them. Rachel was getting plump, she said, and Cecy was too fat for health. Tina shouldn't be so bossy: look where her bossing had got her so far – one daughter run off, one son no better than he ought to be, the other stuck out on a boat somewhere like a hermit.

Becky had made her way in the world. Her patients feared her, her nurses dreaded her. The cost, in terms of appearance, was the loss of that bloom, worn thin by years of starch and scrubbing, disapproval and firmness, and not kissed off by a man's mouth.

She disapproved of them all. Louis's wife was far too beautiful and was bound to come to no good. Cecy's lad, Conrad, gave Sarah looks when he thought no one was watching, and they were not the sort of looks which a decent nephew gave to a decent aunt. What was more, Sarah frequently returned the looks – with interest. Disgusting! Becky would have liked to tell

Cecy and Abe, so that the wrongdoers could be punished, but she was a little in awe of Con. He sometimes made remarks which Becky did not understand, but which Ted grinned over. No, she would not risk bringing Con's annoyance down on her head.

She thought of herself as being good with children, but Rachel's two, Caspar and Miriam, were spoilt. And Simon and Cara were conceited. Desmond had a brood which was too numerous to sort out into its component parts, and Tina's twins were nasty. Knowing and cheeky, they flitted in and out of The Pride, where she was staying, always so polite on the surface, but she could sense the antagonism, the hidden giggles.

She had offered to help to nurse her father, though she despised him too, and pretended astonishment at the huge fuss over the death of one rather wicked old man. Because she knew, if the rest of them did not, that Arthur was dying. He waited, forcing himself to cling to life, but only for Louis. And Louis, she knew with her professional intelligence, could not arrive in time for anything but the funeral.

'Simon, wake up, old boy! Show a leg!'

Simon, fathoms deep asleep after an evening of which his mother would have heartily disapproved had she known about it, stirred and tried to shrug the covers up over his ears again. It could not be time to get up. It would be that wretched Cara, always interfering with him. It occurred to him, then, that it had been a man's voice. His father? He opened one eye, saw a figure bending over him, registered that it was a man, and sat up groggily, knuckling his eyes.

'Whazza matter?'

It was not his father, however, but Uncle Con.

Immediately, his heart hopped in a very uncomfortable fashion.

'Uncle Con! Is Mother ill?'

'No, Simon, I'm here. Are you properly awake, darling?'

He gazed from one face to the other. They both looked serious in the dim light from his bedside lamp. Mother was fully dressed in a dark green woollen dress he had never much liked; when he asked her why she wore it she had said it was warm. Uncle Con was in a sleeveless sweater and plus-fours. Not best things, so they had not been out. They had been roused suddenly, as he had, and pulled on the first things that came to hand. He frowned, unable to come to terms with this sudden awakening. They could not have found out about Pixie, could they?

'What's up?' He shook his head dizzily, trying to clear the fumes of sleep from his brain. 'It isn't morning, is it?'

'No. Simon, Grandpa's dying. The doctor doesn't think he'll last the night. He had another stroke at about nine o'clock.'

'I'm sorry.' Simon looked from one to the other, more confused than ever. What could he do about it? They knew Grandpa was dying. Mother had said so only the day before!

Con leaned forward.

'Yes, but this means that Louis – your father – can't arrive in time, you see.'

Simon frowned.

'But he's at sea! You can't turn him back now, you can't . . .'

'We shan't try to turn him back, don't worry, old son. You've not seen Grandpa since his stroke, have you?'

Simon shook his head. 'No. Mother thought not.'

34

'Mother was right.' Con put his arm round Sarah's waist and Simon, shaking off the last blur of sleep, bristled a little. Who did Con think he was? 'Will you get up and shove some clothes on, old boy? You see, Grandpa's very confused but he keeps asking for Unc . . . for your father. We think, your mother and I, that if he sees you . . .'

Simon got out of bed and dragged on dark slacks over his gaily striped pyjamas, then reached for a jersey.

'Good lad!' Uncle Con handed him socks, then fished his shoes out from under the bed. 'Stick these on, and you'll do. I've got the Rover outside.'

As he struggled into his clothes, it occurred to Simon to ask the time.

'Two o'clock in the morning. A ghastly hour to wake a chap and expect a lively response,' Con said, grinning at him. 'But it's rather urgent.'

'A matter of life and death.' Simon dragged on his socks and shoved his feet into his shoes. 'Except that even if Grandpa thinks I'm Daddy, he'll still die. Won't he?'

His mother had tears in her eyes. Odd, when you remembered that Grandpa was not actually a relative, and that Mother did not cry easily. But he was a good old boy and his mother had never forgotten how kind he had been when Louis had left her.

'Yes, he will. But it means a lot, darling, to know that he's gone happy.' Sarah was smiling determinedly, and her son got to his feet and patted her shoulder. 'Daddy will love you for it, I promise you.'

They made their way down through the silent house and out to Con's car. It went like the wind, with Simon in the back and the adults in the front. They sat too close, it seemed to Simon, aware for the first time of something warmer than mere friendship between his mother and Con. He had not yet considered whether he approved or not, was simply aware that it existed. Besides, he had other things to think about. The strangeness of this wild drive through the darkness had fired his imagination, besides being pulled out of his warm bed in the middle of the night and asked to act a part, an errand of mercy that would grow more dramatic in the telling. It would make a good story for the other chaps when he returned to Pursell's at the end of the vac.

They reached the house in Bishopsgate. Grandpa slept on the ground floor, of course, because he had been crippled in a dreadful fire in America as a young man. Stairs were possible for him, but very hard work, so he had always slept in the big, airy ground floor room overlooking the back garden. They went into the front hall and Auntie Rachel came out of Grandpa's room. She had been crying, he could tell, but she smiled when she saw him.

'Oh, Simon, you're a good boy! Give us a minute.'

He loved Auntie Ray. She was so bouncy and cheerful, she adored her two little kids and was game for anything. All the cousins loved her. He, his mother and Uncle Con waited in the hall and then Auntie Ray reappeared. She was smiling again, and the tears had been banished.

'Come in, darling.' She took Simon's hand and squeezed his damp fingers. 'You're nervous, but don't be. Kindness is never hard when it comes to it. Just say "Poppa", would you, love?'

Simon followed her into the room. It was warm, the fire burning up brightly though it was so late. Grandpa was propped upright but his head lolled on the pillow. His eyes were fixed on the doorway and there was something in his expression which made Simon want to cry, to take that desolate, desperate look out of the old man's eyes.

Instead, he went to the bed, sat down on it and took Grandpa's hand. 'Hello, Poppa!' he said. And then, as if he had, in truth, felt his father's mantle fall on his shoulders, he hugged Grandpa, rubbed the grizzled old cheeks with his smooth young one, and said soothingly, his voice deeper than its wont, 'I'm here, Poppa, I'm here.'

There was a sound from the still figure which was somewhere between a grunt and a snort and it made Simon descend abruptly into childhood again. He wanted to turn and run, far from the quiet room with its crackling fire, the group standing at the far side of the bed. He stared down at Grandpa's hands. They were big and had been strong, but the flesh had fallen away and the tendons and veins stood out, the bones showed. Simon could remember when those hands had represented security, generosity, unfailing safety. He took one of the hands in both of his and smiled down into the craggy, time-abused face.

'I'm here, Poppa.'

Arthur sighed and his eyelids drooped. Auntie Tina moved forward, looked intently down into her father's face, then smiled across at Simon.

'Fine. Off you go, now. He's sleeping.'

He was not. The lids flickered apart, the big, noble head made a tiny gesture of negation. Simon stared hopefully at his aunt. He had done as he was asked; now he most desperately wanted to get out of this stuffy room and escape from the dying ruin of his once-magnificent grandfather.

Auntie Tina leaned over the bed.

'Poppa? Louis has had a long journey and nothing to eat, and . . .'

For the first time since he had entered the room, Simon heard words that he could understand in Grandpa's slurred, hoarse voice.

'I, too, a long journey will have. A few minutes will not hurt; eh, Lou?'

'I'll stay, Poppa.' Simon's courage had come flooding back. He was doing this for Daddy, whom he had loved so very much long ago, and for Grandpa, whom he loved still. Dammit, it was the most adult thing he had ever done, perhaps ever would do. He would not creep out of here and reproach himself to his dying day!

It was over an hour before Auntie Tina came round the bed and told him that he could leave, that there was no point in his remaining there any longer. He stood up, stiff from remaining in one position, and saw that they were all there, the aunts and uncles, the older cousins. Even Josette, the Belgian refugee whom Uncle Louis had brought back for Auntie Tina to adopt after her second daughter had been killed. They were solemn, and the aunts were crying. He smiled at Josette, and then his mother and Uncle Con were ushering him out of the room, out of the house, and into the Rover once again. When she had seen him bestowed, however, his mother lifted a hand and returned to the house.

'You were grand, Simon.' Uncle Con gunned the engine and they started down the drive of the Bishopsgate house. 'I'll run you straight back home now, and your mother will come back later, or rather, I'll bring her. I expect they will find themselves pretty busy now that it's all over, though.'

'Over?' Simon turned in his seat to stare at his uncle's profile. 'Is . . . is Grandpa *dead*?'

'I'm afraid so, old boy. But he died happy, thanks to you.'

'Yes.' Simon thought for a moment. 'Uncle Con?'

'Mm hmm?'

'Daddy won't stay, will he?'

'I very much doubt it, old chap.' Uncle Con swung the car into the drive of the Ipswich Road house and drew up beside the flight of steps leading to the front door. 'I've not said a word to anyone else yet, Simon, but between ourselves, I've asked your mother to marry me.'

'Oh?' Tiredness had caught up with Simon. He felt he could not have cared less who married his mother provided he could get back to his bed and sleep. 'Has she said yes yet?'

Con chuckled. 'I'm glad you seem to take it for granted it's just a matter of time! No, she hasn't, but I share your optimism.'

'Well,' Simon said, getting out of the car, 'I'm sure I hope you'll be happy,' and with that he lurched up the steps and across the hall, never noticing that he had left the front door wide open, certainly not hearing Uncle Con shutting it behind him with a soft click.

Back in bed, Simon expected to fall asleep at once, but instead pictures of Grandpa dying, his father, his mother and Pixie danced round and round in his head. He shoved his face into the pillow and bade himself forget it and go to sleep, but it was hard to forget, particularly when it occurred to him that Uncle Con, presumably, must do to his mother the things which he had been trying so hard to do to Pixie.

That brought him upright in bed, his eyes rounding. It could not be true! Old people could not behave like that! No sooner had he thought it than he realised he was being stupid, not to say childish. Uncle Con and his mother were not old, they were simply adult.

He lay down again, frowning into the darkness. Was

he trying to say that they were behaving like children, or that he was behaving like an adult, then?

Defeated by the complexity of the question, he went to sleep at last.

Chapter Two

Louis was at the funeral. He had been very cast down to learn that he had missed seeing Poppa alive, and grateful to the boy for his intervention, but once he had got over his disappointment he gloried in being home. He had refused Tina's invitation to stay at The Pride, and also a suggestion that he might like to move into the Bishopsgate house. Instead, he booked a room at the Maid's Head, which was near enough to Poppa's house for him to be there when he was needed, but which would still give him some freedom from the family.

He did not, however, understand what had happend to Sarah. Her whole attitude towards him was hurtful and bewildering. Not a day older did she seem, but there was a look in her eyes which had never been present before and it indicated that she had changed, though he was sure he had not. He had expected her to greet him with warmth and affection, if not with love, for they were divorced. Well, if he was being honest he had expected a loving greeting. But she had been . . . wary, on her guard. She had come round to The Pride when Tina asked her to a family get-together the evening of the funeral, had introduced him to his children, and then walked away – walked away! – as though he had never meant anything to her. Louis had been extremely hurt.

Unfortunately, however, no one sympathised with him. When he had complained to Tina about Sarah's attitude she had given him a long, sisterly look and snorted. Yes, positively snorted. And even Ted, the most easy-going of brothers-in-law, had raised his fair brows and given Louis a glance which had combined stupefaction with disbelief. It had been an accusatory glance, and what possible reason could there be to accuse him, Louis, of anything? Anyone would have thought he had left Sarah in straits, eleven years ago. Nothing of the sort had been true. She was rich in her own right and had always been independent and self-reliant. She had taken the bringing up of the children in her stride, she had enjoyed a full and active social life. All she had been deprived of, in fact, was himself, and though he admitted this must have been a cruel blow – for, unlike Con, Louis was still achingly aware of his ex-wife's passionate nature – he reasoned that women were made to withstand the deprivation of sexual enjoyment. How, otherwise, could men go off to war, or spend long periods at sea? The fact that a modern war of eleven years would be unusually lengthy, or that he might, in that time, have circumnavigated the earth six times in a sailing ship, he brushed aside as irrelevant. Women had a capacity for waiting and Sarah had waited. So, now that he was back and had admitted that he had no wife in Australia, why did she not greet him with open arms, press him to stay with her, and start proceedings to get that stupid, hurtful divorce nullified?

Now, however, sitting at the dinner table with the Neyler family, he was careful to keep such thoughts to himself. Instead, he raised a point which had been worrying him slightly ever since his return. He leaned closer to Tina and lowered his voice.

'Tina, I've been wondering, since I got back, what happened to my other kids? Do *you* know? It's odd to think there are half a dozen or so of my kids knocking round the city and I wouldn't know 'em if I met 'em face to face!'

Tina gave him one of her more quelling glances. She was a spunky little thing, he had always known it, but it was no use blinking at facts. He had children other than Simon and Cara, and he was interested in them. In their mothers, too, dammit! He met Tina's look blandly, with some amusement. That would teach her!

'I have no idea, Louis.' She had lowered her own voice to a hiss. 'Kindly remember that not everyone at this table knows about your more sordid exploits, and keep your voice down!'

'I'm the black sheep, aren't I? Isn't it obligatory for the black sheep to have sown wild oats?' But he obligingly spoke more quietly. Louis had never wanted to upset people. 'Poppa knew, because he paid . . .'

'Then you'd better spend some time going through the books,' Tina said, suddenly composed. She looked at him under her lashes. Had he but known it, at that moment they looked very like one another. 'It wouldn't do to ask Sarah, though I daresay she knows, but you could ask Con.'

'Con? You mean Cecy's boy? Why on earth . . . ?'

Tina raised her beautifully shaped dark brows.

'Hasn't anyone told you? Well, it hasn't been formally announced yet, because of Poppa, but Con's marrying Sarah in the summer.'

Louis's fork froze halfway to his mouth. Marrying? He frowned. It was impossible. Con Solstein was a child. There was a wretched, miserable ache somewhere in the region of his ribs, as if he had been winded. Con to marry Sarah? That would mean that he, Louis, would never know the pleasure of having Sarah in his arms again! It was preposterous, outrageous. Someone must be hideously joking.

Carefully, he conveyed food to his mouth, chewed, swallowed. He took another forkful of chicken and glanced at the faces round the table. Des was boasting about the deal he had pulled off or nearly pulled off, Frank was murmuring to Ted, Des's wife Beryl was pushing her food around her plate with her fork and looking sick. Probably pregnant again, if Desmond's past record was anything to go by. The twins were eating with the concentration of children normally condemned to schoolroom meals. The only person watching him was Josette. She smiled at him and, grateful for her interest, he smiled back. He had scarcely noticed her until now, and when her eyes turned to her plate once more he took covert stock of her. She was rather pretty, dark-eyed, dark-haired, with smooth, olive-brown skin and very small, very even white teeth. She must be in her mid-twenties, he supposed. A far cry from the skinny, filthy refugee he had plucked out of a burnt-out bombed farmhouse fifteen years ago! Not his type, though. He favoured fresh complexioned girls, too. His wife – ex-wife, he reminded himself sourly – was dark-eyed and dark-haired, but no one could have a clearer, paler complexion than Sarah, nor a more beautiful and desirable body.

He finished his main course and promptly forgot Josette. He had to see Sarah; he would go as soon as this interminable meal was over! She could have no idea, that was the answer, that he still wanted her! When she knew that he could carry her back to Sydney with him, to a new life, everything would change. She would tell him that it was still he who mattered, and they would break the news to the Solstein boy and go off into the sunset. Yes, that was it. He tackled his iced pudding with renewed zest. Once he had seen Sarah, misunderstandings would disappear like frost in June.

44

'A delicious meal, sister mine.' Louis smiled down at Tina a trifle condescendingly. 'And now I'm going to pop round to Ipswich Road, and see if I can't have a word with Sarah. We've barely set eyes on each other, you know.'

'Yes. But, Lou, don't you think . . . ?' They had taken their coffee through into the drawing-room and Louis could see that Tina felt she must be firm with him, yet was not quite sure how she was to do it. 'Ted, I wonder if . . .'

Louis was not in awe of his brother-in-law, but he did feel that he had put up with quite enough of the Neyler family for one evening. He kissed Tina firmly, therefore, announced his departure, shook hands with his nephews, and then made for the hall, with Tina in hot pursuit. He had borrowed Poppa's car and it stood conveniently close to the front door; as he went towards it he heard Tina give an exclamation and then abandon him, to go, he was sure, to the phone. He chuckled and swung the starting handle, then ran round and jumped in. Let her phone Sarah – what could the girl do? Other than pretend to be out, of course!

He was on the very point of departure, about to drive off, when the front door opened and someone ran out. Quickly, lightly, the girl was down the steps and wrenching open the passenger door. He turned, startled, to meet the gaze of a pair of brown eyes. Josette!

'Do you mind if I come with you? I'd like to see Sarah as well.'

Louis put the car in gear and sighed.

'Was this Tina's bright idea – for you to keep an eye on me? Because if so . . .'

'No, honestly. She didn't say anything to me at all, I

just thought . . .' They were going down the drive now and he saw her put her hand on the door. 'Would you rather I didn't come, Louis? It was only an impulse – I thought it might be a bit difficult, you see, if you went alone.'

He was touched, because it seemed she had thought kindly of him when the rest of his family condemned him. He put a hand on her knee.

'I'm grateful. Sit tight.'

And, in the event, he was grateful, because it was not an easy interview. Sarah was polite and even welcoming, but she sat them down, went to ask the maid to make coffee, and then returned, announcing cheerfully that she would bring Simon in when he returned from his trip to the cinema, and that Cara was at present reading to her grandmother. She would come down at the end of the chapter.

Mary brought coffee and *petit fours* through on a trolley and Sarah had barely seated herself to pour when the front door bell rang. Mary answered it; they heard a murmur of conversation in the hall, and then the door opened and Con walked into the room. He grinned at Louis, sketched a salute to Josette, and kissed Sarah in an infuriatingly possessive manner. He made very sure, Louis noted spitefully, that his inamorata was seated before doing so: otherwise it would have been a case of bring on the stepladders! But the mental dig gave Louis very little real satisfaction. He realised, within a few moments of being in Con's company, that his nephew was now a devilishly attractive man. Dark, with a lively, ugly face, he had charm and something else, which in Regency times had been known as 'address'. It came of being a barrister, Louis supposed gloomily. I have a bedside manner, he thought defensively, which probably knocks Con's into a cocked hat;

46

the only trouble is that it looks as though his address will get Sarah into bed when I shan't be around to try out my bedside manner!

Fast on the heels of this dismaying thought came another. Watching Sarah and Con, he recognised a closeness, a dependence on his nephew which Sarah had never shared with him. She had always been so very independent, perhaps realising that Louis was not a man to lean on.

If Josette had not been there to flirt with, he thought furiously as he got up take his leave without setting eyes on either of his children, he would have suffered a most unpleasant and humiliating half-hour. For whilst Sarah and Con scarcely spoke to each other, certainly did not do so in any sort of intimate way, it was as if they were attached by invisible strings. To counter this, he teased Josette, told her she was the prettiest refugee he had ever rescued, reminded her of childish pranks and exploits, and generally brought a pretty flush to her sallow little face.

Getting back into the car, he hoped that he had managed to fool them both into thinking that he had gone round to the house merely to see his children, that he was indifferent to Sarah. But he doubted it. Con was no fool and, as he well knew, neither was Sarah. He slammed the car into gear and turned out of the drive in the direction of The Pride.

'Do you really want to take me back yet, Louis? Couldn't we go for a run into the country and have a drink somewhere? It was a bit stuffy at Sarah's place; the run would do us good.'

Louis agreed grumpily, but he was naturally an optimist, and by the time they were a mile outside the city he was beginning to cheer up. Sarah had found herself someone else, and that someone else was his own nephew. Well, what the hell? He would go back to Australia tomorrow, instead of staying for three weeks as he had planned. He voiced the thought aloud to Josette, sitting quietly beside him. She shook her head.

'Why should you let anyone push you around, Lou? You've other ties here – family, friends. And there's Grandpa's business, too, that'll have to be sorted out. Stay until you're good and ready to leave, that's my advice.'

He was amused, and grinned across at her in the moonlight, for it was dark now, and there were no street lamps out here.

'You're a funny kid! But you're absolutely right.'

'I'm not a kid, Lou. I was fourteen when you saw me last. Now I'm twenty-five. I'm a woman.'

He drew up at a pub he had once known well and got out, going round to her side of the car to help her alight.

'So you are, and a very pretty woman too,' he said with absentminded gallantry. All he could really think about now was that drink. 'Come along in, then, and I'll buy you a real drink and not raspberryade!'

Once in the pub, with glasses before them and a big fire warming them, Louis felt better. They had taken their places on a settle by the fire, and because it was mid-week the lounge bar was practically empty. Josette snuggled – there was no other word for it – close to Louis. She fixed her eyes on his face, and it struck Louis that they were just as adoring as they had been all those years ago, when he had rescued her. His interest in her as an individual stirred for the first time.

'Are you sorry for me, Josette? It was one devil of a shock, you know, finding that she was going to marry Con. It hurt me.'

'I can see it did.' She looked up at him, and he noticed that her eyes were not dark brown but the colour of very

48

old port, a sort of tawny, reddish, goldish colour. As she looked at him, her pupils expanded and darkened just like a cat's. 'But you should forget Sarah now, Louis; she's lost to you, you know.'

'Yes, but why the devil . . . ? She waits nearly eleven years . . .'

Josette laid her hand on his. Louis looked down at it. It was a small hand, slim and olive brown so that the nails were paler than the skin. A rather pretty hand. In her way she was quite a fetching little thing – pity it wasn't a way which fetched Louis! Besides, she was years younger than he and his niece by adoption.

'I've waited fifteen years, Louis.'

It was said both quietly and modestly, but the glance that she sent him out of her tawny, port-wine eyes was neither. Louis was startled, almost shocked. Damn it, this *was* the child Josette, wasn't it?

'Waited? What for?'

'For you, Louis.'

Louis was used to being the object of blatant female admiration, to being pursued, admired, made much of. But not, he told himself, hurriedly drinking his beer, by girls he had known since they were babes! He looked at her over the rim of his glass and saw that she was looking at him, her eyes giving a message he had received – joyfully – many times before. But she was not his *type*, and he felt, confusedly, that a man should always stick to women who at least fulfilled that criterion. He stood up so quickly that he knocked Josette's sherry glass over, but fortunately it was already empty and she was so busy looking up at him that she did not notice.

'Yes, well, that's very . . . but I'd better take you back to The Pride now. I don't want your mother down on me for taking you drinking.' She had always called Tina

49

Mother; this would remind her, he hoped, that there were certain things which were just not *done*! He almost ran her back to the car, the hairs on the back of his neck prickling erect at his narrow escape. Suppose he had been less experienced, had not recognised the tacit invitation in that smouldering glance? Heavens, Tina's good little adopted daughter, in whose mouth butter had never melted, had been on the verge of making a pass at him!

Back in the car, driving into the city once more, she must have realised how silly she had been, he thought thankfully, for she became good company. She talked about her work, asked about nursing in Australia, and then showed a flattering interest in his own career, the hospital where he worked, the great city where he lived. It was balm to his wounded pride, still smarting beneath Sarah's obvious indifference, and he found himself relaxing, becoming easy with her once more, admiring her poise and grasp of matters medical.

He drew up outside The Pride and Josette jumped out, almost as though she suspected Louis of a desire to grab her. Louis, stung, jumped out too and accompanied her to the front door. When he was thanking her for her company she stood very close, looking up at him, her mouth a little open. She wetted her full bottom lip with her tongue, and her eyes adored. Louis swallowed. She was an odd little thing!

Driving back to the Maid's Head he whistled a tune beneath his breath and felt curiously cheerful, considering what a difficult evening he had had. He had arranged to pick Josette up first thing in the morning and take her out to old Frank's boatyard; he had been meaning to go there himself, and if he took Josette it would turn into a pleasant day's outing. They would take a picnic lunch – he could get the hotel to pack him one – and then Frank could hire them a boat. A treat for the kid! He smiled over his moment of panic in the pub. Josette obviously had a crush on him, but he could cope with that, particularly as she was not his type.

He garaged the car and walked across the darkened yard. He hushed his whistle in deference to other guests, then began to hum the Marseillaise. She was a fetching little thing!

Back at the house on Ipswich Road, Sarah was saying goodnight to Con.

'You were wonderful, darling.' She leaned against him in the hall, gazing adoringly into his face. She had taken off her shoes, kicking them unobtrusively under her chair, and they were now almost on a level. She rubbed her cheek against his. 'Poor old Lou. He was shattered, you know! And now he's gone off with quiet little Josette and he'll bore the poor child all evening by telling her how hard-done-by he is.'

Con took her by the hips and swayed her gently to and fro, smiling at her.

'Poor old Lou, indeed. You know you were delighted! And what's more, he might have bitten off more than he can chew with Josette. She's quite a girl.'

'How can you say such a thing! She's the meekest female in creation! She was always so good and helpful when she and Stell were small. I used to hate seeing Stella take advantage of her good nature, and Tina piling the small jobs on the willing little thing, when they were kids.'

'That, my love, was years ago. At Auntie Tina's request I partnered her to a dance once, when she was home at Christmas. In the car coming back she jolly nearly ate me alive. No, I'm not teasing, I mean it! She was wearing an off-the-shoulder evening gown and it

51

was off more than her shoulder, with no encouragement from me, before the car had been stopped outside The Pride two minutes. She isn't meek with men, I promise you!'

'Well, that'll be just what the doctor ordered for Lou,' Sarah said with a trace of bitterness. 'Though I wouldn't have thought she was his type.'

'Perhaps not. But, you see, all that Josette needs to make a man *her* type in his gender.' He laughed. 'And Lou's got plenty of that! Still, perhaps she still thinks of him as her Uncle Louis, and will respect his grey hairs.'

'He hasn't got any. But I'm sure you're right, and she'll be a good girl. And I bet you jolly well helped that dress, for all your smug denials.'

'When I saw which way the land lay I might have given it a nudge,' Con admitted. 'Here, stop talking, woman!' He kissed her, hard, and had the satisfaction of seeing the colour bloom in her cheeks. He hated leaving her, knowing that she wanted him to stay, but remaining would create more problems than it would solve. Besides, the wedding was not so far off, now that they knew when Louis was leaving!

'Darling Con, thank you for everything. You made huge problems melt away as if they were nothing.'

He laughed and put his arm round her waist, leading her to the front door.

'Just you wait until we're married. You'll have no time for problems then, large or small. Do you mind that it'll be a register office?'

'Mind?' She laughed and blew him a kiss as he got into his car. 'I've had one Shul wedding, and look what happened to that! All that matters, quite honestly, is that I marry you!'

He knew she was watching and waving until the car rounded the bend in the drive and was out of sight.

*

Frank was working in the big shed when his visitors arrived. Or perhaps working was putting too grand a name to it. Business was not good, but they had a couple of orders and he was whiling away an hour sanding down a rather nice table fitment he was making for a houseboat. He was well aware that he was working needlessly, but on certain Saturdays in the month time hung heavy and this was one of those Saturdays.

Patch, skinny and wild-eared, heard them first. His ears pricked and his eyes brightened. He yapped and then stood, stiff-legged, in the wide doorway of the boatshed, staring towards the cottage. Frank straightened and walked out into the yard. People did not come down to the yard on business on a Saturday at this time of year, but he would welcome visitors, provided they did not stay long!

He hoped it was Con. Their friendship had survived some ups and downs, as all friendships must, but nothing would change it, not even Con's marriage. Frank, respecting Sarah and loving Louis, had been hard put to it not to reproach Con with making a reconciliation impossible, but when it came down to it he wanted Con's happiness more than he wanted anything else. Almost.

If it is Con, he thought, gazing across to the cottage, we'll go to the pub for lunch and then I'll explain I've got to make a very important phone call. He'll make himself scarce. Con understands.

But it was not Con. Round the corner came Louis and Josette. Frank walked towards them, thinking how odd it was that they should have come together, because this was the first time that either of them had visited the yard. Louis had a casual hand on Josette's shoulder.

Frank was glad someone was taking a bit of notice of the girl. He had always felt faintly guilty about Josette, for when she had come to live with them he and Des had been glad simply because she had been more or less the same age as Stella and had kept their younger sister off their backs. He had often felt he should have made more of an effort to be nice to this little adopted sister, but then he had never really known her. The first years she had spent at The Pride had been the years when he had been away in the army, fighting first in France and then in Mesopotamia. He had come home, but then she and Stella were teenagers, absorbed in girlish things, and soon after that Daddy had bought the boatyard and he had left Norwich for Oulton, where he had lived ever since. So now he greeted his guests with his widest smile and a great show of hospitality.

'Uncle Louis, Josette, how nice of you to come all the way over here to see me! Come in and have a cup of tea or coffee or something, and I'll show you round.'

'Lovely.' Louis caught his arm as they went into the cottage. 'I wonder, old boy, if you'd mind dropping the uncle? You're catching up with me, you know. We'll soon be the same age, near as dammit, and it makes me feel a fool to hear a chap . . .'

'Yes, sorry, of course. It's stupid really, because I don't call . . .' Frank's voice faded into a mumble. He had been about to say that he didn't call Sarah aunt, but realised, almost too late, that it would be a tactless thing to say. Instead, he turned to Patch, who was sniffing at his guests with the almost indecent enthusiasm he sometimes turned on strangers. 'Leave off, Patch. Here, come and have a bacon bone. That'll keep you mum.'

Josette had come through into the small kitchen and watched with interest as he put the kettle on the top of the Aga and rattled it to bring the heat through.

'I like your place, Frank. Odd that I've not been here before.'

'I was thinking the same,' Frank admitted. 'I'm ashamed that I've never asked you specially, Josette. The trouble was that by the time I got established here you were doing your training, and since then you've only come back to Norwich for short breaks, and I've met you at The Pride either just as you were leaving or just as I was!'

'Yes, I suppose so. I thought you'd have heaps of workmen scurrying round, though. Is business terribly bad? The depression seems to hit everything, but Daddy said you were keeping your head above water.'

'We don't work at weekends – except in the summer when it's really busy – but of course, as you say, the depression's hit us too. Money's short and sales have gone down, but the hire trade – it really is fantastic what people will do to get a bit of a break. They'll manage to find the money for a week on the water, you'd be surprised. Look, what about lunch? I can't ask you to eat here because I always go over to the Wherry on a Saturday, but if you'd like to be my guests . . . well, I'd be honoured. I've a bit of business this afternoon, if you could amuse yourselves whilst I get that settled, but then you could come back here for tea.'

Louis, who had been in the living-room examining Frank's collection of boating photographs, came through and joined them.

'We wouldn't dream of putting you to any trouble, Frank. We've brought a picnic. We're customers, eh, Jo? We want to hire one of your boats and go for a little wander round the Broad. But we'd love to come back for a cup of tea and a sandwich before we go off down to Lowestoft to taste the high life, if that would suit you?'

'That would be fine,' Frank said, relieved. His plans

55

for this afternoon might not sound exciting or important, but they meant a lot to him and did not include either his uncle or his adopted sister. He picked out a reliable boat for them, saw them off, then got into his Bean. Perhaps it was no longer young, but he loved it and had no desire for a more modern car. He would have his lunch as usual, and then come back and make his telephone call. To France. He rang France every other Saturday, regular as clockwork. Except in the first two weeks in September. In September there was no need to ring France, because Mabel was never at her home in France for those two weeks.

Mabel sat in the conservatory of Matthieu's beautiful country home just far enough away from the coast to be quiet and private, but near enough to make a car ride there a short run. She had the big double doors open, since it was a lovely day, and outside, on the wide lawn, Matthieu and her son, André, were playing boule. Through the open doors she could hear a far-off cuckoo, calling plaintively, the sound of André's dog Pepe, scratching, and the low voices of her son and her husband calling to one another. Otherwise it was quiet, sunny, a perfect Saturday.

They were good companions, André and Matthieu. So good that to part them was unthinkable. Otherwise . . . but it was no use thinking about otherwises. She had made her bed years ago and now lay on it with as few complaints as possible. But though she watched the men and listened to their voices her ears were tuned for a different sound. The telephone. The door of the conservatory was open, but only half open. The Ivory room was the somewhat pretentious name for the room behind the conservatory, and in the Ivory room was a telephone. Right now there was a cushion, flung down with seeming carelessness, muffling the bell, but Mabel would hear it. She did not want Matthieu or André to hear because she hated lying to them, and with luck she could slip out, take her call, and be back in her chair before they realised that she had gone. If Matthieu did hear it, it meant more deceit, pretending it was her mother calling, a a wrong number, or her friend Jeanne. One played it by ear.

She sat in her green silk chair, a half-smile on her face, and waited. What a big proportion of her life, it seemed, was spent doing just that! Not literally, of course, because she kept herself busy with the affairs of the house, she still did some translating for Matthieu, and there were the countless ordinary social and sometimes even amusing activities which a rich man's wife undertook as a matter of course. But inside her head she was waiting. For the telephone calls, of course, but mostly for the two weeks in September when she was back in the country of her birth.

Those two weeks meant more lying than all the rest put together, but she did it because she had won that fortnight of freedom and she knew that without it she would no longer be able even to pretend that her life with Matthieu was enough.

The freedom had come about as a direct result of the death of her best friend, Frank's wife, Suzie. At the time, her grief for Suzie had been twisted and soured by the longing which had accompanied it, for Frank. He was free; they were still, in their mid-twenties, young enough to make a fresh start. She had loved him all her life and she felt she could not bear the separation a moment longer. It had gnawed her day and night, making her short-tempered, quick to take offence, prone to inexplicable bouts of tears. As a salmon must return to its birthplace during its life-cycle, so Mabel felt she must return to Frank. But ties stronger than any the salmon could know kept her in France. Matthieu, who had taken her in and married her and, in his way, loved her, when he knew she was carrying another man's child. André, who believed Matthieu to be his father and loved him. She could not grab what she wanted for herself and leave their lives in tatters!

Then Matthieu accused her, without the slightest justification, of having an affair with his best friend, a suave and altogether delightful man who was a good companion, in fact, to them both. She had realised then that Matthieu had sensed her hopeless preoccupation with someone other than himself, and had leapt to the conclusion that she had taken a lover. It was impossible for him to forget that she had, once, had intercourse with a man and borne him a son. He had explained, when he had offered to marry her, that he did not intend to sleep with her and never would. She had been glad at the time, because her one experience of sex had been painful and frightening beyond belief. Later, she had been confused and astonished by her own desires and the muddled, painful way she had tried to rouse Matthieu to some show of physical affection.

The accusation had been the last straw. He had been frightened by her outburst, by her threat to leave him, to take André and return to England and her parents. It had also proved that she had no lover in France, if she was so willing to leave the country, and he knew very well that she could have no lover in England, for she had only been back to Norwich twice without him. When he brought her over on business trips he kept an eye on her; unobtrusively, perhaps, but nevertheless she knew herself watched.

He had been eager, after that, to make amends, and she had seized on his suggestion of a fortnight's holiday by herself, with her parents, in England at any time she chose to name.

Now, she had said, because it was at the end of July that all this had come about, and she could not envisage coping with life any longer without seeing Frank. A whole fortnight, by myself. I will go back to my parents and unwind and live quietly. I'll visit old friends who knew me well once, and old places that I loved. She had glowed with the fact that dreams would become reality, and had been stopped in her tracks by Matthieu's voice, wistful in a way she had never heard it.

'You – you will come back?'

She had hugged him – which he hated – and promised on her son's life that she would come back.

She could not take André, of course. She could never take him back to Norwich now, because his resemblance to his natural father was so marked. His character, she thanked God fasting, was totally different from Desmond Neyler's, but his looks were typical of the men of the family. Thick blonde hair, classical features, blue eyes.

She went, of course, to Frank. She would never forget that journey, culminating in a dreadful rainstorm so that she had arrived in the village saturated and chilled despite the fact that it was still summer. She had gone down through the steadily increasing rain to the jetty and bribed Pat Paterson to row her over to Frank's boatyard. Enveloped in the heavy oilskins which he kept handy for bad weather, she had watched eagerly as they neared the shore and when the door opened and Frank came out, bare-headed into the rain, she had known such happiness that it was a spiritual experience. Childlike, she had promised God that in payment for that one perfect moment, she would be good.

59

She had been good. After that one furtive visit to the cottage they had met yearly, in September because that was a good month for Frank to leave the boatyard in other hands. So far as everyone knew, Frank took a solitary fishing trip in Scotland. He met her off the boat and drove her by slow stages up to the little hotel in the Highlands which he had visited once by himself. They became, as they crossed the border, she used to say laughingly, Mabel and Frank Neyland. Sometimes it rained a lot, sometimes it was fine with that fragile, leaf-fall fineness of pale morning mists and paler sunshine which only seems to come in September. It did not matter. That they were together was all that counted.

Sometimes there were extras. Once, Frank had got up to London when she and Matthieu were there on business and they had stolen a whole blissful day together. Arms round each other's waists, her head against his shoulder, they had gone to the Regent's Park Zoo and looked in the cages and kissed, just as any other pair of lovers might. Except that, then, they had not been lovers. She remembered that day with such pleasure. Even the rain had been lovely, and they had walked and laughed together and wished . . . wished . . .

The muffled shrill of the telephone bell cut across her thoughts. She was up and out of the room, grabbing the receiver off its hook before the sound could alert father and son on the lawn. She had left the doors open, and whilst she waited for the connection to be put through she watched. Matthieu had his back to the house and was strolling down to the long herbaceous border with the apple trees at the back. She suspected that he and André between them had lost a ball in there, since André was already poking half-heartedly with one foot at huge clumps of lupins.

Frank's voice, thinned by distance, sounded in her ear. He wanted to know what the weather was like – it helped if they both knew what sort of weather conditions the other was enduring, though she had no idea why. She could see him so much better, though, in his office in the cottage by the Broad that she had only visited twice, if she knew whether it was sunny or rainy, windy or still.

'It's a lovely day. And you?'

'Nice. Uncle Louis's come back from Australia. He and Josette came over this morning and they've taken a boat out on the Broad. And yours?'

'Playing boule in the garden. How's the business?'

Their talk could never be intimate, not with a servant liable to pop into the room, or a husband or a son. But ordinary little bits of information were good to exchange. Just to hear a voice so much beloved was enough, she knew.

'Old Mr Rose is dead. That's why Lou came back. Mabs?'

'Mm hmm?'

'Con's marrying Sarah.'

She knew what he meant. Sometimes it seemed as though everyone but themselves had the right to get married, live together, be happy. But there was always September. She spoke brightly.

'Lovely, you said you thought they would. They both deserve some happiness, don't they? Remember Loch Ness?'

'Oh, Mabs, my darling!'

She could not risk one endearment, he knew that, but it made her heart bleed to be unable to tell him how she loved and wanted him. And then a movement caught her eye. Matthieu was coming through the Ivory room. She had been talking English but she switched to

French easily, without having to think about it, knowing that Frank would understand what had happened.

'So there you have it, Jeanne,' she said gaily. 'You've had dinner parties like it yourself, so you know what it was like. Yes.'

She listened and Frank said, very quietly, 'Adieu, my dearest love,' his voice sounding small and lost.

'Very true. But look, I'll be in Paris next week. I'll ring you from there, or if you're in town I can pop round.' She laughed. It sounded natural. 'How rude you are. Of course it would be cheaper! Adieu then, Jeanne.'

She put the phone down and turned to Matthieu, the smile fading from her mouth. 'Oh, hello, darling. That was Jeanne. I told her about our dreadful dinner party, amongst other things. Not that she was impressed. Zach is always putting the cat amongst the pigeons and asking people who don't get on deliberately, to make life interesting.'

Jeanne was a good friend; she would not let her down. She knew that Mabel had a 'friend', and since she knew, also, that Matthieu, whilst not a homosexual, was not strictly speaking heterosexual either, said that she had no qualms over deceiving him a little.

'You are taking nothing from Matthieu, for he wants nothing,' Jeanne had said. 'You give to him, to André, just what they want. And to this other, also, you give. To give is good.'

'Well, since you and Jeanne have finished jabbering perhaps André and I could interest you in a little run down to the coast? André thought it would be nice to have *goûter* down there, by the sea. What about it?'

'Marvellous!' André came into the room and she touched his cheek caressingly with her fingers. 'Are you taking bathing trunks? Shall I bring my costume?'

They walked out to the car together presently, and

Mabel remembered the last real remark she had made to Frank. *Remember Loch Ness*. It referred to last September. The best September so far, because during the course of that fortnight she and Frank had become lovers.

The first three times they had gone to Scotland, though she was sure no one would have believed her, they had shared a room and a large old-fashioned bed, had held each other and kissed, but they had never made love. She had begun to think they never would, and to know that though it was much safer for her it was also terribly frustrating, when they had taken a picnic to Loch Ness.

And there it had happened, in that most unlikely of places. Not in their warm bed, not in his large car, but in a ruined castle overlooking the loch, on a dampish, misty day with the sun quite hidden and the grass spangled with wet so that they had brought the rug out of the car and lain it down amidst the ruins, and sat down to eat their picnic rather doubtfully, for if it came on to rain there was no real shelter.

She remembered it more vividly than anything that had happened before or since in her life. The sweet smell of the crushed grass, the mist hanging over the water, and Frank's hands, unbuttoning her blue shirt, lovingly touching her, kissing her, until passion had suddenly blazed in them both and they had joined together at last.

After that, neither could understand how they had managed to spend a total of six whole weeks together without making love. The fortnight had flown and Mabel, laughing, had told him that they had been sleeping together for three years in the literal sense, and now that they were sleeping together in the figurative sense they had scarcely closed their eyes! It was an exaggeration, but he knew what she meant.

'*Maman! Voila!*'

Mabel brought herself back to the present with a jerk. She was in the south of France, with Matthieu and André, and there was the blue Mediterranean stretching out before them. And all she wanted to think about was northern Scotland, and mists, and September weather. And love. And Frank.

Chapter Three

It was a hot afternoon in August, so hot that the players had forsaken a tennis court at The Pride and sprawled, instead, beneath the cedar tree which had cast its shade on the big lawn by the house for as long as anyone could remember. The Neylers were a hospitable family and the twins, running true to form, always held open house during the summer holidays for anyone who wanted to play and to have tea. But this was an unusual party, even though the twins were unaware of it.

For a start, it had split into three groups. One group consisted of Cara, the Neyler twins and Paul Butcher. They lay on the grass on their tummies passing round a peashooter with which they tried, unsuccessfully, to score a direct hit on a huge, tiger-striped tabby cat who lay in the herbaceous border, eyes tightly shut, sleeping in the shade of a clump of delphiniums. Their talk was desultory, for the twins were not fond of Cara and scarcely knew Paul. Also, they wondered what their elders were talking about so earnestly.

The second group was equally ill at ease, though they were just beginning to exchange the odd remark. Jennifer and Martin Bachelow lived next door to The Pride and were friends of long standing, Jenny, who was fifteen, being madly in love at present with Simon. Martin was thirteen and only loved tennis. He wanted to start the game up again but no one else did, so he was sulking, staring at the third member of their little group and wondering why God had made girls as wet as this one.

'This one' was Pixie Hopwood. Pixie lived just up the road from the Butchers in Blofield, and had been introduced into their group ostensibly by James, the elder Butcher. But Jenny, watching Pixie narrowly, fairly bristled with suspicion. Simon liked her, she could tell! Horrible, common girl that she was!

The last group was the smallest and consisted only of Simon and James Butcher. They were right on the outskirts of the shade so that their conversation might remain private, and the reason why they were engaged in such serious discussion, apart from being best friends, was that they had recently discovered they were half-brothers. Not, as Simon had just observed, the sort of information which one could just push into the back of one's mind. He had been gratified to find that James, despite being two years the older, had not known for years and years, but had been told only a few days previously, as he had. Now, with serious faces but with guilty grins lurking, they discussed their new relationship.

'You could've knocked me down with a feather!' That was James, a serious citizen, tall like his father and with Louis's colouring, but otherwise much more like his mother, Sarah Sutton, now Sarah Butcher.

'Me, too,' Simon agreed. He had hero-worshipped James for years and, once the shock of discovery was over, was very glad that they were blood relations. They had been brought up together during the war and had remained best friends ever since, as had their mothers. Simon thought, now, that it must have been difficult to remain friends once they knew that they had shared a man, but they were strong-willed and determined women, the two Sarahs.

'It was hard on your mum, having to tell you,' James ventured presently. 'Mine didn't give a damn.

Laughed, she did, and said Winkie – Dad, you know – always had his suspicions. But your mum didn't know for years, my mum said.'

'I don't think she minds. Not now she's got Uncle Con, and is going to be married to him in a few weeks. She went jolly red, though. You know why they told us now, of course?'

'Can't say I do. Why?'

'Because last time you came over to our house, Cara came prancing in from school, do you remember? We were in the kitchen, you and I and Paul, and she came flirting in and made eyes at you. Remember? I think it suddenly occurred to Mother that if Cara took a shine to you or to Paul it'd be incense. Or something.'

'Well I'm damned!' James was grinning. 'Simon, did your mum tell you that there were others?'

Simon stared, his mouth dropping open.

'Others? Good God, no! No, she didn't.'

James nodded portentously. 'Yes, there are. When he went, back in nineteen twenty, it was because he'd got three other girls in the family way. Mum says they all had sons though, she thinks. Cara's his only daughter.'

'Well, that's something to be thankful for,' Simon said with brotherly candour. 'Girls as nasty as Cara ought only to occur once in a generation.'

'I know what you mean. But she's very pretty.'

'Oh, I'll grant you that. We're all good-looking, you, me, Paul and Cara. And she's the only girl, eh?' He grinned at James. 'At least I shan't have to stare at Pix and wonder if she's my sister!'

'Yes, that reminds me. You do know, don't you, that your mother and aunt and everyone think that Pixie's my bit of fluff?'

'Oh, that! Well, I could scarcely explain I've an interest there myself and expect to get her invited here! I

67

just want her to get her foot in the door and then I daresay I'll be able to swing lots of invites. She's all right, Pixie is.'

It was a statement, but James raised a brow.

'Not your style at all, old boy.' He put on an upper-class accent. 'You public school fellahs shouldn't take up with little floosies like her! You ought to know bettah, boy!'

'She's a sport, that's what matters.' Simon lounged to his feet, for he and James had been lying on the grass like the others. 'I was invited to tea, friends, and it's time it came out! I'll go and remind Ruthie that her favourite guest is starving!'

Val, prone on her tummy with the peashooter to her lips, promptly leapt to her feet in a gangle of long skinny arms and legs. She turned to Simon, her green eyes lighting up. She adored her big cousin.

'I'll go, Sime! I shan't be a tick.'

With Val's abrupt departure, the groups merged into one again. Simon went and sat by Pixie, never noticing the look of blazing reproach fixed on him by Jenny Bachelow. He looked sideways at Pixie's smooth young face with its blue eyes and softly waving fair hair. Her figure was a good deal more mature than her thirteen years warranted, but he liked that; she was definitely his type of girl. She leaned over and touched Simon's fingers and gave him a sultry smile. It was enough to set his heart galloping. What a girl she was! After tea, he might persuade her to stroll in the woods, or on the way home . . .

'Here we are, everyone, tea!' Val came out of the house pushing a huge mahogany trolley laden with food. She brought it to the edge of the terrace then looked doubtfully down at the lawn below. 'You'd better come and eat up here. I daren't let it down the bank.'

'Not necessary,' Simon said. He and James went over and caught an end of the trolley each. 'We'll lift it down into the shade. No point in having roast cakes and sandwiches.'

Ruthie, following with a tray, announced. 'Lemonade here, children. If you want a cuppa tea, you'll ha' to come into the kitchen, together.'

'Thanks, Ruthie, only no one'll want tea, I shouldn't think. It's too hot.' Nicky took the tray from her and staggered over to the cast-iron table beneath the cedar. 'Whew, it's a weight! Oh, there's ice!'

The young people gathered round the trolley and began to help themselves from the piled-up plates. Val poured lemonade into glasses with a chink of ice as it swirled round in the tall jug. Jennifer took some sandwiches and began to hand them round, then put the plate back on the trolley. It was plainly a help-yourself party. Simon saw her put the plate back and gave her a lovely smile, unknowingly making Jennifer's afternoon perfect. She would go away when the party was over and boast that Simon Rose had been 'sweet' to her. Val would giggle, but she would not bother to contradict. Simon was, after all, her cousin, and there was considerable kudos to be gained from that fact at the Norwich High School, where half the girls in the classes above Val fancied themselves in love with him. She would let Jenny have her small triumph.

Pixie was pretty and intelligent, but since she was boy-crazy, enjoying their company more than she liked the company of her own sex, and since in class she thought a great deal more about boys than she did about lessons, few of her teachers thought her anything but a pretty, lazy flirt.

At home, Pixie was kept close. The only child of

elderly and pious parents, she was subjected to endless diatribes on the evils that lay in wait for a modern girl, forbidden to do most of the things she wanted to do, and kept as short of money and clothes as was practicable. Her parents loved her, she acknowledged that, but they did not even begin to understand her. Other girls had parents who talked to them. About clothes, or games, or even about lessons; not about religion, the Bible, and what happened to girls who wore make-up, laughed too loudly, or curled their hair. Pixie's hair curled naturally as it happened, but she suspected sometimes that her mother was secretly ashamed of her daughter's abundant locks and would much have preferred a plain little thing with a straight, mouse-coloured bob. Other parents took their children for outings, played beach cricket with them, accompanied them, on occasion, to the cinema. Yet sometimes, surprisingly, she felt sorry for her parents. The lack of understanding was so total, the impossibility of bridging the gap so complete, that she had to pity their plight. They would have been marvellous parents for the sort of child they should have given birth to – a dull, quiet little mouse of a girl. But they had borne Pixie and for as long as she could remember the expression on their faces as they looked at her had been one of pained bewilderment. The cuckoo in the nest, that's what she felt she was.

'If you carry on like you're bin doing, you'll come to no good,' was her mother's frequently expressed opinion, but since she was never more explicit, and since Pixie had no desire whatsoever to come to good, whatever that might mean, it did not worry her. She wanted a handsome boyfriend, a lot of fun, and her freedom. She could not wait to be old enough to leave home, to buy her own clothes, to have dashing hats, skirts with slits up the sides, sheer silk stockings and high-heeled shoes. To shake the dust of the cottage in Blofield from her heels, and to play all day!

Her parents' reaction to the Neylers' invitation had come as a complete – and delightful – surprise.

'You won't come to no harm there,' her father said. 'Remember how you're bin brought up and you'll do werra well.'

Her mother had been equally enthusiastic. They thought, of course, that she had been invited by Val Neyler, who sometimes came over to see Sally Butcher in the shop nearby, and it was true, in a way. Simon had been instrumental in asking his cousin to invite her, but it had been Val's invitation. She had actually been bought a white tennis skirt and a blouse, garments which her mother normally would have stigmatised as 'fast', and allowed to set off alone on the bus with James and Paul Butcher. When she had tentatively suggested that she might be late, since these affairs tended to carry on into the evening, both parents had told her that would be quite all right.

'Just behave nice, Priscilla,' was the only comment.

And now the party was drawing to its close and Pixie was sure that she and Simon were about to come, if not to no good, at least to some fun! Tentative fumblings and some inexpert but exciting kisses having been exchanged on every possible occasion and in every possible quiet hiding place, Simon had whispered to her that when the party broke up he and she would go off together. He did not say where, and Pixie hugged herself with excitement. Would it be the cinema? She adored the pictures, adored sitting in the back row with Simon kissing the side of her face, her neck, and squeezing anywhere he could reach. Her parents disapproved of the cinema. All that darkness!

At last the goodbye and thank yous had been said and they were walking down the long beech-lined drive. James and Paul were going straight home but Simon, with serpentine cunning, had asked James to nip in to Mrs Hopwood's and tell her that Val had invited Pixie to stay on a bit with some other girls, and would put her on the last bus.

'Well, don't you go getting into any trouble, the pair of you,' James said, looking doubtfully from one to the other. Then he shrugged. 'I'll meet the last bus, Pix. Make sure you're on it!'

'That was a good idea,' Pixie said, as soon as the brothers were out of hearing. 'My mum thinks they're after me. She'll be quite happy knowing that they're in Blofield and I'm in Norwich.' They laughed at such maternal simplicity. 'Where are we goin', then?'

'Up the drive again and into the hayloft,' Simon said, squeezing her hand. 'The twins will be eating soon so we shan't be disturbed.'

Pixie felt the hand that he held grow clammy with excitement and hoped that Simon wouldn't notice. A hayloft! And they would be alone! An unrivalled opportunity for kissing, an exercise that she loved!

They reached the back of the stabling and then it was a simple matter, if undignified, to scramble through a low window whose wooden shutter swung back easily under Simon's hand, and to tiptoe across the brick floor and climb up the ladder into the loft.

Under the eaves, they stared at each other in the dusky, dusty last sunlight which filtered through gaps in the tiles.

'Well?' That was Pixie, lips parted in a provocative pout.

Simon began kissing her.

*

'I didn't like that girl Pixie,' Val said austerely, as she and Nick ate their supper. They were in the kitchen with Ruthie, since their parents were dining out. Ruthie, listening sympathetically, nodded.

'That'd be Master James's friend. Flighty piece, I thought.'

'She wasn't James's friend. It was Simon who brought her,' Nicky said indistinctly through a mouthful of buttered scone. 'You don't listen, you know, Val. They told Auntie Sarah and Mum she was James's friend, but that was all poppycock.'

'She *was* James's friend,' Val said at once. 'Awful girl, she lives near the Butchers. She was making eyes at the big boys all afternoon. I didn't like her.'

'So you said.' Nicky was a thin, tough little boy with a mass of coppery curls and an enormous appetite. Despite being twins, Val was a good six inches taller than he was, but when they fought Nicky always won. Now he reached for another scone and began to butter it lavishly. He turned to Ruthie, watching benignly. 'I do adore butter, in the hols! At school, you know, we can choose, it's either . . .'

'Butter *or* jam, you can't have both,' Val finished for him jeeringly. 'Oh, poor little Nicky, do they starve diddums at Pursell's, then?'

'They jolly well try, but I keep alive on my tuckbox,' Nicky said, unruffled. He reached for the jam. 'Anyway, I don't see why you didn't like Pixie. She was a good sport. And she didn't flirt with me or I'd have landed her one. She just mucked about.'

'She was horrible, and of course she didn't flirt with you, poodle, because you're too small and weedy.' Val reached across the table and snatched the jam dish. 'Leave some for me, you hog!'

73

'Language!' Nick promptly grabbed the dish back. 'Say please!'

'What, to you? Is it likely?'

'Yes, or Vally-Wally won't get any jam!'

'Just you give me that dish back, Nicky Neyler, or I'll cave your head in with the cake tin,' Val threatened. Her face paled as only a redhead's can, then flushed scarlet. She picked up the cake tin. Nicky laughed.

'Go ahead, try it!'

Ruthie tried to get between them whilst Val screamed with temper and Nicky, still laughing, held the jam dish well out of reach.

'Now then, you two!' Ruthie's face was flushed now. 'What the pair of you need is a damn' good walloping, behaving like this in my kitchen! I'll give you one last chance and then I'll tell your pa, sure's my name's Vi'let Ruthven! Val, ask nicely for that jam, and Nick, just you stop irritatin'. Twins! I thought twins never had arguments! Well, you two are the exceptions that prove the rule, that's all I can say!'

'Make him give me the jam! I won't say please! He snatched it!'

'I shan't give her the time of day until she's said please!'

'How dare you, you beastly little squirt!'

'You lanky, ill-mannered gingernut!'

The argument rose to a crescendo and Ruthie added her voice to theirs, threatening, cajoling. The three of them were oblivious of everything else.

In the loft, two more children were quarrelling. Pixie, tears pouring down her cheeks, was crouched against a stack of hay, nursing herself and glaring pitifully at Simon.

'Why didn't you stop when I told you to? You're

cruel, Simon Rose! I feel like you've killed me. I'm sure you've broke me insides.'

'You're daft. Girls don't die of *that*,' Simon said scornfully, hiding his considerable unease. 'I didn't mean to hurt you. The thing was, you were every bit as keen as me until you suddenly started screeching. And by then it was too late. I *couldn't* stop!'

'You could've if you'd wanted. You just liked it,' Pixie said with considerable acumen. 'You did it wrong, that's why . . . well, look at my skirt! You don't think that's *supposed* to happen, do you?'

Simon looked at Pixie's blood-dappled tennis skirt with some consternation. Suppose he had injured her in some awful internal fashion? He knelt down beside her and put his arm round her shoulders, then kissed her cheek.

'Look, I'm sorry I hurt you, but you *know* I didn't mean to! Do you want me to take you home, or get a doctor, or what?'

'I can't go to a doctor,' Pixie said, shocked at such foolishness. 'A doctor'd tell me mum what I'd been up to! And I can't go home – not like this!'

'And you can't stay here, howling in the hay,' Simon said with asperity. Try as he might, he could not think that what he had done could hurt her badly; could it? He shook his head and kissed her cheek again. It was soft and comforting, as was her body in the curve of his arm. How could something that was so pleasurable and exciting to him be injurious to her? He shook her, gently. 'What are we going to do, Pix?'

'Could you borrow me another tennis skirt?' Pixie said nervously. 'They're all alike. Perhaps me mum wouldn't notice. If I can just get back home and to bed without her seeing . . .'

'Yes. I'll nip home and grab one of Cara's. No, it

would take too long. I'll go indoors and find Val and see if she'll cough something up.' He stood up and looked down at Pixie. 'Tell you what, I've got a better idea. You don't have to get back until the last bus. I'll take that skirt down and rinse it under the tap. You stay up here and rest.'

Pixie looked up at him. Her face was tear-streaked and the sparkle had gone from her eys. She looked forlorn and frightened and not a day older than her thirteen years. Simon's heart smote him. He was a kind boy and she looked such a little kid, lying there. He knelt down and kissed her, properly, on the mouth, the sort of kiss she enjoyed. Then he knelt back and smiled at her.

'Poor old Pix! We'll brush through, see if we don't!'

There followed easily the worst hours in Simon's young life. Very much later that night, as he crawled into bed, he decided that he was right off women. As for Pixie, he devoutly hoped he need never set eyes on her again. Blaming him for what she'd been begging him to do one moment, moaning and screeching, setting him impossible tasks . . .

It's taught me a lesson, anyway, Simon told himself as he pulled the sheet up round his ears. He was still trembling from the reaction of his strenuous and misspent evening. First, he had gone downstairs and washed Pixie's skirt. Not expertly, he would have been the first to admit that, but with great diligence. And then, when she had said it was not good enough, he had gone into The Pride, his heart in his mouth one minute and in his shoes the next, and borrowed a skirt belonging to one of the maids. Pixie had put it on and the two of them had limped into the city, for Simon was surprisingly tired even then.

Once in the city, Pixie had disappeared into a ladies' lavatory and had emerged five minutes later with the tennis skirt very wet, but very clean. There was soap, she said briefly, when he questioned her. Then they had gone to the bus station, and he had tried to put her on the bus, but to no avail. The moment she realised he was not going with her her eyes had filled and her lower lip had begun to tremble, so he had got on the bus and gone all the way to the King's Head, dismounting and walking home with her and with James, who had remembered his promise.

She had said nothing to James, which was a point in her favour. All of a sudden, Simon found that he had no desire to tell James what he and Pixie had done. He desperately wanted to ask James about things, but it was no use. James was a marvellous chap, but there was a chance that he might think he, Simon, had been no gentleman.

He had packed Pixie off indoors, with a tale that she had borrowed the skirt to wear over her own tennis dress which had got badly grass-marked, and had then realised he had missed the last bus back to Norwich.

James had lent him his bicycle, and just as he was wheeling it past Pixie's house her bedroom window shot open and the borrowed skirt flew out, draping itself across his head. Pixie had laughed, a smothered giggle behind one plump hand, and that had been *it*, Simon told himself savagely. Oh, very funny, to throw a skirt at a chap when he had been doing his damnedest to see that she came out of it all right. And now he had a ten-mile ride ahead of him, and could not even go straight home, but must detour by The Pride to see that the maid got her skirt.

So, by the time he got into bed, soured and dis-illusioned, not even a distinctly uneasy conscience could keep him awake. At first, his sleep was troubled and he dreamed awful things, amongst which discovery was not the worst by a long chalk. But as morning approached even his subconscious mind decided to give him a break. He slept peacefully.

To give him credit, the first thing Simon did next morning, after he had eaten a substantial breakfast, was to tell his mother that he had borrowed James's bicycle since he had missed the last bus, and arrange to return it. Then, cycling slowly on his own bike with James's led alongside like a captive, he went out to Blofield. James, of course, was working, but the shop was open and Aunt Sally, beaming at him across the counter, took the bicycle in charge and, after a thoughtful look at his pale face, did not tell him that James had been intending to take a bus up to Ipswich Road during his lunch hour and reclaim his property. Simon, she could see, was not quite himself.

Having done his duty by James, Simon stiffened his sinews, summoned up his blood, and, making no attempt to disguise fair nature with hard-favour'd rage, since this did not seem appropriate (he was doing *Henry the Fifth* at school), he knocked, a little timidly, on Pixie's door.

It was opened by an elderly lady of forbidding aspect. Simon unerringly recognised Pixie's mother from the unflattering description given him by Pixie, and hauled his school cap, which he wore when cycling because it had a usefully wide peak, from his black curls.

'Good morning, madam. I'm Val Neyler's cousin, Simon Rose. Your daughter came to my cousin's tennis party yesterday, and she didn't seem too well when she left. Val knew I was coming over to see Paul, so she asked if I'd just enquire after Pixie.'

78

Mrs Hopwood smiled, but there was no disguising the worry on her face.

'That's ever so kind of you, Mr Rose. Priscilla's far from well, but she won't hear of getting the doctor in. I'm goin' to leave it till tomorrow, and if she's no better the doctor she shall hev.'

'I see. I'll call again, then.' Simon gave Mrs Hopwood his most melting smile and remounted his bicycle, his worst fears confirmed. He had done something wrong last night and injured Pixie inside, the way she said he had. By the time he reached the outskirts of the city his sense of guilt was so great that he felt he must find out what was wrong, talk to someone who would under-stand and not condemn. If only, he thought, his father were in England still! Judging from what he and James had been told recently, Louis would be able to explain what had gone wrong, perhaps might even reassure him. But Louis, alas, had gone back to Sydney long since.

As he cycled down past Thorpe Station, it occurred to him that since Con was to marry his mother in less than two weeks perhaps he was the best person – next to Louis, of course – to advise him. It would not be necessary to say what he had done. He would merely ask Con what happened to women when they went with a man. Women in general, not one in particular.

To think was to act. Con's chambers were in Cathedral Street. Simon swerved on to the crown of the road, stuck out a hand, and veered into the side street. He knew the brass plate outside from visits with his mother, and propped his bike against a convenient lamp post before going in through the neatly painted door.

'Yes?' A young woman, well dressed, hair bobbed, cheeks rouged, regarded him over the top of a type-writer. 'Can I help you?'

79

'Is M-Mr S-Solstein in?' Simon stammered, suddenly wondering whether Uncle Con would be alone in the office. It would be impossible to ask him anything with someone else present!

'I think so. Who shall I say?'

'Mr C-Conrad Solstein,' poor Simon said, thoroughly confused.

'No, not *'im,*' the girl said, smiling. 'You!'

'Oh, sorry. I'm Simon Rose.'

'Ah, you'll be the son of the young lady Mr Solstein's marrying!' The girl sighed sentimentally. 'A lovely lady, your mother. Wait a minute, I'll ask.'

She lifted a voice pipe and spoke into it.

'Mr Conrad, you've a visitor, a Mr Simon Rose.'

There was a pause, then a deep voice said something Simon could not catch, though he recognised Con's tones. He looked his enquiry at the girl, who interpreted obligingly.

'He'll be right out.'

Fortunately, for Simon was beginning to think that his bright idea might not have been so bright after all and to contemplate flight, a door opened almost as she spoke and Con appeared. He reached down a coat hanging on the rack behind the young woman and grinned at Simon.

'Hello, old man. Come to have lunch? I'll take you to White's if you're starving hungry, or to the Fye Bridge Tavern if you fancy a pint and a sandwich. Or we can go to the Prince of Wales Snack Bar if you want a quiet chat.'

Simon wistfully declined the Fye Bridge, though in ordinary circumstances he would have loved to go to a public house with Uncle Con.

'It had better be the snack bar, sir, if you don't mind. I've got a – a bit of a problem.'

Once seated in a dark corner with a tiny table piled with sandwiches and meat pies and a glass of milk before him, however, he found it by no means as easy as he had thought it would be to begin.

'Well, cough it up,' Con said, munching cheese and salad sandwiches. 'God knows you must have problems, with me coming into your life in less than two weeks.'

'Oh no, sir. You'll be getting rid of Grandma, that's the main thing,' Simon said ingenuously. 'No, it's just something that I think I ought to know. It's been puzzling me.'

'Right. Just an academic question, eh? Like, if you jumped in the river with both hands and feet tied and your head in a sack, would you drown?'

Simon, vastly relieved by so much understanding, nodded eagerly.

'Just like that, sir. I can't ask Mother, you see, because it's about girls.'

Con lifted an eyebrow.

'Then you're running true to form. Most of our masculine problems are caused by or concerned with the fair sex. Carry on.'

By now, Simon had thought out more or less how to phrase his question.

'Well, sir, if a girl was very young . . .'

He tried not to ramble, and Con was bluntness itself.

'When any girl goes with a fellow, Simon, she can become pregnant and have his baby. It doesn't matter if it's the first time or the hundred and first, the result can be the same. But the first time, whether she's fourteen or forty, she can sometimes get very little pleasure out of a union because every woman has a maidenhead, which a man must break in order to have intercourse with her. That means the woman may lose some blood

81

and suffer some pain. Is that what you were wanting to know?'

'Yes, that's it,' Simon said, his heart lighter. 'I must say I did wonder.' He added, on a note of innocent enquiry, 'If it hurts, as you say, Uncle Con, why do they want to do it?'

Con laughed and pointed to Simon's untouched glass of milk. 'Drink up, old chap. Curiosity is thirsty work! A woman puts up with the pain for the pleasure which follows. It's instinct that brings her to the point in the first place, of course. Every warm-blooded mammal has an urge to mate, otherwise the species would just die out.'

'Put like that,' Simon said, wiping a milky moustache off his upper lip and putting his empty glass down on the table again. 'Put like that it sounds pretty un-romantic!'

'Yes, but between men and women it isn't just an instinct to mate and reproduce,' Con said with a touch of severity. 'Affection first, then joy, then love, lift sex between a man and a woman out of the sphere of mere mating.'

Simon, agreeing blithely, cycled up the long stretch of Prince of Wales Road reflecting guiltily that there had been little enough affection, or love either, in that brief liaison in the loft. But it had all been perfectly natural. No one had done anything awful to anyone else, as he would speedily tell Pixie. And, with the guilt lifted off his mind, it no longer seemed so impossible to see Pixie again with pleasure. He would go over to Blofield, he decided, and break the good news to her that very night!

Back in his office once more, Con avoided his secretary's interested eyes, closed the door, and sank into his chair with a heartfelt groan.

So this was a foretaste of married life, was it? Had he left it too late to back out? For unless he was very much mistaken young Simon, his stepson-to-be, had had his first virgin, and whilst he rather sweetly worried about the blood shed and the pain experienced it was extremely doubtful from what he had said whether the fear of giving the girl a brat in his own image had even crossed the boy's mind. Furthermore, having broken both his duck and her resistance, it was highly unlikely that he would refrain from more such adventures.

Con was in the act of gently beating his brow with the heel of his hand when Andy Felton, his friend and partner, walked in and slung his macintosh across Con's desk.

'Hear you had company at lunchtime,' he said cheerfully. 'Sarah's got you well trained, sending the boy to you already. What did he want?'

Con groaned.

'Andy, you've been a good friend to me, and you were a good friend to Lou once. Simon's Lou's son. If I tell you, in strictest confidence, what he wanted, can *you* advise *me*?'

'Damn it, he's the image of Louis, so I bet it's woman trouble. Why don't you cut and run, old fellow? Sarah's a grand girl, but is any woman worth the sort of worry you'll get from being stepfather to that lad?'

'Yes. She's worth it ten times over,' Con said firmly. 'But, Andy, Simon'll make me a grandfather before I'm thirty if I don't do something about it smartly.'

Andy snorted with laughter.

'Right. Take my advice. Buy the boy a packet of condoms and insist that he uses 'em. Din it into his head that there's no way a decent man can play around with a girl unless he's prepared to take precautions. Believe me, Con, if someone had forced Lou to act responsibly

83

he wouldn't be in Australia today. He'd be here taking care of his own son.'

'I'm bloody glad he's out of the way,' Con groaned. 'You're right. I should have told the boy there were methods . . . but doesn't that encourage him to have sexual adventures?'

'Does he need encouragement? Look, if you're right and he's had a taste of what it's all about, he won't stop there. Damn it, you wanted my advice, take it.' He perched on the corner of Con's desk and produced a cigarette. 'And whilst we're on the question of social mores, can you and Sarah come to dinner next Tuesday night? We've got one or two people coming.'

The conversation became more conventional and soon, having delivered his invitation and received an acceptance, Andy left Con to his reflections.

Con, starting to work, tried very hard not to reflect at all, but it was no good. He would have to do something. He would go round to Ipswich Road tonight and make an excuse to have a private word with Simon. And he would hand him an outsize packet of contraceptives and tell him when they ran out he was to apply to him for more. Hell, it was a thousand times better than letting the boy litter Norfolk knee-deep in little bastards!

But he wished, wistfully, that he could have had an easier introduction to his stepson!

Chapter Four

Half term came, and Simon was back at the Ipswich Road house for the first time since his mother had married Uncle Con. After so long away, he could scarcely wait to see Pixie, she was not a letter writer and Pursell's did not encourage their pupils to fraternise with any of the girls' schools in the neighbourhood. He had been starved of female companionship for a good six weeks.

So on his first Monday he could be seen walking up the street, knocking at the Hopwood door, and enquiring after Pixie.

'Yes, she's off school, fussin' herself in her room, I dessay,' Mrs Hopwood said, half proudly, half accusingly. 'I'll give 'er a call.'

She called, and presently Pixie came downstairs. She was pale and dishevelled, her lovely hair unbrushed, her eyes half closed against the bright light of the morning. Whatever she had been doing, it was certainly not 'fussing herself'. But she smiled at Simon and her eyes opened properly.

'Oh, hello. You're Val's cousin, aren't you?' Simon was about to tell her that he thought this attitude a bit much, all things considered, when he saw the approval in her mother's face. Pixie must know her mother well enough to realise that she would swallow it, he supposed!

She swallowed it hook, line and sinker. She said: 'You did oughter have brought Miss Val with you, Mr

Rose; them gals, they like to mardle on, togither. She could've had a bit of lunch.'

'She isn't a keen cyclist like me, Mrs Hopwood,' Simon said, smiling. 'I was wondering if Pixie would show me the church – my holiday task is brass-rubbing and I know there are some very fine small brasses . . .'

He could not have chosen better. A tight little smile took some of the weaselishness from her narrow face. Nothing could have been more opportune, she assured him, for was not Mr Hopwood at this very moment about his sextonish duties in the churchyard? Pixie knew where the brasses were, but her father could tell Mr Rose the whole history of the church, right from its very beginning way back in the fourteenth century.

Pixie, looking resigned, listened in silence, and then remarked that she must just brush her hair and disappeared up the stairs once more. Simon was invited in for a cup of tea and accepted gracefully. When one wanted something badly enough one took the rough with the smooth, and Pixie was as smooth and desirable as her mother was rough. He sipped his tea and inserted an invitation for Pixie to spend the day with his sister and cousin, assuring Mrs Hopwood that he would ride behind the bus and that Val and Cara would meet them at the bus station and take as much care of her daughter as she would herself. Soon enough, Mrs Hopwood having accepted this suggestion with sufficient alacrity to make Simon smile, Pixie came down the stairs once more, in a clean blue dress, a ribbon tying back her curls and her face shining and pink from vigorous applications of soap and water.

'I'm home for a week,' Simon remarked as they walked, side by side, towards the church. 'I'd like to meet you, if you're off school.'

Pixie looked sideways at him and giggled.

'We're meeting now, silly. Of course I'm off school!'

He took her hand and pulled, but she drew back and snatched her hand away.

'Stop it, Simon. This street has eyes behind every window, you know!'

'All right. But what about meeting for the rest of the week? We could go to the cinema, or catch a bus down to Yarmouth, or . . .'

She sighed blissfully. 'That's good to see you, Simon. I'll do whatever you like, if I can get away from Ma.'

'That should be all right. She's agreed that you can come into Norwich for a day with Val and Cara, just for starters. I'll have to get a hold over Cara so she sees things my way.'

'Oh. In't we going to the church, then?'

'Yes, we are. It was the truth, you frightful girl! I have to get brass rubbings from all over Norfolk for my holiday task. If you ask me, it's just to make sure I visit churches!'

'You're Jewish, aren't you, though?' Pixie remarked. '*Can* you go into churches? What happens at school, during assembly?'

'I don't go into assembly, and I usually go to a Jewish service on Saturday mornings. Otherwise it doesn't make much difference,' Simon said cheerfully. 'As for going to services in churches, I can if I want to, I suppose. You could come to Shul if you'd a mind – the Neylers do, when occasion demands.'

'I see. It's a bit like being a methodist, I daresay.' They crossed the turnpike and headed down the hill. 'I've got an aunt who's methodist.' She glanced up at Simon's dark and curly hair. 'There's a Jewish boy goes to the Grammar. He wears a little cap thing on his head all the time.'

'Some do, some don't.' They turned into Church

Road and there was the ancient flintstone church. It was a huge building, far bigger than such a small village warranted, and the churchyard was beautiful and huge too, set with trees and bushes, the graves well-tended, flaming with autumn flowers amongst which chrysanthemums predominated. Because of the size of the churchyard and the fact that it sloped away towards the river they could easily have missed Mr Hopwood, but Simon saw his back, bobbing up between two grave mounds, and good manners made him greet the older man. Pixie performed an introduction, but to their relief the sexton was too busy to take them into the church.

'The gal Priscilla knows them brasses as well as what I do,' he remarked, grinning at Simon and revealing cheerfully toothless gums. 'She'll show you.'

'He takes his teeth out when he's diggin',' Pixie said a trifle shamefacedly as she led Simon into the church. 'He's afraid he might bury 'em, along of the corpse, if they slipped out.'

'And do they? Slip out, I mean.'

'Well, yes. They aren't a very marvellous fit,' Pixie said as they walked up the long, dim aisle. 'Here, what are we doin', talking about the old 'un's false teeth? Here's a nice little brass. Git out your papers and stuff.'

Simon produced his rough grey paper and a thick, soft pencil and began to work. For a moment Pixie watched him, then she slid down on to the floor beside him, took his hand and began, quite gently, to bite his fingers.

Ten minutes later, a trifle breathless, she and Simon disentangled themselves and Simon finished off the brass rubbing. Then they left the church. Pixie slipped out of the big oak door and pulled it closed behind them, then looked up at Simon through her lashes.

'In't a church hallowed ground, Simon?'

'It is now!'

The pair of them sauntered slowly back up the church path, green with moss and already beginning to clog with falling leaves, towards where Simon had left his bicycle.

'Did you remember to lock the door, darling?'

Con got into bed and leaned over, kissing Sarah on the side of her neck. Sarah put up a hand and stroked his cheek but her dark eyes were anxious.

'Did you lock it? Simon's home.'

'Yes, I locked it, you shy flower! Isn't it a good thing your mother agreed to move into that lovely flat at Mrs Bechstein's house? I daresay I would never have been able to get you pregnant had she still been on the premises!' He settled himself comfortably, then took a book off his bedside table. 'Let's read for a bit.'

Sarah had a book too, but she barely glanced at it before putting it down again and tugging at Con's sleeve.

'I could eat a horse! Why do I always get hungry at night, when everyone else is in bed?' She put a hand over Con's page. 'Who's going to sneak down into the kitchen and get me . . . cheese on toast with grilled tomatoes on top? And hot chocolate? And one of those Viennese whirl cakes?'

'Just because you're carrying my child, woman, doesn't mean you can make me into your slave! I don't believe pregnant women have cravings. They're just a figment of your imagination. Tell yourself you had a good dinner barely three hours ago and that cheese on toast is indigestible, and then we can both get some rest.'

'I can tell myself till I'm blue in the face, but that won't stop me longing for cheese on toast,' Sarah protested. 'Don't be mean, Con! You said you wanted a baby!'

'Think about tomorrow morning, and what'll happen the minute you put a foot to the floor if I feed you now,' Con advised. He laid down his book and leaned over to click off the bedside light. 'I'll take your mind off your appetite and you can satisfy mine, instead.' He slid down the bed and found her face in the dark, cupping it in his hands, kissing her mouth. 'Sweet Sarah!'

'You think I'm foolish to want toasted cheese and Viennese whirl cakes,' Sarah said against his mouth. 'But you're just as foolish, except that you want the same thing every night!'

'That's not foolish, that's logical. I know a good thing when I see one. Anyway, later on I daresay you won't feel like making love, so we have to make the most of our chances now!'

Later, Sarah kissed his bare shoulder, then sat up in bed.

'Those pyjamas were a waste of good money if they're only going to be worn for ten minutes or so every night! I'm going down to toast myself some cheese. Want some?'

Con grunted, then sat up and clicked the bedside light on again. He grabbed Sarah just as she was about to slip out of the covers, forcing her to stay in bed.

'No! You'll be sick as a dog tomorrow if I let you go down there and eat that lot! Darling, it hurts me to hear you heaving and weeping the moment you wake. I refuse to let you make yourself ill. Haven't you noticed you're always worse when you guzzle unsuitable food late at night?'

'I suppose you're right.' Sarah sighed, then yawned until her eyes watered. 'Con, you're so good for me! Have I ever told you how much I love you?'

Con switched off the light and lay down, pulling Sarah into his arms.

'Yes, I'm happy to say you have, but it's something I never tire of hearing. Go on, repeat it!'

Sarah chuckled.

'I love you, even after ten long weeks of marriage. There! Wasn't that handsome of me, when you've just denied me cheese on toast?'

'That's you, handsome. And now, face-ache, go to sleep!'

'It seems strange to have turkey with Christmas only five or six weeks away, but we thought the children would enjoy it.' Tina beamed round the table at her assembled guests. She loved a family dinner party and would have one at the drop of a hat. This one, arranged for Simon and Nicky, gave her special pleasure for it was their first grown-up dinner in full evening dress, to give them something nice to remember during the last half of the autumn term, which began tomorrow. They were the only children present, furthermore, for Ted, who understood the young, had insisted that if Val and Cara attended it would cease to be a proper dinner party and become a romp.

'A turkey's always welcome, Mama,' Des said. 'Redcurrant jelly, too!'

'Yes, that was what we thought.' Tina let her glance wander towards Ted, carving diligently away, and thought how glad Poppa would have been to see this dinner party, for he was a great believer in family and in the virtues of togetherness. He would be here in spirit, she was sure, glad that the Neylers were still hosting parties despite his own absence.

'Would you care for some stuffing, Sarah, my dear? Don't worry, everything's *kosher*!' The familiar, half-joking reassurance made them all smile and Ted, who seemed to be having a bit of difficulty with the bird, smiled too. 'Come on, who else likes sage and onion?'

It was then that Tina noticed the blue and white pottery dish on which the turkey was insecurely perched. She frowned. Whatever was Ruthie thinking about? There was a great silver carving dish which they always used for really big joints and poultry. It had spikes upon which one impaled the meat, making carving a far less arduous task.

It was not like Ruthie to ignore the silver dish, not on a family occasion like this with twelve people seated. To be sure, it was well tucked away in the back of the butler's pantry with its companions, the silver vegetable dishes with the maple leaf handles and the other, smaller silver dishes which made up the set. How odd! Of course they did not often need it; casting her mind back she could not remember using it since the previous Christmas. Food, in the summer, tended to be lighter, with more cold meat at parties than big roast joints.

She dismissed the dish from her mind, save to make a mental note that she would speak to Ruthie about it, and cast an experienced eye over her guests. Everyone was happy, she could tell at a glance. Sarah, her pregnancy not showing at all, was chatting quietly to Rachel, but her eyes strayed now and then to Con and to Simon, with such pride and pleasure in their depths that no one could doubt her happiness. Tina loved Louis, but it was good to know that he had not hurt his ex-wife irremediably, as she had once feared he had. Good to know, too, that it was her favourite nephew, Con, who had brought the spring back into Sarah's step, the sparkle back to her eyes. And Cecy and Abe were happy, now that the marriage was a *fait accompli*, at any rate. They even seemed to take a vicarious pride in Simon's handsomeness and charm, as though he were in very truth their grandson.

'Tina, where's the silver carving dish?'

Ted's voice was plaintive. He had obviously found it hard going, she guessed, to carve the big bird on a plain pottery dish, and one, moreover, which was far too small for the task. She shrugged, and even as she did so a possible solution popped into her head.

'Gracious, that dish was solid silver, and part of a set – do you suppose it could have been stolen?' She glanced apologetically round the table. 'I think I'll just check with Ruthie . . . we had a new kitchen maid back in the summer and only last week a plumber came to fix a new mixer tap in the back scullery . . .' She left her place and hurried out to the kitchen. Ruthie, red-faced, was popping a chestnut soufflé into the oven and Millie was scraping the remains of halibut and shrimp sauce off the fish plates. Annie, the kitchen maid, was laying up the trolley with Tina's Royal Worcester dessert plates. They all looked up as Tina came in.

'Ruthie, the turkey carver . . . ?'

'I'm sorry, Mrs Neyler. I hope I did right to serve it on the pottery dish. It was all I could lay hands on at a moment's notice. I came through to find you, but Mr Desmond met me in the hall and said not to worry, he believed it had gone to be cleaned and re-valued.'

'Oh, but . . . yes, that'll be it, of course.' Tina could not think clearly. Her instinct, now, was to push the whole incident out of her mind and everyone else's. The dish would turn up in the morning, when she had leisure to look properly herself, or perhaps it *had* gone to be re-valued. 'I'll tell Mr Neyler everything is all right – he's managed to carve the bird. Will that soufflé be ready in about fifteen minutes? I'm afraid I held proceedings up a bit, leaving to find out about the dish.

It's a delicious meal, anyway. Congratulations, every-one.'

Back in the dining-room she slid unobtrusively into her place, then picked up her knife and fork so that everyone else could follow suit, for Ted had served them all by now.

'Panic over. The service has gone to be re-valued and cleaned and I quite forgot!' she said gaily. 'We must eat up. Ruthie's just put a chestnut soufflé in the oven.'

Everyone took up their knives and forks and a murmur of talk broke out. But Ted was staring at her, refusing to be side-tracked.

'Has all the silver gone? Did you check the big tureens with the silver maple leaves, and the . . .'

'I don't know. It doesn't matter,' Tina said hurriedly. 'It's gone to be cleaned, Ted, Ruthie remembered. Could I have a little more bread sauce, please?'

'Tina, I . . .' He sensed her desperate embarrassment and picked up the sauce boat. 'Here's the bread sauce.' He turned to Abe. 'Just wait until you taste that soufflé, Abe – it's sheer heaven, I tell you!'

As luck would have it, Simon had been watching Beryl when Uncle Ted had started the fuss over the silver dish. He had noticed her sudden pallor and how, after that, she had not even pretended to eat. Des had leaned over her, his manner almost threatening, but though she nodded nervously in response to his low-voiced remark, and began to poke at her food again, not a morsel passed her lips. Simon was not especially fond of Beryl; in fact he thought her a whiny woman, so pale and colourless that one could not imagine what Des had ever seen in her, but usually she ate quite well. He glanced around the table. Everyone else was finishing off their meal – Ruthie really was a marvellous cook –

but Beryl's plate was embarrassingly full. As Simon watched, Des scooped his wife's food on to his own plate and began to tuck in at top speed. Then he said something else in a low voice to Beryl. She nodded, twisting her napkin nervously in her lap. Beside her Frank, noticing her plate for the first time, nudged her and made another comment. She smiled up at him, then actually took a mouthful of broccoli spears and Frank nodded approvingly.

At that point, Simon's attention was claimed by his mother. Sarah was on the opposite side of the table, and she leaned across to remind him to remember every mouthful, since he would not taste anything half as good for the next six weeks. That made everyone laugh, and he and Nicky began to swop horror stories about school food with Frank and Des, who had also attended Pursell's.

It took the mystery of the silver dish out of the forefront of everyone's mind, if not out of their minds altogether, but it did not stop Simon from wondering. Auntie Tina had looked so very odd – almost guilty – when she came back from the kitchen, and she had shut Uncle Ted up so decidedly that it had been almost rude.

The chestnut soufflé was as delicious as Uncle Ted had promised, and then came dishes of nuts and apples and big, bursting purple plums. The coffee which followed was black, in deference to Jewish dietary laws – dairy products must not be eaten at the same meal as meat – but there was also a jug of milk so that anyone who did not like black coffee and was not Jewish could dilute his drink. Chocolate mint wafers, however, were quite legitimate and Simon, who had watched a little wistfully as Nicky splashed milk into his cup, took three wafers to make up, and sipped his bitter coffee more enthusiastically at the thought of the sweets to come.

When the adults began to push their chairs back from the table, Simon caught Nicky's eye and went over to him. They were both in their best dark suits and grinned a little self-consciously at one another.

'Come out to the conservatory with me, Sime,' Nicky hissed. 'Val's there. I promised I'd bring her some turkey.' There was a bulge in his pocket which Simon viewed with distaste. Really, how the young behaved sometimes! 'Oh, come on, it's pretty dull in here now the eating's over.'

Reluctant to behave with childlike stealth, yet wanting the company of his cousins, Simon hesitated – and was lost. Val was a sporting kid, and besides, he wanted to keep her sweet so that she would ask Pixie to more social functions when the Christmas hols came. He nodded and followed his cousin out into the darkness of the conservatory.

Val was there. She greeted them with squeaks of excitement and gobbled the turkey, indifferent to or oblivious of the fluff it had collected in Nick's pocket.

'I wish you were staying with us, Sime,' she said lovingly, swallowing the last morsel and and wiping her greasy fingers on her dressing-gown, for she was in her night things. 'Remember the midnight feasts we had when Auntie Sarah and Uncle Con were honeymooning and you were staying here? It was fine, wasn't it! Better fun than old grown-up dinner parties, I bet!'

'Yes, it wasn't bad,' Simon conceded, then grabbed an arm of each cousin. Someone was coming out from the brightly lit drawing-room. 'Cave, you two! Into the creepers!'

Afterwards, he marvelled at his childish impulse to hide from grown-ups. Yet if they had not . . .

It was Beryl. She had a hand to her mouth and she was making noises which were horribly familiar to the three children hidden behind the creepers. Beryl might have eaten too much at the party, except that Simon had watched her and knew she had hardly eaten anything. She was closely followed by an angry Desmond. The children could sense his fury though they could scarcely see his face in the dimness.

'What the hell are you playing at, Beryl? Are you deliberately setting out to make me look a fool?' He grabbed her by one arm and swung her violently round to face him. 'Don't pretend to be ill when you know . . .'

'Don't, Des. I . . .'

Des shot a quick, furtive glance at the room behind him. He took hold of his wife by the shoulders and shook her. Then he swung his fist and hit her in the stomach. They heard the air whoosh out of her lungs, saw her double up and begin to retch. Simon could feel Val shaking, pressing against him. Des was her brother, of course. He hardly realised it most of the time, but now it was brought home to him by Val's trembling and by Nick's set, white face.

'Stop that, you sly little bitch!' Desmond stepped back, though, since it must have been obvious even to him that Beryl was genuinely ill now, whatever the case before he hit her. Simon was horrified and incredulous. He had always thought Desmond a lighthearted sort of bloke, all for a good time. He was a very different man when he thought himself unobserved save by his defenceless little wife.

'I'm not . . . Des, please . . . don't . . . it was the silver, when she . . .'

Desmond caught Beryl's arms and dragged her upright. In the light from the French windows Simon could see saliva on her chin and tears on her cheeks. She winced away from her husband, blinking rapidly,

97

plainly terrified, but he did not release her. His fingers dug into her flesh and he shook her so hard that her head jerked like a puppet's.

'I know what it is, you're pregnant again! Damned little slut. No self-control, letting me down, guzzling till you're sick . . . I'll teach you a lesson when I get you home . . . the silver's gone to be cleaned, didn't you hear Mama? I'll make you sorry, you . . .'

Gently, Nick was tugging Simon's sleeve. When he had his attention, he jerked his head towards the house. They were not the only listeners. Uncle Ted stood just inside the French windows, half hidden by the curtains, listening. They could see the tilt of his head, the strained attention in his whole attitude. He could undoubtedly hear every word, but he could not see what Desmond was doing now. He had Beryl's arm up behind her back and was twisting it with the casual cruelty of a school bully, ignoring her whimpers, the way she was beginning to sag forward.

Val acted before her brother or cousin could stop her. She flew out from their hiding place and hit Desmond with all her force in the small of the back. Desmond was over six foot tall and a well-built man, but Val had the advantage of surprise. He staggered, releasing Beryl, who fell to the tiles in an untidy heap.

Simon and Nick rushed out, ashamed that a girl had made the first move. They flanked Val, one on each side, and faced Desmond, who smiled uneasily at them.

'Hello, kids. Where did you spring from? I was messing about with Beryl – do get up, my dear. Here, let me . . .' He lugged her inanimate body off the ground and shook her slightly. 'You frightened her, but she's only fainted. Don't worry, you've done no harm.'

'No, we didn't.' Nicky spoke through clenched teeth.

'We saw you, hitting her, twisting her arm! And we'll tell, so don't you . . .'

'Why, you cheeky young blackguard . . .'

Before Desmond could raise a fist Uncle Ted was there. A hand on Desmond's arm, a cold voice in his ear.

'That's enough.' He took Beryl from his son, held her easily in one arm. He was sixty-one but still immensely strong. 'Get back into the house, everyone, and we'll sort this out indoors. Val, what on earth . . . ?' He had just noticed her night clothes.

They turned towards the house just as Tina and Rachel appeared in the doorway.

'What's the matter?' Simon thought Auntie Tina's voice was shriller than usual. 'Oh dear, isn't Beryl well?'

'Mummy, Desmond's wicked. He was . . .' Val was in tears. Simon took her hand in response to a somewhat wild-eyed look from Uncle Ted. He squeezed her fingers, seeing thankfully that she was about to cry in good earnest and would not say too much. Nicky, on the other side of her, muttered something about 'later', and Val nodded. The three of them followed Desmond and Uncle Ted, who was carrying Beryl like a baby, into the drawing-room. Once there, Beryl began to stir and to weep. Ted laid her down carefully on the chaise longue. Then he turned to the women.

'Beryl fainted. I think she'd better stay here for the night. Des can pick her up in the morning.'

'Right.' Tina bustled over and took Beryl's hand. 'You do look pale, my dear – straight to bed, I think. You've been overdoing it!'

'She's pregnant again,' Desmond said irritably. 'That's all it is. She's not ill or anything. In fact, it's her own fault that she fainted.' His voice became caressing as he turned to Tina. 'I'll give her a talking to, ruining my mama's dinner party!'

99

But for once Tina, it seemed, was not to be easily won round. Simon saw her stiffen and turn to her eldest son.

'I think it's about time your father had a word with you, Desmond, if you think that Beryl's pregnancy is entirely her own doing. Perhaps no one ever told you about the birds and the bees. Though I should have thought that cause and effect would have struck even you by now!'

Simon gaped at his relatives. Fancy Auntie Tina speaking to Des like that, when everyone knew that he was her blue-eyed boy, her favourite who could do no wrong. He glanced at Uncle Ted. Uncle Ted looked . . . old. His face was grey and his eyes tired and lost.

Apart from the Neylers, Simon suddenly realised, only he and Auntie Ray were in the room. Everyone else must have gone through into the billard room or back into the dining-room. He shifted his feet. He felt uncomfortable, a part and yet not a part of the family row that was obviously brewing. He caught Auntie Ray's eye and she grimaced, then came towards him.

'Simon and I will see Beryl up to bed, Tina, if you'll tell me which room she's to go in. And then we'll join the others in the billard room. Right, Simon?'

'Of course, Auntie Ray.' Simon moved towards the door and at a murmur from her father, Val followed suit. Nicky came out after Val. They stood in the hall for a moment, Beryl swaying weakly between Simon and Rachel, and then they all headed for the stairs.

'Val, darling, take us to the spare room, and then I'll see your guest gets some sleep. The boys can go to the billiard room but I really think, darling, that you'd better just pop into bed. And try not to let this business upset you. I'm sure it's all been a misunderstanding – family rows often are!' She smiled at them, but Simon and Nick, going downstairs again, both knew that

Auntie Ray had come on the scene too late to know just how bad this particular family row had been.

In the billiard room, Sarah was waiting for her son.

'Simon? Darling, where *have* you been? It's time we were off. You've got an early start tomorrow!'

Simon did not argue, merely bidding everyone good-night and following his mother and Uncle Con out to the car. Once settled in the back seat, however, he felt he must find out exactly what all this was about.

'Mother, Beryl's pregnant again. And she was sick, out in the conservatory. And there was a row – something about the silver.'

He saw Sarah's head turn as Con's did, but was unable to read their quick glance.

'Ah, yes. Well, your mother and I have a theory about that silver, and I imagine it may be shared by poor Beryl. Did she say anything to Des about it? Beryl, I mean.'

Bluntly, Simon told his mother and Con exactly what had transpired in the conservatory. When he finished speaking there was silence for a moment, and then Con said, beneath his breath, 'Better tell him, love.'

'Simon, I'm expecting a baby.' His mother's voice was flat and lifeless. Simon mumbled something and she turned in her seat and caught his jacket, tugging him forward so that his head was close to hers. 'Oh, darling, I didn't mean to tell you like this! Uncle Con and I want this baby so much, as much as Daddy and I wanted you. I meant it to be . . .' Her voice slowed and Simon knew she was crying. He leaned further forward and kissed the side of her face.

'Don't, Mother! It's all right honestly. I'm jolly pleased we're having a baby, except I just hope it's a boy! I couldn't bear another Cara. She'll be tickled pink whatever it is. As for what happened this evening, I shouldn't have told you. I wouldn't have, if I'd known you were like poor Beryl. I daresay Des . . . oh, hang it!'

'There's a black sheep in every family, and Des is ours,' Con said placidly. He brought the car to a halt outside the house, but no one attempted to get out. Con touched Sarah's hand lightly. 'Poor old darling, what a thing to happen now! But Beryl married him. She must be used to his beastly ways – or at least able to cope with them.'

'I don't think so,' Simon said doubtfully. 'She's scared silly, that's what I think. And you've not said about the silver.'

'Let's go inside, persuade Mary to make us coffee – or perhaps hot chocolate would be better in view of the time – and talk things over.' Con went round and helped Sarah out of the car. Then held the door for Simon. 'I'm sorry your first grown-up dinner party should turn out to be such a disaster, but these things do happen from time to time.'

Once in their own comfortable living-room, with a cup of hot chocolate in his hand and a tray of shortbread near, Simon settled back to hear the explanation. It was not slow in coming. Con had made up his mind, it seemed, that his stepson should not be kept in the dark.

'When Grandpa died, Desmond was at The Pride, and I noticed when Uncle Ted spoke to me later that he was worried by the fact. Well, if you knew your cousin as well as I do, you'd know that Desmond isn't too worried by who owns what, and when Auntie Tina pointed out that the silver carving dish was missing I'm afraid my nasty legal mind immediately leapt to the conclusion that Des might have appropriated it.'

'Des, take the silver?' Simon could scarcely believe his ears. 'But that would be stealing. And from his own parents!'

'It wouldn't be the first time, darling,' his mother said wearily. 'Auntie Tina says that Des doesn't mean to do wrong, but I must admit we see it your way. It's stealing, and a particularly nasty form of stealing, too.'

Light began to dawn in Simon's confused mind.

'Ah, now I think I understand. Des whacked Beryl because he thought she'd give the game away about the silver. And *that* was why Beryl couldn't eat her dinner.'

'That's right. And probably, being pregnant didn't help. Women do get a bit sick and fussy when they're pregnant.'

'Des didn't know,' Simon said broodingly. 'Can you believe it, he said he didn't know? There are enough little Neylers at his house. You'd think he'd know when another one was on the way!'

'You would, but I won't go into that now.' Con grinned at his wife, who was sitting back in her chair sipping hot chocolate, her eyes dark. 'What a family you've married into, my love – and doing it twice! You ought to have a citation for bravery in the face of . . . Don't cry, love! What have I said? Damn it, I was only teasing!'

'Louis wasn't like that,' Sarah mumbled against his shirt front. 'Th-they said he was a black sheep, but he wasn't ever bad, Con, he never hurt anyone, not Lou. N-not even me, n-not on purpose.'

'My God, of course I didn't mean . . . Louis wasn't a bit like Des. I only meant . . . Look, apart from thoughtlessness, there isn't a better man than Lou living! Things got too much for him; that's why he went off and left you and the kids, and if he'd thought for one moment that you *really* needed him he'd have been back in a brace of shakes.'

Sarah, sniffing, dried her eyes on Con's handkerchief and smiled, albeit somewhat uncertainly.

'That's true. I didn't need him really, not ever, and I think he sensed it, poor Lou. But I need *you*, Con. Isn't it odd?'

Over the top of his wife's head, Con smiled at his stepson. It was a comradely smile, a smile that only two men could exchange.

'Good, that's how it should be. I need to be relied on, you see, and Lou didn't. Simon, old lad, you've got a full day tomorrow; do you want to go up?'

'Yes, if it's all right.' Simon touched his mother's shoulder gently. 'Don't go howling any more, Mother. I believe it's bad for the kid. See you in the morning.'

He was actually getting into bed when the thought which must have been hovering in the back of his mind came to the fore, freezing his spine and turning the rest of him to jelly. Pixie had been feeling sickly that morning. She had said as much when he had accused her of being a greedy pig in Deacon's, whither they had repaired for a fish and chip lunch. Thrown up after breakfast, that was what she had said. And though she had eaten every scrap of fish and chips, she had turned her nose up at a cream cake – Pixie, the girl who had once told him she would sell her soul for cream cakes! Then he lay down. Rubbish! Pixie was only a kid. She wasn't a *woman*, whatever Uncle Con may have implied. And besides, he was talking figuratively. When he had said pregnant women were a bit sick and fussy he probably didn't mean it quite as literally as Pixie had. It had, after all, only been that one occasion in the loft . . . He would be sure to take Uncle Con's advice in future, though, and to use the contraceptives his stepfather had so generously supplied.

He decided he would write to Pixie. Not at home; that would never do. Her mother was the sort who opened letters, there could be no doubt about that. But he wrote to James, and could enclose notes for Pixie. That way he could keep in touch, and come Christmas any demands he might make on her would seem less . . . less arbitary.

Comforted, Simon turned over and allowed himself to fall asleep.

'Tina, the boy took the stuff. It's useless to keep denying it – damn it, he's as good as admitted he took it! I know there's very little we can do, but I'm going to stop the value out of his wages until he's paid us back.'

Ted was very angry, but he could tell by the mulish expression on his wife's face that Tina did not intend to believe the worst. They were in his study, facing each other across the desk on the day following the dinner party. Upstairs, in their spare bedroom, Beryl still slept. Ted closed his eyes for a moment and sighed. It was painful enough to admit to himself that Des was a thief and a bully, but to have Tina deny it in the face of all the evidence was worse still, for if she refused to believe the truth, then how could they help Beryl?

'Look, love, we've never been firm enough with Des. That's part of the trouble. See how he treats his wife! If we'd accused him when we suspected . . .'

'He'd have gone, like Louis.'

Ted suppressed a desire to say *good riddance*, and shook his head.

'No. Des knows which side his bread is buttered. We should have faced him years ago, when those Georgian candlesticks –'

'That wasn't Des! It was that awful maid, you know it was! Why, you agreed that she'd have to go and you let me –'

'Yes, and within ten days I knew we'd made a mistake and had to scrape round and find her another job, give her a glowing reference, pay her some money and clear her name generally.' Tina began to protest but Ted wagged an admonitory finger at her. 'It's no good, Tina. The girl had already gone when Sarah missed her silver snuff-box, and as for the car that went missing at the showroom when Des was in charge, you can scarcely blame that on a maid! The boy – damn it, he's *not* a boy, he's a man – the man's light-fingered and until you accept the truth and begin to show him that we won't stand for it you're virtually aiding and abetting him in a life of crime!'

'Crime? Oh, but that's ridiculous – it was only the silver dishes, when all's said and done. The vegetable tureens had been put down in the cellar.'

'By whom? And for what purpose? My dear, if he'd managed to get away with the silver dishes, I'm very sure we'd never have seen the tureens again! Who else would have hidden them behind the wine racks like that?'

'It's that woman, that Zelda. She makes him pay for all her clothes and everything. The other day when I saw her in White's she was wearing an emerald ring with a stone the size of a walnut. The poor boy's under her thumb. He only –'

'Yes, and that reminds me. That diamond solitaire with the high shoulders . . .'

'I *lost* it,' Tina said sharply. 'Des wouldn't take from *me*, Ted, not a personal thing like that ring. And he wouldn't take deliberately from you. It was just a mistake in the book-keeping, that car.'

'You did not lose it. Don't lie, Tina. Make up your mind that Des has to change. If it really is Zelda who's forcing Des to steal, then we must do our utmost to kill the relationship, and one way of doing it is to keep Des so short of cash that he can't support her in the style to which she has become accustomed. Then perhaps she'll turn to someone else.'

'He doesn't steal, Ted he –'

'That's enought!' Ted banged both fists on the desk in front of him and saw Tina's eyes widen incredulously. He knew he spoilt his pretty little wife, even now when she was nearly fifty, but he had never let her do anything which would hurt anyone else. The business with Desmond had gone far enough. 'Desmond is a thief, so don't try to defend him to me, please. And what's to be done about Beryl?'

'Done about her? What . . . what . . . ?'

'Are you going to send her back to Desmond, to let him vent his fury on her? Because make no mistake, he's going to be furious when he knows that his salary is about to be cut. He'll try to take the money out of Beryl's housekeeping, and I won't have it. Nor will I let him continue to humiliate the mother of his children by flaunting his mistress in front of her. So I propose . . .'

'There. You can't take his salary, darling, because we don't want Beryl and the children to suffer! A warning, a severe warning . . .'

'No. We're going to speak to Beryl right now, together. I would have let you go up first, but from the way you've been behaving you'd spend the time trying to persuade her to say Des had never hit her in his life before.' Ted glanced sharply at his wife and could tell by the flush that darkened her cheeks and the way she bridled that she had intended to do just that. 'Come along, my love.' He came round the desk and took Tina's hand. 'We're in it together, remember. We made him together, now we must take responsibility for him together.'

Beryl lay very still in the Neylers' spare bed. It was

comfortably soft, easing her bruises and taking some of the tenseness out of her. It was good to lie there, knowing that no one would make demands of any sort on her for a few hours. She was so tired! When the children were naughty Des blamed her, shouting at her in a voice so full of vindictive hatred that even if he did not touch her she shook for ten minutes afterwards. Yet if she tried to quieten the children he was equally liable to go for her, saying that she would break their spirits with her constant nagging. If she cringed when he raised his fist to her that was wrong; if she managed, with more difficulty than he could possibly have guessed, to pretend defiance that was wrong, bold-faced, an excuse for another slap or punch or curse. There seemed no comfortable middle course she could take which would leave her with peace of mind or body.

Once she had thought about leaving Des, but it never crossed her mind now. Where would she go? Her parents were dead and her elder sister, the one who had insisted she should marry Des years ago, when she found she was expecting little Dessy, had no sympathy for her. Des had spent what little money she had brought to the marriage and he would never let her escape, anyway. She could scarcely believe that she had once loved him, that she had plotted and schemed to be alone with the handsome, blond-haired Neyler boy so that they could make love.

He had tired of her very quickly, and she knew that it was partly her own fault. Never physically strong or mentally alert, she had allowed herself to be swamped by child-bearing, by running a house, by struggling to make ends meet, so that she could not be a companion to her husband.

Not that he wanted her, now that he had Zelda. She hated Zelda with a weary, lethargic hatred which scarcely justified the word. She could not possibly harm the other woman; would not have done so had she been able to. She did not hate her for taking Des away, but for getting all the money which Des should have spent on his wife and children. She had grown used to Zelda's air of casual ownership and scarcely resented the fact that, if she saw Zelda and Des walking through the city arm in arm, it was she who bolted into shops to avoid the embarrassment of an encounter, she who pretended not to notice them.

She had known Des to be dishonest for a long time, had suspected that he stole from the family firm, fiddled the books in his own favour, and then blamed others, but she had not known that he stole directly from his parents, until now. She acknowledged that Des had done very wrong, but she could scarcely concentrate on his sins for fear of what he would do to her when she got home. She had been beaten before, but this time . . . Oh, God, she was so tired! And so afraid!

A discreet tap on the door brought her heart pounding into her throat. It must be Desmond, come to collect her! Please God, she prayed, don't let it be Des, not yet, not so early. I'm not ready.

'Can we come in, Beryl?' It was her mother-in-law's voice.

'Oh, yes . . . please . . .' She sat up a little higher, frantically rubbing her cheeks to make herself look better. If Des thought . . .

The door opened. Tina was there, with Ted hovering just behind her. Beryl smiled brightly. She hoped she looked well, rested; that they would think of something to save them all!

'I'm sorry. I should have got up, but it's such a luxury to lie in. The children wake me . . . well, I woke hours ago, actually, but I . . .'

Ted came right into the room and sat down on the soft little easy chair in the corner, gesturing to Tina to sit on the bed. They both looked rather uncomfortable. Ted spoke first.

'No need for you to get up, dear – in fact, Millie's been told to bring you up a tray of breakfast in about twenty minutes. We wanted a word with you first, though.'

Beryl could feel herself paling. Oh, no! She did not want to talk about the silver, or the way Des treated her, or anything. It would only make things worse for her in the long run.

'Beryl, I'm sorry to tell you that Des did take those silver dishes, but he's going to pay me back out of his salary. Not the whole value, but some of it.'

Beryl could not prevent a small moan from escaping her lips. It would mean even less money to manage on, and another baby coming!

'Don't worry, it won't affect you. I shall pay you your housekeeping direct. So you must tell me what you need and it will be paid to you just like a salary, in an envelope and everything.' Ted smiled at her. 'And now I must extract a promise from you, my dear.'

Beryl shot a nervous glance at him and licked her lips. Sweat was beginning to form on her upper lip and across her forehead. The words *Desmond will kill me* were running through her mind like a refrain.

'I want you to promise me that you'll tell me or Mother if Des ever threatens you again. Or tries to extract money from you. You must promise me that, or else we can't help you. I shall tell Des that we know, you see, and that you've promised.' Beryl began to cry, tears running hopelessly down her cheeks. Tina leaned forward and patted her hand but she said nothing. It was Ted who continued to speak. 'Will you promise to tell us, my dear?'

'He'll kill me!' Beryl heard her own voice, high, shrill, far too dramatic. They would not believe her, no one would, not until . . . Her stomach contracted with fear and within her the child moved, a helpless flutter, as if it shared her abject terror at the thought of Desmond's rage.

'He won't kill you, Beryl, nor hurt you. Not if you tell us! He'll be afraid to do so because he'll know I won't hesitate to see that he suffers a proper punishment. My dear, all it takes is a little courage and resolution.'

Beryl was watching her mother-in-law, and saw the look which cooled her eyes to ice blue. Tina thought her daughter-in-law had neither courage nor resolution. It stiffened Beryl's backbone and made her sit up a little straighter.

'I was brave, once.' She looked Ted straight in the eye. 'But I'm so *tired*, and there are the children – and he can always go to Zelda, you see.'

'I know. Do you think you could be brave again? In a way, I'm asking it for Desmond's sake. He must be made to see he can't go on behaving like this. With your help we can break his relationship with Zelda. I'm sure of it.'

Beryl nodded slowly.

'All right, I promise. But – must I go back today? Now? I don't want to be there when he hears his s-salary is to be . . . oh, dear, you see what a coward I am, but you don't know his temper, how frightening he can be in a rage.'

'I've had an idea!' Tina jumped off the bed. 'Why don't you make it a sort of good behaviour thing, darling? His salary stays the same on condition that he doesn't lose his temper with Beryl or see Zelda.'

Ted sighed. He looked old and tired, Beryl thought, as if his son's defection was a burden heavier than his shoulders could bear. It must have been a terrible shock for him, much worse than it had been for her. Des had always knocked her about, but Ted and Tina had never had to face up to it until last night.

'Very well, we'll try that. But only if Beryl swears to tell us every time he goes off to Zelda or loses his temper. What about the kids, my dear? Does he hit them?'

'Yes, but never as he hits me. I seem to – to irritate him all the time, you see. Not by anything I do so much as by just being me.'

'Right. You'll still get your money separately, by the way. It'll do Des good to know, every time he sees his salary, that he isn't trusted. And remember, at the first sign of anything, Beryl, you must either ring up or come round.'

'I swear it. Father . . .' She had called them Mother and Father ever since she had married Des and for the first time, looking into Ted's kindly, tired eyes, she felt that he was really trying to be a father to her. 'Father, what shall I do if it doesn't work?'

'You'll leave him. I'll find you somewhere to live with the children, and he'll not bother you, because he'll be out finding himself a job, and there aren't many jobs around, especially for people who are sacked by their own father. Because if it happens again, Beryl, he'll not be working for me.'

'I can tell you mean it.' For the first time, Beryl smiled. A little of the heaviness lifted from her heart. 'You really will help me, even though . . . well, he *is* your eldest son. Oh, thank you, thank you both!'

Ted smiled back at her, but Tina turned with a little flounce and headed for the door. Ted followed her, then stopped in the doorway.

'Eat your breakfast in bed, Beryl, and don't get up

until you feel inclined. We'll send a tray of lunch up, if you're still tired. I'll tell Desmond that you're going to be our guest for a couple of days, and then we can really spoil you. I take it your nanny can cope with the children?'

'She's only a youngster, but I think she can.' Beryl sighed and cuddled down, smiling beatifically at the warmth and safety of her nest. 'I'll get up for lunch, really, I want to. But I'll have breakfast here, and then I'll have a nice hot bath.'

The door closed softly behind her in-laws.

Chapter Five

Louis was sprawled in an unlovely but comfortable attitude on his swing seat, full-length on the cushions, with the canopy over his head swaying just a little in the breeze. A book was propped up in front of his nose but he had long ago stopped even pretending to read. He was thinking.

Christmas always made him think. It was, he supposed, being so far from home, for England was still home, and the extreme unseasonableness of the weather. It was very hot indeed in Sydney, which was why he had deserted his small but smart house for the delights of the garden.

He had spent his six weeks in England, the first since he had left it to live permanently in Australia, and he had enjoyed being there, though he had come back to Australia without regrets. Oh, he had been sorry he had not managed to mend his broken relationship with Sarah, sorry that the boy, though obviously intrigued by him, had not attempted to further their friendship. It had been fun to see old Andy Felton respectable and settled, fun to visit old haunts, to catch half-glimpses of girls he had known well, once, as they hurried past him in their hats and respectable matronly dresses in the city.

Nicest of all, perhaps, had been his surprise visit to Say. Stealing into the dim little shop, seeing her look up at him with just that eagerness which had been her undoing so long ago, the way she jumped to her feet, flung her arms about him . . . and remembered herself, scolded him, brought him a cup of tea which he did not want and a piece of rich fruit cake for which he had no appetite.

And afterwards, meeting her out at the back of the village hall, where she had ostensibly gone for a whist drive, taking her down to the river, lying on the bank in the long grass talking, talking, each of them eager to know how the other fared, seeing the changes and the things that had remained the same with equal love, equal interest, because theirs was an old captivity which could neither wither nor die but which could only grow deeper and richer as the years passed.

Sarah Butcher was, of course, the only person in England who knew anything about his life in Sydney, because she had actually visited him there. At the time he had thought she was going to stay with him for good, but that had not materialised. Perhaps he had not even wanted it to. Instead, they had had a marvellous holiday together and she had seen for herself why he could never live in England again.

He had enjoyed meeting his darling Say again, he could still leave her without a qualm, knowing her to be happy with Winkie and the children, knowing that he would go back to Sydney and the life which he loved, hedonistic though he knew it to be. He had a house-keeper who adored him and kept his home beautifully – better, he frequently told her, than any wife could – and a gardener who made his garden the little paradise that it was without Louis ever lifting a finger. His work absorbed him – paediatrics were a thing of beauty and a joy for ever, he thought with a grin – he played hard, made love when he could, accepted as few responsi-bilities as possible in work which was both responsible and demanding.

Yet, when Christmas came nearer, he thought about England. The visit seemed all roses now, though his intelligence could have denied it. There had been the complication of Josette, for one thing. He had taken her on the Broad that first time intending to do no more than give her a few kisses. He had been curious, of course, because it had not seemed in character when the child had almost flung herself at his head, but no more than that. However, they had ended up making love. We seduced each other, Louis told himself firmly, since he had no intention of admitting that he, the experienced black sheep of the family, had been seduced by a slip of a thing like Josette! She had been good, too. Not good in the usual sense, but very good at seductions. Even remembering that afternoon made his insides perform a curious parabola. He could see again the blue of the sky behind her, feel the soft scratching of her fingernails as they passed across his chest, the way she had . . . He scolded himself. He ought to remember the fact that the floorboards of the boat had etched lines across his bum which had still been there twenty-four hours later, or that Josette's nails had scored equally indelible lines across his shoulders, or even, due to her apparently ineradicable delight in *al fresco* lovemaking, the vile and humiliating affair of the thistle.

So he had left England, Say, Josette and his family with mixed feelings – feelings which had crystallised into relief once he got back to Sydney. Josette, whatever her skills, had not been his type and it had annoyed him that she had taken it for granted, after that time on the Broad, that he would want her again. He did, it was true, but that did not lessen his irritation. And once home, why should he regret? The hospital was full of nurses, and women in uniform, especially women with fine complexions and healthy bodies, appealed to Louis.

116

Yet he continued to think about Josette. He had found her fascinating in a way he still could not explain to his own satisfaction. Exhausting – he could admit that now he was well away from her – but fascinating. He had actually written to her once, and had posted the letter, too, which just went to prove that she must have had a very strong attraction indeed since, Louis admitted, with him it was usually a case of out of sight, out of mind. Once he was back in his rightful place, the last thing he worried about was the marriage between Sarah and Con. When he heard Sarah was pregnant he suffered a slight pang, to be sure, but then he went round and visited his current girlfriend and never gave either Sarah or Con a thought for at least a fortnight.

He supposed the fact that he was lying in the sun and thinking about home was mainly due to the other fact that he could not reconcile Christmas with constant sunshine. He felt homesick not so much for England as for snow and rain, a crackling fire, and a family.

Years ago, the children had sent him presents, but he hated shopping and had usually responded by sending Sarah a cheque with instructions to buy the kids something. Since the divorce, no one had bothered. They would not bother this year, not with their own life to absorb them, Con living in the house, the affairs of the family all around them. It was not that he wanted or needed anything, but the habit of Christmases past, when one always made one's way home to one's family, was still too strong to be entirely cast off.

The bell ringing impatiently, brought him reluctantly to his feet. It was Mrs Halliforth's afternoon off; he would have to answer it himself. He strolled across the lawn, over the patio and through the French windows, hoping that by the time he arrived at the door the unexpected and unwanted visitor would have taken himself off. Anyway, whoever it was would be out of luck if he wanted to come in, since he had been on the verge of going down to the beach for a swim for the past hour and now that he had been so rudely disturbed he would act, and get his swimming things.

He reached the hall. Through the glass front door he could see, dimly, the shape of a visitor. He sighed, rubbed sweat off his forehead, and putting on a pleasant, enquiring expression opened the door.

'Hello, Lou!'

For a moment he felt downright odd, as if he was the victim of some insane sort of conjuring trick. Had he thought her into existence here on his front doorstep, conjured her across the thousands of miles which separated Australia from England? Damn it, just by thinking about her?

'Josette? I can't believe it!'

If she thought the remark complimentary she must have been very thick-skinned, for he had spoken without a smile, his voice incredulous, even a trifle horrified, but she smiled sedately up at him, then indicated the enormous suitcase which stood on the gravel by her side.

'Get my case indoors, would you, darling? I can't face having to lift it again.'

'Oh. Right.' He lugged the case – what had she got in it, a body? – into his hall, then turned an accusing eye on her. 'What's all this, my dear girl? You can't stay here, you know.'

'Why not?' She stood on tiptoe and kissed him. Louis, with lively dismay, pushed her away.

'Look, Jo, I'm a respectable bachelor. You can't stay in this house. You'll have to book into an hotel or something. I take it you've got a job somewhere? I remember you were asking about nursing work over here, so if you've got a room in the nurses' home I'll get the car out and run you down there.'

'Well, I haven't got a job yet, and if you're so respectable you'd better marry me,' Josette said practically. 'I've no money. I spend my last penny on a ticket to get me here, and that was a single, not a return. Now come on, Lou, admit you're pleased to see me.' She stood on tiptoe and kissed him again, properly, her arms locking round his neck in a minatory fashion which precluded his eluding her without being downright rude. Louis had never been downright rude to a woman in his life, but as soon as the kiss ended he burst into speech.

'I'll get you a job, and as for somewhere to stay I've got a friend who runs a little boarding-house . . .'

She took his hand. Firmly. Her own hand was small but strong. He noticed, for the first time, that she was flushed, which suited her, and wore a limp green dress, which did not. Her hair was sun-streaked. It looked nice. It smelled nice, too.

'Where's the kitchen, Lou? I want a drink terribly badly – is there a chance of a cup of tea, do you suppose? And then I'd love a bath or shower. And perhaps a rest in my room.'

'Well, we can run to tea,' Louis agreed. 'Here's the kitchen. I'll put the kettle on. But you aren't staying in this house, my dear. My house-keeper's a straitlaced woman, and she wouldn't approve. I'm not jeopardising my entire future for your whim, Jo.'

'Of course not. I'll stay in a hotel until . . . for a little while. You must introduce me to your house-keeper. I'm sure we'll be friends. And as soon as you get me a job I'll start to pay my own way for a bit.'

Later, she sat on his knee in his living-room and told him, caressingly, that she had done her best to forget him, to put him right out of her mind, but that she had been unable to do so.

'I thought of you all the time, Lou,' she said plaintively. 'You obsessed me. All I wanted was you. And now I've come all this way and you won't have me in your house.'

'Not won't, can't! Remember, I'm holding down an important . . .'

'Then let's get married, darling!'

'No! I'm still . . . involved . . . with Sarah. There's a woman over here, too . . . Damn it, you can't just expect to walk into my life after one brief episode over six months ago and marry me!'

'You said it first. You said you were respectable!'

'So I am. I'll get you a job, and see that you've got somewhere to stay for a while, but further than that I cannot go.'

'No?' She unbuttoned his shirt and her fingernails began the insidious, tickling, tingling circles. Louis swallowed.

'No. I mean it!'

'Do you?'

Taking his courage in both hands whilst he could still think straight, Louis stood up, tipping Josette off his lap on to the floor. He expected a shriek, cries of dismay, tears even. Instead, she lay there, looking up at him, the wickedest invitation in her eyes.

'Oh, Lou, look what you've done! I'm a fallen woman! Comfort me, darling.'

Louis bent over her and lifted her up.

'That's quite enough of that! I'll run you down to my friend's guest-house.'

But she lay in his arms, smiling lazily up at him, and somehow, he never quite knew how, they both ended up on the floor again. This time, when he got to his feet and lifted her up too, they both knew where it would end.

'It's just for tonight, mind,' Louis murmured, as he laid her on his bed and began to undress. 'You'll have to leave first thing in the morning, before my house-keeper gets here.'

She smiled lazily, then held out her arms to him.

'Of course, Lou, if that's what you want.'

But even as he sank into her embrace, a little voice warned Louis that he would not escape so easily.

Pixie was relieved when her occasional bouts of sickness stopped. She felt fine for the next few weeks, but just before Christmas she became crossly aware that her brand-new skirt, bought in September, would no longer meet around her waist. She tugged and strained at it but nothing would reduce the new thickness, sturdiness almost, of her waistline. It puzzled her, but she was not worried, for she felt so well, so full of energy, and she knew she was eating too much so that she told herself ruefully she would have to go steady or, come Christmas, she'd be so fat that Simon wouldn't like her any more.

Only one remark had been passed on her waistline, and that was by a girl in the top class, more than a year older than Pixie.

'I never seen no one go like that save my sister Nelly, and she wor in the club,' she announced. 'Seen anything lately, gal Pixie?'

'Seen what?'

'Your monthlies, stupid! Been seein' them regular, have you?'

'I don't, not yet,' Pixie replied truthfully. 'Nor does Joyce.'

The other girl giggled.

'Maybe, but Joyce, she's got a figure like a clothes prop. You're a tidy wench.'

'I daresay, but it's true. I did get one last August, but I haven't had another. My mum, she was the same. Didn't start proper until she was gone sixteen.'

'Aye, you do follow your mum,' the other girl agreed. 'I did. Booth started rare young, we did.'

And there the matter was allowed to drop and indeed to be completely forgotten, for there was all the rush and tumble of the end of term, and then, without warning, Simon came home.

As luck would have it, when he arrived both her parents were out, her father working at the church, her mother laying up the village hall for a whist drive which was to be held that evening. Neither of her parents approved of whist drives since it was gambling, plain as plain, but Mrs Hopwood had recently been employed by the church council to clean at the hall and a job was a job, particularly at Christmastide, when Mr Hopwood would perhaps be unable to dig graves for weeks at a time if the weather was hard, and would, consequently, get fewer tips.

'Simon!' Pixie stood in the doorway, beaming at him, then pulled him indoors. 'Here, come in a minute. Guess what?'

'What?' He eyed her appreciatively and Pixie drew in her stomach and pushed out her breasts, which had suddenly begun to swell in a highly satisfactory manner.

'I'm starting work, come Easter, up at the Hall. Kitchen maid at first, which in't no great shakes, but then parlour maid, if I'm lucky. Well, what do you think of that?'

Simon pulled a face.

'A skivvy! It's awful, Pix, honestly. I'll never see you,

or hardly ever. Why didn't you go into a shop or a factory or something? Then at least you'd get proper time off.'

'Well, how'm I to git a job in a shop or a factory, with work so short?' Pixie looked aggrieved. This was her big adventure and he was pouring cold water on it before it had even started. Just like a fellow! 'I'll be able to buy myself some clothes, boy, get a day off without grumbling from the old 'uns, see a fillum now and then. I can't stay at school for ever, you know.'

'No, of course you can't,' Simon said hurriedly, realising his error. 'But I do like to see you when I'm home. Still, I daresay we'll contrive something.'

'Yes, well, it's all very well,' Pixie said, not willing to forget her grievance. 'When you're here and can put the word out that I'm seeing Val or Cara it's all right. But when you in't here, what do you think I do? No pictures, not allowed to read books with men in 'em, no trips into the city in case I get into bad company . . . well, I tell you, service will be heaven!'

'I'm sorry. I was being selfish.' Simon kissed the tip of her nose, then took her in his arms and squeezed her gently. 'I suppose . . . what time will they be back?'

'Not for a coupla hours yet. I know what you're thinking, but . . . did anyone see you come in?'

'Probably, though it's a gloomy old day. Shall we risk it?'

'The trouble is, every old biddy in the place probably saw you, and I daren't come out with you until they say so. Yet if you stay . . . Oh, Simon!'

Simon laughed. The last two words had sounded less like speech than the frustrated howl of a courting cat! He took her hand.

'Well? Shall we take a chance?'

Pixie was every bit as much of a sport as Simon

thought her. Giggling, she led him up the narrow cupboard stairs and into her own small bedroom. It was a strange little room, scarcely bigger than the bed, with a ceiling that sloped so sharply that even the door had been cut on the slant and a floor wavy as the North Sea. There was a small washstand by the window with a jug and a ewer on it, and the window was small too, barely knee high. Simon glanced round appreciatively as Pixie collapsed, giggling, on to the bed and gazed provocatively up at him.

'What will happen if they come in?' Simon asked rather apprehensively, sitting down on the edge of the bed.

'They won't come up here, that's certain. Dad's never bin in this room since I was born, and Mother don't come up during the day, not with the rheumatics she gets in her knees now. They'll just holler up if they come in, and we'll have to have a bit of a think.'

'We certainly should!' But Simon perked up, she could see that. He knelt by the bed and began to unbutton Pixie's thick woollen cardigan, her cotton blouse, and the waist of her skirt. Then he tugged off her thick vest, staring with unabashed greed at the plump, blue-veined breasts thus revealed.

'I say, they're bigger than I remembered.' He bent over her, putting his mouth to them, and Pixie gasped and clutched his head, pressing his mouth closer to her smooth flesh.

Presently he began to jerk at her serviceable navy blue serge knickers and Pixie laughed breathlessly, but pushed him away.

'Best do the job proper, boy Simon,' she said, and between them they stripped her, and then Simon removed his trousers. He lay beside her for a moment, fondling her breasts, then letting his hand roam lower,

124

to the curve of her stomach. He slid his fingers across it, and then, just as she was reaching for him, froze into immobility.

'Pixie, your tummy's hard as a board!'

Pixie, however, was in no mood for light conversation. She pulled him over her and mouthed his shoulder, then fastened, leech-like, on the skin at the base of his neck and began to suck. Simon jerked free. He was puzzled and a bit uneasy, though he could not have said why.

'Pixie, did you hear what I said? What have you been eating, girl? Your belly's like a rock!'

'So's your thing, but I in't complaining,' Pixie said languorously. She kissed across the flat smoothness of his chest. 'Please, Simon, don't muck about!'

'You mean start mucking about, don't you?' But he dismissed the query from his mind and, in his turn, bent his head to suck the soft skin of neck and shoulder into mauve love-bites, whilst she clutched and moaned beneath him.

'Well, are you coming or aren't you? I want to spend my Christmas money before it all gets frittered away.'

Val's voice was plaintive and she scowled as Nick spluttered at her choice of words. 'Don't be silly, Nick. You know very well what I mean! It's awful when you're given quite a lot of money and you spend it all on little things like sweets and hair ribbons, and next thing you know it's all gone and nothing to show you ever had it. Come with me, do, do!'

Nick and Val were in the nursery, except that it was now known, or supposed to be known, as the children's sitting-room. It was also chilly, because Val had let the fire go right down and when Nick had stirred himself to go down and fetch coal he had put on too much, so that the fire was now smouldering and sending out clouds of evil brown smoke, making the room smell, faintly, of railway stations. Nicky was stretched out on one of the old but comfortable nursery armchairs, but now he pulled a face and sat up.

'I suppose I might as well. Glory, but I get bored here in the winter! Simon's always busy running round after that girl he's keen on, and today Martin's got a dentist appointment in the morning and he's having tea with some horrible old aunt this afternoon. So I might as well come shopping with you.'

'Oh, Nickee,' Val wailed. 'Stop pretending to be grown-up and bored. You know very well you love snooping round the city! Tell you what. We'll go round Strangers' Hall, and the Castle Museum. You like them. And I'll treat you to lunch at Jarrolds.'

'I'm persuaded.' Nick got to his feet. 'Oh well, after all the turkey and plum pudding it'll do us good to be active. Shall we walk into Norwich? Or we could bike.'

Val glanced out of the window. It was a bitterly cold day and the frost which had formed, fairy-like, on the trees and rooftops during the night had not yet dispersed. A walk would have to be very brisk, but cycling would not be practicable.

'Let's walk, or bus. I suppose there's no chance of getting a lift?'

Nick passed a rapid review of friends and relatives before his mind's eye, glanced at his wristwatch, then shook his head.

'No good. If we ask Auntie Sarah we might get landed with Cara, Daddy went off to work ages ago, and if Mother's going shopping she won't set off as early as this.'

'All right, then, we'll bus.'

Val was wearing a dress which had so taken Auntie

126

Ray's fancy that she had bought identical models for her three nieces, Cara, Val herself and Adolphus's brother's daughter. Nicky, glancing at his sister, was mildly surprised that such a striking garment could look so droopy and unattractive, when he had seen Cara looking stunning in it, or rather in its twin, a mere two days earlier. It was black and white wool with a flared skirt and a dropped waist, the skirt itself being set in square pleats. On Cara it looked like a model gown, but Val was too skinny, too narrow-shouldered, all wrong. And she had rucked the skirt up on one side, her petticoat drooped, her stockings were wrinkled round her ankles. Nicky grabbed her arm and shook her slightly.

'Hey, lanky, aren't you going to change? Smarten up a bit, now that your handsome brother has said he's going shopping with you?'

Val turned and grinned and Nicky remembered Simon once saying that whenever Val grinned he waited for the top of her head to fall off. Her mouth, he admitted judicially now, was on the large side! But somehow he could never think of Val as being ugly because she was so bouncy and lively, so totally unselfconscious. Fun to be with, even though she was his sister.

'My *handsome* brother? He isn't coming with me. He doesn't live here any more. It's the little squirt who lives at The Pride still.' She scampered across the nursery and attacked the door, swinging it wide with a shriek of unoiled hinges. 'Anyway, why should I change? This dress is new, and you know Auntie. I bet it cost a small fortune!'

'Well, I suppose you'll be wearing a coat over it,' Nick said resignedly. 'And a hat, of course. Only does it have to be that awful black felt thing with your school colours on?'

'It's that or nothing.' Val reached the foot of the stairs, slid across the polished marble of the hall floor and disappeared with a swish into the downstairs cloakroom. She emerged with her navy blue serge overcoat draped round her shoulders and a green pixie hood in one hand. She flourished it at Nick.

'What about this? It's lovely and warm, and it's probably better than my school felt one. That got a bit dented last term, I don't know how.'

'Possibly because you play hockey with it,' Nick said, removing his own neat serge coat from the hook and noting that Val had somehow managed to tear a triangular hole in the front of hers in addition to spilling something white and sinister looking on the left shoulder. Could it be paint? 'What's that on your shoulder, kid? Honestly, Val, there's no one in the world as untidy as you!'

'There must be.' Val crammed the pixie hood on to her head and scraped all her hair out of sight so that her pale, thin face had a bald look. 'Come on, Nick.'

'Ah, you're getting ready. Well done, children.' Tina, splendid in a full-length fur coat and a very becoming fur cloche hat, emerged from the study, pulling on her brown leather gloves. 'Millie must have absolutely galloped upstairs with my message. She's a good girl.'

'What message?'

'There, I knew you'd forget. Never mind, you're ready to go out. I'm taking you into the city today to get Nick's lightweight coat for the spring term.'

'Oh, no!' Nicky's groan came from the heart. 'Val and I were going round the museums this morning and stopping in town for lunch!'

Tina smiled, but both children knew she was adamant. Clothes were a necessary evil and had to be bought.

'And why not? I'll take you out to lunch, and then, this afternoon, you can go to the museums.'

'What about me?' Val said crossly. 'I won't be much help buying Nick's spring coat. Can I go off by myself?'

'Certainly not! You need a tunic and some more blouses. Heaven knows what you do to your clothes, Val, but you give new life to the clothing industry. I should think at least twelve women have permanent work just keeping you in school things. Come along, both of you. I don't want to keep Mills waiting.'

Val and Nick exchanged speaking glances, but followed their mother down the steps and on to the front drive. Nick stared enviously at Mills, who was whiling away the time with his head under the bonnet of the Sunbeam Talbot which was Ted's latest acquisition. Mills was a new chauffeur, only in his mid-twenties, and Nick envied him his life. Driving the car whenever anyone wanted to go out, maintaining it and the other car the Neylers ran, sometimes helping, in a mild sort of way, with heavy jobs around the house and garden. Yes, a nice life. He caught Mills's eye as the chauffeur realised they were approaching and hastily removed himself from his studying of the engine to open the doors for them. Mills winked, a flicker of his right eyelid, and Nick, gratified by such a sign of masculine unanimity, winked back.

'We'll get out at the Walk, Mills, if you please, and you can call for us at the same spot at two o'clock, after we've lunched.'

'Hey, you can't call for *us* at two o'clock,' Val protested as she climbed into the car and perched on the seat between her mother and brother. 'We shan't come home until later, not if we're going round the museums. We'll get a bus, Mother.'

'Very well, but stay with your brother,' Tina instructed. The children exchanged heartfelt glances, but agreed demurely enough. No use pointing out that Val walked to and from the city each day in summer, and in winter caught the bus, that she was in the habit of spending a large part of her lunch hour in the streets around the Assembly Rooms, where the High School was situated – though it was going to move to Newmarket Road in the near future, if everything went according to plan.

The car drew up by the entrance to the arcade and the children and their mother got out, Tina gracefully, Nick rapidly, Val sloppily.

'Thank you, Mills. Two o'clock,' Tina said dismissively. Then she tucked her hand into Nick's arm, for he was just about the right height for her to do so comfortably. Val slouched along on her other side, her head poking forward, her eyes dreaming down at the pavement as though it were made of fairy gold.

'Well, isn't this nice,' Tina said brightly. 'Shopping with my children! I think we'll try Greens, first. Their clothing is always excellent quality. Come along, dears!'

She led her prisoners firmly in the direction of London Street.

'We'll lunch at the Cafe Royal, for a special treat,' Tina said a couple of hours later to her now exhausted offspring. She laughed at their woebegone expressions. 'Goodness, the modern young have no spirit! You don't know how lucky you are to be able to buy your clothes off the peg. When I was a girl all our clothes were made for us. It was cheaper, of course. First I spent hours shopping for material with Mutti – your great-grandmother – and then more hours at the dressmakers, having interminable fittings. Now you've got the whole thing over in one morning, and you're going to have a delicious lunch and then a quiet wander round the city on your own. I never could have done that.'

Val, rendered furious by the snide remarks of a shop assistant who had made her look ridiculous in a school tunic at least two sizes too big, snorted. But at least her mother had intervened in the woman's avowed intention to fit her out in clothes with she could 'grow into' by telling her that by the time the tunic fitted her she would have worn it to a thread anyway. Some mothers, she knew, would have insisted on the larger garments, in the hope that they might be saved the purchase price of another set in a year's time. And in the end she had been allowed to buy a tunic which the assistant thought scandalously short, some blouses which fitted, and a school tie to replace last term's, which had spent a lot of its time dangling in Val's food or being chewed in maths lessons or having messages inked on to it about prep.

Nicky had an easier time because he was a standard size and clothes looked nice on him. His blazer with its vertical stripes would fit him for another term or two, he had managed to keep his boater unblemished from last year, and trousers and sports jackets lasted until he grew out of them. Fortunately, his clothing had been bought first, so he was only bored and not infuriated by the song and dance over Val's purchases. He had gone through his own particular mill, and when this was over there would be lunch and the museums, or amusing shops. Despite the fact that they frequently fought and argued, he was fonder of his twin than of almost anyone else. She was a good kid. He admired a lot of her attributes – her doggedness, her quick wit, her careless disregard for her own safety and comfort. When he had been a day boy at the grammar school and had walked down most of the way with his sister each morning, he had found her an excellent back-up in a fight, fearless in the face of boots and fists and quite prepared to wade in and thump anyone who attacked her twin. Boarding-school might have created a rift, but it was a rift that always healed within a few hours of their meeting up once more.

'Here we are.' Tina led them through the doors and into the foyer of the restaurant, then paused to remove Val's pixie hood and straighten her coat. Nick had removed his cap as soon as he entered, a sort of reflex action which happened every time he was beneath a roof. Now he stood waiting whilst Tina tried to re-arrange Val's ribbon, and then bade her daughter straighten her stockings and pull them up and not show the whites of her eyes whenever she was asked to tidy herself.

Then, just when they should have gone into the restaurant proper, with its pillars and white tablecloths, someone approached them and greeted Tina. It was Mrs M'Graw, a fellow bridge-player. Nick resigned himself to a long wait; he knew how it was when women got talking. Val, he could see, had gone off into one of her most annoying trances, when she would gaze, open-mouthed and slack-jawed, into the middle distance, dreaming her own dreams and forgetting where she was and why. It would be useless to expect her assistance in moving their mother forward into the restaurant.

It was at this point that Nicky got the feeling he was being watched. He turned and glanced behind him, then towards the staircase which led up from the back of the hall. Sure enough, a face was peeping at him round the banister. A small, oval face, with a broad grin etched on it. Sparkling blue eyes, too, and a fringe of dark curly hair. He could not tell if the watcher was a boy or a girl, but he could see that it was a child. He grinned, then turned back to see what his mother was up to now. Mrs M'Graw had left and Tina was talking to a tall man in a black suit. The head waiter, he imagined.

'Well, madam, if this is a special occasion, perhaps our upper dining-room would be more appropriate. The ceiling is painted very beautifully. People come a long way to see it. A copy of a Michelangelo picture, very fine, very rarely seen in this country, such a ceiling.'

He had a slight foreign accent. Tina glanced interrogatively at her son.

'What do you think Nicholas?'

Nicky would normally have opted for downstairs, food at once, and no painted ceiling. But there was the face on the stairs – what better way to find out who it was than to go up there?

'May we go upstairs? Come on then, Val!' He started up the stairs two at a time, ignoring his mother's startled exclamation at the speed of his departure.

He caught the small person on the upper landing. She was a skinny little girl in a very large pinafore, and she was in the act of fleeing up yet another flight of stairs when Nick grabbed the edge of her skirt and hauled her to a halt.

'Hello! I saw you just now, spying round the banister – d'you live here?'

'Yes. What are *you* doing here? You're only a boy!'

Nick grinned at her haughty tone.

'I'm lunching here with my mother and sister. And you, sprat, are only a girl!'

She smiled reluctantly, then sat down on the stairs. Her petticoat, he realised, was full of peanuts, some in their shells, some already opened.

'Yes, but I live here. You must go, boy. Goodbye!'

'My name's Nicky. That's short for Nicholas. Why have you got all those peanuts?'

She smiled wickedly, looking up at him through thick lashes, then put a finger to her lips.

'Hush, don't shout! I stole them from the chef. My name is Vitty.' She seemed about to say something more but a voice from above interrupted her.

'Vitty? Where are you, you bad girl! Come here at once!'

The voice was slightly accented, as the head waiter's had been, and yet the little girl spoke ordinary English. Could it be her mother calling her? But before he could ask, Vitty was on her feet and racing up the stairs, scattering peanuts as she went. Nicky laughed and returned to the head of the first staircase, to see his mother and sister beginning to mount. What a funny little kid! So self-possessed, and she couldn't be more than nine or ten! Pretty, too, if you liked that sort of thing. Odd, to think that a huge restaurant like this had kids living above it!

The three of them went into the painted dining room, where Tina ordered the sort of meal guaranteed to delight the jaded Christmastide palates of her two young companions, and Nicky speedily forgot the little dark girl and her stolen peanuts. But as they left he glanced up at the second flight of stairs, and was conscious of a vague feeling of disappointment. She was not there.

Chapter Six

Pixie was packing, moving as soundlessly as she could around her tiny room. She was going to run away from home.

At first, when she had realised she was pregnant, she had not had the faintest idea what to do or where to turn. She knew better than to tell anyone. The disgrace would be unbearable, and besides, once her parents knew, it would be All Up. Her father would kill her, if her mother did not finish her off first. Making it go away, as she phrased it to herself, had obsessed her for a few days, but she was hampered by almost total ignorance of how to set about it. She knew, because it was whispered, that babies *were* sometimes persuaded to 'go away', but that this was a risky and uncertain business, involving strange rituals and large quantities of alcohol. Since neither of her parents had ever allowed the demon drink to pass their door, far less their lips, theft was out of the question, and anyway, she did not know what else one did. There was something about hot baths, something else about jumping from a height, yet more about cold baths – she was bewildered and frightened enough by the fact of her pregnancy without adding these other horrors.

Ignorance, in fact, was the worst thing about the whole business. She did not know how babies were born, not even whence they came. There had been talk in the village school that if you looked down the front of a woman's dress you would see a dark slit between her breasts. It was from there, Johnny Halifax said profoundly, that his baby sister had emerged. He had seen her being born as plain as plain. Others thought that it had something to do with one's belly button, still others believed in the depth and profundity of the doctor's black bag. It was only recently, while watching her friend's cat give birth to five kittens, that Pixie had begun to suspect the truth. Babies came because you went with a boy, and then left your stomach by the same route the boy had used to enter.

As if this was not difficult enough to credit, when she thought of the smallness and narrowness of her own body, there were other stories, stories that one had to believe. Cissie Brett had screamed for twelve hours before her boy was born. Mrs Ethel Betteridge had died giving birth to her ninth. The girl from Pedlers End had miscarried and been 'awful ill' for months and months.

Boys, the instigators and perpetrators of the crime of being pregnant, could tell one nothing. They had terribly dirty minds, that went without saying, and knew lots of crude and horrible jokes and stories, but for all practical purposes they were useless. All piss and wind, Pixie thought vengefully, knowing how furious her father would be if he could hear her uttering such a sentiment.

In the end, she had done the most sensible thing. She made up her mind to confide in someone who would not despise her and might even help her. Not the girl from Pedlers End, who was a bit light in the head, nor Cissie Brett, respectably married now to the milkman. But in every small community there s a naughty girl, a bright girl, a girl who attracts boys as honey attracts bees and who is 'no better than she should be'. But though everyone knows about her she's never caught napping, not the village bad girl!

Such a one was Betty Chapman. Pixie, who had never exchanged more than the time of day with the older girl in her life, knew instinctively that she would not appeal to Betty in vain. Betty was kind, generous, and a great one to laugh. She would help.

She did. For a start, she asked Pixie into her gran's warm and friendly kitchen and told her that old Mrs Chapman would be out for an hour or more, so she could take her time. Then she made her a hot, sweet cup of tea and offered her a wedge of fruit cake, just as though she was a grown-up guest.

'Now,' she said, when they were both comfortably settled. 'Wha's up?'

'I'm going to have a baby,' Pixie said.

'Thought so. When?'

This floored Pixie. How on earth would she know a thing like that? She voiced the thought.

'When did you last see your monthly?' Betty asked patiently.

'Oh. August, I think.'

'Hmm. Too late to *do* anything, then. You've got to go through with it, gal.'

'Yes, But . . . where? I can't tell my parents, they'd kill me. And if they didn't, Nurse Fellowes would.'

This momentarily distracted Betty's attention from the matter in hand.

'She would? Why? What's she got agin you?'

'Oh, she sent me home once with a note to say I'd got nits in my hair. Mother was that furious! Straight back to school she marched me, straight into the head's office, and there was old Fellowes, sitting having a cuppa. My mum nearly threw me into Mr Stringer's lap, and defied him to find nits, and of course he couldn't. Nurse'd muddled me with Marlene Boote, and my mum made her apologise. I in't never heard the last of it, not from Nurse. She's been saying I'd come to a bad end ever since.'

Betty laughed loud and long, then sat back, wiped her eyes, and nodded.

'I daresay she'd be well pleased to find herself right this time! But there's no need to let 'em know.' She gave Pixie a bright, wicked glance. 'Not if you don't mind telling a few lies, being away from home for a bit.'

'I don't mind *anything*, if only I don't have to tell them,' Pixie said fervently. 'What'll I do, Betty?'

'Like I did. Oh yes, and no one don't know, see? I went to London, just ran off, like. Wrote to me gran and told her I'd got meself a good job, but I'd be back when I felt like it. Stayed away a year, so's there wouldn't be talk, and came back with no baby, but with some presents and some money.'

'Yes, that'd be fine! But what did you *do* with the baby?'

'I went to this home place where they take care of you, get you over the birth and put you in a job for a few weeks, provided you give the baby for adoption. There's several in London – one in Norwich, for the matter o' that, but you don't want to go there. They'd spot you was only a kid and send you home, like as not. No, Pix, you do as I did, go up to London. Got any money?'

Dumbly, Pixie shook her head.

'I'll lend you some.' She shook her head reprovingly as Pixie began to protest. 'Don't be daft, gal. Someone lent me money all them years ago – I never did ask, what about the feller? Any chance he'd help out?'

'No.' Pixie was firm. She knew Simon was responsible, of course, but she had no intention of involving him in something which she felt was so very much her own affair. 'He's only a lad – he's got no money.'

'Right. Here's five pound. You can give it me back when you come home and tell 'em you were sick of being away so long.'

'That's ever so kind of you,' Pixie said gratefully, taking the money and stowing it securely in her pocket. 'I won't forget you, Betty, not ever. I-I'll send you a card!'

'You can't say more than that!' Betty said, smiling at her. 'And don't let 'em make you feel guilty, gal. All you are is human, after all!'

Before Pixie left her house, she had three addresses which might help her tucked into her coat pocket beside the money, and a great deal of good advice stashed away beneath her curls. Further discussion had revealed the fact that she was supposed to be going into service at the Hall in a couple of weeks. Her mother had been putting it off ever since Easter because she did not think Pixie was well enough.

'Better and better. Leave a note saying service is servitude, or something like that. Say you're going to try for shop work. They'll swallow it, because so many girls feel that way about service now. And don't forget what I say. Don't let *anyone* in London make you feel bad about it.'

And now, a bare two days after the talk with Betty, she was packing, and would leave her home with the first trace of daylight. There was a good chance, Betty had said, of getting a lift into the city once the lorries began to thunder down the turnpike, and they started early at this time of year. After that, she would go to Thorpe Station and take a train for Liverpool Street. She had a little street map of London, worn and elderly, which Betty had given her, with her destination marked on it. She would manage, she was sure of it.

She had not expected to feel anything save

apprehension as she stood, for the last time for months, perhaps, in the familiar living-room, with her hand poised over the bolts of the door which led straight on to the street. Then it engulfed her – the smell which was so much a part of her that she had never, consciously, smelt it before. A trace of lingering damp, for the cottage was old; beeswax, for her mother was a great one for polishing; a whiff of oil from the lamps, coal from the stove, and the scent from a potpourri bowl heavy with rose petals and lavender flowers.

Tears rose to Pixie's eyes, and were dashed briskly away. No use moping, she informed herself severely. It was not as if she were leaving for ever. She would be back in a few months, and no one any the wiser. Just let her have the baby and she would come home again and pick up where she had left off.

She slid the bolts back, slowly, because they squeaked a little. Odd that she had never noticed a sound when her mother drew them. She opened the door and knew a moment's doubt. It was so still and dark out there, and by going she would leave her parents a prey to every passer-by, for she could scarcely bolt the door behind her. But it was just foolishness. The moment she was out, and the door closed, the adventure of it seized her, the glamour of being abroad when all the rest of the world slept. Anyway, once she was out it was no longer dark, for she had got her night eyes and could see the trees against the sky and a light on in one of the bedrooms at the Swan.

The sanded pavement was wide, and besides, she knew it by heart, every hollow and weed patch, every puddle and protruding doorstep. She walked quietly. To the east she could see the lightness in the sky which heralded the dawn. On the main road, headlamps passed. She hurried. She had plenty of time, as the train did not leave for hours yet, but the lorries were beginning already and she did not much want to have to catch the early bus. There was bound to be someone aboard who knew her.

She reached the main road and crossed to the bus stop. Then she stood there, eyes turned towards the oncoming traffic, waiting.

The Butcher's cat came out of the vicarage and stole, like a shadow, along the pavement. His name was Puddin', and he had a mouse between his teeth which he intended to lay right on the doorstep of the shop. Sarah Butcher would come to the door as soon as she got up, unlock it, unbolt it, and open the shop up for the newspaper delivery. When she saw his mouse she would be distracted and scream admiringly, and whilst she was picking it up in the coal shovel Puddin' intended to nip past her and take up his position near the stove in the kitchen where he would be warm and snug and, eventually, fed.

He was a knowing and intelligent animal and his haunts took him regularly across the turnpike road, so when he heard the lorry coming he ignored it until it was almost on a level with him, when he froze into careful stillness. He had never known a lorry to pursue him on to the pavement, but one could not be too careful with such large and powerful creatures.

The lorry slowed, then stopped. The cat turned yellow eyes, slitted against the light, towards it. Odd! The Hopwood girl was standing at the side of the road, and the cat saw the lorry driver lean out and heard him call something softly down to her. She answered, nodded, then climbed up into the cab. The lorry drew away with a roar and the cat watched it out of sight.

Then he took a firmer grip on his mouse and continued to pad softly towards home.

It was midsummer eve and Sarah had been restless all through the long, light evening. She wanted to go out for a run until Con went and fetched her a light coat and said he would bring the car round, and then she changed her mind and decided to stay in. Cross with Cara, who had gone to a dancing rehearsal at her ballet school and come home fifteen minutes late, cross with Simon, who rang up from school to ask if he might buy a new tennis racquet since he had split his own on a friend's head, she was in no mood to be trifled with.

'Simon's thoughtless and selfish,' she stormed to Con as she put the phone down. 'Not a word about the new baby, though he must know it's three days overdue.' She was beginning, she went on, to believe that it would never be born anyway. It was probably just wind, and she had awful heartburn so that she couldn't enjoy her food, and her legs ached, and no one cared a fig for her, not even Con who was, after all, a typical man with no thought for anyone other than himself.

Con, blinking at this totally uncharacteristic tirade, tried to comfort her and got his ears boxed.

'Leave me alone, Con! You think I'm making a fuss about nothing, but you should be the one plodding round the house weighing several tons and having to go sideways through doors and being stared at like a circus freak!' Sarah threw herself down in a soft chair in front of the open French windows, then tried to pull herself out of it, but her heel slipped on the polished boards and she collapsed heavily on to the chair again. 'I hate you all!' she announced, her voice heavy with tears. 'I do, I hate you! It's all your fault that I'm like this,

Con. I never wanted another baby. I've had quite enough children, and besides, I'm thirty-eight, far too old to have a child, and I can't help thinking that . . .' Her voice quivered to a halt.

Con perched on the arm of her chair and hugged her, and then, using considerable strength, for she weighed nearly as much as she thought she did, heaved her to her feet and kissed her flushed and furious face.

'Sweetheart mine, precious one, come to bed!'

Sarah gave a small, angry sob, but leaned against Con's chest.

'We can't go to bed. It isn't even ten o'clock, and besides, I want to go for a walk.'

'Right. It'll do you good. And no changing your mind or I'll roll you down on to the pavement and bowl you along like a ball until you've done a half-mile.'

'No, I won't change my mind.' She put a hand to the small of her back. 'Perhaps it'll get rid of this backache.'

'Backache?' Con's voice lifted. 'Sarah, is it . . . ?'

She had been holding his arm but she released it and pushed through the front door ahead of him, thumping heavily down the front steps on to the drive. She turned towards him. Her momentary softening, he could see, had dissipated.

'No, it is not! For God's sake, Con, I've had two children and you've had none! Please allow me to know best just this once – it can't be too soon for me, you know. I've had enough of waiting. I'm far more sick of it than you could possibly be!' She swung clumsily on her heel and began to stump towards the gate. 'I'm going for my walk, because I can tell it will be ages before anything happens. Weeks. Months, probably. If it ever does.' She turned her head and he repressed an urge to smile at her. She was so furious, poor darling! 'Don't you dare suggest that I'm nearing my time, Con, because I'm not. I'm like the *Marie Celeste*, doomed to sail on and on, until . . .'

He had reached her and was about to make some soothing remark when she said, in quite a different voice, 'That's done it!'

Con followed her gaze. Beneath her feet the gravel had darkened and Sarah was holding out a fold of her dress, half in amazement, half in repugnance. He put a hand on her waist.

'Indoors, sweetheart. Despite your brave words I think something may be about to happen. Your waters have broken.'

'They have not!' Sarah struggled against him, and then gave in, reluctantly, to *force majeure*, and allowed herself to be led back into the house. Halfway across the hall, however, she turned to face him. 'My waters never break until I'm well into labour, and don't you try to tell me any different, Con Solstein, because you know nothing whatsoever about it. Anyway, I want to go for a *walk*!'

'You're going to bed,' Con said firmly. He began to propel her up the stairs, no easy task at her present fighting weight, for she was still struggling and furious. At the head of the stairs he put his arms round her, very gently, and looked deep into her eyes. And knew that Sarah, who was afraid of nothing, was afraid of this birth. Afraid beause she was thirty-eight, because the doctor had warned her that he thought the baby was a very big one, because she was so happy and did not want to leave such happiness behind her.

'Sweetheart, this baby's going to come now no matter how hard you try to deny it. I'll ring for the doctor and we'll fetch Nurse back from wherever she's gone, and then we'll concentrate on giving Solstein junior a hand into the world.'

He left her at their bedroom door, hurried downstairs and made his phone calls, then returned to
Sarah's bedside. It was unfortunate that the nurse had
chosen to go to the cinema tonight, but she could be
paged and brought home by taxi. In the meantime Dr
Phillips would come round straight away, and Cecy
was poised and ready to rush the moment he gave her
the word.

Sarah was sitting up on the edge of the bed, fully
dressed still, and scowling. One hand was on the bed-
head, the other on her waist, or where her waist had
once been. She glanced up as he entered.

'Well?'

'The doctor won't be long, sweetheart. Let me help
you off with that dress and your other things, and then
you can lie quietly and relax until the doctor gets here.'

'I don't want to undress! There's no point. It's a false
alarm, it's . . .' Sarah snuffled and her voice wobbled. 'I
tell you it's nu-nu-nothing. I think it was pressure on
the bladder or something.'

'Never! I've read about it. That was your –'

'Shut up!' Sarah shrieked the words. 'It can't be what
you think. It said in my b-book that dry b-births are
difficult and that women whose waters break before
they go into labour have a hard time! So it can't be that!'

She was glaring at Con, daring him to deny it.
Instead, he took her hands, hauled her to her feet and
began to take her dress off, then her soaked underslip,
her equally soaked underwear. She made no more
demur but stood there like a great, cumbersome child,
her eyes tear-filled and her mouth trembling, until she
was dressed in one of the voluminous nursing night-
gowns she had been wearing lately. Then, when Con
turned back the bed, she climbed into it and arranged
herself decorously with her back to him and

announced, in a muffled voice, that she was going to sleep and did not want to see anyone at all.

'You can sleep in the dressing-room,' she mumbled into the pillow.

Before he had thought of a suitably soothing retort he was saved, quite literally, by the bell. He hurried downstairs, to see the doctor standing on the doorstep whilst behind him Ted was ushering Nurse Maynard out of his car. By great good fortune Nurse had chosen to go to one of the Neyler cinemas and so had been easily routed out, but it was good of Ted to have run her back. Con knew that Auntie Tina had given birth to six children as well as the twins, so Uncle Ted was an authority on pregnancies.

The doctor was sent upstairs, then Con invited his uncle into the study for a quick drink.

'Sarah's in a fearful bate, says it can't possibly have started yet,' he confided as he poured two stiff whiskies. 'I just hope she won't snarl at Dr Phillips and send him away, like she did me. Nor Nurse Maynard, of course.'

Ted laughed and clapped him on the back.

'Like that, is she? Well, Con, it's only husbands who become scapegoats at a time like this. Everyone else is helping to undo the damage you've caused, you see? I remember when Frank was born – and there's barely a year between the boys – your aunt gave me a terrible tongue lashing, didn't want to set eyes on me ever again, and blamed me roundly for everything that had ever gone wrong in her whole life. In fact, to tell you the truth, whilst Frank was being born upstairs I was sitting downstairs in tears, promising myself that I'd treat her like porcelain in future, never lay a hand on her – or anything else – and make sure she never got pregnant again.'

146

'Was that why there was such a gap between Frank and Stella?' Con asked, grinning.

'That sort of resolution, my boy, rarely lasts past the first kiss! No, the gap was me rushing off to America. Here, can I telephone Tina? She'll wonder why I've not come straight home.'

Two hours later Con, pacing up and down on the upper landing, was relieved when the bedroom door opened and Nurse's head appeared.

'Mr Solstein!'

He entered the room and stood just inside the door. Sarah lay on her side, her knees drawn up, her face pink and sweat-streaked. She smiled at him and held out her hand.

'Darling, come here.'

He approached the bed cautiously, then crouched so that their faces were on a level.

'My poor sweet! Is there anything I can do? Rub your back? Get you a drink?'

'You can forgive me for snapping your head off. I'm sorry, truly, but I felt so ill and stupid.' She sank her voice to a whisper. 'And I was scared, which was so silly – I'm not scared now.'

She stopped speaking and he could see rigidity possess her as she strove to conquer the pain that must have been racking her. Colour left her face, then returned in a flood. Nurse, standing nearby, said reprovingly: 'Don't tense up, Mrs Solstein. Relax; let the pains work for you.'

'I will relax more, Nurse, when I can begin to bear down. It's worse when there's nothing you can do to help yourself. Will the second stage start soon?'

'Not long now. How close are the pains, dear?'

'Every four minutes.' Sarah grimaced. 'When will the doctor be back?'

'In thirty minutes. But if you go into the second stage I'm to ring for him. He's gone home to snatch something to eat. The poor man's been on call since breakfast. A busy day.'

Con had been holding Sarah's hand, but now he released it and stood up. 'I'd better go and tell Mother it's still hanging fire; she rang and wanted to come round, but I thought it better not.'

Sarah caught at his hand and gripped it tightly. Con could almost feel the spasm of pain with her as her face whitened. Then she released him, and let out a long breath.

'Whew! Can you come back, Con? I'd like it if you came back and just held my hand for a while.'

'Of course I will.' He left her, to telephone his mother and look in on Mary, who was boiling enough water on the stove for a regiment of babies. Then he returned to Sarah, eager to help in any way he could.

'It's a boy!' Sarah beamed up at Con's face, almost as anxious and tired as her own. Con crossed the room, and thought that for the first time his wife looked her age, her face drawn and lined, still sweat-shiny, her hair lank, the bright eyes dull. Then he saw the baby in the crook of her arm.

He went nearer the bed. The doctor was washing his hands but turned to smile; the nurse was beaming as though it was she who had produced the child; even Sarah looked happy. Only he could not smile. He had heard her screams and been powerless to help her, had known himself responsible for her anguish.

He peered down into the tiny, reddish face. Dark hair, wet still, a cowlick on the puckered forehead.

Lashless, swollen eyelids, a dab of a nose, a little tightly shut mouth. My son, he thought incredulously. Flesh of my flesh created from nights of love, gentleness, passion. Such a tiny creature – and so ugly!

'He's hideously like me,' he said, touching a tiny fist. 'What long fingers he has! How do you do, Sebastian? Or have you changed your mind again?'

'How could I? He looks just like a Sebastian. Would you like to hold him for a moment, Daddy? You could take him down and show him off to Cecy, if she's still here.'

'Still here? Wild horses wouldn't drag her away without seeing him.' Con took the small bundle in his arms. His son felt far too light, yet he also felt just right, as though light was how he ought to feel. 'I won't be gone long, and then he can be settled down. Though he seems to be sleeping pretty soundly right now. Didn't he give a big yell when he was born? I stood outside the door and felt . . .' He glanced at the nurse. 'Oh, well, what all fathers feel at such a moment, I suppose.'

'You'd yell if you'd been held up by the heels and had your bottom slapped,' Sarah said smugly. 'When you bring him back take him straight to his cradle in the nursery, would you? This may come as a surprise to you, but I'm exhausted!'

Dr Phillips, drying his hands, came over to the bed and smiled down at Sarah.

'You've been a very co-operative and helpful patient, Mrs Solstein,' he said approvingly. 'I couldn't ask for a better one. I hope you're proud of her, Mr Solstein.'

'I am.' Con touched his wife's cheek lightly, then turned towards the door. 'And of my son. I daresay they both had a nasty time of it.'

Downstairs, Cecy sat in a basket chair in the warm kitchen where Mary had finished boiling water at last and was using some of it to make everyone a nice cup of tea. Cecy got to her feet as Con came in, bright anticipation on her face.

'Oh, Con, my first grandchild. Is it . . . ?'

'Meet Sebastian Solstein, Mother,' Con said grandly. 'Do you want to hold him?' He transferred the tiny bundle carefully to his mother's eager arms. 'Ugly little blighter, isn't he? You can tell what a conk he's going to have one of these days – and hands like steam shovels already!'

'Who's beautiful, then?' Cecy crooned to the tiny red face. 'Whose daddy doesn't know a beautiful boy when he sees one? Oo's granny knows a beautiful baby, yes she does, and Sebby's the most beautiful baby Granny ever did see!'

'My God!' Con said, revolted by this grandmotherly adulation. 'Don't you go talking like that to him, Mother, or he'll turn out a regular cissie! Here, give him back and I'll return him to Nurse. Where's Cara?'

'At this hour? Fast asleep of course. Aren't you afraid of dropping him?' Cecy enquired, remembering Abe's terror of holding his offspring. 'How's Sarah, my dear?'

'Tired but blooming. Why should I drop him? I don't trot round the court dropping my notes! When I've put Sebastian back to bed I'll give you a lift home, Mother.'

But Cecy, putting on her coat and hat, shook her head.

'No, dear, I promised your father I'd ring him and he'll come round and pick me up.' She glanced hopefully at her son. 'It's his first grandchild too. I wonder – if it isn't too much trouble – well, could he . . . ?'

'Of course he can see the lad! I'll just pop up and make sure Sarah's settling whilst you phone, and whilst I do that . . .' He turned to Mary. 'Do you fancy a bit of baby-holding, Mary, whilst my mother telephones and we wait for Mr Solstein senior to arrive?'

Mary promptly held out her arms and Con passed her the white bundle.

'There! I'll just tell my wife that all's well.'

But Sarah was deeply and happily asleep and the nurse was in the nursery. Only Dr Phillips was left and he was stealing quietly out of the room as Con entered it, so the two men went down the stairs together.

'You've a fine healthy boy there,' Dr Phillips said as they crossed the hall. 'And a fine healthy wife, too. If she wants to have another child, let her. Two will be company for one another, and the age gap between this one and Cara is too wide for real companionship.'

'Well . . . just at the moment, I feel one is plenty,' Con admitted, opening the front door. It was full daylight outside, though early still, and as he shook hands with the doctor and thanked him his father's car, driven a little faster than was Abe's wont, came up the drive and stopped in a scatter of gravel.

Abe jumped out, shook hands with the doctor and then mounted the steps two at a time. His face was wrinkled with smiles, his small eyes beamed.

'Con, my boy! A son, eh? Marvellous, marvellous! Where is he?'

'Don't scream, you stupid girl. You'll worry them others downstairs! Just remember the pain's a judgement, on what you was doing nine months ago, and shut your mouth.' The woman in charge of the hostel for unmarried mothers cuffed Pixie. 'You're not dying, you're in labour, you silly little tart!'

They were in what passed for the hospital wing of the hostel, where the unfortunate inmates gave birth to their babies. Some as easily as shelling peas, others with great difficulty. Pixie was having a bad time. She had strained and strained until it seemed as though her body must split in two, she had clung to 'Melia's thin arm and Mrs Fawcett's thick one and obeyed their injunctions to bear down until she was too exhausted even to weep, and still the child was not born. She opened bloodshot eyes now and looked up at Mrs Fawcett. The broad, bovine face might seem indifferent to her agony, but the sly little eyes rejoiced in it. Mrs Fawcett had never liked Pixie, had resented her brightness, her prettiness, even her willingness. Now she watched as Pixie did her very best to give birth and shouted at her, abused her, hit her. Even her assistant, a one-time unmarried mother herself, was beginning to look worried. Pixie had been in labour now for twenty hours, and there was still no sign of the baby. Mrs Fawcett had done this before with girls she had taken a dislike to, and the authorities were getting suspicious. If this one died and no doctor had been called . . .

'Miz Fawcett, ma'am, 'adn't we better send for the doctor? She's bin at it an awful long whiles.'

'Yes, because she's a lazy slut.' She grabbed Pixie and shook her vigorously, then slapped her face twice, so hard that Pixie's head rocked. 'Get on with it, you cow. We don't want to be 'ere till morning!'

Pixie had bitten her tongue. Blood ran, brightly, down her chin and dripped on to the plain white shift which covered only her breasts and about half her stomach. She gasped, sobbed once, then the pain came again, stronger than ever, and she hitched herself into a more upright position and began to bear down once more, oblivious of the watching women, uncaring that she had been struck and sworn at for hours. She was more animal than human now, reacting only to the pangs and demands of her body.

'You didn't oughter 'ave done that,' 'Melia said, half

152

timidly, half defiantly. 'She's bleedin' inside, see, from her mouth? If she dies . . .'

'There's dozens more. World'd be a better place,' Mrs Fawcett said harshly. She put two beefy hands against Pixie's pointed knees. 'Bear down, you silly bitch, unless you want your face slapped clean off your 'ead.'

'Dr Pienkowski said to call 'im,' 'Melia warned presently, when not all Mrs Fawcett's pushing or Pixie's straining seemed to have brought the baby's head into the birth position. 'You was in trouble over the Yalmer girl; he won't forget that.'

'Shut your gob,' Mrs Fawcett recommended. She dragged Pixie further up the bed and began to press on the mound of her stomach. Pixie, whose screams had ceased earlier from sheer exhaustion, moaned, then took a deep breath and screamed, agony sharpening her voice to an almost unendurable shrillness. Mrs Fawcett advised her, breathlessly, to stow it, and then, when further pressure caused Pixie to give that inhuman shriek again, slapped her face so that scarlet, swollen finger marks showed up sharply against the girl's already maltreated skin.

'Melia hesitated no longer but slipped out of the room. She would not be party to murder, and that's what it would amount to, if they didn't get that doctor here quick! Down the dark stairs she stumbled, and nearly shrieked herself when a shadow detached itself from the other shadows just outside the office door. It was Wilma, a friend of Pixie's. In the dimness her eyes were huge and black in her thin little face, and her claw-like hand clutched fiercely at 'Melia's arm.

'Gawd, 'Melia, them screams! Is she dying?'

'Git the doctor, Wilma,' 'Melia said urgently. 'Telephone for 'im, or run round there. But fetch 'im 'ere, for Chrissake, or there'll be murder done up there!'

Wilma needed no second bidding, and as 'Melia hurried back up the stairs she could hear the telephone being lifted off its hook behind her.

'It's a girl. Good thing. Only good thing she's ever done. Girls is easier got rid of.'

That was the only encomium which greeted the arrival of Pixie's daughter into the world, for by then Pixie was unconscious. The child, her face marked by the forceps which Dr Pienkowski had used in order to get her born at all, lay quietly beside her mother, blood-streaked still, as was Pixie, the bed, the once-white smock.

'Tell 'er to clean 'erself up,' Mrs Fawcett ordered harshly, handing 'Melia a soaped piece of cloth. 'Melia gave the matron a contemptuous glance. How could she do any such thing when the girl was unconscious, knocked out by something the doctor had administered before he cut her to have room to use the forceps? Dr Pienkowski was washing, but he turned and glanced at his patient.

'Clean her up. She'll live. She's strong.' He had a marked Polish accent and was a man of few words in any case. 'The baby's strong, too. She'll go at four weeks, maybe. She's going to be blonde – blondes always go early.'

The two of them left the room and 'Melia began to clean Pixie's inanimate form, though she left the blood-stained smock in position. Pixie would take it off as soon as she came round – they always did. Then she turned to the baby, blanket-wrapped in the cardboard box which was the only cradle it would ever know until it left the hostel. She lifted it out and unwrapped it, and the baby, feeling cool air on its warm, damp skin, muttered a cry. 'Melia cleaned the birth stains quickly

154

and more or less efficiently, then put it back in its box. As she did so, the door opened and Dr Pienkowski and Mrs Fawcett returned to the room, the doctor to pick up his forceps, which he had left in the basin of water, and Mrs Fawcett merely to remind 'Melia, crossly, that breakfast was long over and she was needed to help with the washing up.

In the cardboard box, the baby gave a little cry. Pixie, drowned fathoms deep, now, in exhausted sleep, jerked and muttered but did not wake. None of the three people in the room so much as glanced towards mother or child. They conversed in normal tones for a few moments, then turned and went out.

They were on their own, Pixie and her daughter.

Chapter Seven

'But Pix, you *know* you can't keep 'er! You signed the paper, same's me. That's why they won't give 'er no name or nothin', just calls 'er baby Hopwood.'

'She has got a name. She's Hazel,' Pixie said stubbornly. 'She's mine, Wilma, and they can't stop me taking her when I go. I signed that paper before I knew her, and if they try to stop me keeping her I'll just run off.'

'You mean you'll take 'er? Ain't that kidnappin'?' Wilma gazed with awe at her friend. The two of them were sitting out in the little yard behind the hostel, on the small stone wall, hidden from the house by lines of flapping nappies, suckling their babies. Wilma had a girl too, a tiny dark-haired creature who gave no trouble and had been born after a mere two hours' labour. Hazel, on the other hand, was fair, lusty and lively, always hungry, sometimes noisy, and though only a month old she smiled at her mother, though Mrs Fawcett insisted sourly it was only wind.

'I'm keeping her, whatever anyone says. I . . . must.' Pixie looked down into the flushed little face, warm against the curve of her breast. 'I love her, and I don't trust no one else to love her like I do. My mum and dad would have said they loved me – p'raps they did – but oh, they kept me so strictly in my place! No laughing, no boyfriends, no nice clothes or little chats. With Hazel, it'll be different. I'll see to that.'

'What about that paper? You signed it, Pix.'

'What did it mean, though? Ever since I got here I worked for 'em, skivvying at the big offices, peeling spuds and chopping turnips and grating carrots until my hands was ruined. I scrubbed and mopped and brushed and never a penny of the money did I see, and that was only before. Once she was born they had me at it within five days – more scrubbing, more polishing, more cleaning. Reckon I've paid them back a dozen times over for what it cost 'em to keep me and Hazel.'

'What about the lady what come yesterday and saw 'azel? She 'ad a big posh car, an 'usband, a silk suit. She could give your little' un all sorts.'

'Not love, not like I can. They'd always look at her and remember what her mother had done, and wait for her to turn out bad, like me. No, I'm keeping her.'

'On what? How can you work with the kid along? Where'll you live? Come off it, luv. Let 'azel go where they'll take good care of 'er, and you and me can share a place until we're on our feet again.'

'I'll manage. I've got plans.'

'Is it the farver? You goin' to tell 'im, try to get some money out of 'im?'

Pixie snorted. ' 'Course not! What could he do? No, I've got plans, I tell you.'

The truth was that, though she knew Simon was Hazel's father, she could not believe, in her heart, that he had any connection with this sweet-smelling, golden-haired angel – he was just a boy! A nice boy, who had done exciting and delightful things to her, but still just a boy. She knew that if he walked into the yard right now and claimed the baby, she would deny it. She would lie to him, say she had been with another man and that the baby was his. Because Hazel belonged to no one but her. Logically, she could have argued that she had lost her home, her career, if one could describe

157

the calling of kitchenmaid as a career, and her good name for Hazel. She had suffered pain and indignity and shame for the baby. But none of it counted. All that had been suffered not because of the baby, but because of her own badness. The baby was a beautiful and delightful gift from God to her, and no one, not a rich adoptive mother, not Mrs Fawcett, not even Simon, would take her child away from her.

'Well, what plans? Come on, Pix, tell me!'

'Later. Now, since baby Hazel's full as full, I'm going to get off to work.'

But Pixie had taken fright. Suppose they did try to insist that she had signed a paper, and took the child from her? Suppose they took Hazel whilst she was at work, or asleep? She must go, this very night, before it was too late.

That night she waited until the whole house was quiet, then slipped out of bed. She wore her clothing under her nightdress and only had to take the outer garment off and push it into her previously packed bag, then take Hazel from her cardboard box, make sure that her shawl was warmly wrapped round her, and pad silently out of the dormitory.

No one heard her go. No one heard her patter down the stairs, ignoring the front door, and make for the long window in the dining-room which faced on to Keppler Street. She was out of it in a moment and standing on the pavement, then she reached in for her case and for the baby, lowered the window soundlessly into its original position, and set off along the dark street.

This had been planned for at least two weeks, so she knew exactly what to do. King's Cross station was near, and it had an all-night waiting-room, a ladies' waiting-room what was more, so that she and Hazel would be able to snooze in safety until it was daylight.

She reached the station without mishap and found the waiting-room. Two fat women were asleep in one corner, and a painted prostitute was sitting in the other, changing her stockings, a cigarette dangling from the corner of her scarlet mouth. Pixie settled herself and Hazel in a corner, curled protectively round the baby, and was asleep in five minutes.

It was strange to wake up, to find that the painted lady had gone and the two fat women were now awake and tucking into cold beef and pickle sandwiches. She knew they were cold beef and pickle because she was offered one and accepted gratefully, for though she could feed Hazel she had not thought to provide breakfast for herself.

With Hazel fed and her skimpy blouse buttoned respectably once more, she thanked the countrywomen for their sandwiches and set off, glad that her case was not too heavy since she had only the haziest idea of how far she must walk. She had no money for a bus or a train and, though she knew where she was going, the directions in her head were in relation to one of the big stores in which she had worked and not to the station she had just left.

She was in luck, however. A passing paper boy, when asked, volunteered the information that if she was to take the next turning to the left, walk half a mile or so, and then turn right and right again, she would find herself not only hard by the store, but within a stone's throw of her destination, Catford Street.

One of the cleaners at the store, a Mrs Threadgold, had befriended Pixie when she first went there to work and had told her that, if she ever changed her mind and decided to keep her baby, she might be able to help.

'Twelve kids I've 'ad, me,' she had boasted. 'No

bovver, kids ain't. I'll give an eye to your littl'un whiles you makes a bob or two, and willing. You can kip down alonga my Nelly.'

At the time Pixie had been as determined to have her baby adopted as the other girls, and guessed that Mrs Threadgold had made the suggestion without the slightest fear of its being taken up. Nevertheless, she had seemed a friendly soul. It was worth at least reminding her of her offer.

Catford Street proved to be a grey slum, the tenement blocks on either side of the narrow street full to overflowing with people, mangy dogs and an assortment of pigeons, cats and broken-down prams. But one shy question as to the whereabouts of Mrs Threadgold's flat brought immediate directions.

Up one flight of concrete stairs which smelled rather odd, along a corridor littered with rubbish and broken toys, and there was number 45. It had the number outlined in white paint, which was a good sign, and someone, once, had tried to polish the brass door handle. There was also a worn little brass knocker. Pixie stood her suitcase down and knocked. No harm in trying, was there!

'Yeah?' A skinny girl of about her own age answered the door, hands on hips. She was wearing a filthy wrap-around apron and down-at-heel shoes several sizes too large. Her hair was untidy and badly cut, but her eyes were bright and full of intelligence. They took in every detail of Pixie and the baby, then she held the door open. 'Want 'im minding? Know the rates?'

A strange and extremely strong smell came out of the flat, making Pixie's eyes water protestingly, but she followed the other girl into the living-room which led off a tiny, passage-like hallway. The room was, astonishingly, crowded with small children, many more than Mrs Threadgold herself could possibly have been responsible for. It was also very much cleaner and tidier than she had expected, though the children were neither. Pixie gaped at them, then looked back at the girl.

'I really came to see Mrs Threadgold. She told me to come.'

'Oh, aye? Ma's out. How long d'yer want to leave 'im?'

'I don't, because I haven't got a job. I was doing a cleaning job at the same shop as your mother, and she said, if I decided to keep my baby, to come to her.'

'Oh, you're one of them,' the girl said. She gestured to Pixie to sit down on a patched and faded armchair. 'Make yourself at 'ome. It's three bob a week, and you provide 'is food.'

'She's a girl. Her name's Hazel, and I've got no money at all, not even three bob. But your mother said . . .'

'Yes, I was forgettin', sorry. Why did you come in the middle of the week, though? Usually, gals like you 'ave a free week and pay at the end of it. Look, tell you what. You stay 'ere and sleep 'ead to tail wiv me until you get somewheres, and we'll keep an eye on 'im whilst you work. What say?'

'That would be splendid,' Pixie said thankfully. 'I'm very strong. I can clean and scrub. Do you think I'll get a job fairly easily? Could you tell me where to start looking, please?'

'Naw, I'm stuck 'ere all day,' the girl said, but goodhumouredly. 'Ma knows, though. Or Cissie. Or even our Nelly, if you're lucky.'

'Well, then, when do they get in? And is there somewhere I can keep the baby until she wants feeding? She's too little to play on the floor like the others.'

'Yeah. Through 'ere.' The girl got up and slouched through to another room where a number of thin pallet beds jostled for an inch of space. Each had a cardboard box on it. The girl reached for an empty one and pushed a square of blanket in it. The blanket was thin but clean. Trixie laid the sleeping Hazel inside and replaced it on the bed, then they returned to the living-room and sat down amongst the children.

'There! Now let me interdooce meself. I'm Elsie Threadgold, and you'll be . . . ?'

'Pixie Hopwood,' Pixie supplied. 'Glad to meet you, Elsie.' She smiled tentatively and let a large baby boy with cold sores round his mouth crawl on to her lap. 'You've got your hands full here!'

'You're right, Pixie. Good training for the day I fall for one of me own, though. I got a feller.'

'Oh? You don't look much older than me.'

'Look at you, gal, with a young 'un! I'm seventeen. How old are you?'

'Fifteen, come August. What's your feller like? Are you getting married?'

'He's a sailor. Ginger, they call 'im. 'E's got an 'ead of 'air like a bonfire! I dessay we'll marry, one of these days.' Something in her tone told Pixie that this was wishful thinking, that Elsie herself hardly believed it, but she smiled in a congratulatory fashion.

'I hope you'll be very happy, Elsie. Oh!' A spreading warmth and an increase in the strong, ammoniac smell which had been making her eyes water told her that the child on her lap had puddled on her. She picked him up and put him back on the floor and then stood up herself, her skirt dripping. 'He's not trained yet, I see – can I wash my skirt off somewhere? I'm a bit short on clothes.'

Elsie laughed, but there was no malice in her mirth.

162

'Sorry. Oughter have warned you. The gals know very well they're supposed to bring 'em padded out if they ain't clean, but they don't give a damn, you know. Treat us just like 'ome!'

Pixie, country bred, where children wore nappies until they were trained, was horrified by the assumption that in one's own home one would be quite happy to have small children piddling on the carpets and rugs and perpetually wetting the bed, but she said nothing, merely following Elsie through to a small back kitchen. Outside the window was a balcony, crowded with nappies and other articles of wet linen. Pixie, to whom running water in the house was still a luxury, was pleased to find that there was a proper sink and two taps. She turned one and water gushed.

'Slip right out of that skirt,' Elsie advised. 'Hold it under the tap. We won't 'ave no callers, not at this time o' day.'

And presently, with a clean, if soaked, skirt on, Pixie helped Elsie make a tray of tea with a plate of plain biscuits, which they took through into the living-room so that Elsie could 'give an eye', as she phrased it, to her charges. Whilst they drank the tea and ate the biscuits, Elsie chattered on about her family, giving Pixie information which might otherwise have taken her weeks to acquire.

She learned all about Elsie's eleven brothers and sisters, mostly married now and away from home save for Cissie, who was twenty and worked at the threepence and sixpence store, Nelly who worked for a firm of clothing manufacturers, and Charlie, who worked 'now and again' at the docks. Mr Threadgold also worked at the docks and was, Pixie gathered, a general favourite except when he had had a skinful, when the best thing to do was to keep out of his way.

Drunkenness had never come Pixie's way, though she knew that it existed. No one living almost opposite a public house, as she had done in Blofield, could fail to recognise it. She felt a little stab of fear that a drunken man might share this house with her and her baby, and then dismissed it firmly. He could not be too bad, or mothers would not leave their babies here.

As it happened Pixie was not far wrong, although she failed to take into account the fact that most of the mothers who left their babies with the Threadgolds were drinkers themselves when they could afford it, and would not have dreamed of condemning Mr Threadgold for boozing; certainly would not have taken their children away from a place which was both cheap and convenient just for a scruple.

For the rest of the day, Pixie helped Elsie with the children. Some of the mothers paid an extra one and sixpence a week for a midday meal which consisted of thick vegetable soup, a slice of bread and a drink of sweet, milky tea. The others brought paper bags with various comestibles inside including, to Pixie's considerable astonishment, cold chips sandwiched between two rounds of bread. One small boy came into neither category and was fed, grudgingly, by Elsie with a slice of bread and jam and a drink of water.

'If they bring a kid in twice without 'is dinner, then we won't 'ave 'im 'ere no more,' Elsie said, as she handed Pixie a dishcloth to help wipe sticky mouths and fingers after the meal was over. 'Unless they pays, of course. Awful, it is, when a kid whines for food and you ain't got none to give 'im.'

When everyone was clean and fed, they examined the younger children and changed nappies, both with a speed and dexterity which spoke of previous experience, for Elsie had been 'giving an eye' for years, and Pixie had never let Hazel wear a damp nappy for more than a few minutes if she knew that it was damp.

'They aren't all boys,' Pixie remarked at one point, when, as she removed a sodden nappy, she was faced with incontrovertible evidence of a child's sex. 'Why do you call them all "him", Elsie?'

'Easier than trying to sort 'em out; they're all buggers,' Elsie said cheerfully. She saw that Pixie looked shocked, and gave her a playful push. 'You wait, Pix. You'll learn it's true when you've been 'ere a bit!'

'Simon, darling, it's marvellous to have you home!' Sarah hugged her big son, then stood back and viewed him proudly. 'You've grown yet again. You'll be taller than Louis yet! Do you want to see your brother?'

'Has he changed much? He was a bit weedy when I saw him last,' Simon said gruffly. Babies did not appeal to him. 'Hello, Uncle Con. Hello, Cara.'

'Hello, Sime,' Cara said. She was wearing a deep pink dress with frills at neck and wrist. Simon thought she looked a twerp. 'We've got strawberries and cream for dinner tonight because you're home.'

'Corking,' Simon said obediently. 'Mother, will it be all right if I go over to Blofield tomorrow? I want to see James. I've not seen him since Christmas.'

'But you've only just arrived home,' Sarah protested. 'And it's ages since you were home properly.' Simon had paid them two flying visits, once to see his little brother, the other a mere two days at Easter, for he had gone to Austria on a skiing trip with the school instead of spending Easter at home, as he usually did, and had accepted an invitation to spend half term with a schoolfriend who owned a motor bike which he was quite willing to let Simon learn to ride. But now the summer holidays were here, and Simon wanted to go over to Blofield.

'You go off, old man,' Con said as they mounted the stairs, Simon carrying his suitcase with ease for all its weight. 'Don't let Mother tie you to her apron strings the way she tries to tie Sebastian.'

'Con, how could you?' Sarah turned in the nursery doorway to smile at Simon. 'Uncle Con expects poor little Sebby to start playing golf tomorrow and rugger next week!'

For a moment Simon was conscious of a wistful wish that his own father took more of an interest in his son, then he shrugged the thought off. Ridiculous. Sebastian was only a baby! But the fact remained that Con was not the sort that kissed and ran, like Louis. He would stay here, loving his wife, giving his whole attention to the upbringing of his son.

They went into the nursery and bent over the cot. Sebastian was rosy, powdered, sunk in baby slumber. He wore an embroidered nightgown, the sheets smelled of lavender and he himself emanated cared-for baby smells. His coverlet was hand-knitted in soft silver and blue wool and above his head a row of bright felt animals bobbed so that, should he wake, his eyes would at once fall on something interesting and colourful.

'Ah, Simon, you must meet Nanny Goodrich.'

Simon turned. Nanny Goodrich was, he supposed, about thirty, brisk and capable. She smiled at Simon, then bent over the cot and adjusted the sheet infinitesimally. She loved Sebastian, you could see that. She probably hoped there would be other babies to keep her occupied in this beautiful house where there was plenty of money and, perhaps more important, plenty of love.

'Did you have a good journey, Master Simon?'

'Yes, thank you. My cousin Nick's father collected us both.' He turned to his parents. 'I say, we stopped for dinner at a spiffing place. I had jolly nearly a whole chicken on my plate, and there was so much ice-cream and fruit on the banana split that I felt a pig to eat it all!'

'Well done. You aren't hungry, then?'

'Well, now that you mention it, Uncle Con . . .'

'Right. We'll put your case in your room, you can have a quick wash and brush up, and then we'll go downstairs and put Cook's mind at rest, since she's prepared dinner specially, right down to the straw- berries and cream Cara was talking about.'

Laughing together, they left the nursery. Simon was already beginning to feel that he was not only at home, but a part of it all once more.

Although everyone assumed that he was going over to Blofield to see James, in fact he was going over there on a far from pleasant errand. But Simon had never shirked what he saw clearly was his duty, and now must be no exception. Nevertheless, he rode his bicycle less fast than usual as he neared the village. He did not want to hurt Pixie, but he would have to explain.

The truth of the matter was that he had met a girl during his skiing trip whom he intended to meet again. Oddly, she too, was on a school trip, and once they got talking, which he had managed to accomplish very quickly, they had speedily realised the astonishing coincidence that they both hailed from Norfolk. Not only that, but she was actually a boarder at the Norwich High School and knew Val and Cara quite well, though, as she was so much older, more by sight and reputation than actually to speak to.

She was enchantingly pretty, with rich, chestnut- coloured hair, eyes that matched it, and pale, clear skin.

What was more she was a natural athlete, and very much sooner than the rest of her party she had abandoned the nursery slopes for more exciting terrain. Clad in her skiing sweaters and the tight, figure-hugging trousers which were so flattering to a slim figure and so ugly on a fat one, she had skimmed the slopes beside Simon, frequently beating him at first, manoeuvring with great skill, turning to laugh, until he was head over heels in love.

Her name was Georgina Lennox, but she was known as Georgie, and ever since the holiday she and Simon had been writing to each other. They planned to meet as soon as they decently could, and in the best possible way, too – officially, this time. Simon would tell his mother, Georgie would tell hers, and one or other would then suggest a meeting.

But first, he must see Pixie and tell her that things had changed. She had been on the verge of going into service at Easter, he knew that, and though he had heard from James that she had not been well and her job had been temporarily held for her he was was sure that by now she would be immersed in her work and her new friends. But . . . just in case she still thought of him with affection he would see her before meeting Georgie again.

He leaned his bicycle against the side of the cottage and knocked on the front door, but to his surprise there was no reply. He waited for a moment, then got back on his bike and cycled down to the church. Perhaps Mrs Hopwood was working at the village hall, or in one of the large private houses in the village, but he could be fairly sure of catching Mr Hopwood here.

He did. Simon walked over to where the old man was working and greeted him, and then they faced each other, symbolically almost, over a newly dug grave. Mr

Hopwood looked older, older even than he ought to have done, but perhaps that was because it was a warm day and he had taken his cap off, revealing that sign of the true countryman – a fish-belly white forehead which had been shaded by the cap and a brick-red countenance beneath it. He looked enquiringly at Simon.

'Can I do anything for you, lad?'

Simon went red. The old boy didn't even recognise him!

'Well, yes, sir. I'm Simon Rose. Your daughter Pixie is a friend of my sister's. They met quite a bit last summer, but not a lot in between, except I came over a few times during the Christmas holidays and took her back either to my house or my cousin's place. And she . . . my sister, Cara Rose . . . asked me if I'd pop over and see how Pixie was.'

'She's gone, young master,' the old man said lugubriously. 'Gone these three-four months.'

'Oh, well, I knew she was going to work at the Hall,' Simon said hastily. 'But we thought, Cara and I, that . . .'

'No, she in't gone to work at the Hall. She's gone, left home, run orf,' Mr Hopwood explained. 'One night, she went. Left a note pinned to her piller, just saying she didn't want to go skivvying and could find something better in London. Mother, she had a card from her after a foo weeks, saying she'd got herself a good job and would come home when she was sick of it, but we in't heard since.'

'Gone to *London*?' Simon could scarcely believe his ears. Why on earth should Pixie do a thing like that? To be sure she was sick and tired of living at home, but she was looking forward to working at the Hall, she had said so! An adventure, she had called it. He stared at Mr Hopwood, puzzled.

'But why, sir? I though she quite liked the thought of working at the Hall.'

'Ar, so did we. But that's not what a gal *says* you believe, seemingly.' Mr Hopwood dug his spade into the rich earth mound at the side of the grave. 'We thought she mighta writ to James, but no, never a word. Never a word.'

'I'm awfully sorry,' Simon said uncomfortably. 'I'll tell my sister, but I know she said Pixie never wrote, so she won't be any the wiser.'

He tugged his cap and then turned away, scarcely knowing whether to be dismayed or delighted. Of course it was a weight off his conscience. He could scarcely be blamed, now, for seeing Georgie. But on the other hand he hated to think of Pixie all by herself in London, perhaps having her delicious charm and innocent gaiety turned against her in some mysterious way. He thought of white slave traders; he had heard of them but had very little idea how they worked or whether, in fact, they were real or just bogeys with which to frighten naughty girls. But it was no use wondering. He would go to the Butchers' shop and see when James would be home, and perhaps get some information out of Auntie Sally. She had been his nanny when he was very small and his affection for her still lingered.

He propped his bicycle up alongside the post box and went into the shop, tugging his cap off as he entered the dimness. The door was wide because of the warmth and Mrs Butcher was behind the post office bit of the counter, writing. Her tongue was out, her arm curled round the paper, and it was plain that she had not noticed his entrance and was completely absorbed in her work. Simon stole across the shop until he stood right in front of the counter. Then he said, 'Boo!'

Auntie Sally looked up. One moment she was just the shop-keeper, with an enquiring look in her big brown eyes, her mouth a little open, soft, greying hair falling across her forehead. The next her whole face had changed – not into recognition of Simon, but differently. It looked as if it had been lit up from within. A smile trembled on her lips – not at all the sort of smile she used every day.

'Lou! Oh, Lou, how on earth . . . ?'

'I'm sorry, Auntie Sally, it's me, Simon.' Simon's embarrassment, which he was not old enough to hide, brought the hot blood rushing to his face. He had never thought about his likeness to his father, but now he remembered that people had remarked on it last summer – remembered, too, that Sally Butcher had borne at least one son, if not two, to Louis.

His blush burned, now, in his Aunt Sally's face. Recognition had dawned, joy faded and the glow returned to normal friendliness.

'Simon! I'm that sorry, boy, but you startled me, and for a moment I thought . . . I was just writing a letter, and . . . well, you saw how it was.'

'You're writing to my father, aren't you?' Simon said, shyness sending his voice, which was beginning to settle into a nice deep baritone, up into falsetto for a moment. 'I know about James and everything, you know.'

'Of course you do. Yes, I'm writing to Louis.' She sighed and pushed a wing of her shiny hair off her forehead. 'We're good friends, despite the distance and everything.' She glanced behind her, at the door which led through into the living quarters, but it was firmly shut and there was no sound behind it. 'It's easier for me, perhaps, because I went there once, you know. To Sydney, I mean.'

'I didn't know. It's never been mentioned.'

'No. Well, I didn't say anything to your mother, and so far as the children knew it was just a trip abroad. But of course I told Winkie.' She laughed, and for the first time Simon saw a glimpse of the Sarah Sutton who had captivated his father long ago. 'I won a competition, you know, for selling a good deal of Australian butter and answering a whole lot of questions about Australia. The prize was a month over there, all expenses paid.'

'And you saw my father. Did you . . . ?' Simon stopped, suddenly realising that he could scarcely ask if she had stayed with Louis, but Auntie Sally, smiling still, read his thoughts.

'Yes, I stayed at his flat. He insisted. For three weeks out of the four, in fact, I was there and he treated me like a queen. My path was strewn with red roses, I was entertained and fussed over, and even when I found out why I couldn't be hard on him. People are rarely hard on Lou.'

'What did you find out?'

'That everyone thought I was his wife. They knew he wanted me back, or rather that he wanted his wife back, and all they had to go on was a name, Sarah, and a rather smudged, over-enlarged photograph of your mother taken years before which could easily have been me. I was accepted by everyone. They went out of their way to entertain me, and I had the time of my life.'

The thought which had never, it was plain, occurred to Auntie Sally smote Simon like a fist between the eyes, so that for a moment he could only stand there and blink. Then he found the words to say what had occurred to him, words which were neither censorious nor over-excited.

'Then it wasn't really that Father didn't want Mother to go over to Australia with him once he got established, was it? He *couldn't* ask her, not having deceived all his friends and colleagues the way he did.'

'That never occurred to me, but it's true, of course.' She hesitated, then faced him frankly across the counter. 'Mind, Simon love, he never asked me to go over, either. I just telegrammed him that I was coming and asked him to book me into a hotel for a few nights, until I got my bearings, like. It isn't that your father didn't want you, I'm sure of that. At first, he was working very hard and couldn't have supported you, and later . . . it was easier to let things remain as they were, not to stir up trouble for himself. When I told him I must pack because I was leaving in a few days, he asked me to stay, begged me not to go. But I'd seen his life, how pleasant it is, how he's admired at the hospital and liked by friends and neighbours. I knew that though he would have been pleased enough if I'd stayed he didn't need me; not like Winkie and the children needed me. Not that I had the slightest intention of staying. It was his wanting to please me that made him beg me to stay, because he knew it was what I wanted to hear, even though I had to say no. I'm not putting it very well, but . . . do you know what I mean?'

'I think so. Mother says Daddy was kind and never liked to hurt people, and she said that that was how he came to get into trouble the way he did. I loved him when I was little, absolutely adored him, really, but this time I hardly saw anything of him. It wasn't that he avoided me exactly, but he didn't come round to the house. Did he see much of James at all?'

'Not to know – that is, I didn't tell James who he was until he'd left,' Sally Butcher admitted. 'It was strange, though. James knew nothing, but he was . . . protective, that afternoon. I got the feeling that Louis resented

173

his attitude. Of course, it was only a feeling, but they wouldn't have got on for long, James and Lou. James is too like me.'

'You and my father got on, though.'

'Ah, that's different. A fellow likes a girl to be a bit shy and diffident, not too forceful. But another man . . . well . . .' A shadow appeared in the sunny doorway and Auntie Sally slid her half-written letter under a sheet of blotting paper, then looked past Simon at her customer. 'Yes, Mrs Carter, what can I do for you this week?'

The little old woman hobbled past Simon and put a list down on the counter.

'There's quite a foo items here, Miz Butcher,' she said conversationally. 'My writin' in't that perfect, but I darssay you'll mek it out.'

'I daresay I will. I'll just get the stuff together whilst you go down to your daughter's, and you can pop in on your way back and pay me, then I'll get Paul to run it down to your place when he comes home.'

When the old lady had gone on her way Auntie Sally sat down again and smiled at Simon.

'There, I'm sorry to have run on and almost told you my life story, but I so rarely get the chance to talk about Lou! What did you really come in for, Simon?'

'I loved listening to you talk, because I don't often get the chance either,' Simon said. 'Actually, I wanted to ask you about Pixie. She and I were quite friendly and when I saw her father I asked how she was getting on in service, and he said she'd gone off to London and not kept in touch. I wondered if you knew any more.'

'You've no idea yourself? Not an inkling?'

Simon shook his head.

'She never said a word to me about leaving. Seemed very excited about going into service at the Hall, in fact.

174

I wondered if she might have confided in James, though.'

'Nothing that James passed on. I asked him, tactful like, if anything he'd done could have driven her off, and he said no. If I asked you the same question, Simon, would I get the same answer?'

'Indeed you would!' Simon thought of that summer loving. If anything, he would have thought that what he had done would have kept her here! 'I'm a bit hurt in one way, because we were good friends and saw a lot of each other, and I'd have thought she'd let me know before she just lit off like that. She was a nice kid, though, and I'm sorry if she got into any sort of trouble.'

'She's the sort that comes up smiling through everything,' Auntie Sally said cheerfully. 'She's pretty and self-confident, and even if she wasn't enormously intelligent she was sharp and had quick wits. It's my belief she'll walk in one day dripping furs and jewels and with a husband and a couple of kids behind her. Or we'll see her name in lights! Odd, when you think what her parents are like, but I've always thought that Pixie was born to succeed. Yes, she'll do well, will young Pixie.'

Whoop, whoop. The fearful, racking cough brought Pixie out of her shakedown and across the room to where Hazel lay in her wicker basket. She fumbled for the child, then lifted her up and turned her in her arm in the soft grey light of dawn which stole over the chimney tops and roofs. She had some medicine – it must be time for the next dose.

Pixie crossed the floor, avoiding the creaking boards – there were two – and found the washstand, where the medicine bottle and spoon stood. She must see, this time, if she could get Hazel to swallow the medicine without waking. There was a married couple in the room next door whose antics sometimes kept Pixie awake and often roused the baby when the woman shrieked, but they were always the first to complain if Hazel's cries disturbed the night. What was more, the husband was a violent man and there was something about him which scared Pixie, used though she was to his type. She worked in a pub down by the docks when they were shorthanded and busy, for they paid better than the people who employed her to clean shops and offices, so she had grown accustomed to coarseness, filthy language and the casual blows exchanged by men and women without enough money to feed themselves or their children properly, without hope, who drank to forget the immeasurable greyness of being out of work and never seeing a chance of bettering themselves.

Hazel whooped again and Pixie leaned on the wash-stand and fed her the medicine, drop by drop. The small mouth pursed, then opened, and the medicine trickled down her throat. The baby caught her breath, coughed again, retched, then seemed to sigh and settle down, turning her head into her mother's arm. Pixie sighed too, with relief. She couldn't remember the last full night's sleep she had enjoyed, and there had been times when not even her love and concern for Hazel had been enough to keep her awake, when she had fallen asleep with the child in her arms and had woken, guilt-ridden, to find that Hazel had vomited over them both and they lay in a sticky puddle, the child too exhausted to cry any more, every breath a rasping, agonising cough.

But the worst was over, the doctor said so. Now Hazel would mend and grow strong again, put back the weight she had lost. Pixie gazed out at the rooftops and watched as a pale streak of pink appeared on the horizon. Dawn was coming, the pigeons were uttering their strangled coos as they woke to the new day, and soon the streets would begin to hum with people once more and she would have to get up, take Hazel round to the Threadgolds', and start work. Good thing, she thought now, that she did clean offices, for many a time, lately, she had got through her work only by the grace of God and with the help of the other women. Half asleep over her mop, or keeling sideways as she scrubbed, she could not have held an ordinary cleaning job down for more time than it took for her employers to find her asleep in some unauthorised spot.

To keep herself awake, for it was scarcely sensible to go to sleep now, she sat down on the bed and thought about the breakfast she would have when she finished work. She was always hungry, though she no longer breast-fed the child, for when Hazel had been too ill to suck, her breasts had ached and wept milk and the doctor had given her tablets to take it away or he said she would be ill with milk fever. That meant she had to find money for milk which had, before, been free, but at least it had stopped her having to rush back to Hazel at four-hourly intervals, and meant that when she got a job she could stay until her work was finished.

She had saved a little, when she had got into her stride, but the money had been swallowed up by Hazel's whooping cough. Doctor's fees, medicine, missing work, buying special food, even the dreadful discovery that she had bought herself a thin flock mattress which was infested with fleas, all those things had cost money she could ill afford. In order to buy another mattress alone she had been forced to take on yet another job, and because she was working such long hours she had to pay the Threadgolds more to look after Hazel. It was a vicious circle, a treadmill which, once mounted, was almost impossible to escape.

But a week earlier, when she had been so desperate from lack of sleep that she had felt quite murderous whenever Hazel's little, thin wail rent the air, she had found a solution. A money-lender. A neat little house in a run-down area of the east end, with curtains at the windows, a garden well tended, and a stout woman who had willingly handed over a sum of money sufficient for Pixie to buy the baby much needed comforts – and to buy herself two whole days respite from work, two days to sleep whilst Elsie Threadgold cheerfully coped.

Those two days had renewed her. She had gone back to work a new girl, and planned to work seven nights a week, as soon as Hazel was completely recovered, so that she could pay the money-lender back what was, after all, not such a huge sum. Before I know it I'll be clear of debt, and I'll get saving again, so's me and Hazel can move out into the country, Pixie thought now. Good food, fresh air, then she'll thrive!

Presently, she could tell from the street sounds outside that it was time she began to get ready for the day ahead. She put Hazel, still sleeping soundly, into her wicker basket and began to dress. She took no pride in her appearance now because so few people saw her at this time in the morning, and she had no money to spare for clothes. Hard work in shops, and offices, mostly on her knees, ensured that no clothing stayed decent for long anyway. But cleanliness, besides being next to Godliness, was as good as free, so she poured cold water into the china basin on the washstand, took off her thin little nightie, and began to wash. She began at her neck and conscientiously soaped herself right down to her toes, then rinsed off, rubbed herself dry on a ragged strip of greying towel, and hurried into her working dress, a faded blue and white gingham, her down-at-heel black working shoes and a cardigan with more holes than wool. Through the thin plywood partition which separated her room from the married couple's, she heard him cough, the bedsprings creak, the woman whine that he always took more than his share of the covers.

Pixie picked up Hazel's basket, took the curved glass bottle full of milk from its hiding place beneath her bed, and headed for the narrow attic stairs. Soon enough she would be at work, and the sooner she got there the sooner she would be attacking that breakfast. She knew very well what she would have when it came to it – a good deal of bread, spread far too thinly with margarine, a big pot of strong tea, and an egg. She allowed herself the egg because she got so tired of nothing but cheap, filling food, but sometimes, as she spooned up the rich yellow yolk, she felt guilty. An egg was not essential, it was a luxury.

She reached the Threadgolds' flat and knocked. Elsie answered the door, wearing the dress which Pixie knew she slept in. She took the basket, checked that the bottle was beneath the blanket, then turned back indoors, though she left the door open.

'Come in for a cuppa? I just put the kettle on.'

'I daren't. Today's my day for Mr Puddenham's office, and you know how fussy he is. I love doing it, too. It takes more time, though.'

'Right, I'll 'ave one ready for when you comes back. She take 'er feed last night?'

'Yes. She's better, I can tell.' She waved, then hurried off in the direction of the big office block. She was proud of being the thrice-weekly cleaner to 'do' Mr Puddenham's office, for it was a special room, with a carpet and silver-framed photographs of his wife and daughters, and even curtains at the window and a pot plant on the sill. She felt as if she was cleaning a small, compact home, and took such pains that Mr Puddenham had been moved to congratulate the 'new woman' on her thoroughness. He had noted with special approval the fact that the new woman never failed to clean the silver frames on his photographs.

Now, cleaning them diligently, Pixie smiled at her friends, the Puddenham girls. She had never met them, but had christened them Mathilda and Susannah and wove daydreams round them, even including one in which, years hence, she and Mathilda would meet at a wedding, the wedding of Hazel and Mathilda's imaginary son, who would be called Harold, since it went so nicely with Hazel.

Finishing off the glass with a soft duster, she stood the photographs back on Mr Puddenham's big mahogany desk and smiled at them. Such pretty, fortunate little girls they seemed, such light-years away from her and her life now! They had a pony, and a house in the country as well as the flat in London, and heaps of dresses, she was sure, to say nothing of all the food they could eat. It did not occur to her to wonder at a world which could let the little Miss Puddenhams lead such sheltered and pampered lives whilst she herself had to work and slave and borrow just to keep body and soul together.

Perhaps this was because Pixie thought of the Miss Puddenhams as little girls, never realising that both, in fact, were older than she was. For Pixie, wrapped up in keeping herself and her baby alive, had long forgotten she was young.

PART 2: 1936

Chapter Eight

'Come out of there, Val Neyler! Fräulein said twenty minutes each was long enough for a bath, but you've been in there hours!'

The shrill, complaining voice echoed hollowly round the bathroom and caused Val, lying full-length in the tub despite the rapidly cooling water, to smile enigmatically. So Salka Brecht wanted to have her bath now, did she? Well, she could jolly well want! Val stretched out her big toe and nudged the tap so that more hot water trickled out. Salka would just have to learn patience.

'That isn't fair, Val, to run more hot!' The door rattled. 'If you don't come out right now I'll go and tell. I will, honour bright! You're too ba-ad, honestly.'

It was Tuesday, so the monologue had been delivered in French, according to the rules of this most exclusive of finishing schools where French was spoken on Mondays and Tuesdays, German on Wednesday and Thursdays and Italian on Fridays and Saturdays. On Sunday one might speak one's own language, but with so few other English girls at the school Val scarcely used the privilege. Even one's thinking was done in the language of the day, and it did mean that her French, German and Italian were almost second nature now.

Val settled deeper into the warming water, and thought about rules. They were few, because the staff thought that young ladies aged between sixteen and twenty ought to have sufficient good sense to act responsibly. The Swiss were a law-abiding race, and by and large their attitude paid off, for the conglomerate mix of young ladies being expensively 'finished' here treated even the unwritten rules with respect, probably because there were so few of them. Fräulein had said that twenty minutes was a fair time to spend in the bathroom, but it had only been a suggestion. Val glanced at her wristwatch, hanging from the hook above the sink. She could not read its small face from here, and for all she knew she might only have been in the bath for fifteen brief minutes. She smiled wickedly to herself. Let Salka wait. It would do her good!

'Val, if you aren't out by the time I count ten I'll go down and tell someone. Did you hear that?' There was a short pause, then Salka wailed: 'Why are you being so horrid to me?'

Val considered the question, lying with her chin just touching the water. Why was she being so horrid to skinny, charmless little Salka? Was it just because her friend, Minna von Eckner, disliked her fellow Berliner so heartily? Minna was bright and lively, flaxen-haired, tall, athletic. Salka was little, dark, unsure of herself, prone to tears. Minna made no bones about her dislike of Salka.

'She is not a true daughter of the Reich,' she assured Val. 'She whines when things go wrong. A true daughter of the Reich doesn't behave so: she squares her shoulders and works to make things go right again!'

Salka was no good at games either. In the winter, when they were skiing, Minna had pushed Salka hard at the top of the slope and they had giggled to themselves as the small figure hurtled with increasing speed down the run, to land in an undignified heap at the bottom, all spidery arms and legs. Crying, naturally!

'She should have enjoyed the speed,' Minna had said. 'Marvellous, to go down the run like a bullet, instead of Salka's usual rate, which is like a snail. She should thank me!'

She had not. Nor did she thank Minna for making her run all over the tennis court after the ball when they played tennis, or for deriding her sallow complexion and her funny run. She ran awkwardly, with her feet turned out and her knees turned in, looking a bit like a coolie with an invisible rickshaw in tow.

She was clever, though; cleverer than Minna or Val. And younger than both; at nearly seventeen she was twelve months younger than Val and nearly two years younger than Minna. Her intelligence was formidable, and perhaps Val would have admired her for that and forgotten about her poor sports record if only Salka had not been so serious. She did not understand teasing, never laughed or joked, seldom seemed to enjoy anything but her work. She read the sorts of books that Val avoided, the heavy, serious ones, seemed to have a natural affinity for mathematics, which Val loathed, and never talked about her home or her family in the free and easy way that the other girls did. She was a bluestocking, a spoilsport and a prig!

'Val? Do you hear me? Eight . . . nine . . . ten!'

Salka's voice, sounding serious, brought Val splashing out of the bath at last. She shook herself, her name of dark red curly hair shedding showers of water, and then heard Salka's footsteps pad away down the corridor. Val swore and leapt to open the door. She did not want Fräulein on the scene with her mouth tightening and her brow severe, and anyway, she had been in the water far too long. Her fingers and toes had gone crinkly and dead-looking. She put her head out into the corridor and shrieked for Salka.

'All right, you win, I'm out! Do come back, Sal!'

Salka turned, almost reluctantly, and padded back towards Val. She was already in her dressing-gown, a maroon silk garment, too big across the shoulders, which made her look smaller and more sallow than ever. Her slippers were swansdown and her dark hair was tied back from her face with a length of white silk ribbon, but she still looked plain to Val, standing there with her skin whiter than ever against the dark wet copper of her hair. Val saw that her nakedness embarrassed the younger girl and grinned wickedly. Stupid little prude!

'You are too bad, Val. I'll be late for my music lesson now.'

'You won't, not if you get a move on.' Val seized Salka's arm and propelled her into the bathroom until they were standing by the tub. 'Go on, hop in. You can be out of there in no time. The water's nice and warm still.'

Salka drew back nervously, staring up at Val with her mouth opening a little to show her rather large front teeth.

'Bath in someone else's water? There's a line round the tub, and it's not nice to use dirty water! You're supposed to let it out and clean up after yourself, you know you are!'

'I don't see why I should. I didn't wash in it, I only *lay*.' Val bent and dabbled a hand in the water, deliberately splashing some over Salka's legs and fluffy mules. 'Anyone would think I'd peed in it, which I didn't – or did I? I was startled when you first shouted, of course, so it's possible that I may have leaked a bit.' She frowned. 'Did I pee or didn't I, that's the question? If I did, I daresay you're right and I ought to run this lot out.'

Salka broke free from Val's grasp and grabbed a towel off the rail. She began vigorously rubbing at her legs, her mouth tight with disgust.

'You're horrible! How dare you splash water that you've peed in all over my legs and my mules! You're a dirty girl, Val Neyler, and a cruel one.'

Val was beginning to answer indignantly when a third voice joined in the conversation.

'What is all this about, girls? Miss Neyler, why are you naked? Fräulein Brecht, why did you enter the bathroom before Miss Neyler had finished? Standing there arguing like fishwives whilst the water grows cold is neither sensible nor decent.'

Fräulein Schmidt stood in the doorway, icily aloof and disapproving, her eyes fixed on them with distaste. Val's heart sank. Now there would be trouble!

'Miss Neyler wants me to use her bathwater and I say I won't, and what's more –'

'It was a joke,' Val cut in sulkily. She slitted her big greeny blue eyes at Salka and gave her the most malevolent look she could conjure up. Sneaking little toad! 'Salka's such a ninny, Fräulein. I only said it to tease her.'

'There's nothing amusing about failing to empty and clean the tub after your bath, Miss Neyler,' Fräulein said frostily. 'Nor about your nakedness. Kindly cover yourself.'

Val, used to sharing a small dormitory with three other girls, shrugged mentally but reached for a towel and draped it round her body sari-fashion. At eighteen, she knew her figure was the best thing about her and had no false modesty about her shape. She acknowledged regretfully that she was not pretty, but did not understand that she was something more. Striking, fascinating, exciting: they were all words which could have been applied to her looks, but which meant very little in the context of a young ladies' finishing school. In any case, she would much have preferred a pink and white prettiness. She thought her nose peculiar, her mouth too large, her teeth neither small nor white.

'Now, Fräulein Brecht, go back to your dormitory and wait whilst Miss Neyler cleans up in here. As soon as you've finished, Miss Neyler, run the taps and call Fräulein Brecht, and then you may go and dress. Do you have music before tea?'

Here it came – the reasoned, just punishment for her unreasonable and unjust behaviour. Val braced herself.

'No, Fräulein, but I had planned to play tennis with Fräulein von Eckner in about ten minutes.'

The teacher nodded, but instead of following Salka out of the room she stayed where she was, watching as Val cleansed down the bath with a thoroughness and efficiency which was unusual to say the least. Presently, she spoke.

'You know, I'm disappointed in you, Miss Neyler. Behaviour such as that comes very close to bullying, and what has Fräulein Brecht done to deserve it? Can you give me one reason?'

Val finished the bath and turned to face her. Fräulein Schmidt had a narrow, aesthetic face and faded greying hair. She wore ugly dark clothes with dipping hems and her shoes were bought for their stoutness, not for good looks. But she was a first-rate teacher and Val liked her, as did the rest of her pupils. Now, Val sighed and pushed a hand through the wet mass of her hair, lifting if off her neck for a moment.

'I think she's one of those people who ask for it, Fräulein. She's got no sense of humour and she's so dull and goody-goody that it just isn't true! But I don't want to bully anyone – I'll leave her alone in future.'

The narrow eyebrows rose.

'You'll leave her alone! How charitable – how *English*! Is that going to be your attitude to all your problems, if you leave them along they'll go away? You couldn't try to find her good points, and make a friend of her instead of a victim? It never occurs to you, I suppose, that Fräulein Brecht lacks humour because she has nothing much to laugh about? That, in fact, she is unhappy? Wilhelmina von Eckner decided to dislike Salka and you all followed like sheep. But for that she would be as lively as the rest of you. Well?'

Amazed by the deluge of questions as well as by the force of the teacher's feelings, Val fell back a step.

'Well, it's possible, but surely no one takes *that* much notice of how Minna and I behave? The truth is, Fräulein, that Fräulein Brecht goes the wrong way about making friends. People your own age don't want to be lectured or . . . or made to feel inferior.'

'Oh? And who feels inferior to Fräulein Brecht?'

'Intellectually, all of us, I daresay.'

'Nonsense, Miss Neyler! Why on earth should you feel any dismay because you aren't as clever as Fräulein Brecht? There are other very gifted girls here, but they don't get disliked because of it.'

Val felt herself beginning to flush and gave in gracefully, whilst she could.

'You're right. It isn't really that. I'm sorry, too, that I behaved so badly. Salka . . . Fräulein Brecht, I mean . . . isn't really my type, but I'll try to be friendlier.' She grinned at the teacher. 'If only because I want you to have a good opinion of us English!'

Fräulein Schmidt's face creased into an answering smile. She looked almost attractive when she smiled, so it was a pity, Val mused, that she did it so rarely.

189

'Well done, Miss Neyler. Go and get into your tennis dress and call Fräulein Brecht through. I'll run the bath.'

A week after the incident in the bathroom, Val and Minna were enjoying a hard-fought game of tennis on the school court when one of the young girls appeared with a letter in her hand.

'It's for you, Minna! Who's winning?'

Minna gave an anguished cry as the ball sped past her where she stood at the net, but Val ran forwards, holding out her hand.

'Game, set and match, and don't you *dare* pretend that I wouldn't have won anyway, even without Francine's timely intervention. Isn't that new serve of mine a killer? I swear it rips the grass!'

'Mm hm, when it goes in.' Minna wiped the sweat off her brow and accompanied her friend to the bench by the court where they had left their things. She took the letter with a word of thanks and then flung herself down, stretching out long, sun-tanned legs. 'Run away now, Francine! Val, you play a formidable game sometimes, yet at other times you just can't be bothered. Your besetting sin is laziness, d'you know that? Half the time you won't put yourself out to win. It's only when your temper's up that you wipe the floor with me.' She dropped her racquet on to the grass with a thud and stretched luxuriously. 'I love winning, too!'

'I like the game. Winning doesn't bother me all that much,' Val said honestly, dropping on to the bench beside her friend. 'I know what you mean, though. There are times when it's too much trouble to play all out. In fact, I probably play best when I'm annoyed about something.'

'Oh? What annoyed you today, then?'

'Salka. I had a spat with Fräulein about the way I

190

behaved towards the girl a week ago, and this morning I was determined to be nice. I asked her if she'd like to walk into the village with me this evening, to get some stamps and a new pen, and she just looked at me and said, "No." I can tell you, I was so taken aback you could have knocked me down with a feather. Conceited little prig!'

The tall blonde girl chuckled.

'She probably thought you were going with me – she knows how much time I've got for people of her type. I wouldn't let all the Fräuleins in the world change *my* attitude.'

'Yes, but that's your opinion. I'm old enough to make my own and the truth is that I *was* being led . . .' Val broke off as Minna, who had opened her letter, gave an exclamation. 'What's up?'

'Oh Val!' Minna hugged her friend's shoulders, holding the letter in front of her nose. 'Read that!'

Val pushed the page a little further away from her, focused her sun-dazzled eyes, and then gave a yelp.

'Minna! Oh, oh, your parents are darlings! To stay with you in Berlin for the whole of August, and to see the Olympic Games – that would be the most wonderful experience!' She scrambled to her feet. 'I must go and telephone them at once – my own parents, I mean. Not that there's any doubt about them letting me come. They'll see for themselves what an unrivalled opportunity it is!'

'You're pleased? My dear friend, I wondered whether I ought to warn you that I'd asked them, but I thought a surprise would not be unwelcome.' Minna's fair, tanned face was one enormous beam. 'Let us go at once to the telephone!'

It had been as well that, when the girls had tried to ring

England together, all the lines had been engaged, for despite Val's airy optimism Tina was not at all enamoured of the idea when Val spoke to her later.

'Germany! But, darling, there have been such dreadful stories . . . there's been violence on the streets, Communists and members of Herr Hitler's forces fighting . . . and then there are those concentration camps, the way they've treated Jews . . . surely you can't want to go there?'

'Oh, Mummy, they're just tales, honestly, Minna says so! The Führer's done wonders for the country. They've almost wiped out unemployment, and that's more than can be said for our government, for all their promises!' Val's voice rose to an anguished squeak. 'Mummee, you can't say no. Think of the opportunity to see the greatest athletes in the whole world! Surely you aren't thinking about the war? That was *centuries* ago, and Germany has suffered enough for it, goodness knows. Think of you, when you were young, going off to America with no one to take care of you. You didn't know what you'd find, but I know I've got friends to look after me! Oh, Mummy, don't let me down!'

'Yes, but, Val, remember you haven't been home since last summer, what with skiing trips and Easter in Paris. Besides, Nicky's in the States and we're longing to see you.'

'Mummy, it's only for a month!' Another bribe occurred to her. 'The family has a house in Bavaria, too, and they talk about spending a few days there – Bavaria, Mummy, where Daddy's father came from! Perhaps I could even visit the village he was born in!'

Tina, she knew, was a great one for family tradition; she waited hopefully.

'I don't know . . . Val, Daddy's here. He wants a word.'

Her father's voice came over the wires; deep, sensible, with that trace of amusement which was never far away.

'Val, old darling? It's the chance of a lifetime to see the Games, I know that. And I'll tell you something else, too. Berlin will be cleaned up just like we clean up The Pride before a big party. They'll sweep all their dirty linen out of sight; all the mess and the muddle will be pushed away where no visitors can see it. But just you use those sharp young eyes of yours, and you'll see the dross if it's there. Take care not to get involved in anything though, love, even if you disapprove madly. Promise? That's my girl! See you in September, then, and don't you dare stay any longer than a month. You'd get very swollen-headed if you know how much we missed you.'

So it was all arranged, and Minna's parents seemed to be every bit as good as Minna said they would be in their care of a foreign child.

'My father will buy your ticket home, and a servant will accompany you as far as Calais,' Minna said. 'Vater is somewhat old fashioned. He would not dream of allowing you to take such a journey alone.'

'Yet he allows you to travel to and from school alone,' Val pointed out. 'Does he think a Berliner more capable of taking care of herself than a Norwich girl?'

Minna laughed, shaking her head.

'Not so, my friend. I go to and from Berlin with other girls. Oh, not just Salka and the girls we know here, but others, also at schools in this country. We meet in Berlin or at the central station here and travel in a group. You do the same, I know, until you reach London, when your parents meet you.'

And soon enough, she saw for herself how it worked. The journey to Berlin had been enlivened by several cheery damsels, daughters of ambassadors and embassy staff, who were returning to the capital for their holidays and for the Games. Salka, who travelled with them, could scarcely be said to be of their company, for the other girls ignored her and Salka sat buried in a book for most of the journey. Val, who had tried to be friendly at school and actually seemed to be making some progress, having diagnosed truly formidable shyness as part of Salka's problem, would have chatted to the younger girl, but Salka made it plain that such friendliness would be an intrusion and Val, curious but nevertheless rather hurt, decided to bide her time. Perhaps she would call on Salka in Berlin and see what she was like on her home ground, but probably she would not. This was Val's goodbye to school and Europe. Once she was back in England the only link between her and her friends would be letters and perhaps the occasional visit.

Indeed, once the train drew in at the Potsdamer Bahnhof, she had little time for exchanging addresses with Salka. Minna bounced down on to the platform, hugged a tall, stern-faced man and gestured to a godlike youth with his hand on the shoulder of a fat little German Frau.

'Val, here is my darling Vater, and there is Mutti and my favourite brother Franz. My other brother, Otto, has not bothered to come to the station, but I daresay he will honour us at dinner tonight.'

Val shook hands all round, noticing that they were all as fair as Minna and that Franz, taking her hand, eyed her from beneath almost white eyelashes, with rather furtive interest. She smiled brilliantly at him and he blinked, then blushed. Val was amused by this, but was careful not to show it. Twenty and still ill at ease with women? Or was it just foreigners?

But conjecture would have to wait. They left the station and piled into a long grey limousine chauffeured by a uniformed servant. Val, who had guessed Minna came from a comfortably situated family, revised the estimate. They were rich, and Herr von Eckner was greeted with obvious obsequiousness by the railway staff who had helped the girls with their boxes and bundles. The Potsdamer Bahnhof was a huge station, what was more, not some little wayside stop where the employees might be expected to know the majority of their passengers.

Franz did not join them in the limousine. Minna, smiling, explained it.

'My brother has his own car, a good deal racier than this one! He has a small suite of rooms in our apartment where he can remain and manage for himself when the family moves to Bavaria for the summer months, though we often go there in the winter too, for the shooting. Isn't the city crowded? But I daresay it's just because of the Games.'

As the car drew out from its parking place, Val could see that the busy street was as thronged with cars and buses as the pavements were thronged with people. To her right there were trees surrounding what looked like a small park and in front of them was a clock-tower, supported on half a dozen slender pillars, reminding her that this was a foreign city and she was far from home.

'We live on Neue Friedrichstrasse,' Herr von Eckner told Val kindly as the car began to make its way through the crowded streets. 'I expect both you girls are tired and would like a bath and a good meal so we shall take the most direct route through the city, but another time we will have a more leisurely tour so that Fräulein Neyler may see all the sights.' The chauffeur signalled and the car wheeled to the right. 'This is the Wilhelm-strasse. At number 77 lives our great Führer. You will doubtless see him at the Games. I'm sure he will put in an appearance on most days.'

'Yes, though I expect he'll be a good distance from me,' Val said. She leaned forward, scanning the imposing buildings which lined the street. 'Goodness, who lives in these houses?'

'Palaces, you mean.' Herr von Eckner smiled. 'They're mostly government offices now, but once they were the homes of the German nobility. Now this street – but I will let you guess! What do you think of this, eh?'

'It has to be Unter den Linden Strasse,' Val observed. 'It's so *wide*! Quite the widest street I've ever seen; it makes the trees look little.'

'Just here there is construction work going on for the Nord-Sud-S-Bahn,' Herr von Eckner explained. 'See the Altes Palais? The corner window where the "old Emperor" used to appear to watch the changing of the guard always has the curtains drawn now, as a mark of respect – see the white curtains there?'

'I see. I've watched the changing of the guard in London. It's very impressive. I should like to see it here. Or will it not happen, because of the Games?'

'No, no, the guard will be changed just the same, though it is probably very like your own ceremony. The English and the Germans have a great deal in common, as Herr Hitler is fond of remarking. Not least a love of ceremonial and a great regard for tradition.'

'But Germany isn't a very old country, so we were taught at school,' Val pointed out. 'So where does your tradition come from?'

Minna looked a little shocked and rather apprehensive, but Herr von Eckner smiled quite approvingly at Val.

196

'That is true, yet in a way advantageous. We are an amalgam of small countries, each one of which has traditions and a history stretching back into the mists of time. By the same token, we have not just one capital city but many, each one beautiful and historic. We take the best of our traditions and call them German, though they may be many other things as well.'

Minna, who had been silent throughout her father's explanation, leaned forward and touched Val's arm.

'See there, Val? That's the Ashchinger Coffee House, where all the girls in Berlin go. And all the young men too, of course.'

Frau von Eckner, who had scarcely opened her mouth all the journey, smiled at her daughter with teasing sympathy.

'Ach, Minna, Minna, do you think of nothing but young men? Val will think German girls frivolous and pleasure-seeking if you intend to spend all your spare time at the coffee houses finding admirers.'

'It's what all girls do everywhere, I think, Frau von Eckner,' Val admitted ruefully. 'It's our age. It's like a disease which attacks girls when they are eighteen or nineteen – it will pass!'

Snug in their limousine, the von Eckners laughed.

School had broken up towards the end of July, so that Val and Minna had several days in which to explore the city together before the Games burst upon them.

Val loved it. It was so large and clean, and the sun always seemed to be shining. The shops, too, were full of goods and people were buying eagerly. The depression and poverty at home, though before she had taken them almost for granted, now seemed not only reprehensible, but avoidable. If Hitler had brought full employment, or nearly full employment, back to

Germany, then what was stopping the same thing from happening in Britain? If only the people in government could see the everyday faces in the streets here, she thought eagerly. The contentment, the glow of people who had a goal, was all around her. At home, even the children seemed to grow up with a grey, dispirited look.

She liked the von Eckners, too, and their way of life. They were very rich, very respected, but they were also concerned and involved in a way which, she thought, she had rarely seen at home. Her father was a good employer, caring for his employees, but the man in the street? He scarcely impinged upon him at all, so far as she could judge.

The von Eckners were different. Minna's little brother Gustav was a member of the *Jungvolk*, the junior branch of the Hitler Youth Movement. He was a small, lively little boy and because he attended his meetings with two children of servants in the house Frau von Eckner provided all three with the uniform of the movement and paid all their dues, as well as providing them with meals when they had weekend camps.

Minna belonged to the *Glaube und Schönheit*, having first done her stint with the *Bund Deutscher Mädchen*, the German Girls League, and she had joined both, she assured Val, not because she wanted to but because it was expected that girls of good family should set a good example. As if to prove that she, too, was public spirited, Frau von Eckner went off three evenings a week to teach the G & S girls, as they were known, how to cook cheap but nourishing food and how to keep themselves clean and tidy. Val voiced surprise that Frau von Eckner had ever had to cook economically, especially as there was a resident cook in the big apartment, but Minna said that her mother loved cooking, and in

198

any case she was issued with a huge cookery book, so recipes were no problem. Franz and Otto, at twenty and twenty-two respectively, taught the *Jungvolk* and members of the Hitler Youth Movement the skills that they, in former years, had been taught, as well as supervising various activities such as the weekend camps and the training of runners and other young would-be athletes.

Oddly enough, though Val was living in the same apartment as Franz and Otto, the two young men made very little impression on her. Franz she thought self-opinionated and dull, and Otto, though he had duelling scars which saved his face, at least, from dullness, and dark hair, which she preferred on a man to lint-white locks, frightened her a little. Otto was sombre, sometimes sarcastic, difficult to fathom. Both were polite, punctilious one might say, and good-looking above the average, yet they made no attempt to get to know Val better. It was almost as though they were so wrapped up in their own lives that they had no time to spare for a girl from another country – no time, indeed, for their own sister save for that cold, automatic courtesy. Minna prattled on, sometimes, about her brothers' accompanying them on various expeditions, but Val soon learned to hold her tongue, since such trips mysteriously failed to materialise.

Herr Eckner was a manufacturer. His firm made automobiles and was huge, so huge that though Franz and Otto both worked there they rarely met. Val was quite interested, but no one suggested that she might go over and see the factory, not even after she had said, several times, that her father had a car showroom in Norwich. She thought it was part of the German attitude to women, which was partly to idealise them and partly to treat them like pretty but inferior animals.

No, perhaps not animals in general – more like the way a child treats a kitten! So she was by no means sorry that neither Franz nor Otto showed any inclination to notice her.

On the fifth day of her stay, Minna had to go off to a meeting of the *Bund Deutscher Mädchen*, and though she said Val was welcome to go and watch it was very plain that she hoped her friend would not. Frau von Eckner, obviously feeling that Val could not be left to amuse herself, suggested that Franz become her escort for the afternoon, an offer that Val, with more haste than was perhaps polite, declined.

'It's awfully kind of you, but I'd rather have a quiet afternoon at home,' she explained. 'I've simply got to write to my parents and tell them all about Berlin and what I've been doing, otherwise they'll think I've forgotten them!'

'All right, if you're quite sure.' Minna, dressed in a white blouse and a too-long dark skirt, her hair braided and tied with a thin little lace, looked unlike her usual fashionable self, but Val understood that it was all in the cause of equality. If one was mixing with girls from all levels of society, they were happier to find that they were all dressed alike. 'Don't forget to tell them that Vater got tickets for the opening ceremony.'

'I shan't. I'd like to know how he did it, though! He really does know all the right people, doesn't he?'

'He is a man with many friends, many connections.' Minna looked smug. 'Well, if you're all right, I'll go. See you later, Val!'

For the first half-hour, Val did indeed write letters home. Then she read for a bit. And then, of course, she wanted to go out. What was the good of being in Berlin if she just stayed in a stuffy apartment when outside the sun was shining and the city lay waiting for her?

Although it was called an apartment, the von Eckners' city home was on two floors. Val walked along the white-carpeted corridor, down a flight of graciously curving white-carpeted stairs, and into the large reception hall. No one was about; but the sun, streaming through the open door of the main living-room, tempted her. She peeped into the room. The wood block floor glistened gold in the afternoon light, the flowers in the huge porcelain bowls breathed their scent into the air. On a gold velvet chair Frau von Eckner sat, her knitting on her lap, her eyes closed. A tiny, rumbling snore escaped from her parted lips. Smiling to herself, Val backed out softly. Across the hall was the green baize door which led to the servants' wing. No sound came from there, either. They would be in the kitchen, preparing the vegetables for tonight's dinner or possibly having a nap, like the lady of the house. Whatever they were doing or not doing, they would not miss Val.

The front door beckoned. Why not? After all, at home she went out by herself, and Berlin was such a happy city. Everyone wanted to make a good impression on foreign visitors; she would be made welcome wherever she went. She could be home in plenty of time so that Minna need not even know she had been out – not that it would matter. Minna would quite understand the sudden urge to be outside. What she would not understand, of course, was Val's reluctance to have her brothers' escort, but this problem was neatly solved because they were both at work – or out of the house, at least.

If she needed an excuse, she could say that she had finished her book and had popped out to visit the English bookshop on the Linden. She had been in Asher's the previous day and had spotted a new

Priestley novel. She had her bag with her, so she could buy it, though she must post her letters first.

She posted her letters, wandered round Asher's and bought not a book but a magazine which contained, to Val's patriotic indignation, a lot of made-up stories about the new King and some woman called Simpson. Everyone in Britain knew that the King was young and handsome and could have anyone he chose, so why Europeans should link his name with that of a no longer young, twice married American, goodness only knew. Still, it was interesting to listen to the gossip, or to read it, rather, and to smile to herself at their foolishness.

After that, she simply wandered under the bright sun and thought how lovely the city was and how strange, too, to hear English being spoken by a passing couple, thinking for a startled moment that it was a foreign language, so used to German had she become. Then she decided that she would walk up to the Tiergarten, because it was beautiful and she could buy herself a tall glass of milk and one of the delicious heavy fruit buns at the refreshment stall by the gate. She could, of course, have caught a tram, but the thought of being squeezed into the stuffy interior did not appeal and so she strode out, her mane of hair bobbing on her shoulders, and was very soon through the Brandenburg Gate and entering the gardens. She was in good company, since the place seemd to be thronged with visitors, but she enjoyed walking by the lakes and feeding the ducks with a second bun. Then, when she was beneath the shade of the trees, she decided that she would just sit down for a moment and read her magazine.

She finished an article about the Olympic Games, another about the King's younger brother and his pretty, dark-haired wife. It was nice here! Quiet, with only a couple of impertinent squirrels bounding from branch to branch above her, and the smell of trodden grass and leaf-mould sweet after the dust of the city streets. Val closed her eyes and leaned back in her seat. Pleasant, just to rest for a moment!

When she opened her eyes again the sun had gone from the sky and the pale grey light of evening had sucked the colours from the park. Her charcoal grey silk dress, which had seemed so suitable a couple of hours earlier, felt foolish in the dusk. Val sat up, feeling stiff and shivery, rubbed her arms briskly and got to her feet. She glanced about her. Waking so suddenly, she found herself disorientated, with no clear idea which direction she should take to get to the Brandenburg Gate. A little thought convinced her that to reach the Charlotten-burger Chaussee she should turn right and walk through one particular belt of trees until she saw the lights ahead of her.

Moving quietly over the soft ground, she rounded the trunk of a great tree and realised she was no longer along. In front of her four or five figures were clustered, and even as she approached they laughed simultaneously either at or with some object – or person – that they had surrounded. She could see, now, that they were all youths, and it came to her that she had heard no remark and seen no movement which could have called up that laughter.

She moved towards them unnoticed, for they were concentrating on whatever was in the centre of the group to the exclusion of everything else. She could not tell what they were doing, and now that she was nearer she found that there was something menacing in the very set of the young men's shoulders. Even as she wondered why she should feel this, she knew. A memory of boys in a playground, long ago, clustered

round a cat they had tormented to the point of death
. . . Val began to run across the clearing. That was it!
Great bullying boys tormenting some poor, defenceless
animal! She would not stand for it! Her voice rose, very
clear and shrill.

'Just what do you think you're doing?'

They turned round as if they had been stung. Guilt, of
course. Defensive, they mumbled, crowding together,
hiding their victim from her. She pushed past them – and
gasped.

A small boy stood there, dark hair flopping over a
face which was sickly, unnaturally white, a grey jersey
rucked up round his waist, his tie under one ear. He
was nursing his right arm as if it was injured. Val could
tell it hurt him. The youths closed ranks around her as
she went towards the child, but she cared nothing for
that. Bullies seldom attack anyone who is not afraid of
them, and all her fears were for the boy.

'Were they hurting you? They should be ashamed,
the great bullies. I'll see that they're severely punished.
Come with me. I'll take you home, and speak to your
parents to make sure that these louts get what's coming
to them!' She took the small boy's uninjured hand and
drew him firmly to her side. Together, they faced the
youths. Val gave them the iciest look at her command
and said, in English: 'I shall take this little boy to the
British Embassy on the Wilhelmstrasse and tell them
what you've been doing, and then I'll go to the Rathaus
and tell your own people how I found you amusing
yourselves. You'll be soundly beaten, if not worse!'

Seeing their lack of understanding she gave an
exaggerated sigh and repeated the entire sentiment in
her crispest German.

It had its effect. Before she spoke the circle had been
tightening, the boys standing elbow to elbow, grinning,

triumphant. She was, after all, only a girl. What could she do? But at the dual realisation of her nationality and her intention to complain to a higher authority, the grins faded. The boys glanced uneasily at each other, then at Val's angry face. Then one of them hissed: 'Break for home, lads!' and they were gone, running between trees, crying out as low branches caught them, but intent on putting as much distance as possible between themselves and their former prey.

Val led the small boy out of the Tiergarten. It occurred to her that he was neither crying nor trembling, but she knew he must be suffering from shock. She put her arm round his shoulders.

'My name's Val; what yours?'

'I am Karl.' The words were spoken so low that Val had to bend her head to hear.

'Do you know those boys, Karl? By name, I mean.'

His hesitation, she thought, spoke volumes, but when he did speak his voice was stronger.

'Not really. No.'

'Don't be afraid! Look, I really don't like the look of that arm. Perhaps I should take you straight to the hospital. It might easily be broken, you see, and need setting.'

'No! My mother will be very worried, and besides, my uncle is a doctor who can set a bone. Please, I must go straight home.'

Val could hear the near-panic in his voice and, without fully understanding, she sympathised. One wanted a loving parent at a time like this, not the impersonality of a hospital.

'Right. Where do you live?'

'On the Voltairestrasse. I can go alone. I'll be all right now.'

They had left the park behind them and were at the

Brandenburg Gate. Out here the street lamps were bright and the shop frontages cheerful with wares. The crowds on the pavement were in festive mood, for was not tomorrow the first of August, the day when the world would be in Berlin, watching the Olympic Games? In a few short paces Val heard French, German, English and Dutch spoken. She smiled down at her small companion.

'I'm sure you're quite capable of looking after yourself, but I want to speak to your Mutti; it's my belief that she'll know some of those boys and will want to see them punished. I daresay you wouldn't say a word to her if I let you go home alone. You'd account for the arm by pretending you'd fallen down, or something.'

The small boy sighed, and then looked up at her. She was struck, for the first time, by the size and brilliance of his dark eyes. He was a handsome little lad with an intelligent, sensitive face.

'Very well, and thank you. But I would much rather my mother didn't know. It will only worry her, and there's nothing she can do. We're used to it, you know. Besides, it . . . it is boys' business.'

Val laughed.

'We'll see. Now you'll have to guide me, Karl, because I only know my way to the house I'm staying in, on the Neue Friedrichstrasse. Do you know it?'

'Of course. Voltairestrasse leads off it. I'll show you.' He quickened his pace a little, then slowed again with a grunt of pain. 'I'm sorry, I can't hurry. My arm wishes me to go slowly.'

At a slow walking pace, therefore, they traversed the streets until they came to the quiet side street where Karl lived. He led her along the pavement to a large, modern apartment block and they walked up the stairs together. Outside apartment 4 he stopped, bent down and fished the key from under the doormat.

'I will unlock the door. I daresay my mother is still out, doing last minute shopping, but she usually leaves the key so that we can let ourselves in.'

He opened the door, then pulled Val inside and closed it again before clicking on the electric switch. In its rather faint radiance he smiled at Val, and then raised his voice.

'It's Karl. I'm back, and I've brought a friend!'

A door opened and bright light streamed into the hall. A figure was framed in the doorway. A girl. She began to speak, then stopped abruptly as she saw Val. The little boy spoke quickly, aware of tension.

'It's all right. This lady brought me home. I've h-hurt my arm, and she insisted on coming right home, though I'm quite all right now.'

The girl had been silhouetted against the brilliant light from the inner room but now she stepped into the hall and for the first time Val saw her face clearly. She gasped, and the gasp was echoed by the other.

'Salka! Good gracious, how strange!'

Salka's hands flew to her mouth. She stepped back, pushing open the door which had closed behind her. She said faintly: 'Val? Whatever are you doing here?' and then, to someone behind her, 'It's all right, Mutti, it's a friend from school. She's come home with Karl. I'll take them into the kitchen for a moment.' She came out of the living-room, closing the door carefully behind her, and glanced at Karl, then stared, her eyes widening as they took in his dishevelled appearance, the careful way he nursed his arm. 'Whatever have you done, *Liebchen*?'

'It was done to him. Some boys were beating him,' Val said flatly. 'Can I speak to your mother, Salka? Those boys are young animals and must be severely punished. I think he'll have to have his jersey cut off and his arm set. I suspect it's broken.'

'Broken?' Salka led them into the kitchen, a cheery room with a big, well-scrubbed wooden table and a number of sagging wickerwork chairs. She pushed her brother into one of them and knelt before him, running her fingers gently along the injured arm. 'Can I just slit the jumper along the seam, *Liebchen*, and then we can view the damage?'

'It's my school one,' Karl said, with tight-lipped bravado, as his sister began to cut at the seam with a tiny pair of nail scissors. 'If I get into trouble, Sal, you may have all the blame!'

Salka smiled at him. Val saw that she was quite different here, a practical, cheerful person who knew just what to do when an emergency occurred.

'How kind you are, Karl! However, you *do* have two jerseys, so stop trying to get my friend's sympathy with your stories! Val, I think it would be nice for all of us to have a cup of coffee. Could you stand the percolator on the stove, please?'

'Willingly.' Val saw with pleasure that the percolator was already full of coffee and only needed heating up. She had scarcely realised how tired and cold and thirsty she was, but now, in this warm, familiar kitchen, she began to relax after her trying evening. It had not been easy to stand up to the youths, though she had done so instinctively.

Presently, the jersey off, both girls could see that the arm was bent at an odd angle. Salka nodded decisively.

'I will run down to Dr Spanda in the bottom flat; he'll come up and see to it, Karl.' She turned to Val. 'Drink up your coffee, Val, and I'll come down and get you a taxi. There is much excitement in the streets; it is no time for you to walk home alone.'

Val blinked. It was plainly dismissal, and she didn't want to leave. She felt so at home here, so . . . she glanced round. *Why* did she feel so at home? It was an atmosphere, a smell almost, but she could not quite put her finger on it. Half-remembered pictures kept floating through her mind of parties at Auntie Cecy's house when they had all congregated in the kitchen, perhaps after a bonfire party, for food and hot drinks. What *was* it? Auntie Cecy's kitchen was quite different from this one, about four times the size for a start, and yet . . . She pushed the resemblance out of her mind and turned to the immediate problem.

'It isn't far to Minna's and I want to make sure Karl's all right. Can I run home and then come round again later?'

'No.' It sounded flat and unfriendly and Salka obviously realised it, because she smiled and patted Val placatingly on the arm. 'You must have realised that Minna didn't like me; well, she doesn't like my family, either. She would not approve of your visiting us. Besides, you're here on holiday. You can't just walk out and leave your hostess – especially not to visit a family of whom she disapproves.'

'I'm sure you're wrong. When I tell Minna I've been here, seen you –'

'You mustn't!' It was a cry of such anguish that Val blinked. Salka looked desperate. 'Please Val, promise me that you won't mention any of us to any member of the von Eckner family! Promise!'

'Of course, if that's what you want, but *why*, Salka? Honestly, Minna's parents wouldn't hold a schoolgirl row against anyone, I'm sure. Minna doesn't much like you because you aren't athletic, and you're . . . well, so quiet and meek. But here you're different. I'm sure she'd like you if she once got to know you!'

'She does know me, and she dislikes me very much,' Salka insisted. 'Please, Val, I do have a good reason!'

'All right. But I must come back and see how Karl's getting on,' Val said obstinately. 'He's such a brave kid, and if he has his arm done up in plaster he'll need amusing. Can't I come?'

'I'd rather you didn't,' Salka said slowly. 'It could make more trouble than you know, Val. We're not . . . not popular with the regime. But perhaps I could send you a letter, arranging a meeting. How would that be?'

'Fine.'

They were in the foyer of the flats now, but instead of going outside to find a taxi Salka was tapping on a door. A man's voice said, 'Who is it?' and Salka gave her name and the door opened a crack.

'Yes, dear?'

'Oh, Dr Spanda, could you come up and take a look at Karl? I think his arm is broken. And before you do, could you possibly ring for a taxi for my friend, and give your apartment number?'

The door opened wider. A small, swarthy man glanced out, smiled at Val, and withdrew, tortoiselike, into his home once more.

'Of course, my dear. As soon as I've made the call I'll come right up.'

In seconds he was in the hallway, a black bag in one hand, and he and Salka disappeared up the stairs to the flat above. He had been as good as his word, though, for scarcely had they disappeared before the revolving door of the building spun and a cheerful young man appeared.

'Apartment number one?' Val nodded. 'Right, Fräulein, my taxi's right outside. Where do you want to go?'

Val gave him directions as she climbed into the back of his car, and all too soon, it seemed to her, he drew up outside the von Eckners' apartment. Val climbed out, paid him, and then squared her shoulders and made her way to the ornate front door with the bell-pull beside it. Now she would have to think up some convincing explanation for her lateness – indeed, for the fact that she had gone out at all, for her magazine must have been left behind in the Tiergarten. She felt weary and miserable for there had been no arrangement made for another meeting, and now that she had left the flat she had a shrewd suspicion that the letter from Salka would never arrive. Salka would hope that the Olympic Games and her friends would combine to make Karl and herself seem dull stuff!

She heard footsteps approaching and wished, for one panic-stricken minute, that she had not rung until she had cooked up some convincing story. Then she told herself that all she had to do was tell the truth – that she had fallen asleep in the Tiergarten – and all would be forgiven. Nevertheless, she guessed she had some difficult moments ahead!

211

In the event, however, Val suffered nothing for her truancy, not even the embarrassment of an explanation. The apartment, when she walked in, had been in uproar because Minna's cousin Trudl had arrived for a visit and Minna and Trudl, with Franz in close attendance, were in the spare room, unpacking quantities of clothing and chatting about the forthcoming Games. Val's presence cast a momentary awkwardness for the talk had been, naturally, of Germany's certainty of victory, but this was glossed over in the introductions.

Trudl was a small, fair-haired girl, a little too plump, with a breathless laugh, a tendency to beetroot blushes and a perspiration problem of which she seemed blissfully unaware. She was also madly in love with her cousin Franz and as soon as she realised that Val was indifferent to him she spent a lot of time trying to make the English girl see how wonderful Franz really was. Odd, thought Val, listening appreciatively to Trudl's ecstasies, if you considered how differently Trudl would have behaved had she believed Val to be a little in love with Franz!

But now, their party had taken its place in the enormous new stadium on the first day of the Games. The boom of the last speaker's words was fading away over the excellent loudspeaker system and on the far side a runner, small as an ant, entered with the Olympic torch flaming in one hand. Val knew it had come from the Lustgarten, where it had burned ever since its arrival from Athens, and watched appreciatively as it was slotted into the prepared brazier close to Herr Hitler, who was standing, stern and ready, as another athlete ran up and handed him an olive branch. Good staging, Val thought; but no one had ever denied Herr Hitler an ability to stage large events.

It was a fine afternoon, and the loudspeakers relayed the Olympic oath, immediately followed by the Olympic hymn, specially written for the occasion by Richard Strauss, who also conducted it. And then, as the music faded to a close, there was a clatter of wings, a rush of air, and thirty thousand carrier pigeons were released, to soar their way into the sky, white and gold against the blue, so beautiful and so symbolic of peace and love that Val's eyes filled with tears. Dabbing at them with her fingers, she saw that she was not the only one to be so moved, for Herr von Eckner was blowing his nose and Franz, sitting beside her, had tightened his mouth so that a muscle jumped in his cheek.

'After that, everything else will be an anti-climax,' Val whispered to Minna as they made their way out of the stadium in the evening cool. 'I'll never forget those wings against the sky as long as I live.'

'Nor I.' Minna, jostled by the crowd, clinging to Val and Trudl, still looked dazed. 'I think Herr Hitler is the most wonderful man in the world!'

Val blinked. She thought him an insignificant figure with a harsh and unpleasant voice, but she acknowledged that there was something about him – there must be, if all that Minna told her was true. Making the rich surrender vast tracts of land which they never cultivated or used for any purposes other than hunting, giving it to the peasants together with a cow – or was it a goat? – and enough seed to start them off; that was an imaginative scheme as well as a good one.

However, there had been a note in Minna's voice of which Val did not approve – call it a pash or a crush, it was still equally ridiculous; Minna had been the first to jeer at any school girl who suffered from such feelings. Val nudged her sharply.

'Careful, Minna. There's no future in falling in love with the Führer!'

She expected Minna to laugh, disclaim, but instead Minna bridled and looked defensive.

'All the girls at the *Bund* feel the same – it is good, to love the ruler of your country,' she said stiffly.

'Oh, rot and rubbish – you don't think . . .'

But now the crowd became too thick for arguing or even for the exchange of idle chat, for it was here that the trams were lined up, ready to take the visitors and citizens of Berlin back to the city centre. Franz turned and raised a brow at Val.

'Do you want to go home in the car, Fräulein? For myself, I shall walk. I could do with some movement after sitting still for so long.'

'I'd rather walk, too,' Minna shouted, moving out of the line of people waiting to get into the car park. 'What do you think, girls?'

'I'll walk,' Val said at once, and saw Trudl nod resignedly. 'I wouldn't be surprised if we get home before your parents, Minna.'

'Nor I. Very well, then. Lead the way, Franz.'

At first they walked with a good many others, and conversation was difficult, but as they neared the city the crowd began to thin and presently they found themselves walking a broad pavement four abreast and chatting quite normally.

'What shall we go to see next, I wonder?' Minna

remarked presently. 'Father didn't buy tickets for every day because he thought we would soon get bored. I daresay he'll ask us which events we would prefer.'

Franz snorted. 'The tickets were bought days and days ago, my dear sister. I imagine that Father has our itinerary all planned out, and will tell you what it is to be this evening. Have you no idea of the competition for tickets, nor of the number of foreigners who had to be given preferential treatment?'

'Oh! Well, I wish he'd said. I'd like to see some of the swimming events, for instance.'

'Father will have chosen what's best,' Franz said, and then, relenting at the sight of his sister's crestfallen face, he laughed and continued: 'It would be dull, would it not, to watch only the track events, or the swimming events, or all the events which take place in the *Festwiese*? It is much better that you should sample something in each of these sections.'

'Oh, *much* better!' Trudl cried vivaciously. She was bundling along beside the other three, her short legs fairly twinkling in her effort to keep up, her face glowing with pinkness and perspiration. She tugged at Franz's sleeve. 'Don't go so fast, my dear cousin. We poor females can't stride out like you!'

Minna and Val, both long-legged girls to whom striding out came far more naturally than strolling, glanced at each other and obediently slowed, but Franz tightened his lips ominously before slackening his pace.

'You're out of condition, Trudl,' he said severely. 'Are you a member of the *Bund Deutscher Mädchen*? If so, however do you manage when they have athletics?'

'Someone has to come last, and I'm good at other things,' Trudl said defensively. 'Besides, at home people are more easy-going. No one tries to make me do games.'

'You're too fat. Fat women are a drag on others, as are fat men.'

Minna and Val exchanged astonished glances. How rude Franz was being all of a sudden, when he had seemed quite happy, previously, to accept all the gushing and hero-worship that Trudl could hand out!

'Fat! That's very unkind, Franz,' poor Trudl said, her colour deepening. 'It isn't true, anyway. I walk rather more slowly than you because my legs are shorter. Nothing can alter *that*.'

'All right, all right. No need to get hot and bothered.' Franz patted Trudl's shoulder in a condescending fashion. 'We'll be home in another ten minutes or so and then you can have a rest.'

They had not dined, but the moment they entered the apartment they knew they were about to do so from the good smells which wafted through the green baize door. As soon as they were all assembled in the dining-room a roast goose was carried through, and until they were polishing off the last of a huge chocolate torte there was little talking but much chewing. It occurred to Val that Trudl was quieter than usual, but then they all were; hunger made talking whilst eating out of the question.

When the meal was over, Trudl elected to go straight to bed. That was unusual whilst Franz was around, so Val, feeling sorry for the younger girl, said she was tired too, and Minna, after only the slightest of hesitations, also agreed to an early night. Trudl was despatched to the spare-room, very subdued, and then Val and Minna went to their room. They were both tired, in fact, so got into bed, turned off their light, snuggled down, and then, with typical female logic, began to talk.

'I wonder why Franz was so cross with poor Trudl? He is always so much the gentleman, so kind to all ladies – and perhaps especially kind to Trudl. Indeed, I've always supposed that she and Franz would marry one day.'

Val shrugged. In her view, Franz merely tolerated Trudl. Scarcely an ideal attitude for a marriage!

'Boys get fed up sometimes, and I daresay Franz had been so transported, if that's the word, with the events of the *Reichssportfeld* that when Trudl began to complain he came down to earth with a bump. He was a bit rude, but she's his cousin, dammit. There's no reason why he has to be polite to her all the time. My cousin Simon used to be jolly rude to me and I never got all hurt and dewy-eyed over it. Or perhaps Franz may simply feel that he wants a bit of experience with other women before he settles down and marries a girl he's known all his life.'

'I don't think it's like that. He has plenty of chances of taking other people out. He *is* handsome, and there are always girls swooning over him, but he never seems interested. Look at the way he's behaved with you – perfectly politely, of course, but not at all as though he was interested in you.'

'That's because he isn't, dear Minna! I'm not pretty and I'm a foreigner, and I've not made the slightest play for him, what's more. It might be a different story if I had.'

Both girls giggled.

'Why don't you, then, Val? No, I suppose you can't now Trudl's here. She'd spend all her time whining and complaining if you did. But you could start up a flirtation with Otto!'

It would have been rude to say that Otto frightened her and Franz's calculating attitude repelled her. Instead, Val took refuge in another giggle.

'Don't just laugh, Val. Turn your charm on Otto. It

would be a great challenge, because he's so dull and serious.'

'No fear. He might turn the tables and make me look a fool.'

Minna sat up. In the faint light which filtered through the silken curtains she looked challengingly across at her friend.

'I dare you! I dare you to try to make a conquest of Otto!'

She lay down again, a triumphant smirk on her face. Val, in her turn, sat up like a jack-in-the-box.

'Minna, you beast! I've a good mind to refuse that dare.'

'You've never refused a dare; it's your proudest boast.'

'That was at school, and . . . oh, curse you, Wilhelmina von Eckner!'

But old habits die hard. Both girls knew that the dare had been accepted.

'Otto, Val's never been to the planetarium. She's never even seen one, and she's ever so interested. I don't have time to take her today, because Trudl and I have a *Bund* meeting, but you could take her, couldn't you?'

It was breakfast time and by good luck Otto, who normally ate early and then left for the factory with his father and brother, was still at the table. Val supposed that, since he had been holding the fort at the factory whilst Herr von Eckner and Franz saw the Games, he had been given a day off to make up.

Now, he stared across the table, first at Minna, then at Val, the faintest incredulity in his expression. Frau von Eckner, at the head of the table, stared too, almost as incredulously. Val, smiling demurely at Otto, wondered at their obvious surprise. He was a personable enough young man if you ignored the scars and the air of detachment which seemed part of his nature. Why should Frau von Eckner now look at Minna as though she had done something . . . well, not right or wrong, precisely, but something totally unexpected?

Otto, however, seemed to have accepted the proposal. He stood up and pushed back his chair, not looking at Val.

'Of course.' He clicked his heels together and bowed, a brief, jerky movement. 'I will escort you to the planetarium with pleasure, Miss Neyler. Shall we meet at, say, eleven o'clock?'

Now he was looking at her, the dark and brooding eyes glinting. Was it amusement? Contempt? It was better, anyway, than the usual way his eyes slid over her, as though she were just a child, a friend of his sister's, who would otherwise not merit a polite word, let alone a smile.

'Eleven o'clock will be fine, Otto. Here, in the hall?'

He had very dark, very thick eyebrows, which met above his nose and tilted satanically at the corners. He raised them.

'You would like an escort from the house, then? You have no shopping or small trips you wish to make first? Very well.'

'Oh, no,' stammered Val, thoroughly discomposed. 'You're going out, then? I thought you would be here . . . but it doesn't matter. We'll meet somewhere in . . .'

Frau von Eckner intervened at this point, her smile seeming, to Val, to have false heartiness.

'Dear Val, of course Otto will escort you from the house! I'm sure he meant nothing other than that you might wish to employ the first hours of the morning gainfully in some way. Now, children . . .'

She made shooing motions with her hands and Minna, Trudl and Val made their way obediently to the young ladies' sitting-room, a pleasant, airy room leading off Minna's bedroom where Minna might entertain her friends.

'Now!' Minna bounced on to the couch and patted the cushions on either side of her. 'Sit down, both of you. Wasn't that easy? That's my share of the bargain, Val. The rest is up to you.'

Trudl, now a fellow conspirator, giggled.

'The hardest part is still to come. I'm scared stiff of Otto; I wouldn't flirt with him for the world. What will you do? Wait until you get into the planetarium in the dark and ask him to kiss you?'

Minna and Val exchanged scornful glances, despising Trudl's ignorance, for it could scarcely merit the description of innocence.

'Of course not! I don't want him to kiss me, apart from anything else. I just want him to admire me, glance in my direction when we're in the same room, make a point of talking to me and not just ignoring me the way he does at the moment.' Val pushed her hands through the back of her hair and sighed. 'Mind you, I don't want him at my feet or anything like that. I just want to prove that he finds me attractive. That'll honour the bet, and then I'll freeze him off again like billyo and he'll wonder what he ever saw in me.'

'Otto wouldn't notice you freezing him,' Minna said scornfully. It had been obvious to Val for some time that Minna did not care for her elder brother, though she could not imagine why. She seemed fond enough of Franz, who struck Val very much more unfavourably. 'Otto doesn't have feelings, only prejudices. Not a patch on Franz, eh, Trudl?'

Trudl hesitated, obviously torn by conflicting desires

– the wish to agree that Franz was much the nicer of the two brothers, and a determination to make sure that Val did not decide to try her wiles on the younger boy. She had, if the truth be known, been very much impressed by the way Val's whole demeanour had changed that morning, and for the first time she had become aware of Val's fascination, though she disliked the red hair, hated the freckles and thought Val too tall, too skinny and too big-breasted to have any claims to beauty. German girls, she would have said, did not go in for tiny waists!

'They are very different,' Trudl decided. 'What will you wear, Val?'

The mention of clothes was sufficient to take all three minds off the von Eckner brothers and concentrate them on apparel. All three, with one accord, got to their feet and went through to Minna's room, where Val's clothes hung in the big wardrobe.

'Yet another lovely day,' Minna said enthusiastically, glancing out at the sunshine. 'Führer weather – he'll be attending the Games today, that's for sure. What about your blue silk jump suit?'

'Too warm,' Val said regretfully, fingering the soft material. 'Anyway, what about my new dress? What's wrong with that?'

The new dress was a summer cotton with a flared skirt and the popular cape sleepes. It was black with a tiny white floral pattern, and it made the most of Val's superb figure as well as drawing attention to the whiteness of her skirt and the brilliance of her hair.

'Yes, it's very striking. You should wear some flowers pinned on the breast,' Minna said, rummaging through Val's collection of artificial bouquets. 'These pansies are nice. Yellow looks good against black. Now how about a hat?'

'I shan't wear one, but I'll carry my white straw just in case the heat gets too much for me. And the high-heeled black sandals, though they'll kill me if I have to walk far.'

'I should wear something more comfortable, if I were you,' Minna advised. 'I think you stand around quite a lot at the planetarium, and afterwards Otto might take you walking in the gardens.'

'Not in these shoes he won't,' Val said, grimacing as she slid her feet into the sandals. 'Ouch! The little mermaid has one sympathiser, I can tell you!'

'*Was*?' That was Trudl, who had obviously not been brought up on Hans Andersen.

'It doesn't matter, Trudl.' Val, who had sat down to put on the shoes, jumped to her feet and swirled, making the full skirt bell out around her slender, silk-clad legs. 'How do I look?'

'Very pretty, very elegant,' Minna said, laughing. 'Otto will be most impressed. Usually he thinks my friends gauche and childish, but not today.'

'And my hair? When I get home, I'm jolly well going to have it cut, but shall I wear it up to give me sophistication, or loose, with an Alice band?'

'Just clip it back with two slides,' Minna said, beginning to giggle. 'With it up, Otto wouldn't recognise you! Besides, German boys love long hair, they think it's feminine.'

'Herr Hitler likes it, you mean,' Trudl said crossly. Her own soft fair hair was shoulder length and a source of considerable annoyance to her, since it was so fine and flyaway that it freqently looked untidy. 'Long hair doesn't suit me and I'd love to have it cut, but what *would* Herr Hitler say?'

This was a dig at Minna, but that damsel merely smiled knowingly.

'I doubt the Führer would notice, but Franz would. You just ask Franz what he thinks of girls who cut their hair!'

Trudl sniffed, but Val thought that the question of a bob would not now arise: Trudl would not risk her cousin's displeasure, though she seemed indifferent to Herr Hitler's!

Otto held the door open for her, saw her down the front steps as solicitously as though she had been a hundred and eighteen, and then set off at a fast walk along the Neue Friedrichstrasse. Fortunately, Val could walk fast too, but she did not need to be a mind-reader to know that he was trying to tire her out, trying to get her to ask him to slow down.

She gritted her teeth. She would out-walk him, just see if she did not. But the shoes defeated her. Elegant, yes, but not designed for fast walking or for comfort. She stopped dead in the middle of the pavement, letting Otto get ahead, hesitate, turn. His expression was half solicitous, half amused.

'I'm sorry, Fräulein. Was I walking too quickly for you?'

'Not at all, Otto; but these shoes, alas, are not walking shoes. I was foolish to wear them. Your sister did warn me. However, if you've no objection, I'll just slip them off . . .' she suited action to words . . . 'and then I can keep up with you easily.'

Otto glanced down at her silk-clad feet, then into her face. The pavement was crowded and people were glancing curiously at the girl in the obviously expensive black dress with the flowers pinned to the breast, who stood, barefoot, in the dust, smiling up at her escort.

'No, Fräulein, I'll hail a taxi. You'll ruin your stockings.'

'If you prefer riding to walking a little more slowly, Herr von Eckner.'

Otto hesitated, then shrugged slightly, walked to the kerb and hailed a passing cab. When it stopped he helped her in, gave the driver directions and climbed in beside her. As the car drew away he glanced sideways at her.

'Would you put your shoes on again now, please? It is not far to the planetarium and once inside you can sit down.'

Val dropped her sandals on to the floor and slid her feet into them. Then she glanced at Otto.

'Why don't you call me Val? Your brother does, and your parents.'

'Very well, Fräu . . . Val, I mean. We're nearly there.'

The taxi drew up. Otto got out, paid the driver, then opened the door for Val, clicking his heels and bowing as he did so. When she was on the pavement he took her arm, gesturing to the wide gateway before them.

'That is the zoo. The planetarium is through there also. The lecture begins in ten minutes, so we have plenty of time to take our seats.'

'The lecture?' Val's horror showed, for she saw his mouth twitch. 'Oh, but I thought one just looked at a projection of the night sky! How long does the lecture last?'

'An hour or two, but it won't be boring, for the professor will show one various views of the stars and the planets through the Zeiss projector. Your German is so good that I daresay you'll understand ninety per cent of everything that is said.'

Val squared her shoulders and turned to face Otto. He could scarcely eat her, after all, and the thought of being lectured on the night sky when outside the sun shone and the day beckoned was more than she could stand.

'I'm very sorry, Otto, but I've changed my mind. I don't want to go to a lecture – particularly a two-hour one! You go. I'll get a taxi back to the apartment.'

He frowned down at her, or at least she supposed he was frowning. It was difficult to tell, she realised, with someone whose brows met above his nose all the time anyway.

'Not want to go, when I've given up my day to entertain you? The last thing I wanted to do was go to the planetarium!'

'Good. Then go out and amuse yourself; fight a duel, or hunt the wild sausage, or do whatever you would have done if Minna hadn't trapped you into being polite,' Val said cordially. After all, he had a right to be annoyed; she had behaved badly. 'I'll go to the zoo, I think, and get myself some lunch there, and then I'll stroll around for a bit. That way no one need know you haven't taken me to the planetarium.'

'Hunt the wild . . .' She almost giggled at the puzzled look on his face. 'Oh, never mind. Look, I'll come round the zoo with you for half an hour, buy you a coffee and schnapps, and then I'll take you back to the apartment for lunch. We won't mention the planetarium at all, if that will help matters.'

Impulsively, Val caught his hand. It was cold and unresponsive in her grasp and she dropped it hastily, transferring her fingers to his sleeve.

'That would be lovely, Otto. I adore zoos. What are the most interesting animals? Lead me to them!'

'Come along, you ragamuffin, and I'll buy you lunch,' Otto said belatedly two hours later, as they left the elephant enclosure. 'Walking around barefoot like the veriest street urchin – I'm just glad your parents can't see you now. To say nothing of mine!'

'My parents wouldn't give a damn,' Val said, scuffing her shoes back on again. 'But I expect yours would think it a bit infra dig. You're much more formal people than us, I think.'

The ice between them had melted virtually from the first moment they got inside the zoo. Val's frank and breathless enjoyment, her admiration for the clean and lively state of the animals, had all contributed to Otto's actually beginning to laugh with her and to treat her as a girl and not as a nuisance.

'Are we? I wouldn't know, never having been outside Germany, but if you're an example of British phlegm, then I've been mistaken and you are indeed a less formal nation.'

'I'm a real mongrel,' Val said cheerily, picking up the big menu which was in the middle of the table they had chosen and sitting down. 'I suppose you've never wanted to leave Germany and see how the rest of the world lives – I've heard nothing else since I arrived in Berlin but how happy everyone is to be living here, and how little you envy the rest of the world.' She examined the menu with pleased attention. 'What's Schlemmer-schnitte?'

'It's raw tenderloin with a side helping of Russian caviar. Quite a delicacy. Do you fancy some?'

'Raw? Gracious! I say, the prices are a bit steep, aren't they? Imagine how surprised your mother will be when you tell her you took me out for an expensive luncheon.' She glanced up and caught an expression of such unguarded surprise on Otto's face that she laughed. 'Oh, Otto, what is it? Do you know I was scared of you until today? You seemed so dark and grim, but it isn't that at all: you just aren't very happy! Do tell me what's the matter!'

For a moment she feared that she had caused Otto to

slip back into his shell, for the dark, brooding look returned once more, but then he glanced across at her and she read the naked misery in his eyes and knew he would confide in her because for some reaon he could not confide in his own family.

A waiter approached and took their order, and then, gruffly, Otto began to talk.

'It's a common story. I fell in love with a girl my family considers unsuitable. My father put me on my honour not to see her again and for her sake and mine I know he's right. But I can't forget her. I don't even want to forget her!'

'Go on. Who is she? Why is she unsuitable?'

'Nothing more to tell. That's it. We don't see each other any more.'

'And yet you love each other? That's awful! Otto, I'd never have thought you could be so spineless.'

Otto's face darkened.

'You don't understand. For her sake I said and for her sake I meant, though of course it was an embarrassment to my parents, and would have been for Minna and Franz too, I suppose.'

'But why? How can I help if I just don't understand? Why was she an embarrassment?'

'She's Jewish. You don't marry a Jew in Germany, not if you're an Aryan. She's the eldest daughter so she has to stay at home and help her parents with the youngest ones when she's not at school, and I have to work at my father's factory. We do meet sometimes, but it's difficult and very dangerous; she could be beaten up or deported for seeing me.'

'Jewish? Then it's true that there's been persecution? But I thought that was a thing of the past. I've been here ages and seen no signs of anti-Semitism.'

'You wouldn't, because the city's been cleaned up for

the Games,' Otto said bitterly. 'Before, there were signs in the shops – Jews not welcome here – and on the Ludwigshafen Road, near a dangerous bend, there was a sign saying: "Drive carefully! Sharp curve! Jews seventy-five miles an hour!" Only they've taken it down now, whilst the country's full of foreigners.'

'But why? Why pick on the Jews?' Val thought of her own much loved Jewish relatives and felt sick that such hatred could exist. 'They're just people. What harm have they done to Germany?'

Otto leaned across the table and took Val's hand. Her distress was too patent to be ignored.

'Gently, Val. Because the country's sick, because the Führer wants a culprit and the Jews fit. I keep hoping, from week to week, that things will change and people come to their senses, but I doubt it, somehow. Father and Mother say it's dangerous to know Jews, that if you get mixed up with them, then when they're finally driven out you'll be driven out too. And of course my girl would suffer if they knew she wanted to marry a German.'

'A German? But she's a German herself!'

'Jews aren't allowed to have German citizenship; the Führer decreed it, and it's been law for a while. Hush. Here comes the waiter.' They received their food in silence, but as soon as the waiter was out of earshot Otto continued as though a dam had burst within him, allowing all his fears and frustration to pour out. 'Yet through it all I love her and she loves me. We know there's no future for us here, but somewhere, some-day . . .'

'You must leave . . . go somewhere else. What's stopping you?'

'She is. Her mother's not well and she has to help her father to care for the family. They're quite well off – in fact they've got one of the biggest stores in Berlin – but things are getting terribly difficult. They can't employ Aryan staff in the house, of course, and shopping has been difficult because a great many shops wouldn't serve Jews. Though now because of the Games that at least has changed.'

'Yes, but when the Games are over, what then? The restrictions may get worse, not better. What will you do, Otto? Suppose they drive your girl and her parents out? What then?'

'They never will.' Otto dug a fork into his sauer-kraut and carried it to his mouth. He spoke rather thickly. 'I told you. They run one of the biggest and best stores in Berlin, and they make stuff, too, in a small clothing factory outside the city. The Führer needs them. Some Jewish traders have been forced to close down, but not my . . . my friend's parents. Too many members of the Nazi party patronise them, especially the women. The clothing they sell is on a par with Paris, they say, though a good deal cheaper. In a way I wish they would go, and then I could go too – yes, I would, though God knows how I would support myself – and at least we would be able to see each other now and then.'

'Look, I've had an idea. I'm a foreigner. Say I pretend to know your girl and said I wanted to visit her with your escort – would that be allowed?'

'I'm afraid not. What the Jews most fear is attention being drawn to them, and your friendship could easily bring down the wrath of the Reich on their heads. Besides . . .' He stopped, considering her, and for the first time she saw a look on his face that was almost mischievous. 'Well, it wouldn't do. Minna would find out, and she's very anti-Jewish. Much more so than my parents, who merely see which way the wind is blowing and act accordingly. What's more, she'd tell someone, try to stir trouble up.'

'That's awful,' Val said. 'Is there no way I can help?'

'I'm not sure.' He looked at her under his thick brows. 'There might be a way, but I'll have to think about it.'

'Does Minna know your friend?'

He was eating the last mouthful on his plate, but he nodded.

'And does she like her?'

The dark head shook.

'Oh dear, that does make things difficult. I'll tell you what, though. I do know a girl from school who lives in Berlin. Couldn't I pretend to be visiting her? The fact that Minna doesn't like your girl would be in our favour, since she doesn't like Salka either, and I'm sure she wouldn't want to . . .' Her voice faded and she stared at Otto for a moment in silence whilst things slowly clicked into place in her mind. Her lips twitched into a smile. 'Otto, you're in love with Salka! You are, aren't you?'

'Ssh!' He was scowling, but a smile lurked in his eyes. Don't pretend that you like her, because you treated her very badly at school, she told me when she wrote. I quite dreaded meeting such a bullying, cruel English miss! It's because you don't know her, of course; when she's free from fear she's amusing, affectionate, she glows. But for twelve months now she's lived on a knife edge and all the time she's at school she's worrying what might be happening at home. It makes her different, I suppose.'

'Yes. I saw a difference when I was round there the other night, a good difference. She was firm with me, not afraid nor meek. She told me to go . . .' She broke off. 'Oh, my God!'

'What? What is it?'

'Her little brother. I found him in the Tiergarten . . . some boys . . . I thought his arm might be broken but he wouldn't go to the hospital. They got a doctor from the flat below. Was that. . .? Oh, my God!'

'Beating up is an everyday occurrence, or was before the Games,' Otto said. 'The family is still useful to the regime, but even that can't save Karl from the stigma of being Jewish. Is he all right?'

'I don't know. She said not to go back.' Val hit her forehead with the back of her hand. 'Why didn't I *realise* why she was being secretive, a bit odd? She said Minna wouldn't approve of me being there and though I protested I had a feeling that she might be right.' She thought of her own chequered background and leaned across to pat Otto's hand. 'Otto, shall I tell you a joke, cheer you up a bit?'

'If you wish. I must *think*!'

'Very well. My mother is Jewish by birth, though she attends an ordinary church with my father.'

He stared, then, slowly, a grin spread over his face.

'That's rich – Minna's bosom friend half Jewish! But keep it to yourself, Val. No need to tell anyone besides me. Minna would . . . but perhaps I wrong her. Perhaps she wouldn't count it against you as you're her friend and English into the bargain.'

The waiter approached with the menu again and Val, whose appetite seldom abandoned her no matter how great the provocation, ordered an apple strudel and coffee. Otto followed suit and, when the puddings had been delivered, reverted to the topic uppermost in both their minds.

'Look, I must find out how Karl is and who hurt him. I can do something if it's one of the lads in the Hitler Youth Movement. I can make him smart. But I can't go round to Voltairestrasse without making Salka look conspicuous. If you really want to help you could go round and give her a message, then we'll meet somewhere public – I'll escort you, and you can be the one to do all the talking.'

'Of course. I intended to go back to see Karl, though Salka made it plain that I wouldn't be welcome,' Val said at once. 'I'll go as soon as we've finished lunch, if you like.'

But this Otto would not consider.

'It is best at night, when people are coming out of the stadiums and race tracks,' he assured her. 'Then you can mingle with the crowds and slip up to the flat without causing comment.'

Val agreed, eager to help with this romance that was at once more romantic and grimmer than anything she had imagined. But her efforts were in vain. Though she went to the flats and rang the bell and even called through the letter box, no one came to the door. After twenty minutes she walked back along the Neue Friedrichstrasse, a prey to all sorts of doubts and fears. Berlin no longer seemed a magic city; it had become a place of menace.

Chapter Ten

Against the darkness, the floodlights showed orange and gold, a brilliance of colour that seemed so strong you could almost taste it. But it was excitement that you tasted, Val thought, gazing at the scene before her, excitement and anticipation. There was heat from the crowds and from the lighting, the smell of crushed grass, the sharper tang of the sand in the pit into which the athletes fell as they finished their vaults, lingering food smells of sausages and onions in hot white bread, doughnuts, ice-cream.

Comradeship, too. The emotional warmth of being with people for a whole day, watching events in which the athletes strained every muscle for the honour of their country, and now the pole vaulting, which was continuing into the night because no one could bear to say let it go now, finish tomorrow.

A tiny Japanese was the crowd's idol tonight. So small, so incredibly agile, bouncing like a compact yellow and white ball up into the air, the slowness of his gradual ascent, the quick turn of his body and then plunge down into the sandpit, the fallen angel, white wings fluttering, whilst the roar of the crowd told him that he had done it again.

It had been a lovely day. They had had a picnic lunch, eaten in brilliant sunshine, with the food tasting extra good because of the happiness and excitement of the crowd around them. In the afternoon, the sheer joy of watching the black American athlete, Jesse Owens, win the 100 metre dash, as he had won the 200 metre dash earlier in the week, had brought them to their feet. He was awfully good-looking, Val had thought, and had bitterly resented Herr Hitler's snub, though it had led to explanations from Otto which she was glad to have heard. Racial purity, it appeared, was one of the bees in the Führer's bonnet.

'It is a peculiarity which he now has sufficient power to carry to extremes,' Otto explained. 'The Catholics, the Jews . . . anyone who looks to any leader other than Herr Hitler, even a spiritual one, is dangerous. He thinks only the Aryan race is pure, and a coloured man is scarcely an Aryan.'

'At this rate there soon won't be anyone in Germany he does approve of,' Val observed. 'He doesn't approve of grammar school children, nor university students, nor academics, nor professional men. Oh, and then there are prostitutes, he doesn't like them, nor gypsies, nor . . . what were those others you told me about? . . . Yes, homosexuals. Add Catholics and Jews, and what will he be left with?'

Otto shrugged and eyed Val with a certain amount of caution. He had found it extremely difficult to tell her what a homosexual was, and realised that she accepted his story only because she was in a foreign country where anything might happen. An attempt to assure her that there were such men in Britain as well as on the continent only led to a reminder that he had never left Germany, whereas she had spent the best part of eighteen years in Britain without ever hearing of such goings-on. No one had ever mentioned homosexuality in her hearing, therefore it did not exist. Otto had been quite content to leave the matter there, but he suspected that Val would give someone, probably her twin, a hard time when she got home explaining just exactly what homosexuality was, and why Herr Hitler should rank it with all his other hates.

Prostitution, mentioned in literature and in the Bible, had been easier for her to take in her stride, though she wondered why Herr Hitler did not see that without his strong Aryan customers prostitution would not last two minutes!

But now every eye was on the bar, and on the tall, muscular athlete who was taking his run up. Would he – could he – do it? Could he over-top the tiny man from the tiny island half a world away?

Val held her breath. Around her, she sensed it, the stadium was holding its breath. Waiting, waiting, hoping that the little man would win because he was a little man and had fought with such courage.

The leggy athlete made it, but not neatly nor compactly. In a wild, ungainly tangle of arms and legs he fell and received his roar. With excitement at fever pitch as the bar went higher, with the crowd convinced that he could not possibly do it, the Japanese took a calculating glance up at it, gripped his pole, and began his run. Muscles bunching, skin gleaming like satin with sweat, eyes half-closed, he stormed down towards the challenging bar. There was a brief breathtaking moment right at the top of his swing when it seemed as though he would crash down on to the bar, but then he rolled forward, released his pole, and tumbled down, to spring upright, face split by an enormous beam, waving to the crowd, knowing that his only remaining competitor could not possibly match him.

He could not. The medal ceremony was held, the crowd cheered until it was hoarse, and then began to jostle their way out of the stadium towards the tram stops, for tonight it had been the young people's night, with just Otto and Val, Franz and Trudl and Minna and a friend of Franz's called Walther. It had also been accepted that Otto and Val would go off together while they could, for when the Games were over the family was moving up to the hunting lodge in Bavaria, and Otto very much doubted if he would be able to get away. Minna, at first unbelieving, and then smug, had accepted that Val actually enjoyed her brother's company, and of course she was revelling in parental congratulations. Neither of the von Eckner parents hated Salka, Otto had assured her, but the affair had made them profoundly uneasy and now they were showing perfectly normal parental satisfaction that, to outward appearance at least, their son had got over his first infatuation and was enjoying the company of a perfectly respectable guest.

Or someone they thought was a perfectly respectable guest. Since Otto had begun taking her into his confidence, Val had realised that, in the Führer's eyes at least, she was every bit as racially blurred as Salka!

Tonight, their plan was simple but would prove, she hoped, effective. She had called on Salka again and had managed to have a few words with her, though Karl refused to ler her sign her name on his plaster.

'Put a funny name – Mickey Mouse, or Charlie Chaplin,' he had suggested, so she had done so, given him a large book of crossword puzzles which he had received with great enthusiasm, and gone into the kitchen to talk to Salka. She had wondered, then, how she could have failed to recognise on her previous visit the utterly distinctive atmosphere of a *kosher* kitchen.

'The best time to meet would be after the Games, at a restaurant which is always full anyway,' Salka had said. 'Then, if Odile and I get there first, we can look as though we're saving someone a place and you and Otto can linger until the tables are fairly full, and then come and ask us if you can share.' She smiled at Val's admiring exclamation. 'Yes, it is a neat idea. The waiter will be far too busy to care whether we know one another or not, and if we choose our restaurant right it will be so full of foreign tourists that we stand little chance of being recognised.'

'Suppose something's happened, and they can't get away?' Otto said now as they approached the restaurant's wide portals. 'If her mother is ill or her father decides to disapprove – you must understand that they approve of me, but they know all too well what would happen to Salka if she tried to marry a German.'

'If they aren't there, you'll have to choke down your disappointment, buy me a snack, and then we'll risk it and go round to the Voltairestrasse,' Val said briskly. 'I wish you wouldn't talk all that rot about Germans, too. Damn it, you're both Germans whether you like it or not!'

'But we aren't, Val! It's illegal for a Jew to claim German citizenship.'

'If you're born in Germany of German parents what else can you be? An accident of religion can't take your nationality away from you!'

'No, but Herr Hitler can! You have a proverb, *A man can be born in a stable but that doesn't make him a horse.* Don't you see?'

'No, I don't.' Val shook her head obstinately. 'A child born in Germany of German parents has to be German. What else can he or she claim?'

Perhaps it was as well that at this point they entered the restaurant, and all further argument was driven from their minds, for every table was full and there was a queue of at least thirty people waiting for seats.

Val scanned the room, then clutched Otto's arm.

237

'They've got a table – see? A nice corner one, but they've got another couple with them. Now what do we do?'

It was obvious what had happened. Because of the shortage of tables, Salka and Odile had been put with another couple, a heavy, elderly man and his plump little wife. All four were talking happily enough, though Salka glanced round from time to time, as if searching for them.

'Oh, lord!' Otto was plainly at a loss. 'Shall we go, Val? There isn't much point . . .'

Val took matters into her own hands. High hands, perhaps, but decisive ones. She crossed the restaurant at a swift, confident pace, and approached the table where Salka and her sister sat.

'Salka!' she cried, when a few steps away. 'Darling, this is awful. I'm so sorry I'm late – do introduce me to your friends!'

The man stood up, holding out a hand. He was smiling broadly.

'We're just goin', Miss Neyler – yes, ma'am, we've heard all about how little Fräulein Brecht hasn't seen you in months, and how this meetin' might be ruined iffen you didn't git to sit togither. So Mother and I held on, kinda hopin' you'd arrive, and here you are! I'm Joseph Lawthrop. Mother, shake hands with Miss Neyler. She's come all the way from England!'

'How do you do?' Val shook hands, smiling warmly at the couple. 'Were you at the games today? Wasn't it wonderful to see that little Japanese flying over the bar? We could scarcely tear ourselves away, that's why we're so late – oh, I should introduce my escort. Mr and Mrs Lawthrop, this is Herr von Eckner. Salka, my host, Herr von Eckner.'

'I sure hope you saw our Jesse too, Miss Neyler,' Mrs

Lawthrop said. 'Wasn't he jest wonderful? And that Herr Hitler, walkin' out like that! But there, I daresay I shouldn't criticise.'

'Nor you should, Mother,' her husband said jovially, helping her into a magenta silk coat. 'Well, we'd best be on our way; enjoy your dinner. I will say this; the food's not only good eatin', you get a good bellyful!'

Val waited until they were halfway across the restaurant, and then slid into one of the vacant chairs. She smiled up at Otto, still hovering uneasily. 'Do sit down, Otto. You can see that Salka and Odile haven't ordered yet, so the waiter will be along in a minute.'

'Yes, but . . . what about all the people waiting?' Otto muttered. 'Someone will complain, send for the manager . . .'

'They won't unless you go on standing there looking guilty,' Val said with some asperity. 'Sit down. Everyone understands that foreigners are pushy. That's all they'll think.'

Otto cringed his way into a chair and Val, enjoying herself, picked up the big menu, glanced at it, then handed it to Otto.

'You'd better order for me, Otto. You're better at choosing than I am.' She turned to Odile, a smaller, darker version of Salka. 'Hello, Odile. I'm Val. I wasn't terribly friendly with your sister at school, but I'd like to be her friend now, if she'll let me.'

Odile glared at her.

'Why should she let you be her friend now, after all the things you did? Making fun of her, keeping her out of the bathroom so that she got bad marks for being late for a music lesson, laughing at her when she fell on the ski slopes, imitating her accent when she spoke French . . .'

'Did I do all that? Well, it seems very childish and

very long ago, Odile, and I couldn't be sorrier.' She looked hopefully at Salka. 'Can you forgive me, Salka?'

Salka smiled. She looked really pretty tonight, Val realised. Her eyes were big and bright and her cheeks bore the faintest flush whilst her hair, roughly braided back at school, gleamed like satin with constant care. Even the neat dark dress she wore suited her, and showed up a prettier figure than Val had ever suspected beneath the dowdy clothes she had worn in Switzerland.

'Odile, don't be silly. Val rescued Karl from those brutes; I could forgive her most things just for that. Odile!'

'Sorry, I forgot,' muttered Odile. Then, raising her eyes to Val's face, she added, 'I must say, you don't look nearly so horrid as Salka's letters made you sound!'

Otto grinned at that, but broke into the conversation, waving the menu beneath the sisters' noses.

'That's enough. Now let's think about food! Val would enjoy the veal goulash served with red cabbage and dumplings, since she's always complaining how hungry she is. What will you two have?'

It was a good meal, made better for them all because of the pleasure that Salka and Otto took in each other's company. They smiled, spoke quietly to each other, held hands discreetly beneath the tablecloth. Val, who thought of the relationship between a girl and a boy as being exciting, daring and charged with the secret electricity of sex, now realised that it could be comfortable and reassuring and loving in a way which she had certainly never seen it before. It occurred to her that the difference between the way Salka and Otto behaved and the way her friends at home behaved might be because adversity had matured the former's love. It reminded her of the affection between her parents, the way Auntie Sarah looked when she smiled at Uncle Con, though before she had thought such people to be too old for love as she meant it. Did everyone feel like this, if their love was right for them? But only some showed it? She did not know, and supposed that it was not important. But it was enviable.

So Val ate and laughed and chatted and thought, with the optimism of youth, that there must be a way in which Otto could have his Salka without bringing down the wrath of the Third Reich about their ears. Besides, Hitler must be terribly proud of Berlin at the moment, seeing it peaceful, prosperous, a lesson to the rest of the world. Surely he would realise that absence of prejudice had improved his image more than anything else could have done? He was an intelligent man, or so Minna kept saying. He must leave things as they were!

'Val seems to be having a wonderful time.' Ted leaned back in his chair and absently buttered another slice of toast, then spread it thickly with marmalade. 'Better than poor Nicky. He'd love America, he said, if he just knew more people of his own age!'

Nicky had been despatched to the States to observe for himself certain business methods which Ted wished to emulate. The boy was touring the big car factories, seeing the big retail outlets, and failing, it seemed, to enjoy himself as much as Ted wished him to do.

Tina, who had just finished reading Val's latest breathless and untidy epistle aloud, frowned.

'More toast, darling? You know what you promised the doctor.'

'Good God, woman, you don't grudge me a bit of toast, do you?' In case she said she did, Ted pushed the rest of the slice into his mouth, chewed, swallowed, and then said blandly, 'Because if so, of course I'll not eat it.'

Tina laughed.

'You know I don't grudge you anything, but . . . oh, well, it's too late now, anyway.'

They had had a scare a few months earlier. Ted was sixty-six, apparently hale and hearty, yet he had suffered what the doctor thought had been a mild heart attack. It had been on the very first day that Walters had deemed the grass court fit for use. It had been newly marked, trimmed and prepared and Ted had put on his white flannels and an open-necked shirt, picked up his heavy racquet, and gone for a knock-up with Des, who happened to be visiting his parents.

Des had noticed Ted clutching his arm, and had insisted that they leave the court and go indoors, where he had telephoned for the doctor.

'Pains like cramp in the upper arm and shoulder could just be flatulence, the result of playing too soon after a heavy meal, but they could equally well be a mild heart attack,' the doctor said, having examined Ted. He ordered bed-rest for a few days despite his patient's insistence that it was nothing. 'Keep him quiet for a few days, Mrs Neyler, and I'll come in again the day after tomorrow. No sense in taking unnecessary risks.'

He had spoken to Tina privately, too, telling her that her husband was overdoing it, suggesting that he slowed down a bit.

Tina, terrified, had begged Ted to retire and to hand over the business to the boys.

'I know you couldn't trust Des with everything,' she told him. 'And I know that Frank's too busy with the yard to help much. But Nicky's growing up. He'll be every bit as good a businessman as you, one of these days.'

That was why Nicky had been sent to America, of course, though Ted kept his own counsel about the business. He would retire 'one day', he told Tina, when he was sure he could safely leave his various interests in other hands. In the meanwhile, he would take things easier, and when Nick came back, if he really *was* interested in coming into the business, things would change.

But now, sitting at the breakfast table with the sun streaming through the window from the patio, ill-health and retirement seemed like bad dreams; the reality was so good. Peace, a delicious breakfast, the faint hum of a Hoover somewhere as a maid cleaned the bedrooms, birdsong drifting through the window from the woods. Ted poured himself fresh coffee, eyed the toast wistfully, then turned mild blue eyes on his wife.

'Another fortnight before she even leaves, then! I'll be glad when she's back. I've missed our little madam.'

'Yes. It isn't just Val, of course. The others don't come when she's not here. The garden seems empty, and the house feels dead.'

Ted drained his coffee cup and pushed back his chair.

'And when she comes back? What then?'

Ted wanted his daughter to work, Tina wanted her at home. 'Until she marries,' she was wont to say, with the air of someone betting on a certainty, 'she might as well stay with me, learn to run a household. Someone's got to teach her, why not her own mother? And there are other things, too, which she'll pick up at home more easily than in some stuffy office.'

Now she tutted at him, pushing back her own chair. She stood up, small and compact, with her greying hair pulled back into a tight little bun on the nape of her neck and a pair of rimless glasses dangling on a chain round her neck. Ted, smiling down at her, saw her the way she really was. Eyes blue as violets, hair like ink, figure as slim and supple as the sixteen-year-old girl he had wooed and won nearly forty years earlier. The years might do their worst but to Ted his love never altered.

'What then? What else should she do but stay here with me? Soon enough she'll find herself a husband, go away, live with him and just come back here for visits. Why shouldn't we enjoy her company whilst we can?'

'I think, love, that we must let Val decide for herself. And there must be no moral blackmail, either. Most girls have jobs these days, and they enjoy working. I want Val to enjoy her life, not hang about at home and get bored.'

'Well, when she . . .' Tina broke off. Someone was hurrying across the hall, high heels tapping on the marble. With a leap of imagination and love, she held out her arms, a smile bursting like sunshine across her face. 'It's Val! I tell you it's Val!'

Val shot through the doorway and pounced on her tiny mother like a young tigress, all red mane and russet silk coat. She put out an arm and drew Ted into her embrace as well and for a moment they stood there, content with the physical nearness of each other, before Val gave them one more jubilant kiss each and stood back, blowing out her cheeks and squinting at them.

'Boy, am I exhausted! I've been travelling for hours and hours and I haven't had a bite to eat since yesterday. Wouldn't you know it, the train from Liverpool Street this morning didn't have a dining car? Or rather it had one, but it hadn't been provisioned.' She slumped into the chair recently vacated by her mother and put a hand to the silver coffee pot. 'Don't tell me, it's cold! I see there's nothing left but a couple of bits of leathery toast!'

'Don't worry, sweetheart, Ruthie will make you fresh coffee in a brace of shakes and bacon and eggs don't take more than a few minutes. As for toast, I can make you some of that myself now we've got an electric toaster in here. I'll go and get things organised at once.'

Val watched indulgently as her mother hurried out of the room, raising her voice to give the servants instructions long before they could possibly hear her. She turned to her father.

'Well, Daddy, what's it been like here without me? Peaceful, I suppose!'

'Dull. Darling, why *are* you here? Mama just finished reading me your latest letter and you said quite definitely that you'd be at least a fortnight late coming back as the von Eckners had invited you to visit their place in Bavaria, within spitting distance of the village my father came from. What went wrong?'

Val shrugged.

'I suddenly wanted to come home. I got tired of it all. I wanted my own family round me, instead of someone else's.'

Ted, watching her, saw that she was perhaps paler than even the long hours travelling warranted, and that there were circles, bruised violets, beneath her eyes. He thought he could sense a wariness about her, like a wild creature which finds itself trapped. He walked over to the table and tilted her chin so that he could look into her face.

'Tell your daddy the truth, like a good little girl!'

'I've told you! Well, there is a bit more, but I'd rather come clean when Mama isn't around. It's unpleasant, and –' She broke off as Tina re-entered the room. 'Well, Mama, where's this marvellous spread, then? The bacon and eggs, the coffee, and the hot, crisp toast?'

'It won't be a moment. Ruthie's cooking it now and she says she'll bring it up herself so she can claim a big hug. Why the hurry, anyway? Don't tell me they starved you in Germany!'

She was half turning towards the hall as she spoke, watching for Ruthie to put in an appearance, and did not see the little shudder of revulsion which rippled across Val's face. But Ted did. And it worried him even more than his daughter's words had done.

'It's nice to see you, Val. What did you think of Germany?' Cara's light, drawling voice did not seem to have changed very much, though she was now a married woman. True to her early promise, she was a beautiful creature, but Val was still a little shocked at the thought of her cousin married, and at only seventeen, too!'

'Germany was all right. It's a lovely flat, Cara!'

'I know it. The rent William pays is fearful, but of course it's only for a few months, whilst we're in Norwich. When we go back to London we'll live in his house on the heath. It's huge, with dozens of servants. He thought it best that I got used to a smaller place, first.'

Cara had married an extremely rich widower, and she had a tiny step-daughter not quite a year old called Mira. Mira, however, was still in her father's big house in London, with her nurse and a retinue of servants. Cara's husband had not thought it fair to burden so young a wife with the responsibilities of motherhood so early in their marriage.

'Well, it's lovely, anyway. Can you show me round? I bet the kitchen's a dream, isn't it?'

'It's very modern,' Cara conceded, leading the way out of the living-room with its pale green carpets, white furniture and statuettes in every alcove. 'William's been rather odd over it, actually – he insists that I cook for him, and he's just like a schoolmaster about koshering things. He stands over me and tells me what to do and which pans to use. Honestly, as though Mummy hadn't taught me all about Jewish cooking – and jolly boring it was, too.'

'He's very handsome,' Val said a little doubtfully. It was true, he was very handsome, but at thirty-seven he awed her a little. So high-powered, so at ease with her own father – yet he had actually married beautiful, selfish little Cara.

'Yes, he is. He calls me his child-bride,' Cara said lightly. 'He buys me everything I want. I've only got to mention something and there it is! I'm a rich man's darling, Val, just as I've always wanted to be!'

She opened a door and there was the kitchen, tiled in sparkling yellow, the units chocolate brown. Val, despite herself, gasped. Even the taps were yellow glass, and the window overlooked the square garden. Rows of pans on the wall winked copper, the fridge was bigger than the one in the kitchen at home, and the sink was stainless steel, something Val had only heard about.

'Do you like it, darling?'

'Yes, it's lovely,' Val said truthfully. 'Terribly *grand*, Cara. What do you think about when you're whipping up a nice little cheese soufflé out here?'

It had been a flippant question, but Cara took it seriously.

'What do I think about? Well, if I've not bothered to put an apron on, then I think about my dress and hope I won't spoil it. It we're going to the theatre I suppose I think about the play. Come into the den a minute. I want to show you something.'

Val obediently followed her cousin. Though Cara was a year her junior, she seemed suddenly much the older of the two. Was marriage such an ageing institution, then?

The den proved to be William's study and was decorated rather gloomily in brown with a dark green carpet, as if to prove that men were more serious creatures than women and could only function if their surroundings were suitably serious too. But Cara trotted across the green carpet, flung open a drawer, and drew out a massive photograph album.

'Honeymoon pictures! We went to Sorrento – it was the most marvellous experience, Val, my first foreign holiday. William speaks Italian, of course, which makes things easier.'

'So do I,' Val pointed out, though she was pleasantly surprised to discover that William did something other than make – and spend – money. 'We must have a talk – in Italian, of course!'

'If he has time,' Cara said graciously. 'His Italian probably isn't quite like yours, though – I mean it's all different, isn't it, in different parts of the country?'

Val took this, correctly, to mean that Cara had been boasting a little, and that William's Italian would probably turn out to be a few basic phrases. But she smiled and murmured that she would love to see the photographs some time, but now, since it was getting towards lunch-time . . .

'You could stay for lunch and meet William, if you like,' Cara volunteered. 'This afternoon I've a hair appointment – I thought about having my hair dyed blonde in front, what do you think? – and a manicurist will do my hands, but you could always stay and talk to me.'

'Does the hairdresser come *here*?' Val asked, secretly horrified by the thought. 'And the manicurist? Why don't you go out to a hairdresser, Cara? It's much more fun to be in the shop, surely?'

Cara shrugged pettishly.

'You sound just like Mummy! I much prefer to have them come here, then I never have to worry the wind will disturb my set. Besides, it's rather nice. I sit in the lounge under the drier and the maid brings me a trolley with tea on it, and the manicurist is the most handsome young man, very attentive . . . I rather enjoy it!'

'I'd die of boredom,' Val said frankly. 'Don't you *ever* go out, Cara?'

'I told you I do! William takes me to the theatre and out to dine, and . . .'

'I don't mean with William, I mean by yourself! During the day!'

'Yes, I do quite a lot of shopping, and sometimes I meet people for coffee, only of course none of my schoolfriends are married yet. I really love being married and having my own home, Val, and so would you, if you'd been as lucky as me.'

'Perhaps I would,' Val said politely. 'Well, it's been nice seeing you again, Cara. You must come up to The Pride some time and have tea with us there. Give my regards to your husband.'

'Oh, don't go yet, Val! Gracious, you've scarcely been here any time at all and you haven't said a word about Germany! Look, let's have a cup of coffee and some shortbread – you used to love that – and I'll show you my trousseau. And just one or two of the wedding photos, if you haven't time to see the honeymoon ones.'

Val, who had visited her newly married cousin partly from politeness and partly from curiosity, found that both expired far more rapidly than did Cara's drawling explanations of how she spent her days and how wonderful her honeymoon had been. By the time she made her escape, she was determined to politely refuse all future invitations from that source. She had never much liked Cara, and the married version, in addition to being totally selfish and lazy still, was also extremely boring!

There isn't an ounce of originality or madness in Cara, he'll be as bored with her as I am in a year, she was thinking to herself as she left the flat and walked up Prince of Wales Road. Passing the Regent Picture House, she stopped outside to see what was showing. Cara had suggested that Val might like to dine with them that night and bring her parents, and Val did not intend to comply with the suggestion; one dose of domesticity was sufficient. However, an alibi would be useful. Michael Lanyard in *The Last of the Lone Wolf* might not be everyone's cup of tea, but it would be better than several hours spent listening to Cara's drawl and her husband's doting conversation.

Continuing up Prince of Wales Road towards the car showrooms, Val wondered what Simon thought of his sister's marriage – indeed, what had possessed Aunt Sarah to agree to it? Cara would not reach her majority for another four years; it would have been simple enough for Aunt Sarah to have said that her daughter was too young. But no doubt William Dopmann had been both tempting and forceful – and a bad person to cross.

Still, this was all conjecture, and much of it would be revealed in the fullness of time. Also, she knew she was concentrating on Cara and her marriage to avoid thinking too much – most of all, perhaps, to stop the reflection that popped now and then into her unguarded mind. *You ran away*, the little voice in her head would say accusingly, filling her with guilt. Not that staying would have helped; in fact it could have done nothing but harm. But to run was not what one expected of a Neyler. Neylers were fighters. They didn't flee when trouble came, they faced it and beat it down.

She reached the showroom and swung inside. Mr Fredericks, one of the salesmen, came towards her. He was wearing his professional smile, which just showed how long she had been away. And even when he recognised her, asking how her holiday had gone and telling her that Ted was upstairs in his office, there was a different look in his eyes from the glazed politeness which had previously greeted his employer's daughter.

Val had known him too long to be taken in by his startled admiration, but she was rather flattered by it. She had been sixteen, with flyaway hair and pimples and almost no figure, when she had last seen Mr Fredericks. Now, without so much as looking in a mirror, she knew that the pimples had fled and her figure had arrived – Mr Frederick's nice brown eyes were telling her so with every glance.

Casting him a flirtatious look, she danced past him and up the stairs, banged twice on her father's door, and marched in. Ted, reading a trade magazine over the top of his half-spectacles, gave a grunt of surprise, and then stood up and leaned over to kiss the top of her head.

'Hello, *Liebchen*. Have you come to fetch me for luncheon? I must teach you to drive, then you really could come and fetch me!'

'That's a cracking idea! When can we start?' Val bent and picked up his leather briefcase. 'Where did you park the car?'

'Across someone else's exit, I daresay. We'll go and see if there's a rude note under the windscreen wiper.' Ted, a veteran of such notes, grinned and pushed Val out of the room ahead of him. 'Did you see Cara? Isn't she the perfect married woman?'

At the foot of the stairs Val tucked her hand into the crook of her father's elbow.

'Daddy, if you believe that you must be going senile! I saw her, and I thought it was all deadly boring. I know marriage is supposed to be every girl's goal, but I want to live a bit before I·go down for the third time!'

Ted laughed and squeezed his arm against her fingers. His eyes twinkled at her over his glasses and Val wondered, not for the first time, exactly why he wore spectacles since he scarcely ever actually looked through the lenses.

'If I didn't know you better I'd suspect you were suffering from sour grapes, or that you were trying to placate me and annoy your mama. If you find the domestic round so boring, what are you going to do? There's no financial need for you to work, but I don't like to think of you idling your time away, bored, getting into mischief, when you could be doing work that you enjoyed.'

'I don't know. I'd like to use my languages, and I did typing at school, because the teachers said our hand-writing was so vile that unless we learned to type we'd need interpreters.' They were out on the pavement now, heading up towards the GPO and the Agricultural Hall. Val guessed that the car would be parked on the cattle market – probably badly parked, but at least it was better than his street parking, which was on the casual side. Three feet or five from the kerb, she thought ruefully, on the slant, on the pavement – Daddy really didn't think that it mattered much.

'What about university? Nick wants to go to Cambridge to read English. How would you like to be the first woman in the family to go to college?'

'No fear! Not clever enough for one thing, and I've had enough of school for another. Actually, I'd like to work in London if I could find someone to share a flat. What with the typing and the languages, I ought to get a job easily enough, I should think.'

'Oh yes, a job, but I don't want you taking just any job,' Ted protested. 'That's working because you've got to, not because you want to ! Look at your brother Frank! He adores every minute he spends with boats, whether it's building 'em or sailing 'em. He even likes looking after himself, pottering round the village doing the shopping, lighting up a nice wood fire in the evenings, anything like that. Frank's a contented man. And think of Des! He'd hate anything dirty, like working in the open, and he doesn't think much of office work, but he knows more about films and running the cinemas than anyone else I know. He's got a real knack for predicting what people will enjoy, which films will pack the house. Now you and Nick, you're hovering on the verge of discovering what you'd like to do, and I want you both to choose right when the time comes.'

'But Mama says Nicky's going into the business,' Val protested, as she and her father crossed the cattle market and found the car, parked cornerwise and blocking the exit of a brand-new Morris and a very old Model T. 'I thought it was all arranged. You said he could sell ice-cream to eskimos. I heard you.'

'Ah, could is one thing, would quite another. I'd be kidding myself if I thought Nick wanted to come into the business, and never have I kidded myself.' They climbed into the car and Ted started the engine and crashed into gear. They leaped out of the parking space, grazed a lamppost and trundled, more or less safely, out of the side street and into the main road. 'Other people I kid every day, of course, but not Ted Neyler.' He sighed and planted a palm on the horn, seeming to think this was quite sufficient warning of his intention to turn right. His driving, Val saw through half-shut eyes, had not improved since they had last travelled together. And he intended to teach her to drive? She swallowed. 'So Nick won't be forced into the business. He'll do something else, and the business will just have to get along without him.'

'Yes, but he *might* want to join you, especially if he's good at it,' Val urged uneasily. It upset her to think that she had been wrong about Nick, that he did not want to sell cars, or run cinemas, or do any of the other things that Daddy dabbled in.

'Good at it? An ability as a salesman can be ruined by Nick's other main attribute,' Ted said gloomily. 'The boy's far too honest, Val! Oh, I don't mean I'm a crook, but I add a little gloss to my sales talk, give a big smile, tell the customer what he wants to hear. Nick would never do that.'

'No. I do see,' Val said, after a thoughtful pause. 'But what about retiring, Daddy? You keep saying when Nick comes into the business you'll retire, and, if he doesn't, how can you get away?'

'Well, there's your Uncle Abe; he keeps the books and tells me I'm not yet a millionaire,' Ted said, grinning. 'And there's always Pooter – you've not met him.'

'Pooter? Is that some sort of a joke? Or is it a nickname?' Val knew her father's predilection for irreverent nicknames. But Ted shook his head.

'No, it's his name. Basil Pooter. He's a good lad, he had a good education and he's got prospects with us. He'll go far – or he will if we don't lose him.'

The drive loomed and Ted was interrupted for a moment by the roar of his own horn. He appeared to listen approvingly to the cacophony, then turned to Val again as they approached The Pride.

'What was I saying? Oh yes, Pooter. He's hard working and intelligent and he's already grasped most of the essentials of the business. We were lucky to get him, but work's so tight here that he didn't have the choice he deserved. Tell you what, next time you come into the office I'll send for him. Handsome lad, too.'

'Right you are,' Val said amiably. She had not the slightest desire to meet Basil Pooter, but if it pleased her father that was good enough for her. And if his presence meant that Nicky need not go into the business, that was better still. Her love for her twin was probably the deepest emotion in her life and, though the suggestion that Nick might not want to go into the family business was a new one, Val had always been receptive to new ideas. Now that Daddy had said Nick didn't want to sell cars, she knew he was right, and that Nick had very meanly allowed her to be brainwashed by Mama into simply accepting his desire for involvement. She sighed as Ted brought the car to a flourishing halt outside the front door, and prepared for more questions about Cara and William. And that's the future Mama sees as desirable for me, Val thought with wonder. It just proved how blind parents could be at times.

'I wonder what's for luncheon? I hope Mama remembers my telling her that I don't eat at midday any more, because I don't want hips like a carthorse.'

Ted opened the front door and gestured her through ahead of him.

'Now you mention it, you aren't the stick you used to be, but I don't think you need worry about getting fat. Now me . . .' he tapped the curve of his stomach ruefully '. . . I *am* fat, but I don't worry about it.'

'Nor you should. I like a – a robust man!' Out of the corner of her eye she saw movement and turned in time to see the postman swing off his bicycle and advance over the gravel towards them. 'Hello, letters!'

'Just one, miss.' The postman handed her a thick white envelope addressed to her parents in Nick's decisive writing. 'Welcome back! I saw the Games on the newsreel – they looked suffin' good!'

'They were.' Val smiled at the postman and she and her father went right inside and closed the door. 'I say, Daddy, it's from Nick. Do open it!'

'From Nick? Good lad. I like his letters.' Tina, entering the hall, got a big kiss and an exuberant hug. 'D'you hear that, darling? A letter from the lad and Val home, all in one day. I like Nick's letters. They're full of interesting facts, not scrappy notes written on scented pink lav paper like madam's!'

Tina had taken the letter. Now she opened it and held the pages so that Ted and she could read them together, but barely had Ted got his spectacles organised than she was shaking his arm, her excitement so blatant that Val guessed the news before her mother spoke.

'He's coming home! Oh, Ted, he says by the time we get this he'll be on the high seas! He'll be in England in . . .' a quick calculation '. . . in a week!'

'A week? Here, let me see that!' Ted took the letter from his wife and checked the dates, then grinned impartially at both Tina and Val. 'You're right, a week today! The young scamp!' He turned towards the dining-room. 'Come along. I've a meeting after luncheon and I don't want to be late for it. He's docking at Liverpool – what do you say to motoring up there and meeting him off the ship?'

'Oh, *yes*,' Tina said joyfully. 'I haven't been in Liverpool for years, not since we lived there. I'd love it, and it would be nice for Val to see the city where her brothers were born.'

'Or we could go by train,' Val said quickly, mindful of the fact that her father would never allow a chauffeur to drive them all that way. He rarely allowed himself to be chauffeur driven anyway – it made him nervous, he said. 'That would be more restful for Daddy, don't you agree, Mama?'

Tina, who had the utmost faith in Ted's driving and who thought other people drove dangerously, nodded rather doubtfully.

'Yes, perhaps, but it's a dreadful train journey going cross-country. It would mean dozens of changes, I should think.'

The three of them entered the dining-room to find the round walnut table set for them, with two covered dishes and a silver salver spread with cold ham and chicken ready. The three of them sat together at one end of the table. Ted dispensed the meat whilst Tina and Val helped themselves to the salad in one dish and the potatoes cooked in their jackets in the other.

'We'll have to move back into the breakfast room for luncheon soon,' Tina remarked, helping herself to pickles. 'This room gets very cold with only two or three people at table. But I like to use it during summer.'

Val, helping herself sparingly to meat and salad and refusing potatoes or Ruthie's homemade brown rolls, glanced enquiringly at her mother. It had been a long time since she had lunched at home, but then Daddy's luncheons had been proverbial – something solid, had been his cry, and it had always been answered.

'We have our main meal at night now, dear,' Tina explained. 'Dr Wilson thought Daddy was putting on a little bit too much weight because his blood pressure was higher than it should have been, so we decided to be sensible and cut down. We always have a light luncheon now.'

'We decided nothing of the sort, *you* did,' Ted said, taking two of the largest jacket potatoes and a huge scoop of butter. 'Still, I won't deny I've felt better for losing a bit of weight.' He winked at Val. 'And I stoke up at dinner.'

'And what did you think of Cara and her little love-nest?' Tina enquired as they began to eat. 'She and William are so happy!'

'She thought it was dull and they were boring,' Ted said through a mouthful. 'Boring and domestic, what's more! But there, I've always thought there was more to Val than most.'

'It isn't boring or dull when you're in love,' Tina said indulgently. 'Now, Val, tell us why you came home so unexpectedly! And tell us what's happening in Germany. Is Berlin truly as wonderful as the Germans have been trying to make us believe? It was very odd the way Hitler walked out of the stadium when the American with the funny name won all those races! Everyone remarked on it!'

Val poured water into the glass, sipped, and glanced at her father across the rim.

'Oh, that! There was a lot I didn't care about. Daddy was right. It all looked fine on the surface, but under-neath the peach was rotten. Herr Hitler's a bad man; but they'll find out, won't they? They'll put the country straight again?'

Consciously or subconsciously, it was the child crying to the parent for reassurance that everything would be all right, and Ted responded in kind.

'Yes, bound to,' he said. 'Bound to. One man can't turn a whole nation sour for ever.'

'That's true. Did you see any of those storm troopers that we've read about?'

Val, in her turn, smiled reassuringly at her mother.

'No, or only collecting tickets on the stadium gates or keeping order amongst the crowds. In fact, I left rather suddenly because when we moved to Bavaria I began to notice things that I hadn't seen in Berlin. There were . . . notices in shops, things like that.'

'Oh, darling, I'd hoped . . .' Tina's voice was stricken. 'Was it notices to say that Jews couldn't shop there?'

Val nodded.

'Yes. It was quite a small place, too.' She turned to her mother, her eyes haunted. 'If they couldn't shop there, where else *could* they shop? That was what I kept thinking. So I spoke to Minna about it, said I really would feel more comfortable at home, and she quite understood. There was no trouble about my departure, I promise you.'

'Well, that's something to be grateful for,' Tina said absently. 'Notices in *all* the shops, Val? My God, what will become of us?'

'Only in that village; there were other villages a couple of hours' walk away,' Val said quickly. 'Probably they got friends to shop for them. Minna thought so.'

'I hope so.' Tina helped herself to more pickles, piling them on her cold meat with a child's absorption in something unimportant when big issues were at hand. 'When should we invite Minna back here, then, darling? I had meant to write to you and suggest that you brought her back with you when you came, but you came home so suddenly that there was no chance of that.'

'Have Minna here? How lovely!' Tina was not watching Val's face as she spoke, but Ted was, and determined to have a word in private with Val about her friend Minna. So they had parted in perfect amity, had they? Nonsense! 'Well, give it a few days and I'll write a "bread and butter" and invite Minna here. For Christmas, if you like.'

'Christmas? Well, that's a family time, really. But if you'd like her to come for Christmas, then that will suit us. What do you say, Ted? Should Val invite Minna for Christmas?'

Ted glanced quickly at Val, at the secret amusement which lurked round his daughter's compressed lips and in her eyes.

'By all means. An excellent notion. We'll show Minna what a traditional English Christmas can be like,' he said heartily. Tina opened her eyes a little. Because, hospitable though he was, he disliked having the house full of guests at Christmas; would dislike even one guest. But he knew, of course, that Minna would not come. Not at Christmas, not ever. He was looking forward to hearing why from Val's own lips, though!

'Here's Josie, what's the rush? Don't you have time for your friends no more?'

Josette, in full flight across the pavement towards the shop of her choice, stopped, stared, and then hugged the tall girl with the long blonde hair bleached white by the sun.

'Stell! What're you doing in town?'

By one of those odd coincidences, Josette and Tina's elder daughter Stella had met a year earlier when Stella had come into the Casualty unit with a neighbour's child, but though they corresponded often and telephoned one another now and then, meetings were rare. For one thing, though Stella had no quarrel with Josette, she made it plain that Louis was not to be told where she was.

'Or who,' she had said when they first met up again, scowling. 'I dumped Andy within six months of getting

260

out here, but I don't want Mama to know – she'd gloat, say she and Daddy were right all along. So not a word to Lou – if you're still seeing him, of course.'

But now, in the brilliant sunshine of early summer, Stella and Josette could only grin and hold hands until Josette, recollecting herself, tugged the older girl across the pavement and into the shop for which she herself had been heading.

'Look, tell me whilst I take a look at the dresses, would you? I'm about to strike whilst the iron's hot.'

She led Stella across the main store and into the department which catered exclusively for weddings. Stella stared at her.

'You a bridesmaid or something? Josie, don't say. . . ?'

'You've guessed it. Lou's asked me to marry him. He held out for three whole weeks, Stell, eyeing me with increasing lechery, and yesterday I popped round – it was old Halliforth's afternoon off – and we cemented relationships and we're getting married a month today!'

'Well that's great, if it's what you want,' Stell said a little doubtfully. 'Only he's ever so much older than you, Josie, and has fought like a tiger against being married – do you really think you can make a go of it?'

'I do. First thing I'll do is get myself in the family way. Lou's a sucker for kids, you know, Stell, always was. And don't think just because I've forced his hand this way that I shan't make him happy, because I shall. I'm determined, Stell, and I always do what I'm determined to do.'

Stella looked down at her adopted sister's small brown face with the lips set in a slight smile and felt rather sorry for Louis. Although, from what she remembered of her uncle, he was quite capable of fighting his own battles. Except . . . well, there could be no doubt that Josette loved him. She had had a hundred opportunities to have relationships with men handsomer, younger and a good deal richer than Uncle Louis, and she had never wavered in her determination to have him and no other.

'What do you think of this one, Stell? It isn't white, but I don't want to embarrass Lou, and cream does suit me. What do you think?'

'I think you won't take any advice I offer, so I wish you every happiness. I'll send you a telegram on the day. I can't say fairer than that!'

Chapter Eleven

In the end, Val's suggestion that they should go to Liverpool by train was taken up and Tina decided to stay at home rather than undertake the long and tiring journey. So it was only Ted and his daughter who set off very early on the Tuesday morning on the London train. They had decided, since it was such a long journey, to go via London and to spend a night there, so that Ted might take a look at some property which he had just bought through an agent.

'We'll go up on the early train, spend Tuesday night in town, travel to Liverpool first thing Wednesday morning, bring Nicky back to London, let him take a look at the premises too, spend Wednesday night in town, and travel home first thing on Thursday,' he had said triumphantly. 'Why don't you come, Tina, take a little holiday?'

But Tina, after due consideration, had declined. She was always extremely sensitive towards her husband's wishes, and she knew that he wanted to spend some time with Val, find out what had really happened in Germany. They had both noticed a difference in her, though she tried so hard to hide it. So she said cheerfully that she would stay at home, turn out the study and prepare a marvellous welcome for Nick.

Now, in the train, Ted and Val found a first-class compartment with no other occupants and settled themselves comfortably in the corner window seats.

'We'll be alone until Ipswich, at any rate,' Ted said,

selecting a cigar from his case. 'Mind if I smoke, darling?'

'No, of course not. I like the smell of a cigar.' Val settled down in her own corner. She guessed why her father wanted them to have a compartment to themselves and was glad that at last she would be able to tell him what had happened in Berlin and at the von Eckner's *Schloss*. It had been the worst experience of her life so far, and, though she had not the slightest intention of upsetting her mother by talking about it, it would be a relief to tell someone as understanding and sympathetic as her father.

The train jerked, the guard whistled, and the engine steamed out of the station. Val had a couple of magazines but she scarcely glanced at them. Better was a letter from Nick which had somehow got delayed in the post and had only just arrived. She had read it to Ted in the car travelling down to the station, but now she got it out and read it again, smiling at the picture it conjured up of her twin, sitting biting the end of his pen and trying to gather together any bit of gossip that might amuse her.

You mentioned that Mrs Simpson. The American papers are full of her too, he had written. *All nonsense, of course. She's married and not even a King can change that! I don't say much when people quiz me about Edward and her, but just smile with the air of one who could say a good deal – if he would. This impresses them no end, but they still believe all the rubbish that their newshounds dig out. The next thing we know, they'll start a rumour that Edward is to be named in her divorce. Still, it keeps the children amused!*

'Well, Val? How about telling me what drove you out of Germany, eh?'

Ted's cigar was going well and he was looking across at her with a placid expectancy which Val found touching. He was a darling father!

'Right-ho. Where do you want me to start? At the beginning with the whole chronicle of my time with Minna, or at the end, with what actually sent me flying back to dear old Blighty?'

Ted blew a smoke ring, waited until it was halfway to the carriage roof, then blew a smaller one through it.

'Begin at the beginning and don't leave anything out. We've all the time in the world.'

Val told her story simply and well, to begin with. How impressed she had been at first with Berlin, how prosperous and orderly it had seemed compared with depressed Britain. She admired the planning of the Games, the Games themselves, the cheerful stoicism of the Germans when they were defeated, their honest jubilation when they won.

Then she described her gradual disillusion. The discovery of Karl Brecht in the Tiergarten, the friendship with Otto and the realisation that Jew-baiting was not a figment of English imaginations but a horrible reality, barely hidden beneath the panoply of the Olympics.

'There was a worrying incident before we even left Berlin,' she went on. 'Minna has a younger brother, Gustav. A nice kid, curly hair, handsome, but rather shy and diffident. And not, I gathered, particularly good at sports. But he was a member of the *fungvolk*, of course; I think they have to join, or at any rate, if they don't, they go into a black book somewhere.'

'And he didn't care for it?'

'It wasn't that,' Val said carefully, choosing her words. 'He was forced to join, Daddy, but he was everything the Führer most dislikes, and is teaching the young to dislike. Well, not everything, because he's non-Jewish and he's white, but the family is Catholic – was Catholic, I should say – and Gustav goes to a good school. Apparently, no one said much at first until they thought they were safe, and then they started on him. They gave him no peace. Mental torture combined with judicious physical torture – the sort that doesn't show too much, though, because Herr von Eckner is an important man. I think his mother had an inkling that all wasn't right, because the last weekend we were in Berlin she packed him up a very plain picnic luncheon for a day in the country. I mentioned it because Franz had been boasting about those picnics – how all the children took a packed meal. Rich boys might have roast goose but poor ones just black bread with a smear of lard on it. Then, you see, they put all the packed lunches into a pool and the leader hands them out indiscriminately, so that the rich boy may end up with black bread and the poor one with roast goose.'

'Yes, I see. A good idea, in theory.'

'Only if you don't *think*, Daddy,' Val said, twinkling at him. 'As I said to Franz, some mothers would go to tremendous lengths not to shame their sons and would save all the choicest bits from the family menu for poor little Hans, and then poor little Hans, who hadn't had a decent meal all week, would probably end up with black bread and lard. Franz looked so baffled when I said that!'

'I can imagine. So Mrs Eckner was giving her lad plain food so that he didn't stand out. Very understandable.'

'Yes. Only there was quite a fuss before this particular weekend; Gustav cried, and begged her not to send him, and Minna told him not to be such a little ninny, and Franz told his mother that Gustav was spoiled and that camp would be the making of him. So off he went, poor little mite. And home he came on a hurdle, as the saying goes.'

'A hurdle? What happened? Hurt himself trying too

hard, or was it other boys? Boys can be evil – I should know. I was one once.'

'No, it was self-inflicted all right. Daddy, he . . . he'd tried to kill himself!'

Ted's good cigar was removed. He tapped ash absently, his eyes on Val.

'Are you sure, darling? It seems so drastic – but then children do magnify events. What had he done?'

'Oh, they'd been learning to tie knots, you know the sort of thing, and poor Gustav had made a mess of it and when the rest went on the leader had jeered at him, said he couldn't tie his own shoelaces. Apparently, if you get a working class leader, he can be as vehement against the better type of boy as his charges can. This fellow had been making Gustav's life a misery for months. And then one of the boys said Gustav might as well have all of the rope, since the rest had now passed knot-tying, and hang himself with it. You wouldn't credit it, Daddy, but the poor little beast made a noose, slung it over a stout branch, and was half-dead when someone found him and cut him down.'

'My God! Those poor bloody parents!'

Val, who had never heard her father swear, blinked, then resumed her story.

'Yes. And there was the most terrific row next day, too, because Franz insisted that as soon as Gustav was fit enough he'd have to rejoin the *fungvolk*, though he agreed that the boy should go into a different platoon, or whatever they have. Poor Frau von Eckner did nothing but weep, and Herr von Eckner looked like death, but kept saying that the boy would find his feet easily enough with more sympathetic treatment. Gustav, once he could speak, just said that if they made him go back he'd kill himself properly next time.'

'What happened, then? Is he to go back?'

Val shrugged.

'I don't know. He obviously wasn't fit enough at first, and then we moved out to Bavaria, where no one seemed to expect anything of him. But he'll have to go back to Berlin when the next school terms starts – Minna and Franz were *horrible*, honestly, that was when I started disliking Minna – and I suppose the decision will be deferred until then. But it started me wondering. What sort of parent lets something like that happen without instituting proceedings against someone, or something? Frau von Eckner is weak, I know that, but her husband's a strong man, and an important one. Why did he do nothing? Allow it all to be hushed up?'

'I suppose because one can't fight orders which come from the highest in the land,' Ted said slowly. 'How could the von Eckners criticise something which had happened solely because the boys had followed the lead set by Herr Hitler, and persecuted someone who was different? No; though I disagree with a do-nothing policy like that, I can understand why they thought it was necessary.'

'Can you? I suppose it wouldn't have done any good, and would have plunged the whole family into disgrace. Is that what you mean, Daddy?'

'More or less. Herr von Eckner may have seen that he could do more good for Gustav by speaking privately to someone, making sure that next time he got in a platoon with a sympathetic youth leader and decent youngsters. See?'

'I suppose you're right. But . . . oh, Daddy, I wanted someone to suffer for what they did to that kid!'

'There speaks a true Christian,' Ted said solemnly. 'Well, since that affair, dreadful though it was, didn't send you flying home, I can make a jolly good guess at what did! Go on, surprise me!'

'I suppose it's pretty obvious, really. Minna and I went shopping in the little town nearby . . .'

She remembered it all with almost startling clarity, the golden autumn day, the soft sweetness of the mountain air, and the homely little grocer's shop with its window full of rice and dried fruit and flour. And the notice, the sign in the window. It looked neither old nor new, it just looked . . . permanent. Settled. A part of the scenery. *Fuden unerwuenscht*. Jews not welcome here. People were going in and out, stopping to examine a tray of rosy apples just beneath the sign. There was no reason to be ashamed of such a notice, or embarrassed by it, no reason to stop and stare. It was *ordinary*, taken for granted.

Val had pointed, unable, when it came to the point, to say a word. Minna, eyebrows rising, had laughed, said it meant nothing, that in a little backwater like this there were prejudices but no one took any notice.

'My mother is Jewish,' Val had said, her voice defiantly loud and clear. 'I won't go into a shop with such a notice in the window.'

It had been Minna's turn to be struck dumb for a moment. She stared at Val, her eyes rounding, her cheeks beginning to flush. And then her eyes flickered over Val's red hair and pale skin and she smiled.

'But you're English, Val, so it doesn't really matter. And anyway, no one could tell. You'll be quite all right to go in.'

Telling her father now, some of Val's remembered wrath returned to her.

'The stupid bitch didn't see the point at all,' she said furiously. 'All she thought was that I was scared of being asked to leave the wretched little shop! I just turned round and walked away. We'd come into town in a big, lumbering old car driven by one of the servants and I went straight back to it without waiting for Minna. I told the man that I wasn't feeling well and that he was to take me back to the *Schloss* and then return for Fräulein von Eckner. Once back in my own room I packed in two ticks, went down to the telephone and ordered a taxi, and left a note for my "friend". I did just pop in and thank Frau von Eckner for having me and giving me such a wonderful time, but I don't think she realised I was leaving then and there!' She chuckled. 'Oh, Daddy, the movement I got on that train, I felt so *free*! I arrived in Berlin that same evening and I went straight to the Brecht apartment. I didn't really explain, I just said I'd got to go home, but they didn't ask, I think they *knew*. They gave me a bed for the night – it was Salka's actually, and she and Odile shared – and next morning, Herr Brecht got up and took me down to the station and put me on the right train and bought me magazines and fruit and some chocolate. After that it was plain sailing. I was home in London in eighteen hours.'

Ted's cigar had been smoked down to the band during this recital. Now he crushed it out and threw it through the window.

'I thought it was something like that. That Hitler! A man who puts his own people in prisons or labour camps or whatever they are because he's afraid of them is more dangerous than a striking snake.'

'Why should he be afraid of them? They must be afraid of him when they see what he's done!'

'He's afraid because he's seized power and knows that someone else could do the same – and that if they did there would be very little he could do about it. So he works to have people on his side and he works very cleverly, what's more. He wants to create a Germany whose people will fight for him when the time comes –

die for him, if necessary. And to do this, he is creating factions. He sets all the Germans against the Jews, so that everyone who isn't a Jew feels at one with his fellow Aryans. But he also sets Lutherans against Catholics, board school children against grammar school children, workers against professional men, so that each feels he is a member of a group which he must protect and which, will, in its turn, protect him. In the end, he will have weeded out of all the groups anyone with sufficient intelligence to see through him, and sufficient loyalty to religion or class to act against him. The ones who are left, the "chosen people", will have only one thing in common, and that will be loyalty to Herr Hitler, and a fear of what he does to his enemies. And then he'll begin to reach out further, to turn some other country into an enemy against which he can set the German people, the pure race. God knows where it will end!'

'In a war, do you mean, Daddy?'

'I do, Val. Not next year nor, please God, the year after. But it won't be all that long delayed, not once he's got Germany completely under his domination.'

'Well then, the sooner I learn to do something useful the better! I'd like to make up my mind what sort of job to go for before we get back to Norwich. Though Nicky knows me so well that if I ask him to suggest something he'll probably pick on the one thing I'd like better than all the others.'

Ted laughed and got ponderously to his feet.

'Don't let Nick persuade you into doing something you'd rather not,' he advised. 'Any more than Nick would let you persuade him to a course that was against his conscience. He wouldn't, you know!'

'He would have, once,' Val said, remembering how she had bullied her twin when they were small. 'But now you're probably right. Where are you going?'

'Where do you think? And after that, I'll walk up the train and order us a tray of coffee and some bacon sandwiches. It seems a long time since breakfast.'

'Shall I come too? I wouldn't mind the walk.'

'No need, chicken. You stay here and guard my seat. I shan't be above ten minutes.'

When he had gone, leaving only a faint blueness in the air to show that he had occupied the corner seat, Val opened one of her magazines, but she found she neither wished to read nor to scan the fashion pictures. Talking about Germany had, unfortunately, meant that she had had to think about it, and now she had stirred up all those feelings which she most ardently wished would remain dormant.

Otto's love for Salka – how would it end? What would happen to the Brechts? And Gustav? Changes were coming, Daddy had convinced her of that, but how would such changes affect her friends?

Now that her eyes had been opened, of course, she was noticing other things. Articles in newspapers, bits of gossip from her Jewish relatives, veiled hints on the radio. It was all there, if you knew where to look and kept your eyes open. Jews were leaving Germany all the time, though not every country made it easy for them; England had stopped immigration temporarily, to Val's burning shame. But they were leaving, nevertheless. Otto had promised to write, and Salka too; even Karl and Odile said they would drop her a line from time to time. She would write too – had already written – but how could she, a young girl, persuade an adult man to bring his family out of Berlin before it was too late? She could not do so, but Salka was sensible and at a school outside Germany, too. Perhaps she would make Herr Brecht see reason.

At this point, it occurred to Val that her father had

been gone for a good deal longer than the ten minutes he had promised. She sighed and got up, spreading her magazines out over her own seat and her father's. She had no idea how near Ipswich they were, but knew that the train frequently filled up there. She had better go along to the dining car and see what was keeping him, though she guessed what it would probably be. Ted often travelled up to London on this train and, had she not been with him, he would have sat with friends and business acquaintances in another carriage. Doubtless he had gone past, smiled at them, and popped in for a little chat, forgetting his hungry and thirsty daughter completely.

It was a corridor train all the way along, and as luck would have it they were in the wrong end for the dining car. Val had to walk, uneasily swaying, for what seemed like miles before the welcome smell of coffee and bacon told her that her destination was near at hand. She walked into the dining car, smiled at a couple of men she knew, and accosted the waiter.

'Excuse me, I'm looking for my father.'

The man listened, head attentively bent, to her description, and then smiled at her, his brow clearing.

'Oh, it's Mr Neyler you're after, miss! A gentleman who often travels with us, Mr Neyler is. Likes his eggs boiled, as I recall. No, he hasn't been up here yet this morning.'

'If you're searching for your father, my dear, I should try the first-class carriages,' an elderly gentleman in a blue pin-striped suit remarked. He was tucking into bacon and eggs, and looked amused by her predicament. 'Many a time I've known him spend the best part of the journey to town talking in other people's compartments, usually on his feet because he isn't stopping!'

'I thought that myself,' Val said ruefully, above the clatter of the engine. 'He came up for two cups of coffee, actually, and I'm longing for a drink, so I'd better go and find him.'

'I'll bring two coffees along to the first class just as soon as I've a moment,' the steward promised in a fatherly fashion. 'And a couple of bacon sandwiches? Mr Neyler's fond of them, I do know.'

'That would be lovely. Thanks very much.' Val smiled round at all her well-wishers and set off along the train once more, this time peeping into every compartment that she passed, though without success.

She was only a couple of carriages from her own seat when it occurred to her that he might be in one of the toilets; however, if he was there was little she could do about it, except to wait until he emerged. Anyway, now that the dining car knew he was with her, he would not be allowed to go up there and settle down to breakfast without her!

And then, in the little concertina section where two carriages joined, she had a nasty shock. She had never much enjoyed passing through that particular part of a train, the noise, the dirt and the horrid fear that the carriages might, at any moment, either part and drop you to the track beneath or grind together and reduce you to a jelly being something that every sensitive child must have suffered from. Closing her eyes against flying dust, she stepped forward, hand already out to grasp the opposing door handle, and her foot touched something soft. She lengthened her stride, but the object was too large to be surmounted by such methods. She opened her eyes and in the dim, chancy light, looked down – and felt her heart contract. Someone was sprawled across the floor-space. No, not someone, Daddy!

She dropped to her knees and dragged at the broad, familiar shoulders, shifting him so that she could see his face because she dared not believe it really was Ted, it must be someone like him. But then his head rolled and she looked into her father's face. Grey, grim, the mouth slack, the eyes half-closed. All expression gone. Frantically, she shook him, screamed at him above the roar and clatter of the train, but there was no response.

Clumsily, she got up off her knees, hands automatically brushing the cream linen of her skirt though it was a thousand miles from her mind. She must fetch help. She could not even move him by herself. She patted his shoulder.

'I shan't be a moment, Daddy, don't worry, I shan't be long.'

She struggled briefly with the handle, and then it gave and she was in the corridor once more, uncaring that her little pill-box hat was over one eye, that her suit was filthy. She burst into the first compartment and was relieved to see a man she knew.

'Oh please, Mr Todd, my father's collapsed, could you help me? He's in between the carriages.'

None of the men in the carriage was young, but they all moved fast. Two of them came with her to the connecting door, two more hurried off in the opposite direction, upon what errand she had not the faintest idea; indeed, she did not notice their defection save with the vaguest surprise that four men had risen to their feet yet two accompanied her.

They were quick, too. They would not let her go into the concertina again, but brought her father out and laid him tenderly on the seat in their own compartment. Then Mr Todd turned to her at last.

'Miss Neyler, would you fetch one of the stewards? Get him to bring along a first-aid box, if he's got one, and some hot water or something. Quickly, there's a good girl.'

She hurried as she had never hurried before, and the steward seemed to know at once what was needed. He grabbed a couple of towels, snapped instructions at one of the other white-coated men, and then preceded her down the train at a swift trot. Over his shoulder, he addressed her.

'Won't be long, miss. I told the lad to bring hot water and one of them brandy miniatures. Soon set Mr Neyler to rights. Well I never. I wonder what brought this on? One of my favourite gentlemen, your father.'

When they got back to the compartment, however, Val was not allowed in. The two men who had not helped to carry Ted back to the first class had found a doctor, and he was looking her father over now, she was told.

'In fact, we found two doctors,' one of the men told her cheerfully. 'What about that, eh? Bound for some conference and only too happy to give a hand. Your father will be right as a trivet with two of them working on him.'

'What was it, do you suppose?' Val asked timidly, as she and the unknown man waited, side by side, in the corridor. 'A . . . a seizure of some sort? Or a heart attack?'

'Who knows? You know how the trains sway and jerk. Your father might have fallen, knocked his head. There's nothing in concussion these days, they'll soon have him right.'

'I hope so,' sighed Val. 'Oh, I do hope so!'

The two men emerged when the train reached Ipswich. One of them was pulling a jacket on over his white shirt. He was wearing braces of a somewhat gaudy pattern, Val noticed with a detached part of her mind. He looked at her with pity.

'You the daughter? Well, m'dear, I'm going to have the train held, and I'll get an ambulance here right away. The best place for your father is hospital.'

'H-hospital?' An enormous weight rolled off Val's heart. She felt physically lighter. 'He isn't dead, then?'

The pause was too long before the doctor said robustly: 'Whatever made you think that? We've done our best . . .'

'He's dead.' Her voice sounded different, like the voice of a stranger, without strength or emotion.

'I'm afraid . . . yes, I'm afraid he's gone. It was a massive heart attack, I believe. Probably nothing could have saved him. Come with me.'

She followed him as a lost dog follows anyone who whistles to it. Her mind was in a state of shock, she could *not* take it in. Daddy, dead? Daddy, who was so bright and full of life?

The shock lasted throughout the miserable business which followed, lasted until she had been put on another train, heading back towards Norwich. Phone calls had been made, her mother knew, her brothers. She would be met off the train in Norwich and taken straight home. The kindly man who had put her on it had been a little anxious lest she should break down on the journey, but she had assured him, in her new cool little voice, that she would be perfectly all right.

'It hasn't hit me yet, I don't think,' she said as he settled her in a corner seat, patted her hand and prepared to catch his own train, which would be going in the opposite direction, towards London, where she had planned, so happily, to go. 'Thank you very much. No one could have been kinder. I do hope I haven't ruined your conference completely.'

'Not at all. Goodbye, Miss Neyler.'

He went then, and presently the train pulled out, and

Val was reminded so sharply and violently of that other train, pulling out of Norwich Thorpe, that she was rent by pain. She could hear her father's voice, comfortable, confident. *We've all the time in the world*, he had said. She sat there, useless, foolish tears running down her face because she had lost a whole six weeks of him by staying in Germany with Minna, and now that she was back, with all the time in the world, it was too late. Daddy would not be here to share it with her.

Simon met her at the station. By the time the train got in, she had fought for and regained her composure, but the mere sight of Simon set her off again. She clung to him, tears raining down her cheeks and soaking his shirt-front, shaken by sobs. Simon patted and soothed, and finally took her out to his car and sat her down in the passenger seat.

'I'm not taking you home. We're going to mother's place. She was with Auntie Tina most of the day, but she's come back now, and Auntie Cecy's there instead.'

'Why?' Val turned a tear-blubbered face towards him. Her blue-green eyes showed the slightest tendency to indignation. 'I want to go ho-ome!'

'Because your mother's in no state to see you, not today. Tomorrow, Mother says she'll be better.'

'Oh, but she'll want me! I don't mind, honestly, Simon, I don't mind if she's terribly . . . well, she will be, of course, but I want to be with her!'

'No.' Simon was firm as his stepfather had been firm with him.

'Don't let her persuade you, Simon, or she'll regret it for the rest of her life,' he had instructed. 'I won't have Val see her mother whilst she's in this state.'

'Poor Auntie Tina. I suppose she's terribly distressed?'

Con had looked worried.

'No. She's very calm and collected, in fact. She's laying blame.'

'Laying *blame*? My God, she doesn't think poor Val is responsible, does she?'

Con had shaken his head.

'No. It's a lot odder than that. She blames Ted.'

Tina brushed her hair. A hundred strokes. It lay, thick and glossy, the black intermingling with the white, across her right shoulder. Her skin, she noticed, was white too. But through the mirror her eyes blazed back at her. No tears. Just anger. Oh, yes, she was hurt, but anger was uppermost.

After that first awful shock, disbelief had followed. He could not be dead! He was a part of her; if he had died she would have felt the pain, would have swooned and fallen, would not have simply continued to turn out his study, tidying papers, filing letters, tutting over material which should have been thrown out long ago.

It was unbelievable that she had been so happy. Yet she had cause enough. Nick was coming back, Val was home and likely to be so for a while, the house was looking its best, the garden glowed with autumn. She had been planning a party for the twins, just family and perhaps a few old friends, but it would be nice to have a party to welcome them home. She reflected, as she piled up old newspapers – what had Ted kept them for? – that it had been some while since they had a family party, not counting Christmas, when in any case Val had not been here. She also reflected, with some satisfaction, that family parties were nicer now that Des and Beryl were reconciled. She had never thought it would work, forcing Des to give up Zelda. In her heart, she feared that it would merely drive Des away from them, send him chasing off after the woman, for Ted had made sure that Zelda had left Norwich. She had never been certain how he had done it and if she risked a question he always returned it without a satisfactory answer; she thought he was ashamed of what he had done, but why should he be, when it had proved so successful?

For Des and Beryl, if not happy, were at least no longer at odds with one another. They had some sort of understanding, for Beryl was a little bolder with Des now, answering him back, even showing a certain sense of humour in her dealings with her handsome, difficult husband. Happiness, perhaps, was too much to expect for either of them. Beryl did whine when things went wrong, and Des did take his own pleasures without much regard for the wishes of his wife and children, but then how many marriages were really happy these days? Contentment counted for a lot, and it certainly made family get-togethers more comfortable!

She finished piling up the newspapers and began to collect books. Ted was fond of reading, but not fond of replacing books on the correct shelves, so that the study was always piled with a miscellaneous assortment. When she had an armful, the bell had rung. Afterwards, she realised that it had pealed urgently, but at the time it just seemed a nuisance, an unexpected and unwanted interruption to both her thoughts and her tidying. It was early, too, nowhere near the sort of hour when someone might pop in for a cup of coffee and a chat.

Ruthie had answered the front door, presumably because the maids were busy upstairs, or perhaps out of the house altogether running errands. Tina had peeped round the study door, seen Des running a hand through hair that was a little too long and talking urgently to Ruthie in an undervoice, and had called out to him quite merrily to stop chattering and to take some of the books from her before her arms fell off under the weight.

He and Ruthie had both hastened over, each taking some of the books, and it had crossed her mind that Des looked uncomfortable, no more than that. She had also thought, with an inward chuckle, that had Ruthie been thirty years younger she might have thought Des was having an affair with her and was embarrassed at being caught in confidential talk.

'Mama, there's something . . .'

But she had hurried ahead, crying that Ruthie would make some coffee in a moment, and get the macaroons out of the tin, and then they would have a nice cosy chat in the study, since she was a grass-widow today and had all the time in the world.

She helped them stack the books on the shelves in the billiard room, and then told Ruthie, 'Coffee for both of us, please, and macaroons, and if you've got any of the sticky gingerbread that Mr Neyler likes bring some of that through – you know what a sweet tooth Mr Desmond's got.'

Ruthie had begun to say: 'Very good, ma'am, I'll see to it,' and then instead she gulped and put her hands to her throat and turned away so suddenly, mumbling something, that her ample rear had nearly knocked Tina down.

There had still been, in Tina's mind, no conception of what was to come. She sat down in the big swivel chair that Ted always used, motioned Des to take the visitor's chair, and joked about her cleaning that morning, about the feeling of trespass it gave her to move around here when Ted was out, cleaning and tidying. She had noticed, then, that Des's eyes were hurt and his mouth was trembling, and had wondered, with a sinking feeling, what Des was going to confess. A woman? Another mistake over the books? An unpayable debt?

Then he had spoken. His voice had sounded strange, as it had when it had first lost its childish cadences and began to turn into a young man's voice. Hoarse, oddly disused, a voice new-born.

'Mama, this is going to come as a great shock to you, but I've just had a phone call from Ipswich.'

She must have had an inkling then, surely, just from the words *great shock*, so why had she persisted in teasing him, in saying that he might have told her he had friends in Ipswich, and why did he think she was interested in his calls? But then he had been firm. He had looked straight at her, across the big desk, and there had been tears in his eyes.

'Darling, Daddy's had a heart attack. He's in hospital in Ipswich. Val's with him, but . . .'

She was by the door, every sense alert now, her whole being concentrated on Des.

'Which hospital? I'll leave at once – can you motor me over, Des, or would it be quicker to go by train?'

Desmond looked dismayed.

'Oh, no, Mama, you can't go rushing off. Val said . . .'

'If he's ill, I have to go.' She opened the door, called through it for Ruthie, and then came back and tugged violently at the bell-pull. Ruthie came in and her face was white but her eyes were swollen and pink. She had been crying. Tina had known, then, what she felt she must have known far earlier. That it was no use pretending, neither for her nor Desmond. Ted was dead.

She walked slowly round the desk and sank into the

282

big chair. She was wearing black, feather mules. She stared at them. What small feet I have, she thought in a self-congratulatory way. They really are tiny, like a child's feet, and when you put them into black feathery mules they look even smaller. She did not think of anything but her mules for the next few moments, though she heard her own voice, clear and cold, asking how it had happened, heard Desmond's muttered replies, heard Ruthie, standing in the doorway, breathing harshly, gulping back tears.

Now, sitting in front of her mirror, she realised that she had been the only person not to cry. Sarah had cried, and Des, and Ruthie, and Cecy had been almost an embarrassment – she had ended up comforting Cecy, of all the absurd situations! Perhaps it was because she understood and they did not. Ted had died, he had left her, and it had been because he had not cared enough for her to be sensible, to keep himself fit. He had not loved her enough to forgo a cooked breakfast, or a pile of roast potatoes, or thick, syrupy pancakes after a heavy meal. He had not loved her enough to give up his job, take the retirement he had earned.

And now? She was finished, of course, finished at fifty-four. Ted had been her whole world, her *raison d'être*, ever since she had first met him, and she had no desire to change the habits of a lifetime. If he was not here to partner her, why should she dance?

Grimly, she finished brushing her hair, tied it back from her face with a soft chiffon scarf, and walked over to her bed. Its coldness and loneliness repelled her, but she would have to face it. For the rest of my life, she thought wonderingly, I shall sleep alone, eat, think, walk alone. Tomorrow I shall wear black and I shall go to Ted's funeral, and people will say wonderful things about him and I shall nod, and smile, and pretend to weep. But inside, I shall know that he did it to me because he couldn't take it easy, not even for my sake. Inside, my thoughts will be ugly.

Slowly, she climbed into bed.

Part 3: 1938

Chapter Twelve

It was night. For twenty-four hours the Brecht family had remained behind the closed and locked doors of their apartment, because, in far-away Paris, the third Counsellor at the German Embassy, Ernst von Rath, had been shot.

Otto had lain in wait for Salka as she walked Karl to school and had fallen into step beside her.

'Von Rath's been murdered, you'll see accounts of it in today's paper, and they'll say a German Jew did it,' he muttered. 'Don't take Karl to school today, stay out of sight. My father says they'll take reprisals.'

Salka looked straight ahead, though she longed to turn and look at him.

'Reprisals? Here? But how could any of us help a murder in Paris, even if the murderer was Jewish?'

'That isn't the point; when has the Reich been fair to Jews? Salka, you must get away! Out of the country, I mean. I think Father told me to warn you because he knows that this time there will be no chance of missing out the Brecht family even though you own a business that is useful to the Reich. Tell your father you must all go, I beg of you!'

'Just like that? Otto, how could we? All our money's tied up in the business; and anyway, where would we go? Haven't you heard how many countries are turning away Jewish refugees now? You have to have a sponsor, all sorts of things have to be arranged, and it takes time.'

'Salka? Please? Go home.'

She had gone home. There had been sufficient urgency in his tone to convince her, though she was doubtful if she could convince her father. All along he had kept his faith in the German people, who had harboured the Jews for hundreds of years and who, surely, would see for themselves that the Jews meant no one harm and that, furthermore, they were good patriots, quite prepared to put up with some unpleasantness provided that, in the end, they were given back their citizenship and treated like the decent, law-abiding Germans they were.

But this time, when she told her father what Otto had said, Herr Brecht had neither laughed nor scoffed. Instead, he had declared forcibly that no one was to leave the apartment until he gave them permission.

'What about food, Heinrich?' his wife asked, her little plump face wrinkling into worry frowns. 'I keep a good cupboard, but there's no fresh milk in the house, nor yet fresh vegetables.'

'If Otto is right, and this is the turning point, then soon there may be no one willing to sell you milk or fresh vegetables,' he said grimly. 'It isn't so bad in Berlin, but in the smaller towns Jews are starving.'

'I thought you said those stories couldn't be true,' Odile said accusingly. 'You said it was only one or two stupid, prejudiced people, and that others would sell goods to the devil himself if he came calling.'

'I've opened my eyes, Odile. I must have been mad to keep them closed for so long, but little harm came to us here, nor to our friends. Oh, unpleasant incidents, yes, but no actual harm. And then . . . . What am I telling you this for, young lady? Just you do as you're told, all of you – no one leaves this apartment until I give them leave!'

The family had obeyed, and now they had been in the house for a whole day, a night, and another day. By now they guessed that Otto had been right, for the previous night the synagogue had been burned down, and their neighbour, Dr Spanda, had come quietly up the stairs and warned them that some Jewish-owned stores had been raided and a jeweller's shop and the owner's small flat above it razed to the ground and looted.

'Your premises haven't been touched yet,' he said reassuringly. 'The Nazis need you, so perhaps you'll be safe. Keep your heads down, that's the important thing, until the fuss blows over.'

But tonight the troubles were moving closer. Tonight they knew they should have fled, whatever the cost, whilst they had the chance. It was dark outside, and cold – typical November weather, with a mist hanging over the river and the bare branches of the trees furred with frost. But there was a rumbling growl which was coming nearer, and, bright against the night sky, flames could sometimes be seen between the buildings.

'Do they have a record of where all the Jewish people live?' Odile said presently. She, Salka and Karl were sitting on the big sofa, cuddled close for warmth, like a litter of puppies. They had pulled the sofa up close to the window and were sitting in the dark with the curtains drawn back, so that they would have some warning if the enemy came down the street towards them.

'I shouldn't think so,' Salka said as comfortingly as she could. 'But of course some of our neighbours know we're Jewish; that doesn't mean to say they'd tell, but . . . . well, we don't know who these people are who burn and pillage.'

'Storm troopers,' Karl said briefly. 'The Führer's SS.

And kids. Didn't you hear Dr Spanda saying that a boy of no more than nine or ten kicked the Jewish jeweller as he lay on the floor, then grabbed diamonds worth a fortune and ran off down the street before the storm troopers could catch him? Kids are like that. They'll come in on anything they think amusing.'

'Amusing? Honestly, Karl!'

'I didn't say I thought it was amusing; I don't! But some of the board school brats think any form of violence is amusing.'

'Poor Karl!' Jewish children could no longer attend state schools and Karl, too young to be allowed to simply stop his education, as Odile had done, went to a small Jewish school. For obvious reasons the children did not wear uniform, but there was usually a group of tormentors waiting to accompany them home with shrieks, abuse and blows.

'Oh, I'm used to it.' Karl stared out towards the glow which lit the skyline. 'I suppose this is a pogrom, isn't it? We were learning about the Russian pogroms in school; dreadful!'

'Yes, I suppose it is. They say Mr Vanhauser was killed, and his mother died of a heart attack.' Salka gave herself a little shake. 'Oh, do let's talk about something different!'

'All right. Where's Papa?' Karl, sitting bolt upright, was leaning a little forward now, staring down into the street below them. 'I thought he said no one was to leave the apartment. I'm sick of being shut away up here. I would have liked to go and take a look.'

'Don't be silly, Karl, of course you wouldn't. It's terribly dangerous out there, probably even if you aren't Jewish.' Salka leaned forward too, however. 'What made you say that?'

'Papa's just gone sliding along the wall of the

building opposite, that's why,' Karl said in an aggrieved tone. 'Honestly, Salka, he did say no one was to leave!'

'It was your imagination. He can't have gone out,' Salka said sharply. 'He's in the kitchen, you know he is, helping Mother to make us some supper.'

'All the boys are liars,' Odile said loftily, and then, as her brother waxed indignant, laughed and stood up. 'Sorry, Karlo, I was only joking. I'll go and check up for you if you like, though I'm sure he's still in the flat. In the semi-dark it's awfully difficult to recognise faces.'

But Salka was ahead of her.

'Sit down, the pair of you. I'll go and see what's happening. And I'll ask them to get a move on with the supper, what's more.'

She went straight out to the kitchen. Her mother was there, pouring coffee into a tall brown jug. Toast was steaming on a plate, already buttered. Salka's mouth watered, but one glance at her mother's face was enough to confirm her worst fears.

'Mother, Papa's gone out, hasn't he? He must be mad – whatever shall we do?'

'I couldn't stop him. He was determined to see what was left. Dr Spanda came up about twenty minutes ago and said they were at the store. He didn't think much damage had been done yet, and Father said he must reach the shop before the wreckers do. He knows we'll have to leave the country, and to do that we need money. He's never kept much in the flat, but there's money in the safe and the tills, of course.'

'Yes, but, Mother, nothing's worth the risk! Suppose they decided to burn the shop and Papa with it?' She turned round and took down her dark cloak from its peg by the kitchen door. When she had left school the previous year she had kept the cloak, and she would wear it now with the hood up and just be another girl out on the chancy and dangerous streets. She had no doubt that there were girls and women watching the destruction, half horrified, half fascinated.

She glanced over at her mother and saw that Frau Brecht was not altogether sorry she as going, though there was fear in her dark eyes and her cheeks blanched.

'Oh, my love, I wish you could stop Papa, but suppose they discover you? A girl, alone, unprotected . . . I had better go instead. My life means nothing beside the lives of my children.'

'That's all very well, but I'm more used to moving about the streets than you are, Mother. I'll find Papa and bring him back, and the money too, if I can manage it. I think you'd better give the children their supper, and then pack a couple of cases. Papa can drive us to the station first thing, pretending to be taking a little holiday or something, and we can get out. To France, or Switzerland – anywhere, at first. We can arrange something more permanent later. Keep the little ones amused. I'll be as quick as I can.'

She slipped across the hall and out of the front door and stood for a moment on the familiar upper landing. She sniffed the smell of paint, of cooking, of Mrs Pabst's perfumed face powder, and wondered fleetingly if any of their good, quiet neighbours would sell them to the storm troopers to stop the men from trampling about the apartments. Two days ago she would have laughed the idea to scorn, but someone was helping the trouble-makers who were burning and stealing, smashing and beating up both Jewish-owned property and Jews. If they came here would fat Frau Pabst or lean Herr Stressemann, or one of the other neighbours, ask them in, whisper, send them crashing up the stairs?

It was a question which she hoped devoutly would never be answered as she descended the stairs as quietly as she could and slipped across the lobby and out into the night.

At first, the streets seemed quiet enough. A cat slunk past in the gutter, streetlights lit only the usual quiet suburban scene. But ahead of her lay the burned out synagogue, and to the right of it a store owned by Jewish friends. The friends had relatives in Poland and had talked of going there weeks ago. They had not gone – would it now be too late?

Salka walked on steadily, not pausing by the ravished store as she passed it, for had she been just an ordinary Berliner she would have gaped and wondered at the store yesterday. But a sideways glance filled her with pity. Poor store. The owners had been good business people, had sold as cheaply as they could, given credit to those too poor to buy outright, and honoured their promises, worked hard. And where had it got them? Wincing, Salka averted her eyes from the torn and ruined goods, the empty shelves behind the windows, the air of spoliation and desolation which hung over the place. She could only hope that it was just the material things which had been ruined; that the owners had managed to escape.

She heard the crowd long before she could see it and knew, too, that it was working on the Brecht store. She watched, helpless, as flames taller than a man sprang from the empty, gaping windows where once plate glass had revealed the most fashionable clothes that Berlin had to offer. Not any more. On the pavement, being loaded into lorries, she could see bales of silk, roles of tweed, all the beautiful goods they sold. She stared, scarcely able to believe what she saw. Her father's stock in trade being stolen quite openly by government officials – if you could call storm troopers that.

Others were watching too, cheering as the troopers piled the debris of broken counters and shelving, and the wax models who stood in the windows, on the flames. There was something frightening about those wax models, the way they turned and burned, twisting and melting as if they could in truth feel the heat of the flames. Salka swallowed and looked away. She realised that the brown-shirts did not want to burn the whole store; it would be dangerous so to do because of the proximity of other, non-Jewish-owned property. But they were enjoying the agony of the wax models, calling out one to another that they would make the Jew owner suffer likewise were he here. She shuddered for her father's danger, but could see him nowhere in the crowd. Perhaps he had recognised how hopeless his errand was and had gone back to the apartment. She almost decided to return herself, but then she noticed that the crowd was dispersing. Most of the lorries, heavily laden, were rumbling off, and one of the storm troopers had shouted something about the Kellengers: Jews who owned property some two or three streets away. She felt ill as she realised how her heart had leapt – the locusts were moving on; someone else's fields would be ravaged!

She was hidden, or nearly so, in a dark doorway, so she stayed there, biding her time. Soon, very soon, they would all be gone, and then she could go round the back and see whether they had left anything. She had no keys to the safe, of course, and no idea whether it was worked by a combination, but she did know where the ordinary till-money was kept. It was possible that in their lust for destruction and theft the storm troopers had missed that.

It was then that she saw her father. His face was smoke-blackened and so was his clothing, but she recognised him as soon as he stepped into the street lights. He came round from the back of the building and she was almost sure he had the money; there was a swiftness in his walk which spoke, to his daughter, at any rate, of success.

If success it was, it did not last long. A couple of storm troopers detached themselves from the group waiting to climb into the last lorry and walked purposefully towards Herr Brecht. Salka saw him hesitate, then turn to grasp the blackened edge of the window as if for support. Then he drew himself up once more and walked, steadily, towards the men in brown.

'They hit him.' Salka's voice was very small and remote. She crouched on the sofa with her mother beside her, the two younger children having gone to bed long since, for it was dawn outside; the night was nearly over. 'They swore at him and knocked him to the ground and as he lay there they kicked him in the face. Then they grabbed him and pushed him into one of the lorries. I could only stand there – I dared not move, and it happened so very quickly – I could not think what best to do!'

'Where did they take him?' Frau Brecht's voice was high. 'There must be someone . . . I will go to the Spandas, the von Eckners. They're important people, they could do something! And there is Otto. He works in the factory, he must know people, perhaps someone could help.'

'Not the von Eckners. Herr von Eckner did more than he should when he told Otto to warn us what was coming. Besides, things are not good there. Otto says it is a family divided; they are watched, spied on all the time. They'll take Papa to one of those dreadful prisons, those concentration camps. He's done nothing, but that's what they'll do. I've heard others say so.'

'Perhaps it is against the law, now, to take your own money,' Frau Brecht said dully. 'They will punish him – and us – for that.'

'They don't know anything about the money.' Salka spoke more bracingly. Her mother looked as if she were about to collapse. One of them must be strong! 'Look, Mother, they can't keep him in prison for ever, and Papa certainly wasn't despondent. As the lorry drove off, he turned and winked at me!'

'He *winked* at you? For God's sake, why?'

'I think he guessed I saw him hide the money and he wanted me to get it when the coast was clear. Which is just what I did, and why I was so long.'

'You got the money?' For the first time since her husband had left the flat, Frau Brecht smiled. 'Oh, my love! How? Where? With money we can help Heinrich, perhaps.'

'Yes. And then get away into the bargain. When Papa came out from behind the shop and saw the storm troopers were still there – he must have thought they had all gone because the noise had stopped – he grasped the window frame where it was all blackened and burnt. I saw him let something drop gently down into the charred remains of a bale of silk. I guessed he'd seen me almost as quickly as he saw the storm troopers, and of course the only thing he would bother to hide would be the money. So I moved back into the deep shadow and waited.' She did not tell her mother how the wait had stretched endlessly out, how ice-cold she had grown, nor how fear had very nearly rooted her to that same spot until it would have been too late to do anything, until the early workers had begun to come out of their apartments, when her chance to regain the money would have been lost for ever. But she had forced herself to move at last, forced herself out of her cold refuge to cross the width of the road – how exposed she had felt; the proverbial snowball in hell had her sympathy – and to plunge her hands into the ashes of the silk.

'Yes? And when everyone was gone and it was safe?'

'Oh, then I crossed the road, climbed into the window, and found the money in the ashes.' She produced the small, blackened leather bag from the bosom of her woollen dress. 'And, Mama, though I know you'll say we can't leave, I really think we must. Or at least the younger children must. Berlin is no place for them, not now.'

'Yes, you children must go. But I won't leave your father.'

'I think you should. How will you eat? The money must be for our escape. It's useless to stay here and eat up our chance of life! We can't help Papa until he gets out of that place – then, if we're well situated in a foreign country, we might actually be able to do something for him! We can send for him to join us – bribe the Nazis with money if necessary.'

'Perhaps. I don't know. I'm very tired, dear. We'll discuss it in the morning.' Frau Brecht stood up. She was very pale, all the normal good humour gone from her face. 'Come along, bed.'

'I think I'd better have a good wash first,' Salka remarked. She glanced at herself in the hall mirror as they passed it, and saw her face tired and drawn, with soot marks liberally smeared across forehead and cheeks. She glanced down at her hands. They, of course, had plunged into the ashes after the money; she looked as though she was wearing silky black gloves.

Her mother's eyes followed her glance and she smiled, then drew her daughter into the bathroom.

'Dirt such as that calls for a hot bath! Just you get yourself cleaned up, and then pop into bed. I'll make you a nice hot drink, and I think . . . yes, I'll fetch the little velvet evening bag I used to carry when your father and I were courting. We'll put the money in that and you can wear it under your clothing on a fine cord round your waist. Better to have it on you than hide it anywhere.'

'Right. And tomorrow I'll try to get in touch with Otto and see if there's anything he can do about Papa.' Salka was immensely cheered by seeing a motherly, calculating look back in the older woman's eyes. She had her bath, slipped on her nightgown, and then got into bed, where Frau Brecht presently brought her a drink of hot chocolate and a delicious marmalade sandwich.

'We hadn't intended to let Karl go to school, so we may all lie in, which is a good job as it is already nearly six o'clock,' she said cheerfully, sitting down on the edge of the bed. 'Poor darling, you do look worn out! Eat up, and then you may have eight hours' good sleep!'

But sleep, when it came, was not good. Nightmares had her screaming so loudly that in the end she lay awake, dry-eyed, determined that she would not sleep again to endure such horrors.

And, wakeful, she lay and planned what would be their best course, when she could approach Otto, who else might be in a position to help. She fell asleep unexpectedly in the middle of all her planning, and, exhausted, slept dreamlessly at last.

'Well, well, well, the Brecht place went last night.' Minna, munching toast and sipping coffee, glanced maliciously across the breakfast table at her eldest brother. 'Do you remember them, Otto? You liked the girl at one time – what was her name? Salud? Sala?'

'Salka. Yes, she was a decent kid.' Otto, also munching toast, kept his tone dry and indifferent. He would not give Minna the satisfaction of seeing how heavy was his heart. 'You're glad, I suppose?'

'I think it's amusing. Her family has kept clear up to now, so presumably they've got friends in high places who've covered for them.' Her round blue eyes, in a face now unashamedly fat and pink, scanned her brother's lean, dark countenance. 'But that's all over now. Someone's got their measure. No one should be privileged above another, the Führer says, so of course I'm glad they've been taught a lesson.'

Herr von Eckner, who had been reading the paper and taking no part in the discussion, now looked severely at his daughter.

'Minna, you're malicious. It does not become you.' His tone was severe and the expression on his face not difficult to read. His daughter flushed unbecomingly, her pink cheeks mottling to purple.

'But, Father, they're Jews, they're not like us! Why, they aren't even Germans. You know the Führer took their citizenship away years ago. Why should they live here, getting fat on the money earned by the working people, whilst real Germans know hardship and suffering?'

Herr von Eckner put down his paper.

'The Jews did not know hardship and suffering last night? Today they are rounding up all mature male Jews and taking them to the *Konzentrationslager*. God knows what will happen to them there.'

'They'll keep them out of the way, make them work hard, so that they no longer bleed Germany of her money and goods for their own ends.' Minna helped herself to another round of toast. 'Is there anything about it in the paper, Father?'

'Nothing.'

'Then it cannot be important. No one can have been hurt, just a little discomposed. I don't know where you get these stories of *Konzentrationslager* from, I'm sure, if there's nothing in the paper.'

Father and son exchanged a quick glance, but neither spoke. Frau von Eckner, who had remained silent, merely supplying everyone's breakfast wants, glanced uneasily round the table.

'More coffee, anyone? No? Then if you've finished, Minna, you may leave the table. I believe I've asked you before to sort out the clothing that is no longer any use to you; you can go and do it now, please. The *Bund* is holding a jumble sale and I want to support it.'

As soon as the door closed behind Minna, Frau von Eckner turned to her son and her husband.

'Minna's been disappointed in love, as you both know, and it's made her bitter and sometimes rather difficult. I'm so afraid for her – afraid she'll say something indiscreet to a block leader or . . . well, to someone who'll pass it on to someone else, maybe with embellishments. You must be more careful what you say before her, please! Ever since that sad business with Horst she's changed.'

'It's the regime,' Otto said. 'We're told right from childhood that it's our duty to tell tales, to sneak, and people soon realise that it's a good way to get themselves feared, if not respected. Minna has been odd since the Horst business, I know, but surely she wouldn't inform on her own parents?'

'Oh, no!' Frau von Eckner said quickly. Too quickly. 'It would be an indiscretion only.'

Otto glanced at his father. Herr von Eckner had been looking tired lately, and there was a greyness about him, a stiffness in his walk, which had started around the time of Gustav's death. Ever since they had found their son's body, lying crumpled and small on the tiled bathroom floor and surrounded by what seemed like an ocean of blood, his parents had changed. Neither, Otto knew, could forgive Minna and Franz for their cold and unsympathetic attitude to Gustav and nor, he guessed, could they forgive themselves. Gustav had told them that he could not go through with it if he was forced to rejoin the *Jungvolk*, and had not believed the promises that this time it would all be different, he would find himself amongst people of his own type. Instead, he had slashed his wrists, an action which must have made hideously clear to Herr von Eckner just how terrible his first experience of the *Jungvolk* had been.

Frau von Eckner had lost her complacency, her placidity, her faith in Germany, but Otto thought that with the loss of his youngest child his father had lost more than that. He had lost hope.

'Indiscretions, these days, can be as dangerous and deliberate as cold-blooded revelations,' Herr von Eckner said quietly. 'Minna asked how I knew about the *Konzentrationslager* if there was nothing in the paper, but she must have known that I am told a good deal. I could be called a powerful man, I suppose, but I tell you both, I'm deathly afraid. All the misery that has been inflicted on the Jews, and there are already half a hundred dead, has not raised one voice in Germany. Not a protest in a newspaper, not a voice in a church. Worse will follow.'

He pushed back his chair and stood up. 'God knows where it will end, now that they've seen no one's going to try to stop them.'

Outside in the hall Minna, pretending to fasten a shoe, was stooping by the door, listening intently. As soon as her father finished speaking, however, she ran quietly across the hall and began to mount the stairs. She had no wish to be caught eavesdropping, though she knew her duty well enough. It gave her a good feeling to know that if she chose to pass on what she had heard her father would be severely reprimanded, or might even be taken away for a spell in one of the *Konzentrationslager* of which he seemed to disapprove so strongly. But at the moment she had no desire to upset her comfortable life by letting that happen. Now if it had been Otto who had said things against the state, she really thought she could not have resisted informing against him.

She was in her own room, sorting out her clothing, when it occurred to her that there was nothing to stop her *saying* that Otto had voiced such opinions, for she knew very well that he held them. It would not do yet, of course, because her parents would merely deny what she said, but later on, when things were more . . . more in the hands of people who thought as she did, then he had better watch himself.

Val snuggled down into the collar of her fur coat and drove her small sports car slowly along, peering out through the swirling whiteness of the mist at the tall London houses she could dimly see lining the pavement. *Was* this Granville Gardens? She had visited the place two or three times before, but only either taxi-driven or brought here by Nick, and the last time she had been preoccupied with her hat, a concoction of artificial pink rose petals, and with her temerity in taking part in a clandestine romance.

Nine months ago, when she had last come here, she had been in a taxi with a runaway bride – Simon's runaway bride, to be precise. For last spring she had assisted in what amounted to an elopement. Simon had broken it to her that he was about to be married, and had intimated that it was without the knowledge or consent of either his parents or his fiancée's.

'Who? Oh, *who*?' Val had cried in an agony of curiosity, and even now, nine months later, with the marriage an established fact, could re-live the astonishment she had felt when Simon had told her that his wife-to-be was Jenny Bachelow. Jenny, a girl he had known nearly all his life and a girl who, though pretty enough, was of a type that Val just did not associate with her handsome, rakish cousin. Wholesome, that was Jenny, with her bright brown curls, her soft, smoke-blue eyes and her clear, faintly freckled skin. She would, Val acknowledged, have made most men a wonderful wife. But . . . Simon? She finally concluded that it was Jenny's very ordinary, wholesome sweetness which had captivated Simon, plus the fact that he must have realised that only through marriage could he 'get' Jenny. He 'got' plenty of other girls, Val knew that from gossip and from the evidence of her own eyes, but Jenny was different.

Things had come to a head, too, through her very own Nick. He and Des were suppsoed to be equal partners in the firm after Daddy died, but Des was nearly twenty years older than Nick and had made things difficult for his brother right from the start. Trouble had been inevitable – indeed Abe Solstein and Con had both begged Nick to reconsider his decision to enter the business – but Nick knew how Tina longed for him to work with Des. It was only when Nick's veiled suspicions crystallised in an almighty row over Des's possession of a magnificent (and unpaid-for) Rolls Royce that Tina was forced to see Ted had been right all along.

'Your father said it would never succeed, the two of you trying to work in harmony,' she said distractedly, glaring at her two grown sons. 'Very well, Nick, you'd better do as your Uncle Abe suggested. Use the premises that Daddy bought in London, if you can make anything of them. I was selfish, wanting you here in Norwich with me, and it hasn't worked. For a while, at least, you'll have to go.'

As soon as Simon heard the news, he had rushed round, invited Nick out for a meal, and put it to his cousin that they might go into partnership together over whatever the premises might suggest to them.

'Boots and shoes are soul-destroying,' he said, grinning at his own pun. 'And what's more, I've been looking for an opportunity to get away. Mother's run the business too long to take second place to me, and anyway, there's a good reason for leaving – nothing wrong, I promise you, but a personal reason. What do you say?'

Nick was enthusiastic, so the two of them decided to travel up to London and take a look at the premises. It had been Val's suggestion that she should go with them, and also, she had thought, her suggestion that Jenny might go too and make up a foursome. It was only in retrospect that she saw she had been rather neatly manoeuvred, and that the 'personal reason' why Simon wanted to leave Norwich was that he foresaw endless trouble if he announced that he wanted to marry non-Jewish Jennifer.

Val could still remember the trip – the crisp autumn day, the leaves coloured scarlet, yellow, golden brown, but still on the trees, waiting for the autumn gales to strip them winter-bare. And the boys' faces, as they looked at the crescent of six big, old-fashioned terraced houses right at the end of Granville Gardens. They had turned to one another after their inspection, nodded, and then burst out, simultaneously: 'Car hire, with flats above.'

'Car hire? What does either of you know about car hire? What about demand in this part of London? And the buildings are all *wrong*. You couldn't possibly even get a car into the back, which is where you've got the most space.'

That was Val, practical in such matters because, whenever she could, she had been helping in the offices of the car show-rooms. But Simon and Nick had scoffed at her doubts.

'It'll need converting, of course, but the Neyler Construction Co. isn't just a pretty name, you know, the fellows really know their jobs. Anyway, by having them do it we keep the money in the family. And we've both maintained our own cars for a couple of years now, to say nothing of tinkering with the part-exchange jobs that the firm takes in. This isn't a spur of the moment decision. We've been thinking about it for a while, but we couldn't say for sure until we'd seen the premises.'

'Do you honestly mean that since Daddy bought them no one's been up to see what he'd bought?'

'Basil Pooter came up when we thought about selling them again, and said they were in good condition and it wouldn't hurt them much to lie idle for a bit. I think he guessed that one day they might be used as Daddy had wanted them used. Mama, of course, should have told me, but . . .' He shrugged. 'It's taken her a year to see things in perspective, and it's only now that she's beginning to behave like our mother again.'

Everything had worked out more or less according to

plan, what was more. Simon and Nick had worked like slaves and had forced everyone else concerned to do the same, and the conversion had finally been completed within eight months of the idea first taking root. As soon as the garages were fit for use, they had started hiring cars, and had done so well that any doubts they might have harboured as to the need for such a firm vanished. They bought the part-exchange cars from the Norwich showrooms, did them up, and then hired them for reasonable fees. They had had their share of bad luck – people did not treat hire-cars with much respect – but they had weathered it all. In between hirings, they and Richie Fisher, a mechanic they had brought with them from Norwich, saw to it that the cars were put back into tip-top condition, and that, more than anything perhaps, had paid dividends. Not only casual people but quite large firms were now hiring their vehicles regularly, and Val, who had insisted on putting some of the money she had inherited from Ted into the venture, knew that they were doing far better than anyone had anticipated.

But the question now was, had she reached Granville Gardens, or was she creeping along some other quiet, tree-lined Bloomsbury street? She slowed still further, because the end of the street was coming up and she might have to get out and peer at the name on the last house to see whether she was anywhere near – and then she smiled, doubts at an end. There were the houses, indistinct in the mist, except that visible across the pair of middle doors, white on black, was the legend *Neyler & Rose – Car Hire*.

Val swung on to the forecourt, which had been six tiny front gardens, and climbed a little stiffly out of the car. The air bit at her ears and nose, icy and yet dampish still, and she peered up at the windows of the flats above. Nick, she knew, occupied the extreme right-hand flat, Simon and Jenny the extreme left-hand one, and in between the others were all let, except for one. Val wished violently that she could come and live in that one, help with the new venture, be a Londoner, but it was impossible. Tina could not be left alone in The Pride with the servants. Daddy would have relied on Val to keep her mother company; she acknowledged it even though it irked her unbearably at times.

She had set out from Norwich at four o'clock that morning, wanting to get the journey over with before there was too much traffic about, because it was early December and people would be driving up to town for Christmas shopping. But she had actually arrived before very many people were up – a milk cart, the horse blowing softly into a feed-bag, stood somewhere near; she could not see it for the fog but she had heard the soft clop of the horse's feet and the clink and rattle of the bottles. All the curtains were drawn in the flats. It couldn't be more than seven thirty. If it hadn't been for the fog she would have gone off and found an all-night café and had some coffee and a sandwich, but as it was she did not feel inclined to risk getting lost.

As she hesitated, the checked curtains at the window of what must be Simon and Jenny's kitchen were drawn back with a flourish and a face pressed itself to the glass. It was Simon, barely recognisable through the fog, but he must have guessed who she was, for he shot open the window and hailed her.

'Val, what on earth are you doing at this ungodly hour? Don't hang around down there, you'll catch your death. Come on up!'

'Yes, but *how?*' Val called back, her teeth already beginning to chatter. The flats could only be entered through the garages, which were all shut and, presumably, locked.

'Curse it, you've not got a key, of course. Hang on a moment, I'll come down.'

The window slammed shut and Val turned to lock the car, first lugging her suitcase from the boot. By the time she had it halfway across the pavement one of the double doors beneath Simon's home had creaked back and her cousin appeared in the gap.

'Come on,' he called impatiently. 'I'd give you a hand with that thing, but I'm not dressed for pavement encounters.'

Val hurried over, grinning at Simon's erotic taste in dressing-gowns. He was wearing an ancient pair of paint-daubed flannels beneath it and she guessed that he must have pulled them on when he saw her, since he had obviously already shed his pyjamas – if he wore any. There was a V of bare skin at his neck, anyway. She found this rather embarrassing, though of course she knew that he and Jenny . . .

'Come on up.' Simon padded ahead of her up the stairs. 'Why so early, my bird?'

'Absolutely clear roads until half a mile or so of this place, and not a speed trap for a hundred miles, that's why,' Val said cheerfully. 'To tell the truth I came faster than you'd believe – the needle shot clear off the dial so I can't say how fast. Fancy that!'

'I do,' Simon, veteran of half a dozen speed traps, said ruefully. 'The kettle's on. We'll have a nice cuppa and then I'll take one through to Jen. That's my effort at domesticity, a cup of tea before breakfast.'

The kettle was boiling as they entered the kitchen and Val, putting her suitcase down on the lino with a thump, went over to the stove and lifted it off.

'Where are the tea things? I'll make it if you like.'

'No fear. You get your things off whilst I do it. It'll be quicker.'

Val took off her coat, her driving gloves and her soft green silk scarf, then walked over to the window. Looking into the back yard, she was surprised to see an unfamiliar vehicle.

'Good heavens, Simon, what's that bus doing there?'

'Oh, that. That's our latest venture.'

'A *bus*? But who on earth would want to hire a bus, except a bus-driver, and surely they have enough of driving the things during the week?'

'Oh, we hire it complete with driver. We've got a retired bus-driver, good, steady chap, to drive it. One of the firms who hire with us mentioned that each Christmas they take all their employees into the country for a Christmas dinner – the old-fashioned sort – and said they wanted to hire two or three cars for the senior secretaries. The rest of 'em make their way down to the place by bus, apparently. So I said how about hiring our bus, take them all the way, all together, and probably a good bit cheaper. They jumped at the idea!'

'Yes, but that doesn't explain how you got hold of the bus in the first place,' Val pointed out. 'That's what you used it for once you'd got it!'

'No, it isn't. Well, I suppose it is, but the point is I offered to hire them a bus before we'd actually got hold of one. You might think it was a bit mad –'

'I do!'

'Yes, well, you've got no initiative, then. Anyhow, after two or three rather hairy days we found a bus, and a few days later a driver. We've not looked back, either. We've got a hire for it a couple of times a week until the tenth of December, and then it's out every single day barring Christmas Day itself until after the New Year!'

'Yes, but you can't garage it. It's too big.'

'No, that isn't very satisfactory. It means we have to make extra sure, in this sort of weather, that it's not going to let us down. But that only means getting up an hour or so earlier on the days it's going out.' Simon, pouring tea, grinned at her, a lock of hair flopping over his forehead. He looked very young and unmarried with that guilty, mischievous look. 'I'd like a fleet of them, though. We'd hire them, make no mistake about that! But Nick's a bit cautious still. Here, take this whilst I take one through to Jen.'

Before Val had taken a sip, however, the kitchen door opened and Jenny, clad in a very thin cotton nightie, came quickly into the kitchen and flung her arm round Val's neck.

'I thought I heard voices! Oh, Val, it's lovely to see you – what a natty dress! It's a bit early for Nick so I guessed you'd arrived betimes; Simon Rose, don't just stand there, get me a chair! In my condition I shouldn't have to –' She clapped a hand to her mouth. 'Oh, gracious, I suppose you hadn't told Val, had you?'

Val glanced at her friend. Through the almost transparent cotton she could see the curve of Jenny's stomach and the increased size of her breasts.

'A baby? Jenny, you aren't preggers?'

'I jolly well am, as if you couldn't tell a mile off,' Jenny said, plonking herself down in the chair Simon pulled forward and taking her cup of tea. 'We've not told anyone yet though, neither Simon's folk or mine. We thought we'd do the dread deed at Christmas, if we go home for a few days.'

'I think it's lovely,' Val said, with what sincerity she could muster. She ought, of course, to have anticipated it, but somehow she had not. Simon still did not fit into her imagined picture of a young husband, so the young father image really was mind-boggling! And what about the business? How would Jenny manage to help with the book-work if she had a child to take care of?

Though, on the other hand, it would mean that the question she had come all this way to ask Jenny might be easier!

'Yes, it is, except . . .' Jenny jumped up from the table and dashed for the kitchen door. 'Start the breakfast, someone. I'm going . . .'

'She does that every morning,' Simon said, shutting the door behind his fleeing wife and going into the pantry to emerge with a packet of bacon and a bowl of eggs. 'She'll be sick, and then she'll get dressed and come through, right as rain. All the books say the sickness stops at about four months, but my Jen's the exception that proves the rule.'

'Oh? But she can't be much . . .'

'I don't waste time,' Simon said briefly. 'Are you on the eggs and bacon lark, or are you just a toast and coffee girl?'

'Just toast and coffee, please. And look, you go and get dressed. I'll cope with the bacon and eggs. It will do me good, I scarcely ever get a chance to cook at home. Will Nick be coming over?'

'Yes. He has a cooked breakfast here every morning and we discuss the work for the day. Look, I'll lay the table and get the coffee perking. Nick'll be here in about ten minutes and he likes to eat as soon as he arrives.' He clapped a hand to his head and rushed back to the pantry. 'You'll want sausages, of course, and some mushrooms. Jenny gets nice ones from a man with a lorry who comes round a couple of times a week. Here you are.'

Val, putting the bacon into the frying pan and stabbing the sausages with a fork before consigning them to the grill, glanced curiously across at Simon.

'You know, Simon, after Daddy died, Mama went terribly Jewish again, and she still won't touch pork, or

311

shellfish, though she's more herself now. Do you . . . well, I mean . . . the bacon? Do you eat it?'

Simon laughed.

'No, oddly enough I don't eat bacon, but I break most of the other rules – I'll have those beef sausages with the eggs and mushrooms for instance, though I don't think I'd fancy pork ones. When we married Jenny and I discussed her learning to cook and to *kosher*, and I came to the conclusion that though it had been necessary long ago for hygienic reasons there was no reason for it now. So I eat everything and never wonder how it was killed, which is a lot easier of course.'

'Especially for Jenny; I think it's something you have to be reared to, if you're going to do it without a thought. It's all right if you're Cara, with dozens of different saucepans and lots of servants, but it would be tough on an ordinary housewife.'

'Mm, you're right. How did Ruthie cope when Auntie Tina went all Jewish again?'

'Didn't. Used to say *Yes, ma'am, of course, ma'am, certainly, ma'am*, and carry on just as before. Mama used to potter around the kitchen with her mouth set tight and her eyes beady with indignation, and then she'd forget and drink white coffee after a meal which had contained meat, and hate herself for a bit. It was all mixed up with her believing that Daddy was responsible for his own death, in a dreadful sort of way.'

'Yes, I remember Uncle Con telling Mother that Auntie Tina spoke for a while as though Uncle Ted had deliberately slipped out somewhere without her,' Simon admitted, laying the table with swift expertise. 'Poor Auntie. She adored Uncle Ted, didn't she? It must have seemed like a betrayal when he left her to cope alone.'

'I suppose it did. She'd been spoiled and protected by

him since she was sixteen – that's quite a time. But then one morning, about four months after his death, she woke up and came downstairs, and something Nick said at breakfast started her crying. She cried and cried for two or three hours, I should think, and it was as though she cried all the bitterness and resentment against Daddy out of her system. Much later, I asked her about it and she said the Rabbi had been talking to her and she'd had a dream, but whatever it was it did her good. She can't cope without me yet, perhaps she never will be able to, but she's herself again.'

'She's raised no objection to you coming to us for a few days, though?'

'Oh, no. Actually, she wanted me to come. It's just that she doesn't much care for the thought of living alone. I know she's got the servants living in, but The Pride's a huge house, you know. It could hold another big family easily, and I think if I did leave home she'd feel she wasn't justified in keeping the place. Anyway, she keeps saying that I'll marry one day, which I shall, and she knows I'll have to go then. Unless she has the cosy little idea that my husband and I will live with her!'

'Never that! Didn't Nick say something about a dog?'

'Oh, yes, Maxie. Look, the bacon and mushrooms are done, and the sausages. Shouldn't you go and get Nick up?'

'No fear. Nick's got a key, thank God. Tell me about Maxie; did your mama get him for a guard dog?'

'No, Maxie was what I gave her for her last birthday. Her gratitude was *not* overwhelming! I bought him at the Maxted kennels, hence the name, but the vet thinks there's one born every minute – he says Maxie's too rough for a smooth-haired terrier and too smooth for a rough-haired one. And he's showing every sign of being too large for either. I suspect myself there's a dash of Airedale in there somewhere.'

'It just goes to show. I never thought of Auntie Tina as being a dog-lover.'

Val dished up the bacon and turned the sausages, and began to break eggs into the spitting pan.

'According to Mama's old tales, she had a deprived childhood because Grandpa would never let her have a pet. But what actually decided me was that she began complaining she was nervous when I went out during the evening. She said she was lonely and so on. So I bought her this dear, fluffy little puppy, and she was ecstatic though with certain doubts, and now the doubts may reign supreme but of course she can't bring herself to kick Maxie out into the cold cold snow, so he's found himself a cosy billet and two adoring, if critical, females.'

At this point Nick burst into the kitchen, gave his sister an exuberant hug, shouted, 'Get up Jenny, you lazy little beast!' and slammed the kitchen door shut behind him. He sat down at the table, Simon followed suit, and two pairs of eyes swivelled cookerwards.

'Well, where is it?' Nick said hopefully. 'Where's my sustaining grub, eh? I've a busy morning ahead of me. We've three cars coming back after long hires and they'll all need no end doing to them, oil changes and plug cleaning and so on. People treat hire-cars worse than dogs.'

'It's ready,' Val said triumphantly. She had sliced the loaf, albeit into doorsteps, and she now slid an egg on to each slice of bread, laid bacon and mushrooms taste-fully on one side and two fat sausages on the other and put the plates before them.

'Not bad, for a novice,' Nick said. 'What were you chattering about when I came in? Maxie?'

'That's right. I was telling Simon that though Mama shouts at him for chewing the furniture and piddling in corners and chasing the postman's bike, she's hooked on him. Even when he gave her fleas she forgave him, though she made excuses two weeks running to cancel her bridge party in case her guests left with more than they brought – and I don't mean the silver teaspoons! She takes him for walks on the lead, and she's taught him to beg for a biscuit and not to bark *all* the time in the car, only most of it.'

'Good old Mama! She'll civilise the savage beast! Shall I give Jenny a holler, if that's her brekker you're keeping hot under there, Val?'

'It's ready,' Val was beginning, when the kitchen door opened and Jenny trotted in. She was bright-eyed, her hair neatly brushed, her smock dress with its white Peter Pan collar looking fresh and pretty. She smiled at the Neyler twins and sat down at the table.

'Val, you're a pearl past price. Is mine ready too?'

'Certainly, ma'am.' Val put a selection down in front of her friend and then took her own place with coffee and toast. 'Being an expectant mother suits you, Jenny; when's the happy event?'

'Twenty-eighth of January,' Jenny said between mouthfuls. 'I feel as if it were tomorrow, but the doctor is firm that it's the twenty-eighth.' She glanced up at the kitchen clock and gave a shriek. 'Boys, the garage should be open in ten minutes, and Simon's still in his dressing-gown! Do hurry, you two. I hate the boy having to open up, you never know what he'll *say* to people.'

Simon, sighing and casting his eyes ceilingwards, crammed the rest of his breakfast into his mouth, seized his still full coffee cup, and left the room at an ambling pace. Nick also got to his feet.

'Nag, nag, nag. I might as well be married myself for all the peace she gives us,' he remarked, taking a piece of toast and spreading it thickly with butter and Bovril. 'I'll go down and open up and see that poor young Reggy doesn't put anyone off.' He turned to Val and winked. 'Reggy's got an accent you could cut with a knife, and Jenny thinks other people will have difficulty in understanding him.'

'It isn't that, it's when they do understand him,' Jenny said darkly. 'His language – I'm not narrow-minded, but honestly!'

Nick waved a casual hand and left the kitchen, and just before he closed the door Simon's torso appeared round it. He was bare to the waist and had a tooth-brush, covered with foam, in one hand.

'Don't forget, Jenny, you're on holiday today so you can take Val out on the spree; if you need any money or anything, pop into the office on your way out and I'll see you right.' He winked at Val and disappeared again; there was the crash of a door shutting, the swish and patter of water running, and then his powerful baritone voice was raised in song. Val, listening, seeing the expression of tender affection on Jenny's face, was smitten with a stab of envy so powerful that it made her blink. Lucky, *lucky* Jenny! Loved by and married to Simon, living freely in London and being teased and spoiled to death by two young men – it seemed there was more than one sort of marriage, and this sort would be nice to have. One day.

'Well, Val, what would you like to do?' Jenny enquired, as they sat and sipped a last cup of coffee in the sunny kitchen. The fog had miraculously cleared as they ate and now it was a brilliant winter's day, with a clear sky and just enough nip in the air to be invigorating.

'There is something I very much want to do, but it's a bit dull for you,' Val said. 'Actually, Jenny, I want to ask you a rather big favour.'

'Carry on. You know I'll do it if I can.'

'Oh, I know. But this is . . . oh, dammit, it's an odd sort of thing to ask.'

'Then cough it up. How can I say yes or no when I don't know what you're going to ask me? It isn't like you to hold back. You usually come straight out with things, no matter how outrageous.'

'All right. Did you read in the papers about the pogrom the Nazis carried out in November against the Jews? The night of the long knives, they called it.'

'Yes, I read about it. I thought it was awful. I felt worse, I suppose, when I read about the adult males being sent to those concentration camps and thought that if it was here, Simon . . . You see, he's sure there will be a war and he says when it comes he's going to join the Air Force. Well? You heard more than there was in the papers, I daresay, from your friends in Berlin?'

'Yes. The Brecht family lost pretty well everything and Mr Brecht, who was so kind to me when I ran away from the von Eckners, is in a concentration camp. We can't do anything about him, I'm afraid. Salka writes that they've moved heaven and earth and can't get his release. But Otto, my friend, you know, the one who's in love with Salka, says they must get out. Only they can't get very far unless they have a sponsor, because Britain is afraid of being swamped by refugees who'll just be a charge on the state. Mama is sponsoring Frau Brecht and Karl, he's only a child, so he can come with her. Mama's put in for a mature woman to be her housekeeper and she's got her three refusals from employment agencies, here, so that one is going ahead. But . . .'

317

'Three refusals? Why on earth?'

'Oh, didn't you know. The British government says the refugees must have a job, but because of the high unemployment problem here they also say they can't take a job which an English person could do. So you have to have written confirmation from three employment agencies that they could not find you anyone to do the work. And then, armed with that, you can apply through the Bethdin, in London, for a refugee from Germany.'

'I see. How on earth did Auntie Tina manage to get three refusals, though? I should think quite a lot of women wouldn't mind being housekeeper at The Pride.'

'Don't know, didn't ask, but people are a lot nicer than you might think, sometimes. It isn't just a job, you see, it's their lives. I think a good many people realise that, and, when they see that they can save the life of some poor little Jewish woman stuck in Germany, then they'll bend the rules a bit. So anyway, Mrs Brecht and Karl will be here quite soon, and Odile's being sponsored by Auntie Sarah, who's applied for her as a nursery maid. The thing is, though, it's awfully difficult to do these things from Norwich. It means coming up and down to London all the time and writing interminable letters and so on – you have to present your case in London, you see. And we wondered . . . Oh, Jenny, I desperately want to get Salka out, but I'm single and I live at home . . .'

'I'll do it,' Jenny said eagerly. 'Val, I'd love to do it, I'd be proud! Couldn't I say I wanted a nanny for when the baby's born?'

'That would be ideal. I couldn't do anything until we'd arranged for the rest of the family, because Otto rang up and said it was clear that Salka wouldn't budge until all her family were safe. Apart from Herr Brecht, of course, and I'm afraid we can't do anything there until he's served his time or whatever they have to do.'

'I wish we could help him, too,' Jenny said wistfully. 'I don't have to tell you how tight money is, because the boys plough every penny back into the business – larger cars, a bit more advertising. But we're not penniless by any means, and we did intend to get someone quite soon really, because I want to go on helping with the office work and answering the telephone and so on. So when the baby's born a nanny will be really useful.'

'Right. Only Mama's going to pay Salka's wages. No, don't try to go all independent on me. I very much doubt if Salka will be a good nanny – she's far too brainy! The hard work is getting her here, and Mama will be saved that and will gladly pay the wages for as long as Salka stays with you. It won't be Mama really, either; it will come out of the business, and that's partly mine and partly Nick's. So just accept it as a gift, Jen, from us Neylers to you Roses.'

'All right. Thank your mother very much. Now, what do I do?'

'Well, first we try the agencies. Mama says the best thing is to word your request in such a way that it's difficult for them to find you someone. Since you're applying for a nanny, say you want one who can speak French and German; that'll stymie them.'

'Gosh, yes, I might easily get three refusals that way!' Jenny got to her feet and began collecting the dirty dishes and carrying them over to the sink. 'You haven't unpacked yet, have you? Well, go and do that whilst I wash up, and then we'll set off. I can think of two . . . no, *three* employment agencies quite near here where we'll certainly have a job to find a tri-lingual nanny!'

Chapter Thirteen

It was five days before Christmas, and the flat was gay with decorations. Holly, scarlet-berried, was massed behind the mirror and coloured paper chains were looped tastefully across the ceiling. The lights had been transformed by Chinese lanterns in a variety of brilliant colours, the little Christmas tree was hung with silver and gold baubles and the tip of each branch was decorated with a tiny red wax candle.

In the kitchen, Jenny and Val were working. They had planned the meal carefully because it was a welcome for Salka, and because it was Christmas and the entire family would foregather in The Pride in a few days to gorge themselves on turkey and plum pudding.

'Something light but delicious,' Jenny had said. And of course it had to be *kosher*, too. In the end, they had decided on a roast chicken, because that was easy, with fruit jelly and pears in red wine. Coffee would be served black for those who could not take cream. The soup which preceded this repast would be Tina's own recipe, chicken soup with *pfarvel*, and it smelt delicious already as it simmered on the stove.

'I just hope I've done everything I should,' Jenny said now, peering into the pan through wreaths of steam. 'It's hard to cook *kosher* with only Simon to advise you. I know all about what meat is allowed and what isn't – he got his mother to write me out lists. But there are other things; I had to pay more for this chicken because it had been slain in the right way, whatever that may be. I just hope I've not done anything unforgivable.'

'It won't matter, you know. Salka was at school with me, remember, and she ate what the rest of us ate, though I do remember that she wouldn't have custard with her fruit pie if we'd eaten meat,' Val said comfortingly. 'What happened about Cara, anyway? I thought Auntie Sarah advised you to get her to give you a hand?'

'Yes, she did. Well, she is Simon's sister, so you might have thought she'd help me out, but not a bit of it! She said she was going to a charity ball, of all things, and needed time to get ready. And when I hinted that her cook might give me a few tips, she was quite emphatic that *William wouldn't like it*, which is absurd because William's the most generous of men!'

'You know him much better than the rest of us, of course. He's nice, is he? I'll grant you that he's handsome!'

'He's really nice, one of the nicest men you could wish to meet. I can't imagine . . .' Jenny broke off, suddenly conscious that Val was Cara's cousin after all. 'Let's have another look at the bird. I don't want it cooked before they've even arrived!'

'Cara's terribly pretty,' Val said. 'Shall I take the cocktail snacks through into the living-room? The drinks are out on the trolley, aren't they?'

'Yes, we're pretty well organised now. And then we can get our aprons off and tidy ourselves. We might even treat ourselves to a drink whilst we're waiting.'

Both girls were swathed in the dark overalls which the firm provided for Jenny to wear when she was working in the office since, no matter what precautions were taken, oil and grease seemed to appear there from nowhere. Val's was belted neatly round her slim waist, but Jenny's gaped unbecomingly over her bulge, and when they took them off and hung them behind the kitchen door it was possible to see that Jenny, in a green smock dress with a floppy artist's bow at the neck, was heavily pregnant. Val, in a figure-hugging earth-brown dress and jacket with cream collar and cuffs, smiled approvingly at her friend.

'That's a very natty dress, Jen! I'm bringing Curtiss down to Norwich, you know, because he's been staying with his elder sister, and his mother means to remain there over Christmas. You've not met him, but you'll be as impressed with him as he will be with you.'

Curtiss was the latest in a long line of devoted boyfriends. Jenny sometimes wondered if she herself, by marrying Simon, had marred Val's life, but she knew that a marriage between Val and Simon would never have worked: they were too alike. Simon needed someone sober and sensible, someone to make him see the dull side of life, not a sweet, dizzy mayfly like his cousin.

'I like all your boyfriends. Come on. I feel we've earned that drink I mentioned.'

They were in the hallway between the kitchen and the living-room when the front door bell pealed. The two looked at one another.

'It can't be Nick and Simon back with Salka, it's still too early,' Jenny decided. 'Help, suppose it's Cara, having changed her mind? Oh, glory, did I do enough potatoes? I suppose I'd better go down and see.'

'No you don't. You go through and start pouring our drinks. I'll see to the door,' Val said. She had done her hair in a new style, piled up on top of her head in a rich bunch of curls, and looked very sophisticated. Jenny half hoped it would be Cara. It might take her down a peg or two to see Val looking so lovely. Jenny knew that Cara despised her, thought Simon wasted on her. She had once called her a *goy* when she thought Jenny out of earshot, and there had been no doubt from her tone that it was meant as an insult. But though it would be nice to see Cara looking ordinary and even a little dull beside Val, it would not be worth the misery of actually having her to dine!

Standing by the drinks trolley, Jenny heard the door open, then Val's voice, then another, smaller one. Then Val spoke again, her voice louder, amusement in its cadences.

'In that case, you'd better come upstairs and speak to your friend yourself.'

Well, if the word friend had been mentioned, it could not be Cara. Neither could it be Salka, since Salka was Val's friend and had never yet set eyes on Jenny. Curious, Jenny went and stood by the living-room door, watching the stairs. She could not think who her visitor could be!

It was a small girl. She came up the stairs, crossed the hall, and stood, smiling up at Jenny, her rosy face framed in honey-blonde hair. For a moment, Jenny could not think where she had seen that little face before, then she smiled and held out her hands.

'Hello, sweetheart! You're from the Broad Street Orphanage, aren't you? You're the one who's usually last in the crocodile. You often stand and stare at the garages and if I look out we wave!'

'That's right.' The little girl nodded vigorously, her gaze fixed on Jenny's face. She was clutching a small parcel. 'I come to sing you a carol and give you me card. And I made a . . . a *fing*, for your Christmas box.'

'Oh!' Dismay was stronger than pleasure in the exclamation, for Jenny was a generous creature and her

323

fingers immediately itched to give the child a present, but the little girl was absorbed in detaching the card from the small parcel and handing it over. She looked about six or seven and was clad in a thin little grey coat with patched elbows. Her mittens were frayed and much darned and her small black shoes old and cracked. But her face shone with the joy of giving.

Jenny opened the card. It was a brilliantly crayoned picture of the crib scene, with Mary wearing blue, the Babe all white and gold, and the animals a variety of soft browns, greys and orange. It had been roneoed on to the paper so that the children could colour it for themselves. Jenny, opening it, saw the legend *A Happy Christmas* written in wobbly capitals and beneath it, in pencil, *To my frend*. Very much touched, she looked up just as the child started to sing. Clear and true, the small voice soared in the carol that should be sung to every expectant mother at Christmas.

Once in Royal David's city stood a lowly cattle shed,
Where a mother laid her Baby, with a manger for his bed.

Jenny stood quite still, listening. What on earth had possessed the little girl to bring her card and her carol here, to a stranger?

The song finished, the child held out the small, clumsily wrapped Christmas box.

'Here y'are. I made it meself. You can make something for your muvver, or for someone else if you want. I made mine for you.' She watched as Jenny fumbled with the paper. 'Steady on, miss, don't tear it!'

The present was a red tissue-paper rose, lovingly fashioned, with a stalk made by winding green wool round and round a length of wire. Jenny put the flower carefully against the green of her dress, then dropped to her knees and kissed the child's cheek.

'What a beautiful flower. Thank you so much . . . what's your name, dear?'

A triumphant smile lit the small face.

'Same's yours! Rose! That's why I give you the flah!'

Several pennies immediately dropped. So that was why the child so often stared at the lettering on the garage doors. Neyler & Rose! She was Rose, and she had looked up at the flat or across to the office and seen another female and had assumed that this other person must be Rose, as she was. Indeed, assumed rightly, in a way.

'Thank you very much, Rose. I'm having a very special party tonight and I'll wear your flower on my dress. But actually my name's Jenny Rose. What's your second name?'

'My second . . . Oh! I'm Rose Mackay, miss. I fought you was Rose like me, Rose Suffink.'

'No, I'm afraid I'm Jenny, but we still have the same name, don't we?' She turned to the little workbasket which stood just beside the drinks trolley, opened it, and produced a pin with which she attached the rose to her dress. 'There! It couldn't be better! Did you really make it all yourself?'

A glance at Rose's face was sufficient to tell that this was the response she had dreamed of. Her eyes glowed with such pleasure and joy in giving that she made Jenny feel old and soiled and rather wicked.

'Yes, I made every bit meself. Do you really like it?'

'I really do. So much that I'm going to invite you to have something to eat whilst I ring the orphanage. There are peanuts and raisins, salted almonds, crisps . . . and you can have some soda water with orange juice in it for a drink.'

But the thought of being the subject of a telephone call made Rose's joyful look disappear. She clenched her hands tightly and glanced with wild appeal from Jenny to Val.

'Oh, no, miss, they won't like it, they'll send round and fetch me back, I won't never get that sody water! Cou'n't I just drink it up and 'urry back?'

'I'm going to ask the home if you may dine with us. I don't think they'll refuse; they've got a lot of children of their own and won't grudge me a loan of you,' Jenny assured her.

Rose, not at all convinced, sighed and dug her hand into the proffered salted almonds with only moderate enthusiasm.

'Awright,' she said. She glanced round her at the decorations and spoke to Val as Jenny disappeared. 'Cor, ain't it luvly, though? Like Aladdin's cave, ain't it?' She paused for Val to murmur assent and then her curiosity got the better of her. 'Who are you, miss? Are you my friend's sister?'

'Not really, I'm just a friend. Well, your Mrs Rose married my cousin, so that almost makes me a relative, I suppose.' She was about to tell Rose about Simon and Nick and add that she was a Neyler when the door bell rang again. A quick glance at the clock confirmed that it was likely to be Salka. 'Just you sit down, Rose, and eat your nuts. I'll go down to the door!'

Salka got out of the train and stood on the platform, blinking under the bright lights of the station. She glanced round her, but could see no one she knew; indeed, it would have been surprising had she done so, for the station was crammed with people, those who had travelled by the boat train as she had done, and others bound for more prosaic destinations.

She had a small hold-all in which reposed a change of under-clothing, a toothbrush, some toothpaste and a

326

piece of soap. Otto had brought her these things and had supplied the hold-all, but she had scarcely seen him before she left Berlin; it would have been too dangerous. He had come round to the block of flats and they had met in the little, cramped foyer, kissed once, lovingly, and then parted, for how long God alone knew. She had wanted desperately to stay for his sake, but there could be no future for them in Germany, and her mother, Odile and Karl were waiting at the other end of her journey. So she had done as she had been told, she had boarded the train, shown her passport with the big red J across it, got out at frontiers, got in again, until this moment, when she stood in Victoria Station and wondered where Val and this other girl, this Jennifer Rose, were to be found.

'Just stand still, as near the clock as you can get,' Val had said when she had telephoned. 'Don't worry about finding us. We'll find you.'

She was still there five minutes later when she saw two young men watching her. For a moment she went cold with terror. She felt as vulnerable as a bird amongst cats, standing openly on the station platform. No one could have realised how she had skulked, these past months, so that even crossing the street had become an effort, for to cross the street meant that eyes might be upon you, watching you, seeing that you were Jewish and therefore fair game.

They were nice-looking young men, but that meant little, in Berlin. Some of the storm troopers were nice-looking young men; that made it all the more frightening when you saw their faces change, their mouths droop with revulsion. She clasped her hands tightly on the handle of her hold-all. Not here, don't say it's like that here!

'Umm . . . . excuse me . . .'

The fairer of the two was addressing her, and at once she knew who he was. His grin was very like Val's and so was his voice. She smiled, immensely heartened to realise that this was no prying stranger but Nick, Val's beloved twin.

'Mr Nicholas Neyler? I am Salka Brecht.'

He took her hold-all and looked round for the rest of her luggage, seeming to realise that there was none by her demeanour alone, for he did not embarrass her by asking for it.

'How do you do, Miss Brecht? This is my friend and partner, Simon Rose.' The three of them solemnly shook hands, and then Nick took her elbow and began leading her out of the station. 'Val had planned to come to meet you herself, but Simon's wife isn't used to dinner parties, and she felt she needed Val's support.'

'It is quite all right. I saw who you were because you are, in some ways, very like Val.' Nick pulled a face and Salka smiled. 'But she is very pretty, your sister!'

'And you think I am, too? That, Miss Brecht, is no compliment!'

This time, Salka laughed out. What a relief it is, she thought, to be able to afford the luxury of laughing aloud, with a young man's hand on your arm – and how she wished Otto could be here to share it!

'I did not mean you were pretty, Mr Neyler. And please call me Salka; I have heard from my brother and sister, and I'm sure you call them Karl and Odile.'

'We do, actually.' Simon, who had been walking on her right whilst Nick walked on her left, slowed beside a small car. 'Good thing you've not brought all your worldly goods, Salka, or they would have overflowed the boot!'

She was ushered into the front seat, Simon got into the back and Nick climbed into the driving seat. He revved the engine and was about to pull out when he thought of something.

'We'll go through Piccadilly, I think, up Regent Street and along Oxford Street; then Salka will be able to see all the lights and the Christmas trees.'

'The traffic will be awful at this time,' Simon warned him. 'But it's the most direct route, I suppose. And Salka will like to see the lights.'

Although it was chilly, the streets were crowded with shoppers. Salka saw Piccadilly Circus, admired Eros, and gasped at the shops on Regent Street, and then the little car turned into Oxford Street. She had a good opportunity to see the brightly lit windows, indeed, when the traffic lights turned to red and stopped them just as Nick had been about to draw out and pass a bicycle, so that they were in front of the traffic queue.

Simon was beginning to speak when suddenly Salka gasped and clutched Nick's arm. 'What on earth is happening? My God, those poor men! They will all be killed when the lights change to green once more!'

'What ever can the fools be doing?'

Nick peered through the windscreen at a crowd of working men who were marching into the middle of the road and lying down on their backs. Head to toe and eight abreast, they formed a living carpet across the intersection, and even as they watched posters were spread over their recumbent forms. On the pavement women screamed and one girl fainted, keeling over so dramatically that she lurched into the side of a bus before being attended to by a friend. In the small car, Nick, Salka and Simon gazed incredulously at the scene before them.

'What do the posters say?' Nick said, unable to read them properly at such a sharp angle. 'Aha, I think I know! Listen! The NUWM strikes again!'

The lights changed to green unnoticed for not a wheel moved, and Nick wound down his window the better to hear what the men on the roadway were chanting.

'We want work or bread!'

'We want extra relief!'

Salka wound down her window too, but could make little of the raucous voices, for people at the back of the queue, who could not see why the traffic continued to remain stationary even when the lights changed to green, began to hoot their horns and rev their engines.

'What is it that they say, Nicky?'

'They're members of the National Unemployed Workers' Movement – the NUWM,' Nick explained. 'And they say they want work or bread, or extra relief. Fair enough – I hope they get it.'

'I thought they did get extra relief in the winter,' Simon objected from the back seat. 'I read something about it in the paper.'

'Yes, if they're eligible, but the vast majority of the unemployed aren't able to claim it,' Nick said briefly. 'Lord, but this'll snarl up the traffic horribly – aha, here come the police. They'll soon move 'em.'

'Get up, you fellows, you're holding up the traffic,' a burly inspector shouted, to the accompaniment of roars of amusement from the men in the road. As more police arrived, the uniformed men began to drag the recumbent NUWM members out of the roadway and on to the pavement, but as soon as they were left so that the police could pull someone else clear, they went back and lay down again.

The burly inspector turned to the crowds who were now watching.

'Come on, fellers, lend us an 'and,' he shouted, but no one stirred. Even those motorists being held up had no desire to get out and move the protesters.

'What will happen to them?' Salka whispered fearfully, as it became evident that the men in the roadway would not move and the police began to grow impatient with them. 'Surely they will be harshly dealt with when they get them into their power?'

'Happen? Why, nothing. This isn't Nazi Germany,' Nick said cheerfully, distressed by her pallor and the darkness of her eyes. 'Anyone can peacefully demonstrate, and that's all they're doing. You watch, and presently you'll see them begin to get up and go off home. No one'll try to stop them.'

'She won't watch for long, because once they go we can move,' Simon said. 'I hope to God Jenny isn't worried out of her mind.'

'Move? That's comic, old lad – we shan't get clear of this little lot for an hour or more. In fact, if you're worried, you might do better to walk. Think what's happening behind us, with traffic held up for miles and queueing across the lights and all sorts. See, they're moving, getting up from the road, but we shan't go just yet!'

That was how Simon came to be knocking on his own front door with Salka beside him, both rosy from the walk and amused by their predicament.

'Sorry I didn't use the key, but I didn't bother to take it out with me. I thought we'd be using Nick's, and his, of course is on the ring with the ignition key,' he said as Jenny kissed him at the top of the stairs. Val and Salka, their arms round each other, came up behind them. 'Honestly, poor Nick's still in Oxford Street and likely to remain there! Salka's first experience of England, and it has to be a protest which is causing a mammoth traffic jam!'

'It was a wonderful experience,' Salka said, slipping

331

out of the dark cloak which had been her friend for so long. 'Unbelievable, Val, to see policemen *ask* men to get up from the roadway, without anything terrible happening. It has done more to make me feel easy here than anything else could.'

Jenny took her cloak and kissed her warmly.

'Welcome, Salka, my dear! I've only just put the phone down, so my guest doesn't yet know she *is* a guest. Val, perhaps you could explain to Salka about Rose whilst I put Simon in the picture, and then I think we ought to eat, even if we have to put Nick's share in the oven to keep warm, because that chicken is done to a turn.'

'Of course. Come with me, Salka.' Val and Salka left the Roses, and Jenny turned to Simon and took his hand.

'Look, a little girl came round. She brought me a Christmas present she'd made herself. She's from the orphanage; I often wave to her. I felt awful, Simon, because there was nothing I could give her, so I asked her to dinner. Is that all right?'

'Of course it is, you cuddly, delicious little fatty,' Simon said, hugging her and planting a kiss on her soft, unprepared mouth. 'I'm so hungry I could eat you right here and now. What's the kid's name?'

'Rose. That's what attracted her to the place and to me. She thought my name was Rose too – well, it is, of course, but she thought it was my first name. Anyway, I rang Matron and got her permission for Rose to stay here to dine. I said we'd run her home later, and I promised her we'd bring some sweets for the other kids. It-it's an odd set-up, Simon.'

She had rung the matron as she had said, and had been a little shocked to discover that Rose's absence had not even been noticed. It was strange, the way the child had just come out of the blue, strange and rather disturbing. A happy child does not make presents for an unknown face at a window, learn a carol for someone who simply happens to bear the same name, and leave her home and her playfellows on the first day of her Christmas holidays (Jenny had learned all this from the matron in the course of the telephone conversation) when there is an Entertainment planned, and all the children had been promised jelly for their tea.

'Well, I've asked her to stay to dinner with us,' Jenny said when the matron had explained how they managed not to miss Rose. 'We'll deliver her safely back to you in the car about nine o'clock. She seems a dear little girl and I'm sure she'll be no trouble. In fact, I'd like to see more of her, if that's all right by you.'

There was an incredulous silence at the other end of the phone before Matron, in a slightly cautious voice, revealed that Rose MacKay, though a pretty-enough child, was a limb of Satan and by no means an ideal orphan.

'She hasn't always been an orphan, that's the trouble,' Matron said as though, by definition, children who had always been orphans were always good. 'Discontented, she is. Always running off after that mother of hers, and if the mother had wanted her why leave her in the first place? Went off with a man, I believe, and left the child with the landlady. Be no good to Rose if she did find her, but you can't convince a seven-year-old of that.'

'No. Well, I don't think she'll run away from me,' Jenny said briskly. 'I'd like to bring something nice for the other kiddies when I bring her back; can you suggest something suitable?'

'There's thirty of 'em,' the matron said doubtfully, but her voice sounded warmer. 'They're fond of sweeties, very fond, and few enough they get, for try how we may the money won't stretch to luxuries of that sort. A few sweeties would give everyone a thrill.'

'Fine. I'll get some and pop in with them, if I may, when I bring Rose back at nine.'

Telling Simon all this, she led him through into the living-room, introduced him to Rose, and returned to the kitchen to begin serving up the meal. Salka and Val joined her there presently, both eager to assist, so that when she popped her head round the living-room door ten minutes later, it was with the news that dinner was on the table.

Simon was making Rose a rabbit out of his pocket handkerchief. Rose was standing very close, leaning against his knees, totally absorbed by the miracle of manufacture which was happening before her eyes. She glanced up as Jenny entered and smiled, but her attention immediately returned to the rabbit. Jenny thought that Simon had all his father's charm for children, and congratulated herself on choosing a good father for her own child. If he could so happily settle down to amuse an unknown little girl, how much better he would be with his own flesh and blood!

'Dinner?' Simon stood up, thrust the rabbit into his pocket, and held out a hand to Rose. 'Come along, Miss MacKay. Let's see which of us is really the hungriest!'

'I bet I am,' Rose boasted. 'I bet I could eat the whole of that chicken what Mrs Rose 'as cooked.'

'You won't, because Mrs Rose has made some lovely soup first, and when you've eaten your share of that you won't have room left in your little tiny tummy for much else.' Simon patted his own midriff. 'But I, being so much larger, will have plenty of space! Wait and see!'

'And when we've eaten, Mr Rose will go down to the corner shop for me and buy me some sweeties for all the children at Broad Street,' Jenny said cheerfully, leading the way into the dining-room. 'Perhaps you could go with him, Rose, and help him choose!'

'Blimey, that I could,' Rose said, staring with all her might at the dining-table. 'Cor! All them knives and forks and fings!'

'And flowers,' Simon reminded her. 'Nearly as pretty as the one you made for my wife.'

Rose beamed and stood behind the chair that Jenny indicated.

'That's right. I made it all meself!'

It was a good meal, rendered even more enjoyable by Rose's obvious delight in every mouthful, which made it easier for Salka not to feel greedy as she rejoiced in the good food. She had been hungry for months, it seemed, and had been forced, once her mother and Odile and Karl had left, to subsist on as little as possible, for she was deathly afraid to go shopping in Berlin alone.

As soon as the meal was over, she offered to wash and wipe up and make herself useful, but Jenny assured her that though she certainly would not prevent her from helping there would be no question of her doing it alone.

'I'll wash, you may wipe, Salka, and we'll let Val put away,' she said. 'Simon, if you and Rose could go down and get those sweets, I'd be very thankful; my money's in my purse.'

'Don't be silly, sweetheart. I'm going to pay for the cushies,' Simon assured her, putting on a Norfolk accent. 'There in't nothing like a foo cushies to make a feller happy!'

Rose pricked up her ears.

'You sound like someone I knew, once. Can I come to choose them sweets?'

'Of course,' Simon went out and fetched her coat. 'I say, this has seen better days, young lady – will you be warm enough?'

'Yeah, it's what I always wear,' Rose said laconically. Nick, who had managed to join them in time for the main course, frowned down at her.

'Here, borrow this.' He wound a huge, striped scarf round her neck and offered her a vast pair of driving gloves, which promptly fell off, making her give a squeaky giggle.

'Gawd, mister, they're huge,' she announced. 'I'm better off wiv me mittings.'

'Perhaps you're right.' Nick took his gloves back, patted her head and held open the door for the pair of them. Simon, winking, put Rose's hand into the crook of his arm.

'Shan't be long, Nick! Come along, Rosie, step out!'

'They don't believe me muvver will ever come back,' Rose announced, as she and Simon, having selected their booty, returned the way they had come. 'Them others, they've been orphans always, or elst they 'as real muvvers what come to see 'em. But they've got it all wrong. My muvver didn't run off like Matron says. Aunt Elsie sent her away, so she don't even know I bin sent to Broad Street.'

'Sent her away? How? Had she done something wrong, perhaps?'

'Nah!' Rose said scornfully. 'She was in 'er bedroom, Mum was – I asks you, what's wrong wiv that? – and Aunt was out at work, only she come back early, and up the stairs she runs, two at a time, and in she bursts, into me mum's room. I was in the kitchen playing wiv one of them monkeys on a stick that the feller had brought me, see, and I watched through the doorway. So Aunt

336

bursts in and starts to shriek like a mad thing, and me mum run out and so did the feller, both shoutin' that Aunt was makin' a big mistake. The feller, he had red hair and a scritched-up sorta face, and Aunt went at 'em both wiv a broom, and then she grabbed a knife, and they run out of the house – well, wou'n't you, like? – and they never 'ad time to take me wiv 'em.'

'Good lord,' Simon said mildly. 'And then what happened?'

'Oh, after about a week or two Aunt took me round to Broad Street, said she'd been landed. It seems I wasn't 'er relative at all, she was just a friend to me mum. Acourse, I knew she can't have told me mum where I was, else I'd 'a been fetched by now.'

'Well, I wouldn't be too sure of that,' Simon said. 'I'm sure when your mother comes back that woman will tell her what she's done with you. It stands to reason; otherwise your mother would accuse her of all sorts of things.'

'Ho, yes, so you might think,' Rose said. 'But I run away, back to me old 'ouse, a few months after I got sent to Broad Street. And there was new people in the old place what didn't know me or me muvver – they said as 'ow Aunt 'ad gone as soon as she got rid o' me. Moonlighted, like as not.'

'Well, even so, the orphanage will have advertised and so on,' Simon said soothingly. 'And the police stations and other places will have your name. I'm sure your mother's only got to ask.'

'Is that so?' Rose said, agreeably surprised. 'I 'opes they use me old name, the one Mum used – me name's Hazel wiv a haitch, only they've got an 'azel in Broad Street already, so they calls me Rose. Why didn't they tell me in Broad Street about the police? It would 'ave saved me no end of trouble. 'Cos she'll come back, I know she will.'

337

'Of course she will. Here, can you fish my doorkey out of my pocket and unlock for me? I don't want to get Jen trailing down all those stairs again.'

'It is wonderful that you have brought me here, and I will do everything I can to take good care of Jenny's baby when it is born,' Salka said, as they sat round the fire later that evening whilst Rose, squatting on the hearth rug, toasted a shovelful of chestnuts in the embers. 'Naturally, I long to see Mutti and Odile and Karl, but most of all I hope to see again my father. He is very strong man with great courage, so I hope that we shall see him before too long.'

'I'm sure you will.' Val patted Salka's hand. 'Your father was so good to me, Salka; as soon as we can do something we will. Besides praying, which we do all the time. After all, they can't hold him in prison for ever for doing nothing.'

'Can they not? I hope you're right.'

Salka thought of Otto, and of his promise that he would do his best to get her father out. She wished most fervently that he had promised to get himself out too, but it seemed he could not do that. It would, he had said, make too much trouble for his family, and anyway, whatever he might think of Herr Hitler and his Third Reich, he was a German and he loved his country as much as he hated its present governors.

' 'Oo wants anuvver nut?' Rose, oblivious of tensions, lifted a flushed face from the warmth of the fire and offered Salka a chestnut burned black on the outside but done to a turn within. 'Take some salt, miss!'

'Thank you.' Salka took a nut and began to peel off the blackened shell. Jenny, watching her, sat up suddenly, making Simon groan since she was sitting on the arm of his chair, leaning heavily against him.

'Salka, I meant to ask you to tell me if I give you food that isn't what you should have! Don't hesitate, my dear. Simon's got very careless about *kosher* food, but I don't want to make you uncomfortable.'

'You won't. We were not strict about the dietary laws,' Salka said. 'Only about meat, really – we ate no pork or shellfish.'

'Can't you eat pork?' Rose interrupted, gazing at Salka. 'Does it give you belly-gripes?'

There was a universal chuckle at this, but Val, taking pity on Rose, gave her the answer.

'No, it isn't that, Rose. Salka doesn't eat pork for religious reasons, and there are some other foods that she shouldn't eat, either. Mr Rose is the same, he won't eat pork.'

'Well, is that so?' Rose stared curiously from Simon to Salka and back again. 'Me muvver, when she was a gal, 'ad a feller like that.'

'A Jew? Well, I suppose it's quite possible. The east end's full of 'em,' Simon remarked, but Rose shook her head.

'Nah, not rahnd 'ere! Me mum came from Norwich.'

'In Norwich? A Jewish fellow in Norwich? Whereabouts? What was his name, Rose?'

The questions came from several throats but Rose could only shake her head.

'I dunno, me mum never said. Only said she used to like 'im, but was glad she 'adn't never married 'im. Too fussy by 'alf, she used to say.' She paused, to unpeel her own nut. 'I fink that feller was me farver,' she finished nonchalantly.

Only half understanding, Salka wondered at the silence which followed this innocent remark. It was a remarkably alert silence, almost a listening silence. But before she, or Rose, had time to comment, Nick jumped in with some joke or other and everyone was at ease again, talking, laughing, opening the hot chestnuts.

The moment had passed.

'Well darling, how did you think it went? Salka's nice, isn't she? And that little Rose MacKay is a regular poppet. I've told Matron we'd like to see a bit more of her when we get back from Norwich after Christmas.' In the warm darkness, Jenny moved uneasily against Simon's back. 'Wasn't it odd, her mother actually coming from there? And that bit about her father – I daresay Jewish lads are as apt to blot their copybook as any, but it was strange, wasn't it?'

'Bloody strange. I daresay it wasn't only me who racked his brains at that point. I bet Val and Nick did a bit of wondering too. They know the Congregation very nearly as well as I do. How old's the child, did you say? Seven? Well, that puts the hanky-panky around thirty-one; I wonder what my papa was up to then? No, that's no good, he was in Australia. Well, that leaves the field open for the rest of 'em – all those righteous Shul-goers!'

'Mr Rose was at home in 'thirty-one, actually,' Jenny said out of the darkness. 'Wasn't that the year your grandfather died? Mr Rose was home for a couple of months then.'

'By all that's wonderful, you're right! Mind you, she's very blonde to be one of my Papa's byblows. She looks more like a Neyler! You don't suppose that Des pretended to be one of us just by way of disguise, do you?'

Jenny stifled a giggle against his back.

'Fool! What about that thin, gangly chap with glasses and frizzy pale hair. What's his name? Daniel Streissman, what about him?'

'In 1931? He doesn't have a lot of charm now, but *then*

he was an awful weed. I doubt his ability to father a child! He was about seventeen then, I suppose, so it could have been him, but . . . well, the mind does rather boggle.' He turned over and pulled her into his arms, pushing his head up under her hair so that he could blow on the side of her neck and into her ear, a prelude, as Jenny well know, to lovemaking. 'I'll give it some thought when I've a moment. A good thing I was a mere child at the time or you'd be looking suspiciously at me!'

'True. Hey, be careful, love.' She shifted clumsily as his knee nudged against her. 'Mind you, child though you were, you did have a girlfriend in 'thirty-one; remember who is was?'

'Of course I do. Georgina Thingamebob. Marvellous skier, that's what attracted me to her.' He chuckled against his wife's soft flesh. 'That and a couple more things.'

'Not Georgina; she was later. Little Patsy or whatever her name was. James brought her over to The Pride from Blofield. She was blonde, and fast, too, by the look of her. She looked stunning in her little white tennis skirt and she didn't half know it. Remember her?'

'Oh, yes. Pixie, not Patsy. But she was only a babe, darling, about thirteen or something. Nice kid. And *now*, Mrs Rose . . .'

Christmas was a great success for Salka and her family, though they could never be really happy whilst Herr Brecht was in the German concentration camp.

'But they will have to release him,' Frau Brecht said with fierce conviction, as though her belief alone was enough to free her husband. 'How can they continue to hold an innocent man?'

Salka knew that Frau Brecht was finding exile much

harder than her children. She spoke no English and, though she tried very hard, it was not easy to learn a language for the first time when you were fifty. She loved going to Shul and could get by there with Yiddish, but Tina had forgotten most of her Yiddish and consequently the two women tended to spend long hours in silence, waiting for Val to come home to translate for them. Karl was at school and doing quite well – he had friends and his English was excellent – and Odile, living with Cecy and working in the Solstein & Neyler offices, was perhaps happiest of all, for she felt she had a purpose in life with a proper job and proper wages.

'Odile is paying Karl's school fees,' Frau Brecht told Salka almost tearfully. 'She's so good, such a comfort! But I am not even a very good worker any more. I've never done so little in my life. I feel that kind Tina is paying me for nothing, giving me and Karl a home out of . . . well, out of charity.'

'Nonsense, Mama. Besides, later, you'll learn to speak English and will be a real help to Mrs Neyler. And once Papa joins us . . .'

'Ah, then it will all be different,' Frau Brecht admitted, smiling. Now, *Liebchen*, tell us how you got out.'

'There were several moments when I thought I wouldn't be allowed to go,' Salka admitted. 'There was talk of the Jewish debt to society which must be paid off by all able-bodied Jews, just as if the Reich had not already ruined us. But then I got a notice to appear before the councillors at the Rathaus, and I asked Dr Spanda how best to conduct myself. I took his advice, which was to make up my face very white, and to draw dark smudges beneath my eyes. Stand hunched up, keep shivering and cough a lot, he said, and that's what

I did. They insisted on a medical examination, but again I was fortunate in that Dr Spanda did it for me. He wrote me down as being of a tubercular tendency, he told me, and that decided them that I was better out of the country. I got my passport the next day.'

'Was it like ours, with a big red J stamped across it, so that everyone might despise us? The memory of it all disgusts and terrifies me. I feel I'll never be safe from that malice.'

'I know. I try not to let myself think about it, except to remind myself that I'm lucky just to be alive, and free.'

'Well, we're here, and together, but for Papa. And we must all pray very hard indeed. Surely God wouldn't save me, yet allow my dear Heinrich to be sacrificed?'

'Hasn't it been a lovely Christmas, Simon?'

Jenny, cuddled down in their own bed once again, squeezed close.

'Good enough. Though I don't know how Martin stands it. The day with your mother was pretty tough.'

'She's been difficult since Father died. But it wasn't even a whole day. We left right after lunch, and the rest of the holiday was bliss, wasn't it?'

Simon thought of the big, comfortable Ipswich Road house, the way Sebastian had driven him mad by pretending to be a car roaring through the house in first gear and how Cara's step-daughter had fallen downstairs and twisted her ankle, making life hideous, first with her howls, and then with her constant demands to be piggy-backed everywhere. Yet despite it all, they had had a marvellous time.

'Yes, love, it was bliss. And you've got over the myth that Jewish people don't celebrate Christmas, I hope?'

Aunt Cecy's party had been, if anything, more fun than Aunt Tina's.

'Yes, I have – you get the best of both worlds, don't you? But I thought you were quieter than usual. Is it the responsibility of expecting a baby? Poor darling, does it weigh on you?'

'Heavily. It wasn't that, though. Jenny, I know it may come as a bit of a shock to you, but I want to join a flying club.'

'Oh, Simon, no!' Jenny sat bolt upright in bed and clicked the bedside light on, staring down at Simon. 'Why can't you join the ADGB, like Nick?'

'Idiot, I want to join the RAF when the war comes, not the army. You know that!'

'Yes, I know, but . . . why not wait until the war? Don't forget, it may never come, and then I'll have had all the awful worry of you being up in the air for nothing. Honestly, Sime, if you want to join the RAF if there's a war I wouldn't dream of trying to stop you, but now, in peacetime, I can't bear it! You're thinking of Salka and all she's been through, but that may be just a temporary madness. Don't do it, love, not now, when I'm edgy anyway, because of the baby. Think of last September, the war that never was!'

'I keep thinking of last September, that's the trouble. We handed the Czechs over bound and gagged, Jen. We let Hitler threaten and hustle us into believing we'd win world peace if we'd just let him go a little further, but it was the thin edge of the wedge. First we let the Austrian Anschluss happen, because the Austrian regime was corrupt and Austrians are almost Germans anyway, then we let Chamberlain tell us that it was madness to fight a war because of a quarrel in a far-away country between people of whom we knew nothing. But we *did* know something: we knew the Nazis were the aggressors and that the Czechs had our word that we wouldn't let them be overrun. All bullies are the same, you know; the more you back away the fiercer they get. We're making a monster and some day we're going to have to face up to what we've created. When we do, Jen, I want to be prepared to fight for my country, my wife and my baby. So I must learn to fly now!'

'All right, then. I know I can't stop you, but I hate the idea.' Jenny clicked off the light and lay down again. 'Now shut up and let me get some sleep.'

Simon put his arms round her and kissed the back of her neck, then settled down to try and sleep himself. But he hated the fact that they had quarrelled, a thing they did rarely. Had it really been about his learning to fly, or had she sensed his desperate uneasiness? Did she wonder, as he had been wondering, whether Rose MacKay could by any awful chance be his child? He had never known a girl called MacKay, but girls did take other names when they got into trouble, and he could not help remembering that he and Pixie, young though they were, had got up to some rather adult games. And she had gone away to London, though it seemed incredible that something as important as a baby could have resulted from the inexpert embraces of two children – for he and Pixie had been little more. Ever since she had mentioned a father in Norwich, though, he had been haunted by a fleeting resemblance. Rose was rather like Pixie, or was it just his guilty conscience? Or perhaps all blonde good-time girls were a little like Pixie, and Rose's mother, if she turned up tomorrow, might prove to have a slight likeness to his one-time inamorata too.

It occurred to him as he was on the very brink of sleep that Rose had said her real name was Hazel, which would make her Hazel Rose. His heart gave such a jerk at that that he was afraid Jenny would feel it, but she was asleep, snoring a tiny bit, and he tried to relax once more. That did not explain the MacKay – why call herself MacKay?

On the other hand, Hazel Hopwood had a certain naturalness, a swing to it. Oh God, suppose she was his child, then it followed that he should make every effort to trace her mother. Only, if he did so and found her, what a rich tapestry of complication, misunderstanding and pain would result!

He turned over in bed and Jenny sighed and turned over too, snuggling close. His heart contracted with love for her. Dear, *good* Jenny, who was prepared to love him knowing his faults, who had happily given Salka a home and a job, who was willing to spread the mantle of her loving kindness over a little orphaned girl – would fate hurt Jenny so? Of course not!

Illogically comforted, Simon slept at last.

Chapter Fourteen

The baby was born on the second of February, and
named Marianne. Simon took Jenny into hospital and
stayed with her until they turned him out because the
birth was imminent, and then he went out with Nick, in
an agony of worry and fear, and got so drunk that, on
his return to the hospital to see his wife and daughter,
the matron refused to allow him to so much as peep at
them.

'Take Father away, Mr Neyler, and make him drink
strong coffee,' she advised frostily. 'We can't allow him
to upset our patients.'

'U-ups-s-s the pa-pa-pash-sh-sh . . .' Simon howled,
outraged. 'I won' upsh-sh-sh-sh . . . Where's my
Jenje . . .'

'Come along, sir, you'll feel much more the thing
after that 'ot coffee,' the porter advised, taking Simon's
arm. He winked at Nick. 'Gotta car, sir? No? Then I'll
hail you a cab.'

The cab journey back to the flat was no picnic, with
Simon alternately maudlin because he was a father and
furious because he had not yet been able to see his
offspring. When they arrived, the cabby very decently
helped to get Simon, who seemed to the harassed Nick
to have suddenly developed legs made of spaghetti and
as many arms as an octopus, up the stairs and into the
living-room.

'Sit down, Simon,' Salka said, pushing him into a
chair. 'I'll make some coffee.'

'Gimme a drink,' Simon mumbled. 'All's I nee's a hair of dog, then I'll be ri's rain!'

'Yes, all right, but drink the coffee first.'

Simon drank the coffee and promptly threw up all over the hearthrug. Salka, casting a despairing glance at the ceiling, got down to clearing up whilst Nick, who had been obliged to take a drink or two himself, giggled and got Simon through to the bathroom by easy stages so that he might divest his cousin of his sticky and digusting clothes and put him to bed.

Fortunately, Simon's aggressive period seemed to be over, but he was still difficult to handle, being at once floppy and slithery, as Nick described it to himself. Finally, he was forced to apply to Salka for assistance and she lugged Simon's outer clothes off whilst Nick kept his cousin more or less upright.

They had just bundled him into bed, where he began to snore in almost musical comedy style, when the door bell rang. Salka, hot and cross, with coffee stains all over her grey wool dress and a red bump on her forehead where Simon's flailing hand had caught her, ran downstairs, muttering in German so that Nick should not understand her. Of all the madmen, Simon Rose had to be the worst – what a way to celebrate the arrival of your first-born!

Salka opened the front door and raised her brows at the boy standing on the doorstep. He looked vaguely official, but she was learning to subdue her fear of officialdom here, where they all seemed to act pleasantly towards her. Anyway he was very young, with fair hair flopping over his pimply face.

'Yes?'

'Telegram for Brett, miss.'

Salka was used to hearing her name anglicised, but her heart did a heavy thump. She held out her hand.

'That's me. Thank you.'

She took the little yellow envelope, then hesitated. One should tip the boy, she supposed; she had seen Simon's stepfather do so at Christmas when he had received a greetings telegram. But the boy was just standing there, and she had no money. She looked at him, puzzled.

'Is there an answer, miss?'

'Oh! I d-don't know. Wait.'

She turned and ran up the stairs, tearing open the envelope as she did so and spreading out the thin sheet. For a moment, the words danced before her eyes, then she steadied herself and read them deliberately. *Herr Brecht released as soon as guarantor found*, she read. *Please arrange stop Letter follows. Otto.*

She was still standing there when Nick, hearing the telegram boy whistling impatiently at the foot of the stairs, came out of Simon's bedroom. He took in the situation at a glance, though he misread it.

'Salka? Not bad news? Lor', doesn't everything happen at once; look, I'll deal with the boy for you.'

Salka dragged herself out of the daze she was in and thrust the telegram into Nick's hand.

'Not bad news, wonderful news!' She sighed tremulously. 'Oh, Nick, isn't it the best thing ever?'

'It is indeed. You must send a reply, though, love. Quick, get a pencil and a piece of paper and you can dictate whilst I write it down.'

'Yes, but what can I say?'

'It's simple – *Guarantor found, writing. Salka.*'

'Oh, but I've not found a guarantor, Nick, and it isn't so simple, not now; there's money needed, and lots of forms to fill in, and Mother said she's been trying to get someone interested but the responsibility is too much for ordinary people and important people don't want to get involved, especially since there's been so much in the papers about refugees taking jobs that the English need for themselves.'

'Look, you don't think we'd let your father stay in that place one day longer than he need, do you? Simon and I will guarantee everything necessary – and Jenny, of course.' He handed over the piece of paper. 'That all right?'

'Oh, Nick!'

'Don't cry, idiot, just take this down to the boy. Oh, and give him a couple of bob, he's brought good news.'

'A couple: I giff him all I havv!' Salka's English was deserting her. Happiness seemed almost too much, as though to allow oneself to hope was asking for trouble. She fished in her purse, found five shillings, and took the piece of paper.

'I can't thank you properly, Nick, but you know what is in my heart.'

Nick grinned.

'I know. A baby daughter and a father all in one day! This household is lucky just to be near. After this I wouldn't be surprised if Simon doesn't even have a hangover tomorrow!'

The corridor was long and the counters at the end menacing in their impersonal efficiency but Jenny, halfway at last, longed for nothing more than that they might reach them. The queue of patient, shuffling people was so sad and their errand so urgent, for this was where they would answer the questions and fill in the forms which would result in Herr Brecht's release.

After that, if all went well, if the Bethdin backed their application and the Hebrew Immigrant Aid society took over, then it would not be long before Herr Brecht was with his wife and family.

'You're all right, aren't you, Jenny? I feel so guilty, with poor Marianne scarcely two weeks old and you having to stand here. But we are getting nearer the front! The only thing that worries me is when they close. It's getting awfully late and I know you'll have to go at six to feed Marianne.'

'No I shan't. Marianne can go hungry for once. Oh, Salka, *don't* worry, I won't run out on you!' Jenny squeezed her friend's hand and Salka sighed convulsively. 'After all, if we stay here now, and are seen, then we shan't have the worry of returning tomorrow.'

A man in front of them, who had obviously been listening to their conversation, turned round. He wore spectacles so thick that his eyes looked bigger than dried peas and he was so dark that his chin was blue with bristles, but he smiled at them, though his unprepossessing countenance was drawn with worry.

'I cannot help to overhear – they close at eight, *Mädchen*. We will be seen today unless we are very unlucky. The others will come back when the bureau opens tomorrow at nine. By the time the clerks arrive the queue will already be a long one, because people come early, at dawn, to wait. We wait for something worth waiting for, eh?'

Salka nodded wordlessly and Jenny answered for her.

'Yes, I suppose everyone feels that; a last chance to get a loved one out. Are all the people here waiting to get relatives out of concentration camps?'

'This young lady has a relative in a camp?' The man's face, at Salka's nod, became so full of pity and love that ugliness fled, and for a startled moment Jenny saw that he was beautiful, with a beauty of soul that transcended the thick lips, the little eyes, the heavy, blue-jowled face. Then he was ushering them in front of him, gently

351

but firmly. 'Go before me; those who wait for prisoners must go first.'

'Oh, but . . . it's my father,' Salka whispered, allowing herself to be moved forward. 'You're so good. I hope you'll be lucky, too.'

'My brother will come, now that I've found a guarantor.' He patted the arm of the woman with him, a skinny, big-nosed woman in a vivid peacock-blue coat and hat. 'We help each other, eh?'

'You're both very good,' Salka was beginning, when a little fat woman ahead of them turned towards her.

'Your father is in a camp? Forward, *bubeleh*. I can wait my turn for one little moment longer.'

It happened right up the line. The whispered word that the young lady had a father in a camp was sufficient to see them passed along like parcels until they were both in tears and almost at the front of the queue. Jenny looked into the faces and read the urgency of their longing to see their loved ones safe, knew that by giving up their places they might delay their applications by a whole day, and could also see that they did this willingly for one of their own less fortunate, even, than they.

The clerks at the counter were talking in low voices to the men and women seated opposite them and the few people now ahead of them turned and told the girls that they, too, were waiting to apply for the release of prisoners. It was very quiet. Everyone was concentrating now on what he must say when he reached the counter.

Life or death, Jenny found herself thinking. I didn't even realise it, but we're patiently queuing for a man's life. It made the wait seem nothing.

'Phew!' Jenny and Salka emerged into darkness, though

352

the street lights were bright enough. 'That was quite an ordeal, Salka, but we won! It won't be long now before Herr Brecht is back with you again.'

'I hope you're right.' Salka tucked her arm into Jenny's. 'Shall we get a taxi? You have waited so long, and you shouldn't have to stand about like that. Thank heaven for the chairs once we reached the counter. I was so frightened that you might faint!'

'Nonsense. I'm made of tougher stuff than that! But I think perhaps you're right and we ought to get a cab.' She stepped off the pavement as she spoke and flourished a hand at an approaching taxi. 'Good. We'll be home in no time at all now. And we'll have good news for the boys, too. They both felt awfully guilty that they couldn't come with you in my place, but it was just impossible today; they were both committed far too heavily. Still, we did the thing!'

In the taxi, however, Salka voiced feelings which she had not admitted until the afternoon.

'Jenny, I'm worried. I hadn't thought until those wonderful people made me do so, but why are the Nazis releasing Papa?'

'Because he's no more use to them. He'd had his property confiscated and all his money taken, and I think we agreed that Otto must have paid to have him released. Otherwise, he's just another mouth to feed. Don't you think?'

'I did,' Salka said slowly. 'Yes, that was what I thought. But . . . that wasn't what they thought, the people in the queue. And even the clerks on the desk gave me the same sort of look.' She closed her own eyes tightly, then opened them so wide that Jenny could see the milky white all around the dark irises. 'He's younger than my mother, you know. He's not yet fifty, and as strong as strong, though he's not very big or tall.

I heard talk before I left of making Jews labour on the roads and in the mines, menial tasks. The inference was that the hard work without hope of an end or any sort of break would finish them off. Why, then, should they free Papa?'

Jenny shrugged helplessly. She, too, had read the depths of compassion in the eyes of those who waited, a compassion greater, surely, than the release of a healthy man warranted?

'I can't answer you, Salka. We'll simply have to wait and see.'

They knew why Herr Brecht had been released as soon as the train carrying him drew in at Victoria. He was on a Red Cross stretcher, and Jenny could tell by Salka's expression that had there not been a piece of paper pinned to the blanket with his name and the Bloomsbury address printed on it she would not have recognised him.

He was unconscious, an emaciated, white-haired old man who could have been eighty, his face seamed and yellow against the grey of pillow and blanket.

'No, you can't take 'im 'ome, miss,' the official said when they approached him. 'He's got to go straight to 'orspital. For a check-up,' he added hastily, as Salka's face crumpled. 'Only a check-up – probably he's just been a bit sickly like on the crossing.'

'A bit . . . my father is forty-nine years old,' Salka said fiercely, looking down into the weary, tormented face. 'How old did you think he was, sir?'

'Forty-nine? I never would've credited it, but, well, miss, he's come from one of those terrible places . . .' He patted her shoulder awkwardly. 'Look, you get back 'ome, have yourself a hot cuppa, and then go straight round to the 'orspital. They can tell you better than I can

354

what's wrong.' He glanced appealingly at Jenny. 'You tell 'er, miss, no point in worrying till you know what to worry about!'

'It's true enough, Salka.' Jenny took her friend's arm. 'We'll catch a bus, then we shan't be home too soon, have that cup of tea, and then bus back to the hospital.' She had been given a printed card with the address of the hospital on it and now she glanced down at it. 'It isn't too far. It won't take us long.'

Back at the flat she made the tea and pushed Salka into a chair. All around them, the flat sang of the happiness Salka had felt earlier that day. A big notice, scarlet lettering on a silver ground, proclaimed: 'Welcome, Papa!' and Jenny's spare room had been made up by Salka, at her own expense, into a bedsitting room, with a wireless set, flowers in a bowl, fruit in a dish and a biscuit barrel full of chocolate biscuits.

'They won't have given him chocolate biscuits in one of those awful places,' she had said blithely to Jenny as she filled the barrel. 'And he's always had a sweet tooth.'

Now, their illusions shattered, they could only sit and sip their tea and avoid each other's eyes. When, presently, Nick and Simon came thundering up the stairs to see their visitor, Salka found herself unable to explain and Jenny, red-eyed, drew them out of the living-room and into the kitchen.

'He's desperately ill, that's why they released him. He's gone straight to hospital.'

'Poor Salka. Where's Mari?' Simon asked, glancing round the kitchen. Jenny's hand fled to her mouth.

'My God, what an awful mother I am! Mrs Blitnell offered to have her. I suppose I ought to go and fetch her back, though we're off to the hospital as soon as we've drunk our tea.'

Simon, however, shook his head.

'No, Jenny. It won't do any good to arrive there too early, whilst they still sorting out the admissions and settling people in. Just you leave it until about three o'clock this afternoon, when they've got time to tell you what's happening. I'll go and tell Salka whilst you fetch Mari.'

'But, Simon, Salka's so worried. I think she'll go mad if she has to wait so long.'

Simon shook his head.

'No, she won't, she's a sensible kid. I'll explain carefully to her that one way to irritate the hospital staff is to turn up before they're ready and ask a lot of questions, and so on. And I'll point out that Marianne has to be fed and watered, and so do Nick and I. I know she'll realise that we could wait, but she'll see the point of all this, you see.'

She did. When Jenny returned with the baby in her carry-cot, Salka was composed and smiling once more, though she was still very pale.

'I'm sorry, Jenny. Simon is quite right. Now, what can I do towards lunch?'

'The sister says you can see him now.' Salka came out of the small room where her father lay and spoke softly to Jenny. 'Only one at a time, you understand, because more than that tires him.'

'All right, but what about the language?' Jenny spoke no German and realised that she had no idea whether Herr Brecht spoke English.

'Papa speaks very good English, don't worry. He's very weak, because he did a lot of talking yesterday, telling Mother what he wished us to do, giving her addresses and so on. But he wants to thank you for all you've done.'

356

It was not quite a week since Herr Brecht had arrived in the hospital, and though he had eaten what he could and taken quantities of milk and other liquids, the doctor had been quite certain that he was dying.

'The body can only stand so much abuse,' he had explained to the two girls the first afternoon. 'Vital organs have been maltreated, and we cannot undo the harm that has been done. But he seems to be content.'

So now, tiptoeing into the room, Jenny knew that the first time she saw Herr Brecht conscious would probably also be the last. What time he had left he would need for his wife and children. She went and stood by the bed, smiling down into the weary eyes.

'Good afternoon, Herr Brecht. How are you?'

He smiled at her. He had an extraordinary impish smile. It seemed to light up his whole face, and when it did so Jenny caught a glimpse of the Herr Brecht that Salka had waited for, the fit and capable man.

'I am not so bad, Jenny – you don't mind I call you Jenny?'

Jenny shook her head.

'No, of course not. Everyone does.'

'Good, good. I wish to thank you for what you have done, not just for me, but for mine child, mine Salka.'

'I've done nothing for her, and she looks after me and my baby very well indeed,' Jenny protested. 'And all we've done for you . . . oh, Herr Brecht, I wish it could have been more. I wish we could have brought you here sooner!'

'Sooner?' His voice was little more than a whisper, yet it held humour, affection, even gratitude. 'What matters, Jenny, is that I'm here. To die amongst friends – ay-y-yi, how good that is!'

'Oh, but . . .'

He shook his head at her, a tiny movement, but it stopped the words in her throat.

'To die amongst friends is all I ask, my child.'

The Jewish cemetery in Highgate was a quiet and lovely spot on a fine spring day with the whole of London spread out below, misted, beautiful, like an illustration by Dulac. Val and Nicky had brought some flowers for Herr Brecht's grave, as they had promised Salka they would, but having visited the plot, the earth over it still raw, they did not immediately turn and leave again. It was so beautiful here, with the spring flowers budding in the long wild grasses which grew between the graves, and the silver birches, bare still but with their branches colouring, moving in the breeze. Peaceful, as Herr Brecht would have wanted it, Val thought, and moved the daffodils so that they covered more of the earth. Salka had seen the grave only fleetingly before she left. By the time she saw it again it would be a grassy mound, less a reminder of the cruelty of his death than of the contentment he had carried with him to the last.

'There's a bench over there, Val. Let's sit down for a bit before we go.' Nick led Val over to the bench which flanked the overgrown gravel of the little winding path. 'It won't hurt you to rest; we've had a hectic time of it lately, haven't we!'

It was a statement, not a question, but Val agreed as she took her seat beside him.

'I wonder how the Brechts like the States? Lucky them! Although of course the people they've gone to are as much strangers to them as we were – more so, in some ways.'

For Herr Brecht's last wish had been that his family should leave Britain and go to cousins in New York. He had done his best to make what arrangements had been

358

possible, though these had consisted mostly of dictating a number of letters to Salka and of living long enough to receive the replies.

'They will take you in gladly,' he had told her wearily, on the day before he died. 'They can even promise accommodation, and work. You must go, Salka, with your mother and your brother and sister.'

Salka had known, of course, that she could not refuse to leave, even though she felt she was treating Jenny badly. But Jenny had not thought so.

'Honestly, Salka, what can you hope for here? You've got work, all right, but only looking after Marianne, and you don't have a home of your own or a place you can entertain your friends. No, your father was right. You've got to go to New York and see what it has to offer. Herr Brecht seemed quite certain that your family are people of means, who can afford to give you a good start. Seize it with both hands, and remember, your mother will never be truly happy without a home of her own.'

Val, seeing more of Frau Brecht's dilemma than probably anyone else, backed Jenny up and then the whole affair was clinched by the arrival of tickets for the entire family.

'Who bought them?' wondered Salka, but she was told, briskly, that it did not matter who had bought them. It just reinforced Herr Brecht's determination that they should leave.

In truth, Neylers and Roses had waved the Brechts off with almost no regrets. It was difficult having a nursemaid with about twice as many brains as you had yourself, Jenny remarked as she and Simon went home afterwards. And Tina, they knew, had been infuriated by poor Frau Brecht's inability to cope with English, her frequent bouts of tears and depression, and her habit of constantly apologising for everything she did.

Now, sitting on the bench and looking out over London, Val turned to Nick.

'I wonder what they'll make of America? We'll find out soon enough. I've heard from Otto, you know – via Spain, admittedly, but still a letter in his own handwriting.'

'Oh? What did he have to say? Is he going to cut and run for the States?'

'No. He's joined the German air force. He thinks there's bound to be a war. Odd to think of Otto and Simon, both learning to fly, but for different sides.'

Nick plucked a long grass and began to chew the soft yellowy stem.

'Odd to think of German youths saying just what we're saying. I wonder whether they justify themselves in some way? I can't imagine how!'

'I don't think Otto does; I think he's very unhappy. I also doubt whether he had much choice. He'd just be told where he was go, though I'd have thought that the factory could have kept him employed as usefully as the air force. Oh, Nick, what a mess it all is!'

'Yes, I see what you mean. Well, I'm off next week myself to see what sort of training the territorials are offering. Fancy, a month away from the business! Are you sure you and Simon will be able to cope? Richie's marvellous on the mechanical side, so perhaps you'll get by. Jenny, of course, does the books and keep us up to the mark, and she'll probably work twice as hard. She's got a nanny for Marianne now, you know, because it was so hard when Salka first went and she was trying to do all the work and cope with the baby as well.'

'I ought to cope, so long as no one expects me to know

anything about a car's innards,' Val said. 'I'm eternally grateful to you actually, Nick, old fellow, for going off and getting me away from The Pride for a bit! Mama didn't really enjoy being with Frau Brecht, but nevertheless I couldn't have left her alone. It was positively providential Auntie Cecy suggesting that the pair of them take a holiday together, now that neither of them has a Brecht living in! Not that I'd have chosen Tunbridge Wells – but it's a spa town and it's within nice easy commuting distance of London so that they can come up for a day, see a show, and still get back to their hotel in time for bed.'

'Just as long as she doesn't keep popping into Granville Gardens and putting you and Jenny off your stroke,' Nick said forebodingly. 'Our dear mama, sister mine, can be very officious when she's in the mood.'

'Not over business matters – or not your business matters, anyway,' Val said, laughing. 'Actually she's a very astute lady, but she feels that she's got so much on her plate watching brother Desmond play the fool with whatever he can lay hands on that she doesn't need any more.'

'Does she watch him, or does she try to stop him?' Nick enquired, but before she could answer he got to his feet, stretched, and held out a hand to her. 'We'd better get a move on, or Jenny will be thinking herself deserted!'

'The answer to your question is that I honestly don't know,' Val said. 'I work in the office sometimes, but I only type letters and things. I don't know much about what goes on. Basil Pooter sometimes pulls a face, but although he's only about our age he's very discreet.' They set off down the path towards the city once more. 'Perhaps Des is discreet, too, now that Mama's made it clear she wants to know what he's doing with things.'

361

'Perhaps.' The long, winding downward path was tempting. Nick glanced sideways at his sister. 'Race you to the gates!'

'Oh, Nick, it's a cemetery. We really shouldn't . . .' She grinned at him. 'Herr Brecht wouldn't mind. Ready, steady, go!'

Tina had agreed to go to Tunbridge Wells partly to please Cecy and partly because she knew how much Val longed to go to London and help Simon and Jenny whilst Nick was away on his silly training course that the army had arranged. But now that she was here, she found herself enjoying it more than she had enjoyed anything since before Ted's death.

The hotel was a good one, the food excellent, but best of all she felt she had recaptured her girlhood friendship with her sister. She and Cecy had been close as children. It was only later, when Tina married, that jealousy and rivalry had entered their relationship. Now, two middle-aged ladies of fifty-four and fifty-six, they seemed easier together. Perhaps it was the fact that Cecy had been aware that of the two of them Tina had made the better marriage which had made her bitter. Whatever it had been, it was there no longer. They were friends once more.

'What did you think when Louis wrote that he'd married Josette, Tina? I was shocked, though of course they never were blood relations. But she was your daughter, as good as; you must have felt it more.'

'I did. After all the pain and misery he'd put poor Sarah through, and the children he'd fathered – and Josette such a dear, good little thing. But what's done is done. They've been married a while now, and the photographs of their home and their darling twins are a great comfort. What's more, you know, they were instrumental in putting me in touch with Stella again.'

'Were they, indeed? Well, Josette and Stella were always close. Do you hear much from Stella? She re-married, didn't she? But no children, I understand.'

'No. Between you and me and the doorpost, Cecy, I don't actually know if she re-married, or if she just lives with Mr Fairbrother. But it doesn't do to enquire too closely into things like that.'

'Of course not,' Cecy breathed. She loved conversations like this; they were interesting but not taxing. 'It's not like when we were young, though, is it? Imagine a girl living with a man then! Mind you, Josette married Lou, and the twins came twelve months later, isn't that so?'

'Oh, certainly. Lou has become very respectable. It's odd, when you think of it,' Tina continued thought-fully, 'how full Australia is becoming of our . . . well, our slightly black sheep! There's Louis and Josette, and Stella of course, and then there's Mark's son, Johnny – do you remember Mark?'

Cecy screwed up her brow for a moment, then smiled.

'Of course, Ted's younger brother from New Zealand, the one who married a Chinese girl! But I thought they had a daughter, Emma.'

'That's right, but they had a son first. He must be in his mid-thirties now. Ran away and went to Australia when he was only a youngster. Ah well, that's families for you, a skeleton in every cupboard. Shall we go up to London tomorrow and see the children and do a bit of shopping?'

Cecy clapped her hands softly and nodded.

'Oh yes, and do a show, perhaps. I dearly love the theatre.'

'Yes, we could do that. And I need a new summer dress. Well, I could do with several.'

Cecy smiled at her sister. It was a warm, sympathetic smile.

'Of course you could! Do you realise, Tina, that you've scarcely bought a thing since you lost Ted?'

Tina thought, biting into a crumpet, then nodded.

'You're right. It didn't seem worthwhile.'

'Well, if this little holiday has made it seem worthwhile, then it's done some good, at least.'

'I don't want to get dowdy,' Tina said, avoiding the issue. 'And I'm glad we've had this break, Cecy. I've got a feeling that it'll be our last holiday for some time.'

Cecy raised her soft brown brows. Her round eyes looked rounder.

'Not because you think there's going to be a war? Oh, dear, you said you didn't believe it. You said it was just scare-mongering.'

'I don't want to believe it. But, Cecy, I can't see this National government wasting money on training my son to be a good soldier unless they foresee that they're going to need good soldiers fairly soon.'

'Oh dear,' Cecy remarked. 'You've quite spoiled my tea, dear!' She took a slice of rich fruit cake from the dish and nibbled at it. With her mouth rather full, she repeated: 'Quite spoiled my tea!'

'I'm back, you lucky people!' Nick flung himself down in a chair in Jenny's living-room and smiled round at them. 'Well, how did you get on without me?'

'Fine. You look marvellous, old Nick,' Simon said. 'Bronzed and fit and all that. Are you now a hardened soldier of the old school, or are you one of these new, mechanised jobs we hear about?'

'Neither. We're still – hush-hush – very short of

equipment, rifles and so on,' Nick disclosed. 'But they did their best. We learned how to use various weapons, how to drink beer all evening and then go on guard duty, how to crawl on our stomachs across a piece of ground with blank ammo whistling over our heads.' He grinned at them and lounged to his feet. 'I want coffee. Can I go and forage?'

'I never thought to have to tell you to sit down and shut up in my house,' Simon said plaintively. 'One of my women will get us coffee. Shall it be the lovely Valentina, or the gorgeous Jennifer?'

'Neither. I'll call Ivy and she'll do it,' Jenny said, smiling.

'Darling girl!' Nick blew her a kiss and then turned to Val, who was lying back in her chair and watching him. 'Well, and how did twinnie enjoy working for her living?'

'Prime. I really loved it. I wish I could do it for ever. I was good too, wasn't I, Simon?'

'You were, lovely.' He turned to Nick. 'She could sell ice-creams to eskimos as your father used to say. Anyway, she managed to persuade every person who came and enquired about car hire to hire one. I can't say better than that.'

'It was surprise, to be honest,' Val admitted. 'They didn't expect to be met by a young woman and it rather knocked them for six. And whilst they were gasping, I was all but signing the forms for them.'

'That sounds good.' Nick winked at Simon as Jenny returned to sit down again and pick up her knitting. 'When war comes, we'll know what to do about the business – get Val and Jen to run it between them!'

'It might come to that,' Val said. 'Don't think you're joking because it could happen. Anyway, Nick, what did you do apart from shooting guns and squiggling on your tummy across wet meadows. Break any hearts?'

'No-o,' Nick admitted. 'But an odd thing did happen. Do you remember, Val, absolutely aeons ago, me telling you that I'd met a kid called Vitty? It was at the Cafe Royal. Mama took us there for a treat, for lunch after we'd been shopping. And this little kid was hiding from her parents on the stairs. I don't think you saw her, and I only did for a minute. But I remembered her for ages. Pretty little thing.'

'Well? So what?'

'She was down there, working behind the bar where we went in the evenings. The Wild Pheasant, it was called. Odd, wasn't it?'

'Very odd. How did you recognise her?'

'She hadn't changed all that much, actually. But of course it was the name that gave it to me. Vitty. Unusual. She's Italian, of course. Vittorina Magrelli.'

'What was she doing in the Wild Pheasant, beside serving behind the bar, I mean?' Jenny said curiously. 'Why wasn't she still in Norwich? The Cafe Royal's still in London Street, isn't it?'

'Yes, but she's left there.' He grinned at Val. 'I took her to the flicks – get a load of me!'

'Good lord, don't say you've found someone who interests you at last!' Val said. 'Trust you to choose an Italian – is she dark and greasy and passionate?'

'No. She's got blue eyes, actually, and she's . . . well, perhaps you'll meet her one day.'

'I say, you're serious, aren't you?' Jenny broke in. 'He's watched you breaking hearts with contempt, Val, but now he's started himself.'

'No, I haven't. I'm not serious, either. I just think she's rather a nice girl.'

But Val was not deceived for one moment, and when

Nick went back to his own flat that night she walked over with him, her arm lightly linked with his. He unlocked the door, sniffed a trifle disconsolately at the stale-seeming air, though Val and Jenny had taken it in turns to keep the place fresh by opening windows each day, and then went into the kitchen, closely followed by his sister.

'Want a drink?' He put the kettle on, then turned to Val. 'Right, I know why you're here! She's run away from home, that's why she's in Hertfordshire. Said she couldn't bear life with her stepmother a moment longer.'

'A stepmother? Poor little Cinderella.'

'No, you're wrong there. She's a most independent little creature. You'd like her. She's younger than us, only eighteen, but she's living in digs and keeping herself by working as a waitress during the day and a barmaid at night.' He paused, eyeing Val. 'I'm seeing her again. Naturally.'

Val raised a brow. 'Of course. How could I expect otherwise? You, my dear brother, are as different from me as chalk from cheese.'

'Am I? How do you mean?'

'Oh, I'm light-natured, I flit from flower to flower – or from man to man, if you prefer it. You're the sort that finds one you like and sticks.'

'Yes, I probably am. But Val, you do rather carry it to excess, you know. You must have had a dozen boy-friends in the past six months! What makes you so – so hard to please?'

Val stared at him. Her big green eyes were mocking, her mouth curved into a sarcastic smile, but Nick, who knew her better than he knew anyone but himself, could see that she was putting on a mask.

'I'm not hard to please, in fact. My trouble's always

367

been that when I find the right man, he's already spoken for. Enough of that, or you'll have me in tears.'

'Val, poor old Val. I've often wondered . . . was it Simon?'

'Oh, not since we were kids. Well, he was always my dream-man, but I can see that Jenny's perfect for him and I wouldn't have been. He wouldn't have suited me, either, not in the long run.'

'Well, who, then?'

Val sighed and plucked the kettle off the stove just as it began to boil.

'Oh, no one you've ever met. Let's change the subject. How do you rate my chances of leaving home, now that Mama's survived without me for a whole month?'

Rose was standing in Hyde Park, watching the soldiers. They had a thing which looked like a telescope, except that it was on three little legs, and they were milling round it and shouting to each other, for all the world as though they were kids like the ones at the Broad Street home. Just behind her, she knew, was Ivy, with Marianne in the pram. Rose was fond of Marianne and she got on well with Ivy, but she only came out with them because Jenny was too busy to talk to her. And it went without saying that Simon was busy. Simon was lovely! She adored him, and now that he was flying aeroplanes at his flying club she spent a lot of time at weekends just gazing up into the sky, wondering if he might go over and waggle his wings at her. She knew he waggled his wings, because he had told her so.

But today, the only thing in the blue sky was a barrage balloon, and she was too used to seeing that to worry about it. She rather liked barrage balloons, so big and fat and grey, like cushiony elephants. Simon said they guarded London against attacks from enemy aircraft, though why they should be necessary no one thought to explain. Nor what they would do if an enemy aircraft hove into sight. She could not imagine a barrage balloon suddenly becoming aggressive, unless they sort of *barged* the aeroplanes out of the sky?

She glanced behind her, to where Ivy sat with one hand on the handle of the pram, rocking it gently up and down, and the other grasping a paperback novel. She often read in the park, but she always kept a good hold on the pram, she told Rose, for fear it might drift away whilst her mind was occupied.

Rose looked at her and checked that she had her gasmask, and that the baby's Micky Mouse mask was also shoved untidily into the pram-basket. Her own gasmask, a torture-object, bobbed on her shoulder in its small cardboard box. She hated and feared it, but had got over the stage of screaming that she would rather be gassed, which was how she had felt when it was first issued last September. Now, six months later, she was almost accustomed to the odd, rubbery smell and the constriction round her face and chin. Anyway, she didn't see why she still had to cart it about with her. She might not be very old, but she could remember when all the grown-ups had thought there was going to be a war, and how they cried with relief when it had turned out to be some sort of joke. She had been taken to see the men digging trenches in Lincoln's Inn Fields, but though they had not dug more trenches they had not filled any in, either. She supposed the gas-masks were a bit like that; they couldn't be bothered to take back the masks nor to fill in the trenches, and they left the dear, cuddly barrage balloons floating in the sky, too. It was either laziness or a precaution, she supposed.

She liked the soldiers' uniforms because they reminded her of Nick's. He was a soldier too, and went off at weekends to practise his soldiering, sometimes in his khaki uniform and sometimes in ordinary clothes. Nick believed a war was going to come and so did Simon and so, though she hardly ever talked about it, did Jenny. Of course, they did not say when such a thing would happen – probably when I'm ten, Rose thought vaguely, since ten – double figures – seemed a lifetime away.

Behind her she head Marianne begin to mutter and turned in time to see Ivy push her book beneath the pram blanket, and then straighten her hat and her navy blue coat and glance over to where she stood.

'I'm going to walk for a bit, Rose,' she called. 'You comin'?'

The question was rhetorical, since when she was out with Ivy she was in Ivy's charge and must do as she was told, but Rose answered that she was, and went and took hold of the pram handle.

She had gone walking with Ivy once and had thought she saw her mother. In a moment she had forgotten the new kindness she was receiving at the hands of Jenny and Simon, the new trustworthiness she had vowed to maintain which meant that Matron allowed her more freedom. She had simply put her head down and run like the wind along the pavement after the pretty yellow-haired lady in the scarlet and white walking suit.

It had been quite half a mile before she had realised not only that the lady had escaped her, but that she was lost, and a good two hours before she found her way back to Granville Gardens.

Jenny had been really cross with her.

'When you're with any of us, we're responsible for you, Rosie,' she had explained over tea. 'We promise the home that we'll look after you, in fact, we're what they call in *loco parentis*. That means that we're taking the place of your parents, just whilst you're with us. So when you go out with Ivy or me or Simon, you must tell yourself that however like your mother someone looks it's no excuse for running off, because we're looking after you *for* your mother. See?'

Rose, sharp as a needle, saw one thing. If she wished to continue her lovely friendship with the Rose family, she must never again run away from one of them, no matter how great the temptation. And to give her credit, she never had.

Now, they began to stroll along the path towards the soldiers. Rose smiled to herself. Ivy was sixteen and liked men. She particularly liked soldiers, sailors and airmen – men in uniform, in fact. Now, if Rose was any judge, they would walk along where the soldiers were, and then Ivy would pick the baby out of the pram and try to get her to wave to the men. Marianne, a fat and cuddly baby with a sweet smile, would coo and beam and get the men's attention, though at twelve weeks she was scarcely old enough to wave, and then some- one, sure as check, would say something nice about the baby to Ivy, and they would be off. Ivy was pretty, with fair hair which she tortured into curling pins every night and pale, rather goggly blue eyes. Though she was sensible with the baby and helpful to Jenny, almost her entire conversation away from the flat was to do with men, and Rose found her supremely boring. However, she watched her technique with interest, for it was quite impressive to see how Ivy always managed to attract some man over to speak to her, even if it was not the one she was aiming for!

Today, it was a nice, thickset young man with gingery hair and an attractive grin. He came over to admire the baby and to tell Rose she was the prettiest girl he had seen for many a year. Rose dimpled at him, knowing herself to be a pawn in the game about to be played between Ivy and the gingery one and not minding in the least. She *was* pretty, she knew that, and one day she would have boyfriends of her own. Until then, she had no objection to helping in Ivy's campaign!

It was Saturday afternoon, so when the plane noise came from directly overhead she naturally looked up, gazing into the windy, cloudy sky, hoping for a glimpse. And that was how she came not to notice that Ivy had caught a bigger fish than she had either desired or expected. The first Rose knew of it, indeed, was when a voice she knew well remarked sarcastically: 'Taking the baby for an airing, Ivy?'

It was Nick. In his uniform, fiddling around with the object which she now knew must be an anti-aircraft gun, Nick had looked just like any other soldier to the short-sighted Ivy, and she had undoubtedly ogled him for his nice figure, his crisply curling hair, and his air of quiet efficiency.

Rose, every bit as startled as the nursemaid, blinked up at Nick, her mind working furiously.

'Hello, Nick,' she said affably. 'Ivy wanted to show Marianne what the soldiers do, and when we saw you there she *had* to tell Baby it was her Uncle Nick!'

'So I did!' Ivy squeaked valiantly. She had been holding the baby against her shoulder but now she turned her round. 'See, Mari? There's your Uncle Nick!'

Nick sighed and shrugged.

'Nice of you to notice me, Ivy. And now I suggest you get back to the flat before Marianne catches a chill.'

'That wasn't very nice,' Ivy grumbled to Rose as the two of them made their way, considerably chastened, back to Granville Gardens. 'It's all rubbidge, gals not being allowed boyfriends! What do they think I am, made of stone?'

'But you've got a boyfriend, and no one minds,' Rose said, surprised by this approach. 'I don't suppose they'd care if you met Fred!'

'Ho, wouldn't they? That's what you think, Miss Smarty!' Ivy said. 'They wouldn't like it if I met Fred when I was walkin' the baby in the park. Meet 'im in your own time, they'd say!'

'Well, it was daft of you to try to flirt with Nick,' Rose said, one hand on the pram handle as she had been told. 'Lucky for you I thought of an answer!'

'Oh, we *are* pleased with ourself!' Ivy said crossly. Her cheeks were still flushed from the unexpected encounter with Nick. 'I tell you, I'll not live in and skivvy again, not on your life! Soon's I can afford it, I'm going to be independent!'

'I wish I could be Marianne's nanny, then,' Rose sighed. To her, life could hold nothing more desirable than living in the same house as Jenny and Simon. 'Just you wait until I'm . . . say twelve, Ivy, and I'll 'ave your job.'

'Mari won't need no nanny then, you 'alf-wit,' Ivy grumbled, but Rose's experienced eye could see that she was looking less flushed and that her voice was losing its shrillness. 'You ain't a bad kid, really; fanks Rosie.'

With their gas-masks banging against their sides, the two of them pushed the pram on towards Granville Gardens.

Chapter Fifteen

It had been a rainy July, but then, as if to make up for it, the weather had turned brilliantly warm and sunny, and on the third of these sunny days, Tina and Val decided to have breakfast out on the terrace.

Accordingly, they got the maid to help them carry one of the wrought-iron tables out on to the crazy paving, selected a couple of sagging but comfortable basketwork loungers, and settled themselves outside in the early morning sunshine.

Maxie approved of the scheme; he enjoyed al fresco meals, which so often meant handouts. It also ensured that, should the postman arrive, he would be in the best position not only to hurl defiance at him for daring to ride up the drive on that abominable red bicycle, but to actually see him off, preferably without a piece of his ugly serge trousers.

Val, settling herself and reaching for the jug of orange juice, eyed Maxie crossly. She knew exactly what thoughts were predominant in his small, shaggy head, but it was a lovely morning, and he always shared their breakfast. It seemed a shame to confine him to the conservatory when it was actually sunny.

'Has the postman been, Mama?'

'I don't know, but it's quite early. Why?'

'Just look at Maxie's expression! He knows very well that he's always kept indoors until the post's been delivered, and he thinks this is a heaven-sent opportunity to teach the postman a lesson.'

Tina looked, then laughed.

'He's a calculating animal, isn't he? Now I come to think of it, though, the postman has been. He brought nothing but circulars, mind, but I riffled through the pile on the hall table before we came out. Poor old Maxie, foiled again!'

Maxie, in sublime ignorance, stalked, stiff-legged, across the terrace so that he was nearer the drive, and listened. No sound yet; he would have to wait a bit. Whilst waiting, he raised a leg and watered the lavender, unperturbed by the cries which immediately broke out from the breakfasters. Stupid women!

Assured of peace, Val sipped her orange juice, then buttered a slice of toast. Up in the cedar tree a dove cooed. No other sounds disturbed the air except for a faint tapping. Val squinted up into the sunlight trying to see the dove, and was rewarded, instead, by a glimpse of the tapper. She leaned forward and nudged her mother.

'See that? It's the woodpecker! The times he's woken me up, clonking away, and I've gone to the window but never caught a glimpse. Gaudy, isn't he? You wouldn't think I could miss him!'

'Yes, I love seeing him. The best time is just when dawn's breaking and the sun's coming up and dispersing the morning mist, then you can hear him breathtakingly loudly, and many's the time I've seen him, hammering away. I read somewhere that he's searching for the insects which live under the bark of trees. Oh, what a nuisance. I didn't pick up the paper as I came through the hall.'

'And the wireless is through in the breakfast room. Not that the news is likely to be good; it never is these days. I listen to the news every morning though, just in case the announcer says we're at war.'

Tina snorted and applied herself to her boiled egg.

'War! That's all you young things think about. It won't come to that. Look what happened last autumn. If that didn't end in war, when we were all prepared, why should war come now, when we're all thinking peaceful thoughts?'

'Peaceful thoughts? With Nick in the territorials learning to defend his country, and Simon a pilot, albeit only in his spare time? It'll come, Mama, the only question is when.'

'They find the thought of war exciting, that's why they prepare for it,' Tina said, spooning yolk. 'I wish you'd eat a better breakfast, darling. I'm sure it isn't good to have nothing but orange juice and toast.'

'And coffee. Then you don't think we'll go to war? Not even with the Italians bombing Albania without so much as a word of warning and King Whatsisname in exile and his poor little Queen and her new baby forced to fly to Greece?'

'Zog,' Tina said absently. 'That's other people, though, not us. We've got more sense; we can remember last time.'

'Zog? Mama, what are you on about?'

'King Zog of Albania. And we've got anti-aggression pacts with half the world. They're signing one with Russia at this very moment, probably, so there should be no fear of war. What was it Chamberlain said?'

'Lots of things, and most of 'em silly. Peace in our time, is that what you're thinking of? Or Hitler's missed the bus? Tell me, if he believes Hitler's missed the bus and left it too late to declare war, then why are they conscripting men of twenty and twenty-one?'

Tina sighed. It was a sore point that Britain was actually conscripting men in peacetime, because it had always been said that the British wouldn't stand for such a thing.

'Oh, that. They're saying that it's healthier for young men from the slums to be under canvas, learning to take care of themselves, rather than hanging about all summer because they can't find work. Why, one of the papers asked its readers what they thought, and nearly all the young men said they were glad of it!'

'The papers! What about the wireless?'

'Warmongers. They're all warmongers at the BBC. *Punch* says so.'

Val laughed and poured coffee into two cups.

'Milk, Mama? You shouldn't be allowed to read *Punch* if you can't see a joke! The whole *point* of that cartoon was to show that the BBC tells the truth so gets branded as warmongering. Did you know that Jenny and Simon have cancelled their holiday? They have, honestly. Jenny says it's no time to be gadding off to France with the world in such a state, though Simon thought that it might well be their last holiday before Europe's closed to us.'

'Is that so? How strange, because Frank's just booked himself a fortnight's holiday in France! And your elder brother, my dear, is the most level-headed of men. What do you say to *that*?'

'You're kidding! Frank never takes a holiday! Not old Frank!'

'Frank isn't thirty-nine yet, and it's absolutely true,' Tina snapped, nettled by Val's tone. 'Mind you, I believe there's some business involved, but he's decided to combine it with a holiday. He isn't drawing back because the world's in a mess.'

'Well, blow me down! Good old Frank!'

'Frank? Do listen to me, lovely, *handsome* brother Frank!

I should have thought you'd have been falling over yourself to give your little sister the chance of a two-week holiday in France! I shan't interfere with your business pursuits, whatever they may be; I just want an excuse to get out of the country for a couple of weeks. It's three whole *years* since I was abroad last and I miss it terribly, but Mama won't hear of my going alone and she won't come with me. Besides, I'm such a fluent French speaker that I could be awfully useful to you – I bet you're no good at all!'

Frank groaned inwardly. He wished, devoutly, that he had never let himself be jockeyed into giving Val a day's boating on the Broads. If he had known that she would turn up in a snappy yachting costume, insist on being allowed to steer on some of the busiest water, and then try to persuade him to take her to France, he would not have allowed her to come within a mile of him. He looked balefully at her across the spindly tea-table. They had lunched at the White Hart, gone along the New Cut to Reedham, and were having tea at a pretty thatched cottage with an old-fashioned garden, having moored the boat at the bottom of the long lawn and walked up to where the little tables were laid out beneath scattered apple trees.

Frank had done his best to give Val a good day because she *was* his sister and he felt he ought to like her and be kind to her, but in reality he had always considered her a spoiled brat, had never admired her looks, and now thought her a proper little nuisance into the bargain. Badgering him to take her to France, making googly eyes at him as though she were neither eighteen years younger than he nor his sister!

'I'm not bad at French. I get by. Are you ready for a cake yet, or would you like another scone? They're very good.'

He had ordered a lavish tea, still thinking of Val as a

schoolgirl though she would be twenty-one in November and had had more boyfriends than he had had hot dinners. Now, she picked up the teapot and poured herself another cup of tea, looking up at him under her lashes. He could willingly have slapped her!

'No cake, thank you, nor a scone. I'm watching my figure.'

He considered being gallant and saying that so were half the male customers present – it would have been no more than the truth – but he did not want to inflate her ego even more. He just took another scone himself.

'Frank, *why* won't you take me to France? I accept that you won't, but I would like to know why.'

'Because I'm going on business and I prefer to go alone.'

He was so irritated by her persistence that he longed to shout *Because I'm going to meet my mistress and you would be confoundedly in the way*, but he still retained enough self-control not to actually do it. He flashed a glance – under his lashes, had he but known it – across the table at his sister and imagined that he could read her mind. *Good old Frank, dull old fellow*, his little sister would be thinking, *he must be the only man in Britain who would go off to the south of France on business!*

'That would be a good reason, Frank, if I meant to haunt your footsteps. But I wouldn't, honestly. I'd be off on my own affairs all the time. All I want is your company on the journey there and back, so that Mama would believe I was with you. I'm perfectly capable of taking care of myself.'

'Really? I doubt that! Anyway, the question doesn't arise, because I won't take you.'

'If you don't take me, then I'll go with Gaston. I'll probably have to pay his fare, but I'm sure he'd be glad to get back to France again!'

If there was one thing that all the family agreed over, it was that Val's latest acquisition was a fatal mistake. One and all they disliked Gaston, his patent leather hairdo, his too-even tan, his neat dancer's figure which seemed to be joined more loosely at the hips than a human body should be. Frank, however, was not to be drawn.

'As though Mama would let you go anywhere with that greasy dago! Horrible little lounge lizard. If that's the kind of man you like then you wouldn't want to be seen dead in my company.'

Val looked daggers at her brother.

'How dare you call Gaston names, just because he's a marvellous dancer! And because he's got a fatal fascination for women! No woman ever looked twice at you, Frank Neyler, and it's obvious why not. You're dull and righteous and so selfish you don't even notice when other people are upset!' She jumped to her feet, knocking over her small chair. 'Take me home at once. I don't want to stay here with you!'

Other couples were staring, nudging, tittering. Frank calmly helped himself to a cake. It was a chocolate eclair, thick with cream. He knew eclairs were Val's favourites. There was another on the plate.

'We'll go when I've finished my tea and not one moment before. Sit down and stop making an exhibition of yourself. The trouble with you, young lady, is that you've been spoiled rotten; no one's ever said no to you before and you just can't believe it's happening.'

'I'm going back to the boat!'

Frank shrugged.

'Please yourself. I was going to make a suggestion, but it doesn't matter. Do you know, this must be the most delicious eclair I've ever tasted? I think I'll have another cup of tea; you might pour me one before you flounce off.'

Defeated by her own sense of humour, Val giggled, sat down again, and poured the tea.

'Well, I've told you what I think of you, and I shan't retract one word of it. But I might as well stay here and eat an eclair as wait for you in the boat.'

She took the cake, bit into it, and then leaned back in her chair.

'Sorry, Frank. I shouldn't have blown up like that. I know I'm spoiled in some ways – Nick's always telling me so – but in others I'm quite sensible. I suppose I thought it would be easy to persuade you and when it wasn't I lost my temper. I won't mention it again, I promise.'

But it had occurred to Frank that whatever his plans to meet Mabel might have been, they certainly had not included any reason for calling on her at home, or for taking her off on expeditions of pleasure. And since he was going to France for the sole purpose of persuading Mabs to come back and live with him, it would be much better if he had someone along who could visit Mabel without causing comment. Val, moreover, could speak very good French – had she not lived in a partially French speaking society for years? – and would be ideal in other ways as well. What, indeed, could go wrong if he did take her with him? She would be his link between Mabel's home and wherever he happened to stay.

'I've been thinking. It might not be a bad idea for you to come to France with me.'

Val choked on her eclair, coughed, and had to be patted on the back. Finally, with streaming eyes, she spoke.

'Frank, I love you! But why this sudden change of front?'

'Because something tells me I can trust you not to blab what I'm going to tell you all over Norwich. Am I right?'

381

Val nodded vigorously and leaned across the table, elbows spread, eyes shining.

'A secret? I'm an oyster.'

'Hmm. Look, Val, this is a *real* secret. If you did let it slip out, then you could ruin everything. Understand?'

'Oh, *yes*. Do tell!'

'All right, here goes. I've got an old friend who's lived in the south of France for years. I've kept in touch with her, but now I want to go over there and see her, talk to her, persuade her to . . . well, that isn't important. What matters is that I must talk to her without her husband finding out and interfering. That's where you come in. You won't remember her but she knew you well when you were a baby, though she only met you once when you were older. She told me you and Nick were in the sandpit . . .'

Val's unflattering astonishment melted before a faint, faraway recollection. Of a sandpit, a sunny afternoon, of cherries which fell, ripe, into the sand. There was a little boy in the memory, a child with almost white hair, and a woman. Elegance personified, she had been. She had black hair, big black eyes, a profile like the picture of Minnehaha in Val's Hiawatha book. A French-woman, yes, she remembered that quite clearly. She had been smoking a cigarette and Stella had come and they had talked in riddles in the infuriating way that adults were wont to do. Val frowned. For years she had remembered that woman, wondered about her, envied her the blackbird's wing hair, the slender brown wrists with a small fortune in gold bangles, the thin, fragile ones, which jingled when she moved. A name . . . there had been a name, if only she could remember. But it wouldn't come. She sighed and looked across at Frank.

'I do remember someone. She had black hair and eyes

and jingly gold bangles. She came and spoke to Nick and me. There was a little boy, too, her little boy. They both spoke French.'

Frank's eyes softened, and for the first time Val acknowledged that he was a handsome man. She smiled at him.

'What's her name, Frank? You did mean that lady, didn't you?'

'Yes. That's Mabel.'

'Mabel?'

Val almost shrieked the word. She had been brought up with the spectre of the Walters' perfect daughter, who lived in France and who entertained her parents over there twice a year, ever since she could remember. So that was Mabel Walters! No wonder her parents were so proud of her. She had come a long way from being the gardener's daughter at The Pride!

'That's right, Ada and William's girl. She and I . . . I suppose you know the story. It's ancient history now.'

'I don't!' But Val was eager to right the omission. 'All I heard was that there was a mystery about the Walters girl. She ran away, I heard, and married a rich Frenchman. The kitchen-maids used to tell each other about her.'

'That's all you need to know.'

Val gave an anguished moan and Frank relented.

'Perhaps you're right. I'm asking for your help, so you should know the whole story. We thought a lot of each other, Mabs and I. We were going to get married, but something happened, I never did know what, and she ran away, to France. She got married to this fellow, Matthieu de Recourte, and had a son, André – I've never seen father or son – and we lost touch. You remember Suzie?'

'Oh, *yes*, she was lovely, such a darling! I've always

383

thought that you were so in love with her that no one else could compete, and that's why you never married again.'

'No, you've got it all wrong. Suzie, poor darling, was just a substitute for Mabs and I'm pretty sure she always knew it. After she died, I started seeing Mabs again. Not often, just once a year. I've been seeing her ever since.'

'Not your holiday in Scotland?' Val breathed the words, her eyes fixed on Frank's. She was still sprawled halfway across the table, scones, sandwiches and cakes pushed to one side. 'And we all thought . . . oh, Frank!'

'I couldn't very well tell you, could I?' Frank said reasonably. 'I could hardly say: "I go off to Scotland each September with my mistress, who's married to someone else." Even Daddy would have been shocked, and Mama would have gone straight up and never come down again.'

'I don't see why. It wouldn't have had anything to do with them.'

'Be your age, Val. You can't go through life shocking and hurting people. Anyway, we couldn't risk it getting back to Matthieu, because he would have been terribly hurt. Mabs says that he married her when she was desperate and brought up the boy as if . . . that's to say . . .'

'I thought you said she married Matthieu and had André,' Val said accusingly. 'I can tell how it was. She married him, but he wasn't the boy's father. Am I right?'

'A guess as accurate as that hints at a misspent youth,' Frank said darkly. 'Yes, you're right. She fled to France for whatever reason and got taken in by some rotter. I've always imagined it was the fellow who took her across on his boat, though goodness knows why.

And then she got a job with Matthieu's firm and when he found she was pregnant he offered to marry her, though he told her it would be a business arrangement. He wanted a child, you see, but I don't think . . . well, from what Mabs told me he and she don't . . .'

Val cut across his embarrassed mumblings.

'Don't live together. Lord, Frank, I'm sorry I said you were dull. You must have been burning up with passion for years, probably since before I was born!'

'I don't see why I'm less dull because I've admitted to loving the same woman for twenty years,' Frank said stiffly. 'Nor why her unhappy circumstances should affect how you think of me! It's when I hear you talking like that, Val, that I begin to think perhaps I'm mad to trust you.'

'I'm sorry,' Val said, full of remorse. 'I didn't mean it rudely, honestly I didn't. It's just such a surprise!'

'Yes, I can see that. Now look, though I said I was going to France to see Mabel, that's only partly true. I'm going all right, and I'd hoped to see quite a bit of Mabs, but I've not actually made any plans at all, and though she knows I'm going to be in France we haven't discussed meeting because we've not had time to do so yet. And it occurred to me just now that it would be a lot easier for you just to walk into her house and ask to see her, for old times' sake, you know. You could arrange to meet her for lunch or something, and then I could step in.'

'What about the son, André? He's about my age, or a couple of years younger, I suppose. Couldn't we use that angle?'

'Afraid not. He's at university in Paris, but actually at the moment he's on some sort of course in Dublin. Part of the trouble is that I can't write to Mabs except through a third party, it's far too risky, and, though we

385

exchange telephone calls, again we have to be terribly careful. It isn't easy to make plans. But you could write quite openly, say when you'll be in France and ask if you can visit her. She's bright, is Mabel; she'll twig what's happening and ask you over in a moment.'

'It's a deal.' Val shook Frank's unresisting hand. 'I can't tell you how I'm looking forward to it. Dearly though I love Mama, being stuck at The Pride with very little to do can be extremely enervating! Here, do you want any more cakes? Then perhaps you'd better catch the waitress's eye and pay the bill.'

'I'll take the rest of the cakes for my supper,' Frank said, eyeing them. 'Are you telling me, Val, that you didn't stay on at The Pride because you wanted to learn to be a good housewife, as Mama said?'

'*Did* she now? She's a devil, isn't she?' Val said appreciatively. 'No, of course I didn't. Can't you remember how you felt at twenty? All I want is to get away, show everyone that I can cope on my own. I'd *love* to be in London with Nick and Simon and Jen all the time, I *adored* the month I spent there, but whenever I get desperate I think of Daddy. He would have implored me not to leave Mama alone, you know he would. At first, I thought Frau Brecht might be the answer, and then I thought Maxie might do the trick, but there's no substitute for a daughter. It had to be me.'

The waitress, answering Frank's wave, came over at that point and there was a temporary lapse in the conversation whilst Frank paid the bill, got a bag so that he could carry away all the remaining cakes, and tipped the girl. But when they set off again towards the boat, he gave Val a more appreciative glance than any he had yet bestowed on her.

'You're a kind kid.' He helped her down into the well of the boat, admitting to himself as he did so that the yachting costume, though eye-catching, was also practical with its short, full skirt. 'To go back to what we were saying, surely you won't be the spinster daughter who stays at home for ever? I do think, Val, that there are some sacrifices no one would ask of you, particularly Daddy. He'd be horrified to think of you tied to The Pride.'

'Oh, it won't be for ever, just until something turns up,' Val said with the airy optimism of youth. 'If there's a war I shan't stay at home, I'll do something useful.'

'Yes, but you should be training for it. Nick's training, and Simon. I reckon I'd be pretty useless as a modern soldier, but I've put out feelers and when war comes they want me in the boat building industry, so you could say I'll be useful in my way.' He had started the engine and cast off; now he steered his craft into midstream. 'You could make use of your languages, mind.'

'Yes. I see myself as a latter day Mata Hari,' Val said smugly. 'Though Mama would have a seizure if she heard me say so! No, I'm only teasing. I wouldn't have the nerve to be a spy, but there must be other jobs I could do better than most because of my languages. Perhaps I could break codes!'

'Well, whatever you do, it won't be in Norwich. How would you start? By joining the women's services?'

'Probably. Don't tell Simon, but I've got an urge to learn to fly an aeroplane. Amy Johnson did, after all.'

Frank snorted.

'Yes, but not in wartime. I'm going to head for home now, and when we've moored the boat I'll run you over to The Wherry and we'll get the details of our trip cleared up over a decent meal.'

Val giggled.

'A decent meal? You've done nothing but eat ever

since I arrived at the yard! First it was coffee and gingerbread, then it was that enormous lunch at the pub, then it was tea, and you're already thinking of filling up again.' She glanced at his lean figure. 'It isn't fair. If I ate like that I'd be as fat as a pudding.'

'I don't always eat a lot, only when I'm entertaining sisters that I hardly know. Women like you, Val, terrify me. Smart clothes, loud voices, heaps of self-confidence – they're all the things that scare quiet men like me.'

'Then how come you get on with Mabel? From what I remember she was smart – Paris smart, what's more.'

'Is she? Not to me, she isn't. Here, pass me that cake with the pink icing on. I could do with a mouthful!'

There was a gale blowing when Frank and Val motored down to Dover, but they had the hood of the car up and they bowled along very comfortably, both in a holiday hood. Perhaps because of the tensions and worries over world affairs, a holiday in France seemed not only highly desirable but very sensible, too. After all, it might be their last chance for a long time to come.

'If the war starts whilst we're in France,' Val said blithely, 'Con says all British motorists will be given sufficient petrol to get them back to the Channel ports, free. What about that, then?'

'If war starts I shall kidnap Mabel and bring her back with us,' Frank said. 'I remember France last time – it's no place to leave the woman you love.'

'You're right. Now let's forget war and enjoy what's left of the peace.'

In her beautiful country home, Mabel waited. She was waiting for Frank, waiting to know what the future would hold for her; but she was also waiting, as was the rest of the world, for a war which she believed to be inevitable. Would it be fought on the French soil she had learned to love, or would the French hold the Germans back with the help of their allies and the Maginot line? Hitler had taken Austria and then Czechoslovakia, Mussolini had occupied Albania, Italian and German intervention had given Spain to Franco. Hitler was now threatening Poland. God alone knew where it would end.

Surely the Maginot line would hold off invasion, though? Matthieu had little faith in it, but at least it was there in all its glory. Then the Germans had a strong navy; if they invaded from the sea the de Recourtes would have to leave this house. But they had other houses, a flat in Paris, a place in Brittany.

She had received the letter from Val, showed it to Matthieu, and greeted his suggestion that she ask the girl to lunch with mild pleasure. She was sure that Matthieu's interest in Val would not last long, since he seldom stayed at home when she was entertaining women friends. Once alone, she would suggest a trip down to the coast in her car, and she would then meet Frank and arrange other rendezvous. She appreciated why he had come; many years ago she had promised Suzie that, one day, when she felt she had worked off her debt to Matthieu, she would go to Frank. She had lived with Matthieu for nearly twenty years and she knew that the time had come, if it was ever to come, for her to take the plunge. André no longer needed her – it was doubtful if he would ever live at home again – and Matthieu, though he was fond of her and liked to have his pretty wife running his home and entertaining his friends, could scarcely accuse her of not keeping her side of the bargain. It is not for myself that I would leave Matthieu, she thought now, but for Frank. He has been punished for my fault for twenty years; surely the time had come for him to have some happiness?

The ringing of the doorbell brought her abruptly back to the present. She got leisurely to her feet, for a servant would bring Val through, if it really was Val at last.

She heard a murmur of voices and for a moment was stricken with icy terror at the thought that Frank might have ignored her wishes and have come as well. Frank and Matthieu must never meet. It would lead to the most awful complications. But the door was opening and François was ushering a young woman into the room.

'Mademoiselle Neyler, madame,' he said.

Mabel blinked. Was this a Neyler? She was like none of them. She had red hair, thick and curly, very large green eyes and an equally large mouth. She was made up extravagantly too, with lots of lipstick and mascara, and her small, imperious nose was dusted with face powder to hide the faint freckling. Ugly? Ye-es, and yet . . . Val smiled and bounded forward, both hands held out. She was wearing an absurd little green velvet pillbox hat with a tiny veil and a green silk suit. Mabel registered the fact that Val had one of those enviable hourglass figures and then she was caught in the girl's embrace, hugged, and held back so that Val could beam at her. Mabel blinked again, a victim, though she did not know it, of Val's fascination. She would never think Val Neyler ugly again.

'Mabs – may I call you Mabs? – it's wonderful to see you after so many years! You're a legend in our house, did you know that? The perfect daughter, the one who made good and gives her parents super holidays and never a moment's anxiety. A wonderful wife, a marvellous mother.' The green eyes shone with wicked complicity. 'And you look so *young*, as young as you looked when I last met you – do you remember the sandpit, and me and Nick?'

'How could I forget? Thanks for the compliment, but I fear I can't return it. You've changed out of all recognition since those days – for the better, I must add!'

'Yes, I was a hideous child, wasn't I?' Val said, twinkling. 'Now where's Matthieu? I feel as if I know him already. Your son's away, I believe.'

'Yes, I'm afraid André's in Dublin still. My husband's just gone out into the garden for a moment; he wanted to tell the gardener something. Shall we go and fetch him in to pour us a drink? And this afternoon we'll take a drive and talk over old times.'

'Spiffing, as Nick would say.' They went out through the French windows and on to the long lawn. Val dropped her voice. 'There's a hotel called the Miramar, down on the coast, do you know it? Frank's going to wait for us there at about three o'clock; he'll entertain us to tea, he says. If that's convenient, of course.'

'Marvellous. Ah, there's Matthieu! Come over and let me introduce you, my dear.'

'A little more *pear au vin*, Val? Or would you rather try some of the *mousse de chocolat?*'

Matthieu, showing Val the creamy delicacy of the mousse, was very taken by their vivacious guest, to Mabel's secret amusement. Far from finding her liveliness trying and her bright colouring too garish for his Gallic taste, he had obviously fallen for her charm. And his undeniable good looks, though his hair was grey and his waistline thickening, had made an impression on Val, too. She flirted with him, laughed at him, and behaved so delightfully that she made Mabel feel old. How long had it been, Mabel wondered, since she had bothered to flirt with a man! But times had changed;

when she, Mabel, had been twenty she would have been thought disastrously fast to flirt with a man as Val was flirting with Matthieu.

'Alas, monsieur, I dare eat no more, or you will have to roll me to the door like a hoop! Besides, one should not eat too much before bathing, and I hope to persuade Mabel to bathe with me down by the sea. Why don't you join us?'

'One day, perhaps. But today I must return to my office. A colleague is coming all the way from Paris to see me so that I may sign some papers for him. Some other time, though, I would enjoy swimming with you. If you would care to, I could teach you to swim underwater so that you can see how the fishes live beneath the waves.'

He got to his feet as he spoke and Val, abandoning her coffee, jumped up also, holding out her hand.

'That would be very nice, though I daresay you'd find me a poor swimmer compared with girls who live on this coast all the year round. *Au revoir*, monsieur. I hope to see you again.'

'*Au revoir*, my dear. You may be sure we shan't let you stay here and not visit us!' He shook Val's hand, then strolled round the table and dropped a light kiss on his wife's cheek. '*Au revoir*, *chérie*. Take good care of our guest.'

'*Our* guest! Val, you're an enchantress,' Mabel said as her husband's car roared off down the drive. 'Matthieu is a serious man, no more liable to flirt with little girls than to fly. You really do know how to make a man feel special!'

Val, who had sat down again, smiled and picked up her coffee cup.

'This is the most delicious coffee. May I help myself to some more?' Pouring it, she considered the remark seriously. 'Men *are* special, though, aren't they? And I like men, or most of them. I liked Matthieu.'

Mabel laughed.

'And he liked you! I can't ever recall seeing Matthieu so at ease with a woman.'

'I'm not sure whether that's a compliment or not. He's very handsome, though, so I daresay he's used to flibbertigibbets setting their caps at him.'

'I don't think so. He can be very formal; I've actually seen him totally annihilate someone he thinks is angling for him with an icy glance. But you mustn't be too charming, or you'll find yourself invited to stay in the house! I could see that it was on the tip of his tongue to ask you.'

'That really would put the cat amongst the pigeons,' Val said, amused. 'However, I did think he might be persuaded to escort me round seeing the sights whilst you and Frank catch up on your unfinished business or whatever the phrase is.'

'My dear girl, how can he? Remember, when I'm chatting with Frank, I'm ostensibly with you.'

Val finished her coffee and smiled at her hostess.

'Not necessarily. If I've gone off somewhere with Matthieu, making sure I keep him occupied, then there's no earthly reason why you shouldn't just go for a quiet stroll by the sea, or a solitary meal – anything.'

Mabel stared, then a slow smile crept across her face.

'Val, you're a genius! But won't you be bored to tears with Matthieu?'

Val shook her head reprovingly.

'How can you say that? Matthieu's an interesting person, Mabel, as well as being so terribly handsome that I'll be happy to be seen with him. I like him and he likes me, which means we'll entertain one another very well, I promise you.'

393

'If you can persuade him to take you out,' Mabel reminded her guest, pushing her chair back from the table.

'That'll be child's play!'

Frank had found a tiny, curved bay where no one else ever seemed to go. It was an enchanting spot with pine trees which grew right down on the sand and an array of ancient, salt-encrusted fishing boats pulled up in the trees' shade. He and Mabel were sitting on the sand, leaning against a fishing boat and chatting comfortably. Val, bless her generous heart, Frank thought, had traipsed off to Nice with Matthieu; he was going to show her the casinos. They would not be home until very late, Mabel had said, probably long after she was in bed, for the casinos didn't really come alive until about eleven o'clock. So now they felt as safe and secure in each other's company as they did in Scotland – Mr and Mrs Neyland.

'All right, Frank. I've heard your arguments and they're pretty much the same as mine. André doesn't need me any more; Matthieu has had a good run for his fathering of my child. I've never told you why I left all those years ago and I never shall, because it's totally irrelevant. All that matters is that I did go, and gave you a lot of unhappiness. I think we both deserve better than what the years would have in store if I stayed here, so I'll come and live with you. If you'll have me, that is.'

Frank had a casual arm round Mabel's shoulders; it tightened and he pulled her closer, then leaned over and kissed her mouth.

'If! You know what it will mean to me, to have you there. Will you tell Matthieu, or just come away with us when we leave at the end of the fortnight?'

'Neither. I'm not telling him because I can't bear to, or

394

at least not until I'm all packed and ready to leave. For our September holidays, you know! Then I'll tell him that I don't know whether I want to come back. I'll talk about the possibility of war, my parents getting old – you know!'

'But will he swallow it?'

'I think he will. He may suspect that there's another man, but I don't know that it'll hurt him all that much. He dreaded losing André, you know, they're such good friends, but he must know he won't do that. André adores his father, and he's a Frenchman through and through, he wouldn't ever want to live in England. Matthieu won't even miss me terribly, not now. He has excellent servants.' There was a trace of bitterness in the last words.

'Right. And you needn't lose André; he can come and stay with us whenever he wants.'

'No!' The reply was almost too vehement, but before Frank could comment Mabel continued: 'I'd rather you didn't meet, much rather; that really wouldn't be fair to Matthieu. Now let's forget it and enjoy the sunshine. Because I really am coming back to England to stay, this time.'

Frank closed his eyes and turned his face up to the sun.

'Dear God, I can't wait for September!'

'There's a telegram for you, Nick. I've not opened it, but I can guess what it is.'

Jenny was sitting in a deckchair on the forecourt, basking in the brilliant sunshine. The pram containing a sleeping Marianne was parked close by. Jenny had been working, somewhat desultorily, on the books, but now she closed the ledger in her lap and smiled up at Nick, holding out the little yellow envelope.

Nick strolled over and took the telegram. He opened it and spread out the flimsy sheet.

'Yes, it's mobilisation at last. I leave for Stanstead tomorrow. I'll drive down, I think. Then I can come home whenever I'm off and give a hand with this place. By and by, the school has hired two buses for the twenty-ninth of August, so that's satisfactory, provided neither of our drivers get called up, of course.'

'Not likely; they're both in their fifties.' Jenny stood up and handed the ledger to Nick. 'Even so, we're not actually at war, are we? We'd have heard! It could drag on and on. Look at last September.'

'I wish people would stop looking at last September and think of now for a change,' Nick remarked. He took the handle of the pram and began to push it towards the Roses' flat. 'I suppose it's possible that we shan't get down to brass tacks before Christmas, but very improbable, I'd say.' He looked excited, as though the thought of imminent war pleased him. 'Anyway, if you think there isn't going to be a war, why did you buy all that black cotton material?'

'The black-out stuff, you mean? Well, because if I hadn't, then there would definitely have been a war. But since I spent money we could ill afford on the stuff there probably won't be one. And if there isn't, it'll be worth wasting the cash, don't you think?'

Nick, trying in vain to unravel this statement, shook his head wryly and parked the pram at the foot of the stairs which led up to their flat.

'I need notice of questions like that! Do you mean you think that if you . . . no, it's just too complicated. What time's tea today, or is Ivy getting it?'

'No, it's Ivy's day off. She's gone to see her mum. Simon's not had his telegram yet, but I daresay it'll come within the next two or three days. And if you mean why aren't I upstairs preparing tea, it's because it's all done. It's cold meat and salad and a trifle, with ice-cream on top, and there's a cake, too, because Rose is coming. It's no secret that they're going to start evacuating children from London any day now, war or no war, and if she's off I want to say a proper goodbye.'

'Yes, she's a nice kid,' Nick said. 'Shall I carry Baby or will you?'

'I will.'

Jenny plucked the drowsy, smiling infant from her blankets and draped her across one shoulder so that she was facing Nick as they climbed the stairs. At six months, Marianne was plump and smiling, an ideal baby, now rosy from sleep, her soft, dusky plume of hair sticking to her forehead and her white broderie Anglaise bonnet rucked up round one ear. She knuckled her eyes, rubbed her head against Jenny's and then smiled at Nick. He stroked one fat little hand.

'Hello, pet. Who's had a lovely snooze in the sun, then?'

'I just hope she sleeps as well tonight,' Jenny remarked as they entered the kitchen. 'Here, Nick, put her in the high chair, would you, and keep her amused whilst I do her a rusk? Then you can put the kettle on whilst I change her – I'd like to have her cleaned up and fed by the time Rose gets here.'

'Where'll you go, Jen, if the government decides to get all women and children out of London?' Nick asked presently, as he poured them both a cup of tea. Marianne, bibbed and brushed, was chumbling on her buttered rusk with a good deal of dribbling, casting roguish glances at him every now and then. 'You couldn't all stay in your mother's new house, could you? There wouldn't be room!'

'No, and I wouldn't, either.' Jenny did not like the

tiny house on Harvey Lane which her mother had bought after her father's death two years earlier. 'Mother's got Auntie Prue living with her. Even Martin's away from home now. They couldn't possibly fit me and Mari in, let alone Ivy! But your mother's very good. I'm sure she'd let us stay at The Pride if we were desperate, then I could keep Val company and perhaps do some work at the showroom if they needed extra help.'

'I'm sure Mama would love to have you and the tiddler there; as for the showroom, when the war starts they'll ration petrol and they may requisition cars, too, so there won't be any sale for them. But if Simon's in England, you could move into digs near him, or perhaps there are married quarters, I don't know.'

'We've considered that, and of course we're hoping to kill two birds with one stone. Norfolk's covered in aerodromes and if we're lucky and Simon gets posted there, then we could live in Norwich and be near him. You expect to go abroad, I suppose?'

'I imagine so, probably to France. You can't have an army sitting at home. They've got to be out there, stopping the enemy from attacking.' Nick began to lay the table, first with a white tablecloth, and then with the appropriate cutlery and crockery. 'When will Simon be back? By the way, guess what they want the buses for? The school, I mean.'

'Tell me,' Jenny invited, picking her child out of the high chair and taking her over to the sink to wipe off the remains of the rusk. 'I never was a good guesser.'

'To round up their evacuees. They're being sent out of London round about the end of August. Of course if it *is* just a false alarm they may be brought back again, but it's a pointer, isn't it?'

'Mm hmm. Where are the kids going? I just hope our buses are up to it.'

'Oh, only Waterloo Station – or is it Paddington? After that, God knows, though the school must have been told. It might be anywhere rural – perhaps it's Norfolk.'

'Not from Waterloo or Paddington,' Jenny said, ever practical. 'But some will go to Norfolk, of course. My aunt lives at Brooke. She's the evacuation officer for her area, and she's been up to her eyes in administrative work.'

'Yes, Mama was talking about it. She's had an air raid shelter dug out in the grounds, and they've done improvements to the cellars. Do you remember those wooden stairs, when we were kids?'

Jenny shuddered.

'I do. I hated your cellars, that awful, earthy, mouldy smell and the flicker of the torch on the whitewashed walls, and the size of the spiders! But the stairs were dreadful, so slippery and steep; it's a wonder we never broke our necks.'

'Yes, well, Mama has had them replaced, she said in her last letter, and had shelves put up and a beam put across to strengthen the ceiling. Poor dear, having stoutly denied rumours of war for months and months, she's suddenly decided to open her eyes and stop hiding her head in the sand, and she's talking quite cheerfully of stocking the shelves with necessities, whatever that may mean, so that if the family gets trapped down there when a bomb falls they won't starve until they're dug out.'

'Which family? She's only got Val at home. And me, if the worst comes to the worst.'

'All the family, my child! Remember, if Des and Con go off to fight, someone will have to keep an eye on the families that are left. Mama plans to be that someone. She's always been a superb organiser. I can tell she's raring to go.'

'I wonder what my mother will do in case of air raids? That house won't have a cellar, or not a large enough one for a siege!' Jenny chuckled, then cocked her head on one side. 'What's that, Mari?' She swung the baby up in her arms to face the door. 'Who's coming to see his best girl, then?'

Simon and Ivy entered the kitchen together, Ivy somewhat flushed.

'I'm sorry, Mrs Rose,' she said apologetically, mopping her streaming brow with a handkerchief, 'but what a rush I've had! Can I have the day off, come next week? Me mum's a bit upset. They've told her that the two youngest have got to be 'vacuated to Surrey.''

'Of course you can, but why did you rush back? You know I don't mind if you're late on your day off.'

'Fred's got 'is call-up papers. I wondered if you'd mind . . . he leaves ten o'clock tomorrow morning. He'd like it if I was on the platform to see 'im orf.'

'That'll be fine, Ivy.'

Ivy took Marianne from Jenny, cuddled her, let Simon pull a funny face at her, and then turned to leave the kitchen.

'I'll give her a nice bath, Mrs Rose, and then she can have her feed. Don't you worry about me tea. It's cold, isn't it? I can get it for meself when I've got Mari tucked up in bed.'

'She's not a bad kid,' Simon said when the door had closed behind her. 'I went along to the council offices about the business, as I said I would. They were very helpful, actually – said that mechanics were always useful, especially if they were in well-equipped garages and workshops. Said I needn't worry, there would probably still be a place for hire-cars and buses even when war did start, but that even if we found it necessary to close down for one reason or another they'd keep an eye on the property, probably even requisition it, and save it from being torn apart by thieves or vandals.'

'That's a relief, because my telegram's come,' Nick was saying absently, when the doorbell shrilled. 'Aha, that'll be Rosie! Shall I . . . well, would you look at that?' Simon had already gone and could be heard thundering down the stairs. 'He does like kids, your old man, Jen.'

'I know it; he dotes on Mari, too.' Rose burst into the kitchen, hugged Jenny, beamed at Nick and darted out again without a word. 'She's every bit as bad! Does she say hello? Not before she's gone through and paid her respects to Mari!'

Presently, however, respects paid, Rose returned to sit in her place at the table and watch hungrily as Simon piled her plate.

'Well, Miz Rose, we're off, just like you said,' Rose remarked as she began to eat. 'It won't be long now, they reckons. We've been told all sorts, had an extry vest each, and a card, all labelled, so's we can write to Matron soon's we arrive. Reckon it's somewhere real far off!'

'Oh, Rosie, I wish it was near where we might go,' Jenny said. 'But you never know, stranger things have happened. Don't forget we're going to Norfolk. Will they take you all into one house, or what?'

'Nah, we'll go all over the place,' Rose said cheerfully. I'm glad, I am. I don't want to be together, like in the 'ome. I want to be in real 'omes, like this one.'

'So you should,' Simon said approvingly. 'Have you still got the card Mrs Rose gave you? Don't forget to post it off as soon as you reach your new place, and then we can write back.'

'Some chanst of me forgettin'!' Rose said scornfully. 'I'll write quick as a flash, you bet. You'll write back quick too, won'cher?'

'As quickly as I possibly can. Mr Rose will write too, from wherever he is. Oh dear, I hate all this talk of friends parting.'

'Never mind, Miz Rose, it won't last long. All be over inside six months,' Rose said cheerfully. 'That 'itler won't last long once Mr Rose gets 'im lined up!'

'It hasn't even started yet, and it may not,' Jenny reminded them, but Simon, helping himself to bread and butter, pointed to a pile of black material lying beside the kitchen window.

'Oh, yes? Then why did you buy black-out stuff?'

'Don't ask her,' Nick groaned. 'Feminine logic is baffling.'

'I bought it to insure that there won't be a war,' Jenny said triumphantly. 'I worked out what I meant just now, when I was feeding the baby rusk. If there isn't a war, I'll have wasted my money, but I don't mind wasting money if there isn't a war. And if there *is* a war, then I'll have done the right thing by getting hold of the material before all the prices go up!'

'Nick, it's as clear as daylight,' Simon said reproachfully. 'My old darling's hedged her bets, that's what she's done. Whichever way it goes, she'll be pleased she acted as she did. I wonder when *my* telegram will come?'

Chapter Sixteen

'A bit lower, Ruthie. I don't want to make it an inch bigger than it has to be. My goodness, this house is going to cost me a fortune to black out completely. I bought a whole roll of material and it isn't nearly enough!'

Tina and Ruthie, armed with scissors, a tape measure, swathes of black cotton stuff and a step-ladder, were in the living-room. The floor to ceiling windows in here were proving exceedingly awkward. Black-out curtains were essential, of course, if there was going to be a war, and not the most determined optimist could doubt that war was in the offing, but the amount of material needed in this room looked like proving prohibitively expensive. As it was, Tina and Ruthie laboured on, knowing that their material was going to run out even before the ground floor windows were fitted, though they had sent Val into the city to search for fresh supplies.

'I wonder if we'll have to make blinds, like we did last time?' Tina said, perched on top of the step-ladder and stretching her tape measure across the big central panes. 'It isn't as effective as curtaining, but if you remember, Ruthie, last time we stuck black paper down each side of the window and across the top and bottom, and that sufficed. We could make rollers with garden canes, I suppose.'

'Yes, and we'll ha' to replace the light bulbs with totty little old things,' Ruthie contributed. 'And carry torches, of course.'

'That's right, torches are essential. Do you remember the muddle in the spring when they had trial blackouts? We don't want guests leaving the house and breaking their ankles before they reach their cars!'

'There'll be petrol rationing, so that's on the cards there won't be no cars,' Ruthie said pessimistically. 'What about them refugees, m'm? Do they be going to send us some?'

'Perhaps, but we're rather near the city, I think. I expect they'll save us until later.' Maxie, wandering into the room, saw her up on the ladder and promptly began to bark. 'Be quiet, you bad dog! Aaargh!'

Maxie, predictably, had attacked the ladder, which was wobbly to start with. Tina lurched, Ruthie grabbed her, the ladder tiped sideways, and mistress and maid landed on the floor. Maxie, an opportunist ever, grabbed as much black-out material as he could cram into his mouth and made off, trailing his booty behind him. Tina used her only swear word and scrambled to her feet, giving Ruthie both hands to help her up too.

'Damn, damn, damn that damned dog! I'm sorry, Ruthie, but it's more than flesh and blood can bear!' She headed towards the door. 'Come on, we must get him before he tears that material to ribbons!'

But even as she crossed the room there was a commotion from the hall, a laugh, another swear word, and Val appeared in the doorway, the erring Maxie beneath one arm, another roll of black-out material beneath the other.

'Whatever's going on here? Help me untangle this stuff from his tonsils, Ruthie!' She turned to her mother. 'I got another roll, Mama, though I had to pay three and tenpence a yard. What did you say you paid a couple of days ago?'

'Two and eleven; profiteering already.' Tina examined

the new roll of material. 'It's thinner than mine, too. Oh, well, at least it's something. If you ask me a lot of people will be making do with black paper. They did last time, though it isn't nearly so efficient.'

'I think you'll have to settle for blinds,' Val opined, slapping Maxie half-heartedly and putting him out of the room. 'This stuff has to be the last in the city. I had an awful job running it to earth, and no one else had any at all. If you do blinds, though, it ought to do the lot, even the conservatory.'

'Not the conservatory, Miss Val!' Ruthie, who knew she would end up making the blinds, showed the whites of her eyes. 'What about blast? Mr Frank was talking about blast, saying the conservatory would be dangerous in a raid.'

'Yes, you've got a point there. But what on earth made Frank mention the conservatory in the same breath as a raid?'

'Me,' Tina said complacently. 'I just happened to mention that if we were in the living-room and enemy action started then the quickest way to the dug-out would be through the conservatory. Which it would, and there was no cause for Frank to be so rude to me. I didn't say I'd go that way, I just pointed out that it would be quickest.'

'I can't imagine anyone voluntarily going down into that dug-out,' Val said, shuddering. 'I'd opt for the cellar, any time.'

'That dug-out cost a lot of money, and if I say we use it, then we use it,' Tina said grandly, rather spoiling the effect by adding, 'Well, in summertime, anyway.'

'Right. Perhaps the war will be over by then.'

'That in't started yet,' Ruthie reminded them. She picked up the new roll of black-out material. 'We're finished in here. Shall we go through to the study?'

But before anyone could move the door opened and Ada's skinny, aproned figure appeared in the doorway.

'Sorry to bust in, Miz Neyler, but hev you heard the wireless? Them Germans have gone into Poland and they've dropped bombs on Warsaw!'

Tina crossed the room quickly and put her arm round Ada's thin little shoulders.

'Oh, my dear, and you're worried sick about poor Mabel! But she's coming home quite soon, isn't she? Surely someone said she'd be coming back in September some time. And the Germans will be too busy in Poland to worry about France, particularly as they've got to tackle the Maginot line.' She turned to Val. 'Did you see the Maginot line, darling, when you were in France?'

'No, I didn't, though I saw lots of photographs and read lots of articles. But Matth . . . someone I met who had seen it didn't think it would prove insurmountable. He said it was built by German labour, so Herr Hitler would know all about it.'

'Well, it isn't supposed to be secret, it's supposed to keep Hitler and his storm troopers out,' Tina said, glaring at her tactless offspring. 'It'll do that, surely?'

'Of course, of course,' Val said hastily. 'Anyway, the French know what they could be in for; my friend said he'd get his wife and family to the north coast as soon as hostilities broke out, and then, if necessary, he could get them out right away.' She turned to Ada. 'Don't worry, Mrs Walters. The Allies won't get embroiled if they can help it. Hitler will probably see sense and withdraw. He may be as mad as everyone says he is, but he won't want to fight the Allies over Poland, surely!'

But Ada, little meek Ada, was shaking her grey head, her face set and determined.

'No, miss, I'd rather we had it out with him this time.

We're had enough of talk, and saying it's for the best to hold back. The time's come when we're gotta say enough, if you ask me. But I'd like my gal back, I would.'

'There's time,' Val said. 'Didn't you say she was coming on Monday, anyway? She'll be here before you know it.'

Ada sighed and turned back to go into the kitchen again. For the first time, Val noticed that she held a potato in one hand and a small paring knife in the other.

'I don't know, miss. She're got her hubby to consider. He won't expect her to leave at a time like this, to say nothing of the boy. But I can't help wishing she was back here!'

At six o'clock that Friday evening, Frank stopped work and went into the kitchen to get himself a meal. September had come in like a lion, with the Germans invading Poland, Chamberlain sending them an ultimatum, and the government sending him plans of a craft they wanted built. They were good plans too. He and the other men had decided to get on with the job at once, leaving less urgent work, and already, out in the yard, signs of an imminent new task were there for all to see. Frank was glad, because he loved building boats and too much of his time, lately, had been taken up with repairs, although he was building big yachts for export still – or had been, until the spring, when it seemed as though the crisis in world affairs had at last trickled through to the yacht-owners.

The knock on the door took him by surprise. Patch had died two years ago and, though he knew it was silly, he could not bear to replace him with another dog. Patch had been special. It did mean, however, that he had no warning of visitors until they were upon him and, in a cottage where the front door opened straight into the living-room, this could be quite a disadvantage.

He got up and opened the door, and found himself looking down into the dirty face of a small boy. His hair looked as though it had been cut with blunt garden shears, he wore trousers too short to be longs and too long to be shorts, and his feet were only partially encased in cracked and ancient boots.

'Hello! Lost your way?'

It was an absurd question, but he could think of no other reason for this visitation. The child was no villager, he knew them all.

'I was left,' the small boy said, his voice thick with unshed tears. 'All them others was claimed, but I was left. They brung me 'ere and give me this.' He held out a paper bag. 'She says she'll be rahnd later.'

'Oh! Well, you'd better come in.' Frank was completely mystified but he could see a piece of paper sticking out of the child's pocket; no doubt it was an explanation of sorts. 'Do you have a note for me?'

'Oh, yeah!' The note was handed over and proved to be from Mrs Matthews. Frank would have recognised that big, commanding handwriting anywhere even without the signature. It was brief and to the point.

Lenny's an evacuee, one more than we were promised, the note read. *Can you manage for a night or two?*

Frank felt his hair prickle on the back of his neck. Poor little blighter, to come such a long way from home and to find himself unclaimed at the end of it. He threw the note into the fire, for he lit a fire in the evenings against the damp, and smiled at his unexpected guest.

'Well, that's clear enough. You're going to stay here, Lenny, for a day or so, until they find you a home with a lady in it who can take care of you properly. I'm afraid that, until then, you will have to put up with my

408

housekeeping, which isn't very marvellous. But I daresay we'll manage. Do you like beef stew and sponge pudding with custard?'

'I sure do!' Lenny was blooming in the warmth like some exotic flower. He was also beginning to smell rather strongly. 'I eats *anyfing*!'

'Good, then let's get on with a meal. I was in the middle of mine when you arrived, but there's plenty left in the saucepan. Come into the kitchen with me and you can tell me how much you can manage.' The two of them went through into the lean-to-kitchen and Frank got a plate and spooned beef stew, rich with meat and vegetables, on to it, then added a pile of floury potatoes. He looked at the child. 'How's that!'

'Gawd, that's summink like!' Lenny's eyes glistened and Frank felt almost embarrassed by such enthusiasm. It was only beef stew, after all!

Later, when they had eaten, he asked his guest some pertinent questions.

'I know you're Lenny, but did anyone tell you who I was?'

'You're Mr Frank. They didn't *tell* me, I heard 'em whisperin'.'

'That's right. Sharp as a needle, that's you. Tell me, Lenny, can you swim?'

'Nah.'

'Row a boat?'

'Nah.'

'Then they shouldn't really have sent you here – did you see the water at any time? Yes, I thought you'd have noticed it. Well, if you were to stay here, you'd have to row across that water every morning to get to school. You could go round by road, but it's a much longer journey. If you stay anywhere in Oulton Broad, in fact, you should learn to swim and to row, because there's water everywhere.'

'Go to school in a *boat*?' Lenny's eyes gleamed with as much appetite as they had shown for beef stew. 'Gee!'

'You think you'd like that? Well, there's a possibility that you might stay here since . . .' He was thinking of Mabs; if she came, this would be regarded as a normal home, presumably, and as such might take a refugee. Unless, of course, the moral aspect of it struck them as unsuitable. But Lenny was staring at him, waiting for him to finish the sentence. '. . . since they're very short of cottages with a spare bedroom, I believe,' he finished lamely.

'A spare room? Cor!'

'Let's go through, then, and I'll show you where you sleep.' He had not looked into the paper bag but now he did so and found it contained a shirt which had seen better days and some socks whose reek made him push the bag quickly behind the scented geranium which stood on the kitchen windowsill. Phew! They would have to be washed – or burned, he wasn't sure which would be best!

He opened the spare room door and Lenny peered in, eyes rounding.

'Ain't it huge, then? 'Oo else sleeps 'ere?'

'No one. Just you. I've got the room next door. If you're frightened during the night you can bang on the wall and I'll come through.'

'I ain't scared of nothing,' Lenny said loftily. 'Only . . . I never slept alone before.' He subjected Frank to a long stare. '*In* the bed, is that where I sleeps?'

'That's right.' Remembering the smell of a fire-warmed Lenny and the fact that the bag had not contained such niceties as pyjamas, Frank added hastily: 'When you've had your bath, that is.'

'Barf? I 'ad a barf. A bed to meself, eh?'

'That's right. Why do you ask?'

'At 'ome there's seven of us, four in and free under.' Lenny's voice was matter-of-fact. 'I don't need no barf, mister! Me mum give me a good wash-dahn this morning.'

'Did she?' Frank examined his grey-skinned guest doubtfully. 'Perhaps the water wasn't very hot. I have a bath most nights,' he added in a consoling voice.

'*Do* you? 'Oo makes you?'

'I like it,' Frank said briefly. 'So will you, really. I'll stay with you so's you don't drown.'

He had meant it as a joke, but thirty minutes later, emerging from the bathroom almost as wet as his victim, it no longer seemed so funny. Lenny had not enjoyed his bath, or not the soap and washing part of it, though once he had got over the natural nervousness of a person who had never before been immersed in water he had thought it great fun to sit in the bath and push a laden soap dish, shiplike, from one enamelled bank to the other.

Frank lifted him out of the now grey, scum-laden water and carried him through into the living-room to get dry in front of the fire. Then he lent him an old shirt and a sweater and got out a pack of cards. They were still playing pelmanism, with Lenny winning hands down, when there was a knock on the door. Frank, opening it, grinned at Mrs Matthews's guilty expression.

'Come in, Mrs M. I'm just about to pack our young friend off to bed.'

Lenny went willingly enough, his eyelids heavy after a day of such strange and unaccustomed happenings as a train journey, a meal which included beef, and a bath, and once he had gone Mrs Matthews and Frank settled down on either side of the fire for a talk.

411

'There wasn't another bed in the village,' Mrs Matthews assured him as soon as Lenny had disappeared. 'I felt awful just sending him in, but I had a score of kiddies to take to the outlying farms – we were told they'd arrive on the second of September, and here it is, still the first – and I just drove down here, aimed him at the door and fled. I couldn't stop for explanations, but I'll take him off your hands first thing tomorrow, if you can't manage, I swear it. He'll have to go into Lowestoft and see if they can find somewhere for him.'

'No! He's not a bad kid. If you want to leave him and he wants to stay . . . well, I'll be glad of the company, in a way. Look, tomorrow's Saturday. We don't work Saturdays; I can take him round the village, show him the school, let him find his feet a bit. How does that sound?'

'Very fair!' Mrs Matthews seized his hand and shook it, pumping it up and down until Frank felt quite breathless. 'You've no idea, Frank, how I'd hate to fall down on this job. It'll be a feather in my cap if I find places for all of 'em.'

'You're a sport, Mrs Matthews, even to take it on,' Frank said sincerely. 'How many have you got?'

Mrs Matthews groaned.

'Four, two adults and two youngsters. I can see we'll have trouble. I believe the women are tarts; they're certainly sluts! Smoked all through supper, kept shrieking because the house seemed too large, too lonely, all wrong, cuffed their kids at the least excuse . . . I don't mind the children, but the adults are a different kettle of fish! By the way, did he bring his rations?'

'Rations?'

'He didn't, then. It was just a tin of condensed milk, a tin of bully beef, and a few apples. We were afraid that people might be caught without sufficient food in the house. But you've managed, I can see. What about clothing?'

'What clothing? He's gone to bed in my shirt and an old jersey. He's got trousers which once belonged to a fellow at least twice his size and I should think he's worn them from birth, a shirt in a similar state, no underwear, and two pairs of socks – one on, one off – which I shudder to describe. I think they ought to be burned. And there's something very odd about his hair. When I was washing it I noticed sort of fly things coming out of it. And it's full of little white specks.'

Mrs Matthews drew in her breath sharply.

'Can it be head-lice? Of course it can. Send him down to me first thing in the morning, my dear fellow, and I'll deal with that problem. As for the clothing, someone in the village will help you out – you want vests, under-pants, shirts . . .'

'Everything,' Frank interrupted firmly. 'Just say everything and you'll be all right. How old is he, anyway?'

'Eight,' Mrs Matthews said, after perusing a sheet of paper which she produced from her pocket. 'Lenny Cripps, aged eight.'

'I see. And where's he from?'

'London. East end.' Mrs Matthews stood up. 'Hey ho, who's next on my list? Aha, it's your Madge. She's taken two girls. Her little cottage must be bursting tonight. One of 'em is a Cripps, too.' She consulted her list again. 'Vera Cripps, aged twelve.'

'Why didn't she take them both?' Frank enquired as he saw her out. 'It seems a bit hard to separate brother and sister.'

'No, no, can't mix the sexes,' Mrs Matthews said briskly. 'That wouldn't do at all.'

She waved and disappeared into the night, leaving Frank a prey to wonderment at the oddities of the official mind.

During the night the excesses of the previous day made themselves felt and Lenny, weeping dolorously, was extremely sick in his bed. Sticky, and disgusting, he made his way, dripping, into Frank's room.

'I'm ill,' he quavered wretchedly. 'I've been poisoned.'

Frank, woken from a deep sleep, had to work very hard to control a desire to shout, but he knew, of course, that the fault lay with his beef stew, to say nothing of sponge pudding and custard. However, he got out of bed, stumbled into the bathroom, and made the small sufferer decent in another clean shirt.

'You haven't been poisoned, old lad,' he said patiently, as he offered Lenny a drink of water. 'I expect the stew was a bit rich after that long journey.'

'That stew come up,' Lenny announced bitterly, 'all mixed up with the chocolate what they give me on the train and the mince pies what we 'ad at the village 'all. I ain't never going to eat bloody mince pies again. I reckon they was *bad*, that's what I reckon.'

'Well, never mind, it's over now,' Frank was saying consolingly, when Lenny suddenly clutched at his stomach and rendered up the remainder of his previous day's guzzling all over Frank's feet and the bathmat. 'Couldn't you have sicked into the basin, old man?'

'I dunno *where* I'se going to be sick,' wept Lenny, plucking at his now thoroughly soiled shirt. 'I don't like bein' sick!'

'And I don't like you being sick either,' Frank said in heartfelt tones, getting yet another clean shirt out of his second drawer. 'Now, do you feel empty? If so, we'll both get into my bed and try to get some sleep out of what's left of the night.'

'I'm 'ollow as a bleedin' drum,' Lenny said, hoarse-voiced. 'No one ain't never been 'ollower.'

'Right. Then try to sleep.'

In the end, the pair of them slept so well that they were only woken, at ten o'clock, by Madge popping her head round the bedroom door. Lenny, to be sure, merely sat up, muttered something, and lay down again, instantly asleep once more, but Frank lurched out of bed and stumbled into the kitchen.

'What time is it, Madge?' He slumped down at the kitchen table and put his head in his hands. 'My God, what a night!'

'Have you been celebratin' down at the Wherry, bor?' Madge asked, with a giggle. 'Or hev that Lenny kep' you up till all hours?'

'This is not a hangover,' Frank said frostily, then looked up to grin at Madge. 'Poor kid, though, I've never seen anyone so sick!'

'You didn't give him that beef stew?' Madge said. She giggled again. 'Glory be, Mr Frank, that was rich – I'm surprised he in't inside-out this morning!'

'I know. But at the time I didn't think.'

'Well, no more did I,' Madge confessed magnani-mously. 'I give mine sausage-meat pie with swedes and the big 'un was suffin' sick.'

'Perhaps the mince pies the village worthies handed out *were* poisoned,' Frank said with faint hope. 'Lenny swore his food had been tampered with.'

'Ah, that'd be just like a boy's sauce to say so. No, t'were food being unaccustomed rich. How did he sleep?'

'Like a top, when he wasn't throwing up all over the bed. By the way, Madge, if it was your idea that I might put him up, then I don't mind admitting there's a pile of sheets and things in the bath, soaking and dreadful. Was it? Your idea, I mean.'

'That it were, so I'll wash the sheets gladly.' She paused, eyeing him. 'Mr Frank, did your lad say anything about the bed and that?'

'Rather! He said . . . you'll scarcely credit it, Madge . . . that at home they sleep seven to a bed, four in and three under. He must be making it up, mustn't he?'

'Not unless he and his big sister's making up the same thing,' Madge said grimly. 'Well, did you ever, Mr Frank? We don't know the 'alf, tucked away down here.'

'Nor want to,' Frank said fervently. 'When do you think we ought to wake him?'

'I'll put a nice pan of porridge on, that'll line his little belly,' Madge said. 'What do you fancy? Bacon and eggs?'

'Porridge will do nicely, thanks,' Frank said, repressing a shudder. 'I don't know why, but I'm not terribly hungry. I say, switch the wireless on, would you? Chamberlain sent Hitler an ultimatum telling him to get out of Poland or else. I want to hear his answer.'

But no answer came that day, and in the hurly-burly of finding new clothing for Lenny, showing him the school, the village and the house where one of his sisters was lodging, Frank found that world affairs tended to take a back seat. He stayed in for an hour on the Saturday afternoon, but Mabel did not ring. Why should she, when she would be on the boat on Monday, heading for England at last? He comforted himself with the thought.

Rose looked around the farmhouse kitchen. She had never dreamed of a room like this one, but if she had

416

known about it she would have. She liked it more than any other room she had seen, that was why. There was a huge, blackened range at one end, a stone sink with two wooden draining boards at the other, and in between a scrubbed wooden table, a red-tiled floor with rag mats dotted over it, and a dresser gay with blue and white china.

There were chairs, too. The sort of chairs with wooden seats and backs that you used up to the table, and the sort of chairs with chintz covers on that you relaxed before the fire in.

She had been here for only one evening, because the journey was a long one, taking the best part of the day, with their school teachers who had accompanied them harried and almost as lost as they. But as soon as they had arrived on the platform of Barnstaple station, she had known a foretaste of what was to come. The very air seemed different, softer, milder, and the leisurely accents of the ladies who had come to welcome them and arrange where they were to go filled her with a sense of home-coming.

Mrs Riley, the farmer's wife, had come to pick up her evacuees in the pony trap. She'd taken two strapping fourteen-year-old orphans who could help on the farm, a thin boy called Roy with a mop of fair hair and glasses, and Rose.

'You'm my treat, maid,' she had said as they wended their way through the rich country lanes in the early evening. 'The lads will give Tom an 'and, but 'ee'll be with I.'

In one evening, Rose had discovered that the Rileys had three strong sons, all grown men, that Mrs Riley had yearned for a daughter ever since she could remember, and that they were people to whom fairness meant a great deal.

'Joseph and Sam'll pay their way, I reckon,' Mrs Riley had said as they ate their tea. 'You youngsters are make-weights; 'tes only vair.'

The Rileys were quite different to look at. Mr Riley was small, skinny and tough as old boots. He was not garrulous, ate like a starving wolf, and would have worn his cap at mealtimes – Rose suspected that he probably did wear it in bed – had his wife not been firm. Mrs Riley on the other hand was a big woman, fat and cuddly as the goose-feather bolsters on Rose's new bed, fair-haired, blue-eyed, rosy-cheeked. Both were in their mid-fifties, though Rose, had she thought about their ages at all, would merely have classed them as 'grown-ups', together with everyone else of her acquaintance over about sixteen.

Rose had got up early that morning, but even so, the men had eaten and gone long before.

' 'Tes harvest,' Mrs Riley had explained laconically, when Rose remarked on their absence. 'They be out early. 'Tes a fine day, zee?'

Rose, spooning porridge with clotted cream on it, did not enquire further but remembered her postcards. The farm was in the depths of the country. Hills rolled away in all directions, but there was scarcely a house to be seen. She had been told to post her cards at once – but where?

'Us'll take they in, come ten o'clock,' Mrs Riley said comfortably when Rose put the question. 'Mrs Cuthbert du like fresh-laid eggs. Would 'ee like to fetch 'un for I?'

Rose found that it was a lot easier to understand Mrs Riley's odd way of putting things if you didn't think what she was saying, but just took in the gist of it.

'Fetch the eggs? Where are they?'

Mrs Riley chuckled and surged to her feet. She had

418

eaten with the men, but had sat down with Rose 'for company' and drunk two cups of very strong tea. Now she took off her flowered apron and made for the back door.

'I'll show 'ee.'

Rose had read in books that hens laid eggs, but she had never actually thought about it. Now, bent double, she was in the shippon, ferreting about in soft, dusty piles of straw and hay, in and out of carts and mangers and a lethal looking machine which Mrs Riley said was a turnip cutter, and finding 'shop eggs', cunningly hidden, in the most unusual nooks and crannies. She also found a hen, swollen, scarlet-faced and furious, which had attacked her when she bent to examine the straw in which she squatted.

'She'm broody,' Mrs Riley had said, with another of her plump, bosom-wobbling chuckles. 'There'll be chicks for 'ee, soon.'

Chicks! She had seen a picture in a rag book when she was very small; chicks were round and yellow. They went, according to rumour, *cheep cheep!* She stared up at Mrs Riley, open-mouthed, and saw that good woman's mouth twitch.

'There's calves, in the pens; shall us go there next? I fed 'em, earlier, but tomorrow . . .'

Rose scuttled in her wake, her cards all but forgotten. This place was heaven! When Roy, who was nine and had overslept even more efficiently than she, joined them, inclined to cavil at the feather-bed into which he had sunk, she had no time for such behaviour.

'That ain't nothing. Wait'll you see the animals, Roy!' To her own ears, her voice sounded sharp and foreign after Mrs Riley's leisurely tone. 'They'm lovely,' she said carefully. 'They'm wunnervul!'

Jenny heard the alarm go and groaned, then sat up and stared suspiciously at it. This was Sunday. Why should she be woken on Sunday? If there was a hire either Nick or . . . she groaned again and swung her feet out on to the floor. Damn and blast it, how could she have forgotten? Simon had not merely got up and gone out to see to a hire; he was miles away, in Surrey somewhere, doing whatever newly called-up Royal Air Force men did. And Nick, of course, was in Stanstead, being a soldier.

She began to dress, then remembered that she had not washed, and sighed, but padded out to the bathroom, only to find Ivy in occupation, with Marianne cooing to herself as she lay on her back, naked, and watched the light fitting overhead.

'Morning, everyone,' Jenny said cheerfully. She leaned over the baby and butterfly kissed her cheek, then plonked a real kiss on her bulging tummy. 'I'll go and wash in the kitchen rather than disturb the pair of you.'

'Why so early, Mrs Rose?' Ivy asked. She folded the clean nappy, slid it dexterously beneath Marianne's small body, and pinned it neatly in place. 'I thought Sunday was a quiet day?'

'Yes, it is, only my alarm was set and . . . oh, God!'

'What've you remembered, eh?' Ivy said to Jenny's disappearing back. 'Someone coming to lunch?'

'No, I wish it were! We've a bus hire for nine o'clock and I promised to open up and make sure everything was ready to roll. I'll get dressed and wake Ritchie.'

Ritchie and his family had moved into one of the flats so that he could help her to take care of things. She was grateful for his help and company and adored his wife, Minnie, who had no sooner moved in than she got herself a job at a nearby dress shop. Minnie, with her broad Norfolk accent and her commonsense approach to each day was a joy to be with, and when she wasn't working in the dress shop she often came over to Jenny's flat for a chat, or to give a hand, as she phrased it, with the office work. A thoroughly nice woman and the sort of neighbour that everyone dreams of having.

As soon as she had dealt with the hire of the bus, Jenny came back to the flat and rang her mother-in-law. Sarah was also suffering from a lack of husband, since Con had joined the army, but she was her usual cheerful self in spite of having to manage the naughtiest child ever born, as she phrased it.

'Worse than Simon?' Jenny had said teasingly, last time she rang.

'Oh, far worse. Simon was a *dear* little boy, when he was a little boy, I mean. It was just that I couldn't cope with his teenage carryings-on. But Sebastian's only seven and he defeats me already. I suppose it's my age.'

But this morning, she had other news.

'William's joined up, dear. Jews, you know, feel far more loathing for Hitler than anyone else because they know more. We listened to what the Jews in Germany were saying, we saw the type of decent, intelligent professional man who was having to leave, and we knew the Führer was a monster. That's why William's gone, of course, because I imagine he could have waited a bit longer if he'd wished to do so, or even pleaded that his work at home was worth more than anything he could do in the army.'

'I understood what Hitler was after I'd seen Herr Brecht die,' Jenny said. 'English people have been saying for ages now that he's mad, crackers, fit for a loony bin, but ever since March I've known he was more bad than mad. Anyway, it helped when Simon

421

left to tell myself that he was fighting evil, and I expect it'll help Cara, too.'

'I don't know that it does.' Sarah's voice was light, but Jenny could tell from its tone that she was not pleased with her daughter. 'She ranted and raged at him, accused him of deserting her and his child, and then didn't even stay in London to see him off, but came flouncing down to Norfolk in that chauffeur-driven Rolls of theirs, full of grumbles, expecting me to take her side and demand that William be released from the army at once. Just as though she were still a child. I've no patience with her.'

'The trouble is, Cara married far too young and never had any real responsibility. I mean, you stopped taking care of her and William took over, and she seems to have stuck at about seventeen. What are you going to do with her?'

'I sent her back to London at once, with a flea in her ear. I told her that as a married woman her first responsibility was to her husband and stepdaughter. She wasn't best pleased, but she went.'

'Gracious!' Jenny assimilated this. 'You mean she had left Mira in London?'

'Yes. She said she couldn't take her away from her nursery school, of all the absurd excuses. What she meant, of course, was that Mira wasn't even considered; all she thought of was herself. Anyway, she's back in town now, so I thought I ought to warn you that she'll probably descend on you some time today, full of self-pity and hating her mother. If she does, dear, do you think you could try to talk some sense into her? I really dread what she might do without William to keep her in check.'

'Well, I'll do my best if she does come round. What sort of thing could she do, though?'

'I shudder to think! Remember, Jenny, she had no ordinary courtship or anything like that, she simply married William straight from school.'

'I often wondered why you let her,' Jenny said a little shyly. 'Or did you really think she was head over heels in love?'

'Oh, *no* Jenny, Cara isn't like that! But William was absolutely besotted and Cara was determined, so I just said go ahead and spent months with my fingers crossed, hoping that I'd done the right thing. I'm sure it would have worked beautifully, too, if only William hadn't had to leave her.'

'What do you think she'll do, then?' Jenny laughed. 'Make up for lost time? Play the field?'

'She might, at that. Cara needs admiration and someone who adores her and sees no fault in her. And though I knew I must send her home, when I think of her in London, alone except for servants, bored, with time on their hands, I get quite scared enough to consider sending for her and having her to live here.'

'She wouldn't come, so I think you're safe there! Unless they actually bomb London, in which case she won't be the only one fleeing. What about the flat off Prince of Wales Road? Did William keep it on, or did he let the lease lapse?'

'Bless you, my child!' Sarah said fervently, her voice lightening. 'I don't know, but I can find out. Once William's left – if this war does happen, I mean – then she could come down here with all her entourage and live there. I'd be able to keep an eye on her without actually being driven mad by having her in the house. I'll go now, and ring round and see if I can find out. 'Bye, darling!'

Jenny rang off and went into the kitchen in a thoughtful frame of mind. So William had enlisted, or whatever they called it, had he? And Cara was on the warpath? She heard Ivy bringing the baby through, and poured milk into a pan ready for Marianne's cereal. She also turned the wireless on. Best to be prepared for news, when it came.

Mabel had packed and unpacked her cases a dozen times in the last two days, but now she unpacked for the last time, and put the case away. It was no use. She could not possibly leave Matthieu and go flying off to England without knowing what was going to happen. It would look so strange to go now. Matthieu had taken it for granted that she would go until Hitler had moved into Poland, and then he had taken it for granted that she would not. He did not know, of course, that she had meant to leave him for good. He thought it was just a holiday, and, plainly, one did not go away on holiday with the threat of war hanging over one's head. But now, just as she was resigning herself to wait only a few more days, the blow had fallen. Mme Frenaise, abandoning the preparation of luncheon, had rushed out of the kitchen and into the living-room, a skillet still in her hand, the smell of roasting chicken accompanying her.

'Madame, the Allies have declared war on Germany!'

Mabel's heart plummeted.

'Are you sure, Mme Frenaise?'

A stupid question, but one, Mabel was sure, that would be asked in a number of homes today. Mme Frenaise, however, a stolid Breton, merely nodded.

'Yes, madame; it was on the wireless.'

'Very well. Where is my husband?'

'He's on the telephone, madame. Shall I ask him to come to you here when his call is finished?'

'Yes, that would . . .'

But at that moment Matthieu entered the room,

patted Mme Frenaise dismissively on the bottom and turned her towards the door, then spoke to Mabel.

'Pack up everything you need, *chérie*, and we'll be off this afternoon. What a mercy André is in Paris and not in Dublin. He's only been back two days. I heard the announcement and rang him, and the Paris office too, of course. How soon can you be ready to go?'

'Go? Where?'

For a moment her heart sang with the hope that he was going to pack her off to England, but his next words killed all that. 'Brittany, of course, where else? I shall go back to Paris, but I would prefer to think of you in Brittany.'

From Brittany, it would be a simple matter just to go; to slip across the Channel to England and home. She took a deep breath. She had waited twenty years; a few more days, a few more weeks, even, would not hurt her.

'I'll come to Paris with you, if you please, Matthieu. I've no intention of being packed off to safety like a child, and anyway, we don't know that it will be any more dangerous in Paris than anywhere else! I could be useful, I'm sure, particularly as all the young men are being called up for military service.'

Matthieu, never demonstrative, patted her shoulder.

'You're a good wife, Mabel. It would be far pleasanter for me if you were in Paris, too, but at the first sign of danger you *must* go to Brittany! I've always faced facts, my dear, and I'm nearly sixty; you are thirty-five.' He hesitated, then looked down at her, his face working as if he might burst into tears. It frightened her a little because Matthieu never showed emotion. 'I want your happiness, *chérie*, whatever the cost to myself.'

'Then I'll come to Paris,' Mabel said, smiling at him. 'I'd be happier to be at the hub of things than outside them. For a time, at least.'

425

When he left her, however, she sat down in a chair by the telephone and picked up the receiver, her mind in a turmoil. She must put in a call to England and let Frank know that her plans had received a temporary setback, but then she must acknowledge that, however careful she had been, Matthieu knew. Oh, he might not know that she had intended to leave him, but he certainly knew that her happiness did not lie with him, either in Paris or Brittany. And he had, in a few words, offered her her freedom. Strange that by so doing he seemed to have tied her here more effectively than by forbidding her to go!

She dialled, but when the operator answered it was only to tell her that there was a three-hour delay on all calls abroad and that she would be rung back in due course.

Baulked of even the pleasure of hearing Frank's voice, Mabel went into the kitchen and told Mme Frenaise that they would be leaving for Brittany later in the day. Mme Frenaise, basting a fat capon, smiled at the news and promised that she and the other servants would be ready.

'Is Brittany safer, when there is war?' she asked. 'Will monsieur be joining us there, madame?'

'No, monsieur and I will be going to Paris. But we'll probably come down next weekend.'

Mabel glanced affectionately round the kitchen, and then returned to the Ivory room, where she picked up the receiver and tried to call André in Paris, though without result. Every telephone line in France seemed to be busy.

She had done her best to put off the evil hour, but now she must pack. She went to her room and dragged out the suitcase, feeling all the misery of her cancelled holiday flooding over her, as she had known it would.

To be packing, not for England, but for Paris! Dully, she began to put her folded clothing into the case.

Nick was in the pub in the village when the news came over the wireless. He scarcely heard it, in fact, because the White Hart was so crowded that the small voice speaking so sombrely was lost in all the other voices. But he knew it was war. Men who had waited a year for this moment were garrulous now that it had arrived and they shouted and drank and showed relief that at last the waiting was over. Now they could get down and do the job, show Hitler and his storm troopers that bullying did not pay.

Nick's friend John grabbed his arm, and in so doing sloshed the best part of Nick's pint on to the floor.

'Hear it? It's come! No more peace in our time, old boy, we're at war with Germany!'

His tone was triumphant, and triumph was the prevailing feeling amongst the men crammed into the old-fashioned public bar.

'We're at war, Rose! What do you think of that?'

Roy had been in the kitchen with Mrs Riley, both of them listening to the wireless, whilst Rose, outside on the tiny lawn before the farmhouse, made her first-ever daisy chain. She was going to hang it round Mrs Riley's neck at lunchtime. Now, she squinted up at Roy, whose glasses seemed to blaze with excitement, trying to take in the import of what he had said.

'At war? Is it with the Germans?'

'Of course! Blimey! Wish I was older!'

'Does that mean we'll stay here, then? That they won't come and fetch us back to London?'

'That's right. We could be here *years*.'

'I say!'

Speechlessly, the two stared at one another. Roy, too, was an orphan from the Broad Street home. They grinned like idiots, then Rose jumped to her feet and hugged Roy, only it turned into a wrestling match and they both fell heavily on to the patch of grass, the daisy-chain, forgotten, squashed beneath them. War could be wonderful!

Val and Tina missed the wireless announcement because they were halfway to Desmond's house, where they had been invited for Sunday lunch. Val, driving, was trying to warn Tina that she had every intention of joining one of the women's services in case of war, but Tina, who did not intend to lose her daughter without a fight, was pointing out in what she thought was a calm and sensible tone that Val would have to give up any silly schemes such as the one she was propounding and help to run the business.

By the time the car slowed down to turn into the drive of the Earlham Road house, both occupants were flushed and furious, though still perfectly willing to continue the argument. Except that there was some sort of commotion on the drive before them, a tangle of arms and legs which presently resolved itself into the figures of Desmond's younger children, Eddy and Emily. They had been fighting fiercely, but as they saw the car they broke apart and hailed their relatives.

'Give's a lift, Auntie Val!' Val drew up and the two children grabbed at the door. 'You don't know what *we* know!'

'I know you won't get a lift if you don't stop fighting,' Val said.

Eddy promptly picked his small sister up in his arms and deposited her, with a jarring crash, on Tina's lap.

'There you are, Gran! She's a dirty German and I'm a British soldier, like Uncle Nick.'

'I'm not, I'm not,' Emmie wailed, hitting out at her brother with a furious fist. '*You're* the dirty German!'

'Shut up, both of you,' Val commanded. 'Hang on tight, Eddy, and you can ride on the running board. What's all this fighting in aid of, anyway?'

'We're at war, Auntie,' Eddy shouted, the breeze of their going blowing his yellow hair up into a crest like a cockatoo's. 'That old man said so a moment ago, on the wireless. Mummy's crying and Daddy's telling her not to be a fool, and Bea's saying a good job too, only her boyfriend's still in Germany and he'll be called up, and they'll be on different sides, so she'll probably be snivelling soon.'

Bea was a German refugee, a plump, motherly creature who had settled easily into the Neyler household and created order out of chaos, too. She was not a Jew, but her father had been a Communist and poor Bea had fallen into disfavour with the Reich and had been smuggled out of Germany, according to her, in a lorryload of cauliflowers. Eyeing her ample proportions, the Neylers thought they must have been mammoth cauliflowers, but they loved her anyway.

'So we're at war.' Tina sighed and settled Emmie more comfortably on her lap. 'I wish Bea's young man could have got out, but if he's safe that's something to be thankful for.'

'Daddy says he won't be called up because he works in a factory that makes aeroplanes,' Emmie remarked. She was a tough little thing – Desmond's children had to be tough – and had not shed a tear over the rough treatment her brother had handed out. 'What about you, Auntie Val? Will you go off to the war?'

'No, she won't,' Tina snapped as the car drew up outside the front door. 'She's needed at home just as badly as Bea's young man is needed at the aircraft factory.' She fumbled for the door handle but Eddy was before her, opening it and then gambolling off towards his father, who was coming down the front steps whilst Beryl hovered behind him. Val came round and helped her to stand Emmie down and to get out herself, and then Des was holding out his hands to her, a smile of genuine affection lighting his handsome face.

'Good morning, Mama; good morning, Val. Did you hear the news before you left? Hitler hasn't answered the Allies' message, so we're . . .'

'. . . at war,' Tina finished, standing on tiptoe to kiss his cheek. 'The children told us. Well, well, when the worst happens it's sometimes almost a relief.' Two more of Desmond's children, Art who was eighteen and Maude, who was seventeen, appeared beside their mother. They were both so fair that they looked almost albino, with very light blue eyes and paper-white skin, but despite appearances they were as hardy as the younger children. Art grinned at Val.

'Hello, Auntie!' It amused them all that a mere three years separated their ages, but it was a family joke only. The older children always called her Val.

'Morning, Art. Hello, Maudie. What do you think of the news?'

'A relief,' Maud said and Art added: 'Absolutely, a great relief. Know where we stand, what?'

Beryl kissed Tina as she entered the house, then smiled at Val. She was pale and red-eyed, the only person present who did not look happier for the Prime Minister's announcement.

'Good morning – isn't the news dreadful? I confess I had a little weep.'

'Mummy's a baby. I didn't cry,' Emmie announced, bounding into the hall. 'Why didn't you bring Maxie, Auntie Val? I love Maxie!'

'Because he's an ill-mannered beast,' Val said briefly. She had been bounced on by Maxie that very morning and he had ruined her cream linen skirt and a pair of silk stockings. 'What's more he chases cars, so he shouldn't be allowed to ride in them.'

'And the postman has warned us that if Maxie bites either him or his bicycle once more he won't deliver the post,' Tina added. 'Can you imagine, having to walk the length of that drive twice a day just to pick up the letters? We'd have to have a box fitted to the gatepost, which would be so shaming, such an admission that we couldn't control our own dog.' She cast Val a malevolent look. 'Thank heaven *I* wasn't responsible for bringing him into our lives!'

'Well, he's a dear little dog in other ways,' Beryl said hastily, sensing a quarrel. She moved towards the living-room. 'Would anyone like a sherry before we sit down to the table? No, Emmie, darling, not you. You can go and ask Bea for a nice glass of milk.'

By eleven o'clock Jenny was cooking the lunch whilst Ivy took the baby for a walk in the park. It seemed silly to be roasting a chicken just for the two of them, but on the other hand the chicken had been bought before she knew that neither Simon nor Nick would be able to get home this weekend. The only comfort was that there would be plenty of cold meat over, and she and Ivy both loved chicken. What was more, Mrs Fisher and their two daughters had gone off for the day to visit friends down in Wimbledon, so she had told Richie to pop up and share their meal and he had promised to do so, if he got back in time. So there might be three people eating, after all. She had done plenty of potatoes just in case, and was even now preparing runner beans enough for a small army. When one had been accustomed to cooking

431

for two hungry young men, it was difficult not to overcater.

When the doorbell rang, Jenny glanced at the kitchen clock, but it could not possibly be Richie – he had been hired to drive a party of pensioners down to a village in Somerset where they would stay until the authorities thought it safe for them to return to the capital. He could scarcely have got there and back by now. Sighing, Jenny abandoned her beans, shed her pinafore, and hurried down the stairs. Whoever it was they would have to come into the kitchen and watch her stringing beans, otherwise lunch would be late.

As soon as she reached the foot of the stairs, however, the mystery was solved. Through the glass panel of the front door she could see the sleek dark hair and the pale face of her sister-in-law. Cara had come calling, as her mother had thought she might. A little reluctantly, for she and Cara had never really seen eye to eye, Jenny opened the front door.

'Cara, how lovely! Can you stay to luncheon? Do come up and I'll get you a drink. Simon and Nick couldn't make it this weekend, so I'm all alone. Did you drive, or come by tube?'

'Darling, are you ma-ad? I was driven, of course. Carstairs is out there now, parked in front of your doors, waiting for me.'

Jenny stopped so abruptly that Cara nearly cannoned into her.

'Should we ask him up, if you're staying for a bit? He might like a beer or something.'

'What a socialist remark! One doesn't drink beer with one's chauffeur in the kitchen! I don't suppose I'll stay long, anyway.'

They reached the kitchen and Jenny held the door open for her sister-in-law.

'Sorry to bring you in here, but I'm stringing beans and I want to get on with it. Ivy's taken Marianne to the park – where's Mira?'

Cara was wearing a pale, golden-coloured fur coat and a tiny violet silk hat. She flung herself into a chair and yawned, showing her small, perfect white teeth and a very pink tongue. She reminded Jenny of a cat.

'Mira? At home, with Nanny. I'm deathly bored because William is away, that's why I came round.'

Despite herself, Jenny laughed.

'Cara, you're incredibly rude! You never care what you say, do you? Would you like a drink?'

'I'll have a sherry. What makes you think I'm rude? All I said was . . .'

'I heard! You implied that had you not been deathly bored you would never have come to visit me. See?'

Cara smiled, catlike once more. She also shrugged, a feline gesture when Cara peformed it.

'Darling, don't be si-illy! I'm sure you lead a very busy, interesting life, but I don't find hiring cars particularly fascinating, and babies are terribly boring, and so's housework.' She stood up and dropped her fur coat on to the nearest chair. 'Shall I go and pour my sherry, darling? I know where Simon keeps it.'

'All right. Pour me a little one, too,' Jenny said. 'Look, Cara, do stay to lunch. You can easily ring home and tell them you won't be back until later. If you're so bored, it might be the best thing to do.'

'Well, I could, except . . . what's for lunch, anyway?'

'Roast chicken and so on. Oh, I was forgetting the *kosher* business, but at least it isn't pork, and I've not made a pudding yet, unless you count a jelly.' Abruptly, she remembered her invitation to Richie. 'Oh, one of the boys promised to come in if he could, but you won't mind that.'

'Who? Not that terrible little fellow Simon brought up from Norfolk?' At Jenny's nod: 'Dear God, Jenny, what's happened to you? When we were children your mother was so terribly fussy, even fussier than mine. You wore what was best, you went where she allowed you to go, you only met people she approved of – the *fuss* when Simon brought some little tart to a tennis party and your mother saw her and thought you'd be defiled by her company! I can remember heaps of times when your mother and Auntie Tina almost came to blows over what was "right", and what was not!'

'They say we all try to be different from our parents, and Simon's very broadminded,' Jenny said as patiently as she could. 'As for you Cara, you're the end! There's nothing terrible about Richie, though I know he does get greasy when he's doing up a car – and I wish you wouldn't just trot out remarks about Simon's "little tarts", either. He *is* my husband, you know.'

'Yes, so you must know he had little tarts,' Cara said, going through into the dining-room. She returned presently, carrying the bottle of sherry and two glasses. 'Simon's my brother as well as your husband, remember, and I don't mind if people knew he had affairs before he was married. Besides, I daresay it was mostly talk and there was nothing between him and all those girls.'

'Are you staying to lunch or not?' Jenny's voice, which she was striving to keep calm, came out a little higher than usual.

'Not. I wouldn't mind, but I'm not eating a meal with that horrible greasy man with the broad Norfolk accent. I wouldn't be able to enjoy a mouthful. Besides, I bet you muddle your pans when Simon's not here to watch you.'

'I probably do,' Jenny snapped, shooting a malevolent

look at her elegant little sister-in-law, standing there so smugly in a simple black dress which had probably cost sixty guineas. 'Simon isn't fussy about pans, so why should you be?'

'Because I wouldn't want to break the dietary laws,' Cara said self-righteously. 'William wouldn't want me to, either. Oh, do stop glaring, Jenny, just because I don't like your greasy little employee.'

Jenny picked up her glass of sherry and swigged it so quickly that her eyes watered, but she was so annoyed with Cara that she hardly noticed.

'All right, Cara, you've made your point. You won't stay to lunch and you think I'm putting Simon's soul in mortal sin by not being careful over my cooking pans, but just tell me this! How is William managing in the army, do you suppose?'

The smug look left Cara's face. She frowned.

'I suppose they're making him special food, aren't they? Of course, they give Catholics fish on Friday all over the place, it's always on menus, so they'll be providing *kosher* food for Jews.'

Jenny laughed loudly, then winced. Could it be the sherry making itself felt?

'For one man in every five thousand? Don't be ridiculous!'

Cara sipped her sherry.

'Do you mean to tell me they won't provide *kosher* food? Well then, William could get out of it right now, on religious grounds. It isn't as if we were at war!'

'That reminds me.' Jenny crossed the room and turned the wireless up. 'Mustn't risk missing any announcements. I don't know about getting out of it – why should he? You may be sure that William knew what joining the army implied even if you didn't.'

'You mean he's been eating non-*kosher* food at those

435

weekend courses?' Cara's eyes rounded. 'You can't be right!'

Jenny, triumphant, was just racking her brains to see how she could prove how right she was when the music coming from the wireless set stopped and a voice began to speak. Quickly, she went over to it and turned the volume up.

'Wait a mo, Cara, this may be important.'

It was Chamberlain speaking. Jenny recognised his voice only too well. He was talking about the ultimatum which had been sent to Hitler demanding that he undertake to withdraw his troops from Poland.

I have to tell you that no such undertaking has been received and that, consequently, this country is at war with Germany.

Even as the voice ceased, the ominous ascending howl of an air raid warning rent the air.

Cara set her glass down carefully on the table. She was very pale.

'Well, that's that. I don't suppose William could get out of it now even if he wanted to. What are we supposed to do when the siren goes off?'

'Go to the shelters, I suppose.' Jenny ran to the open kitchen window and leaned out. 'You go, Cara, I'll wait here. I can't just rush off when Ivy might bring Marianne back at any moment.' It was a sweet, autumn morning, the sky blue, the sunshine bright. 'There's no sign of them outside yet. Oh, and perhaps Carstairs ought to take cover. I bet he won't like to leave the car without permission.'

'I'll go down to him and come straight back. Will it be all right, Jenny, if we both lunch here after all? Carstairs and I?'

Jenny swung round from the window, her mouth dropping open.

'You *and* Carstairs? Good God, has the war turned

you into a human being already? Or are you frightened to go home because of the siren?'

Cara poured herself more sherry and sipped at it.

'I'm not frightened, because it's far too soon for anything to have happened, but I can see that it'll change things,' she said. 'William was cross with me last weekend. He said I was nothing but a spoiled child. I think I'll try to be a bit more like you, Jenny.'

She turned and left the kitchen and Jenny, biting her lip, went to the oven to check her chicken, and then began to lay the table for five. War was a terrible thing but at least there were good reasons for fighting. Herr Brecht and others like him had to be avenged; the Poles, the Czechs, even the Austrians, had to be saved from the terror of the Third Reich. And war was not only terrible, it was a great leveller – look at Cara, actually offering to sit down for luncheon with her chauffeur and a motor mechanic! If the war humanised Cara, there was some good in it.

Slowly, Jenny began to do her own bit for the war effort. She began, for the first time in her life, to carve the Sunday bird.

A Selected List of Fiction Available from Mandarin

☐ 7493 1045 6	**Body and Soul**	Marcelle Bernstein	£4.99
☐ 7493 0494 4	**The Hour of the Angel**	Alexandra Connor	£3.99
☐ 7493 0595 9	**Mask of Fortune**	Alexandra Connor	£3.99
☐ 7493 1107 X	**The Well of Dreams**	Alexandra Connor	£3.99
☐ 7493 0554 1	**People of this Parish**	Rosemary Ellerbeck	£4.99
☐ 7493 0779 X	**The Future is Ours**	Margaret Graham	£4.99
☐ 7493 0561 4	**A Fragment of Time**	Margaret Graham	£4.99
☐ 7493 0500 2	**A Measure of Peace**	Margaret Graham	£4.99
☐ 7493 1069 3	**Only the Wind is Free**	Margaret Graham	£4.99
☐ 7493 0385 9	**The Barleyfield**	Sue Sully	£3.99
☐ 7493 1066 9	**House of Birds**	Elizabeth Tettmar	£4.99

NAME (Block letters) ....

ADDRESS ....

....

☐ I enclose my remittance for ....

☐ I wish to pay by Access/Visa Card Number

Expiry Date

Signature ....

Please quote our reference: MAND